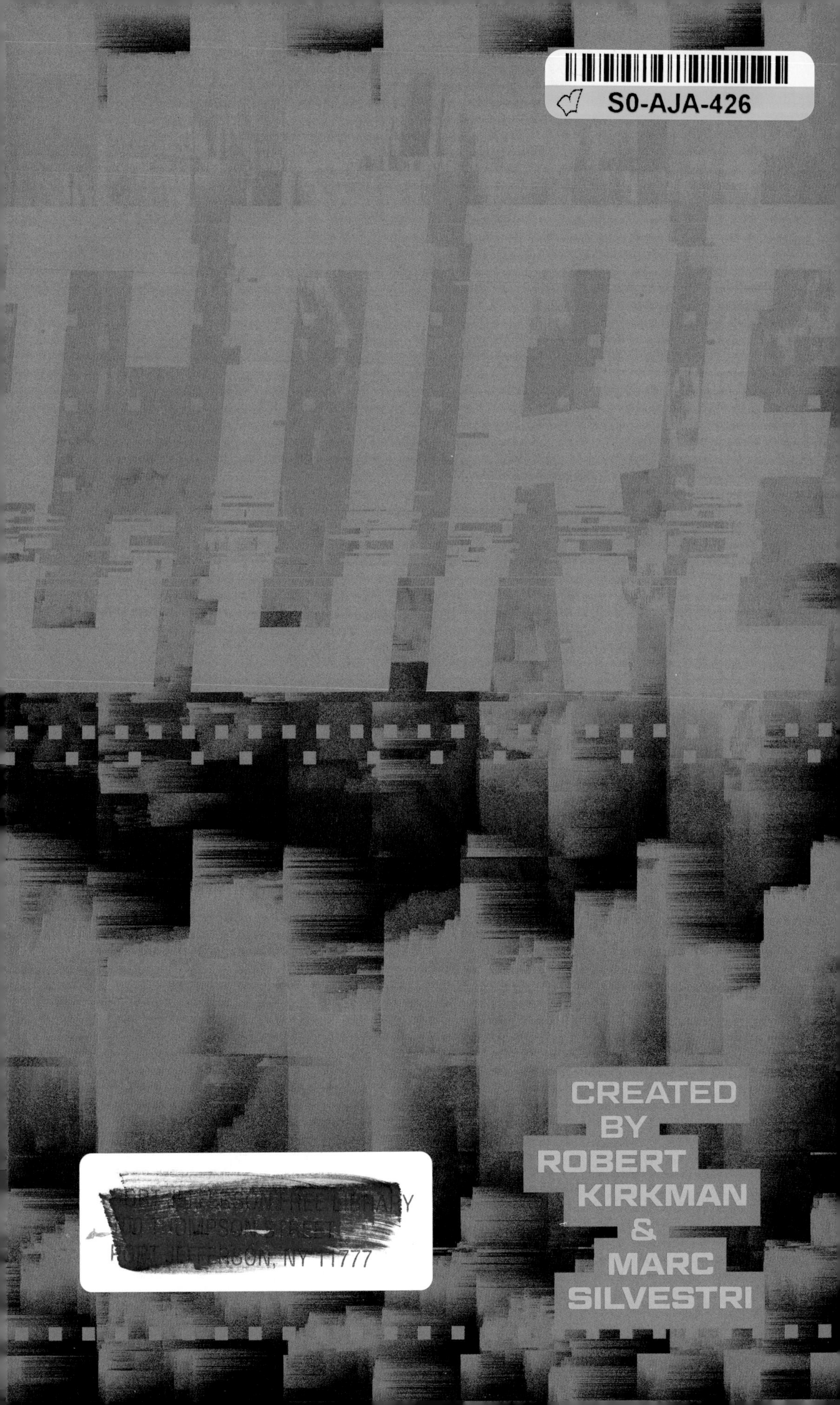
CREATED
BY
ROBERT
KIRKMAN
&
MARC
SILVESTRI

SKYBOUND

> FOR SKYBOUND ENTERTAINMENT
ROBERT KIRKMAN_CHAIRMAN
DAVID ALPERT_CEO
SEAN MACKIEWICZ_SVP, EDITOR-IN-CHIEF
SHAWN KIRKHAM_SVP, BUSINESS DEVELOPMENT
BRIAN HUNTINGTON_VP, ONLINE CONTENT
SHAUNA WYNNE_PUBLICITY DIRECTOR
ANDRES JUAREZ_ART DIRECTOR
ALEX ANTONE_SENIOR EDITOR
JON MOISAN_EDITOR
ARIELLE BASICH_ASSOCIATE EDITOR
CARINA TAYLOR_GRAPHIC DESIGNER
PAUL SHIN_BUSINESS DEVELOPMENT MANAGER
JOHNNY O'DELL_SOCIAL MEDIA MANAGER
DAN PETERSEN_SR. DIRECTOR OF OPERATIONS & EVENTS
FOREIGN RIGHTS INQUIRIES: AG@SEQUENTIALRIGHTS.COM
OTHER LICENSING INQUIRIES: CONTACT@SKYBOUND.COM
SKYBOUND.COM

> FOR IMAGE COMICS, INC.
ROBERT KIRKMAN_CHIEF OPERATING OFFICER
ERIK LARSEN_CHIEF FINANCIAL OFFICER
TODD MCFARLANE_PRESIDENT
MARC SILVESTRI_CHIEF EXECUTIVE OFFICER
JIM VALENTINO_VICE PRESIDENT
ERIC STEPHENSON_PUBLISHER / CHIEF CREATIVE OFFICER
JEFF BOISON_DIRECTOR OF SALES & PUBLISHING PLANNING
JEFF STANG_DIRECTOR OF DIRECT MARKET SALES
KAT SALAZAR_DIRECTOR OF PR & MARKETING
DREW GILL_COVER EDITOR
HEATHER DOORNINK_PRODUCTION DIRECTOR
NICOLE LAPALME_CONTROLLER
IMAGECOMICS.COM

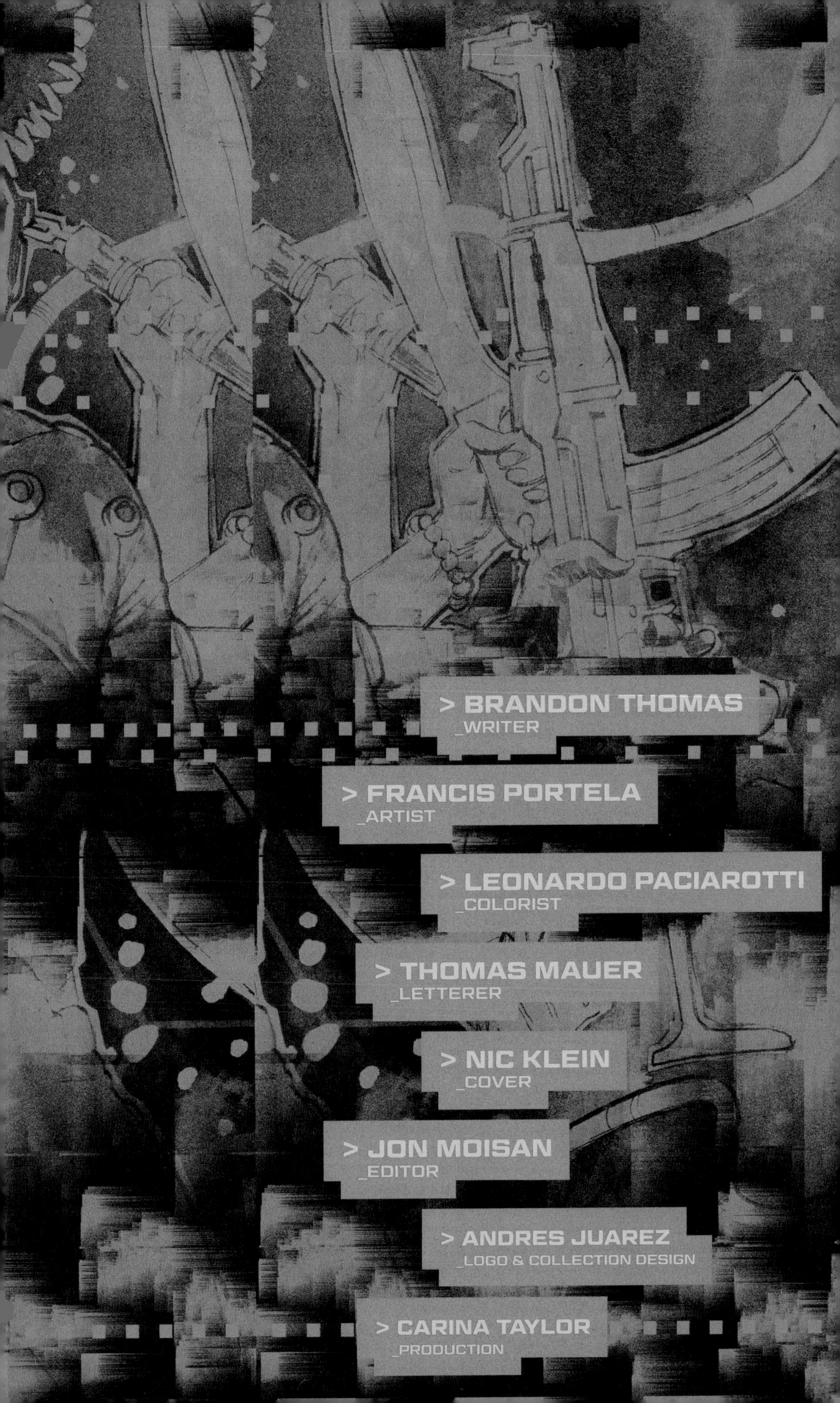

> BRANDON THOMAS
_WRITER

> FRANCIS PORTELA
_ARTIST

> LEONARDO PACIAROTTI
_COLORIST

> THOMAS MAUER
_LETTERER

> NIC KLEIN
_COVER

> JON MOISAN
_EDITOR

> ANDRES JUAREZ
_LOGO & COLLECTION DESIGN

> CARINA TAYLOR
_PRODUCTION

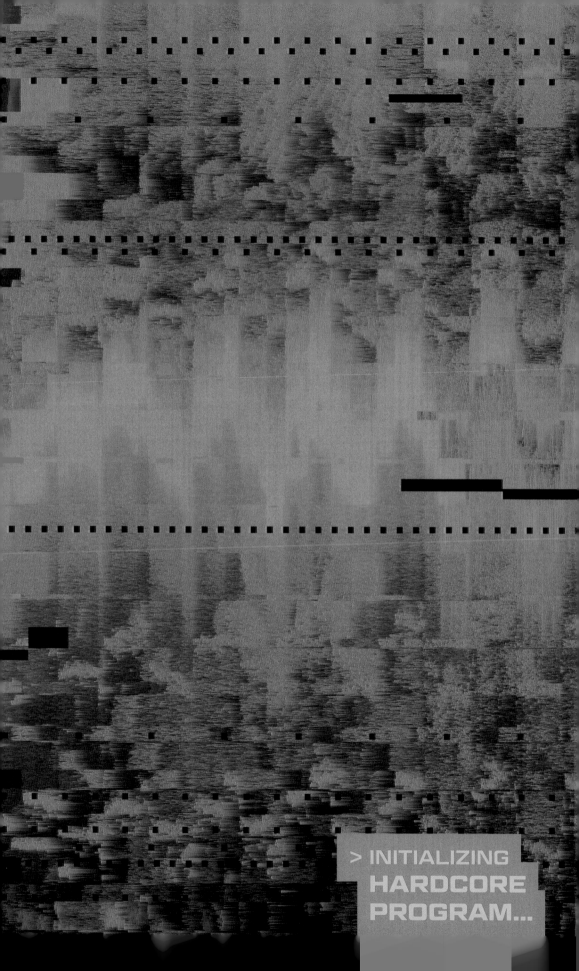

> INITIALIZING
HARDCORE
PROGRAM...

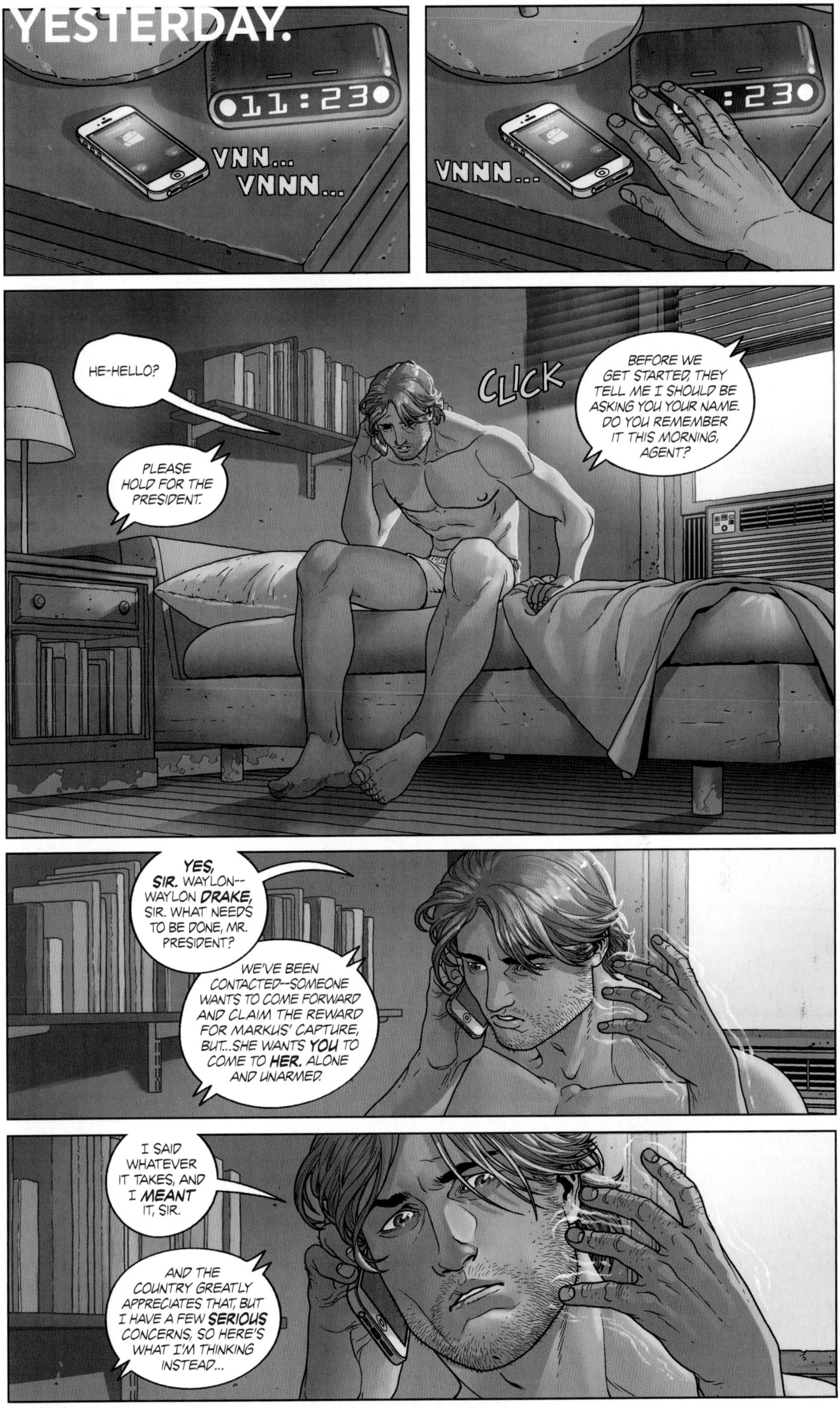
YESTERDAY.
11:23
VNN...
VNNN...
11:23
VNNN...
HE-HELLO?
PLEASE HOLD FOR THE PRESIDENT.
CLICK
BEFORE WE GET STARTED, THEY TELL ME I SHOULD BE ASKING YOU YOUR NAME. DO YOU REMEMBER IT THIS MORNING, AGENT?
YES, SIR. WAYLON--WAYLON DRAKE, SIR. WHAT NEEDS TO BE DONE, MR. PRESIDENT?
WE'VE BEEN CONTACTED--SOMEONE WANTS TO COME FORWARD AND CLAIM THE REWARD FOR MARKUS' CAPTURE, BUT...SHE WANTS YOU TO COME TO HER. ALONE AND UNARMED.
I SAID WHATEVER IT TAKES, AND I MEANT IT, SIR.
AND THE COUNTRY GREATLY APPRECIATES THAT, BUT I HAVE A FEW SERIOUS CONCERNS, SO HERE'S WHAT I'M THINKING INSTEAD...

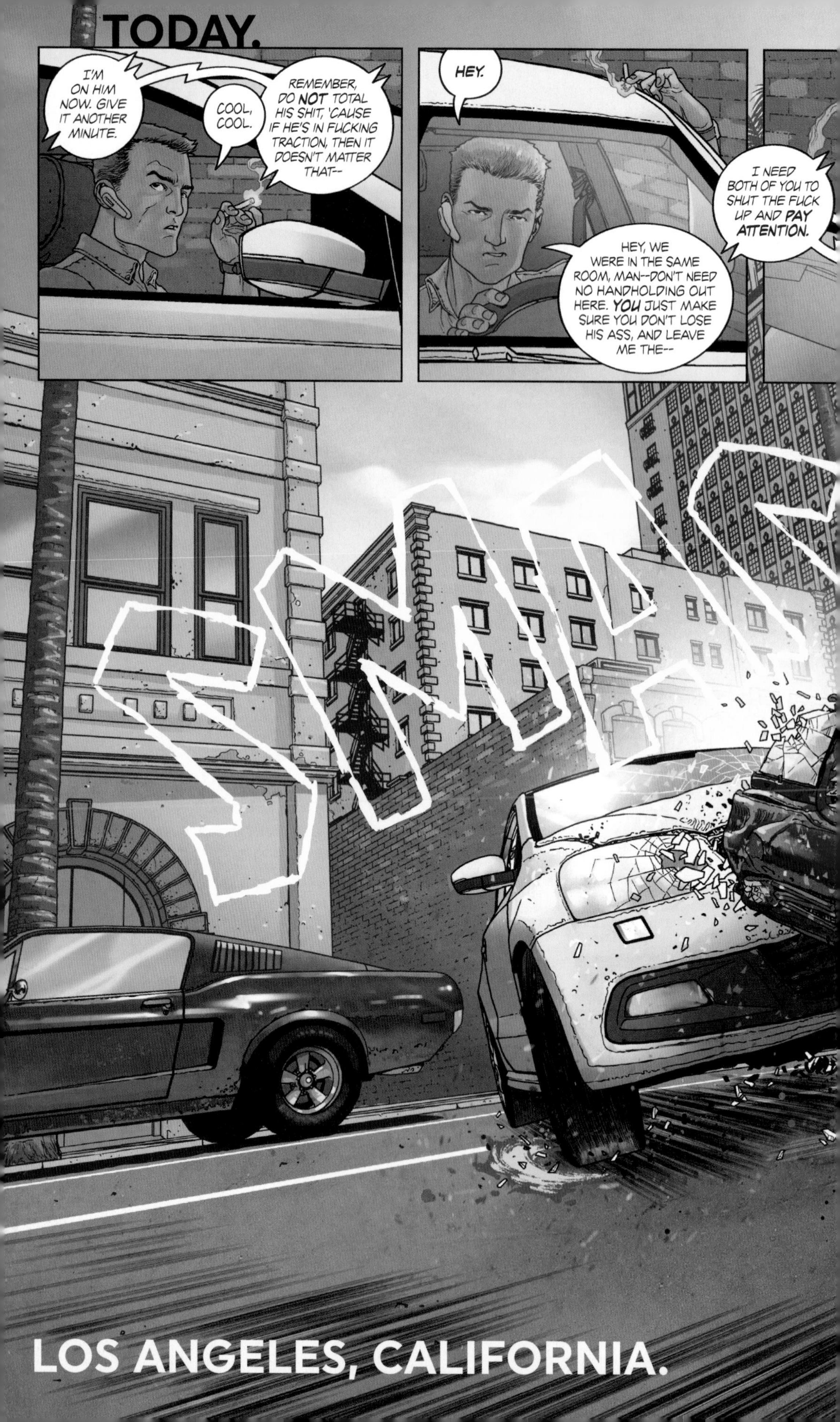
TODAY.
I'M ON HIM NOW. GIVE IT ANOTHER MINUTE.
COOL, COOL.
REMEMBER, DO NOT TOTAL HIS SHIT, 'CAUSE IF HE'S IN FUCKING TRACTION, THEN IT DOESN'T MATTER THAT--
HEY.
HEY, WE WERE IN THE SAME ROOM, MAN--DON'T NEED NO HANDHOLDING OUT HERE. YOU JUST MAKE SURE YOU DON'T LOSE HIS ASS, AND LEAVE ME THE--
I NEED BOTH OF YOU TO SHUT THE FUCK UP AND PAY ATTENTION.
LOS ANGELES, CALIFORNIA.

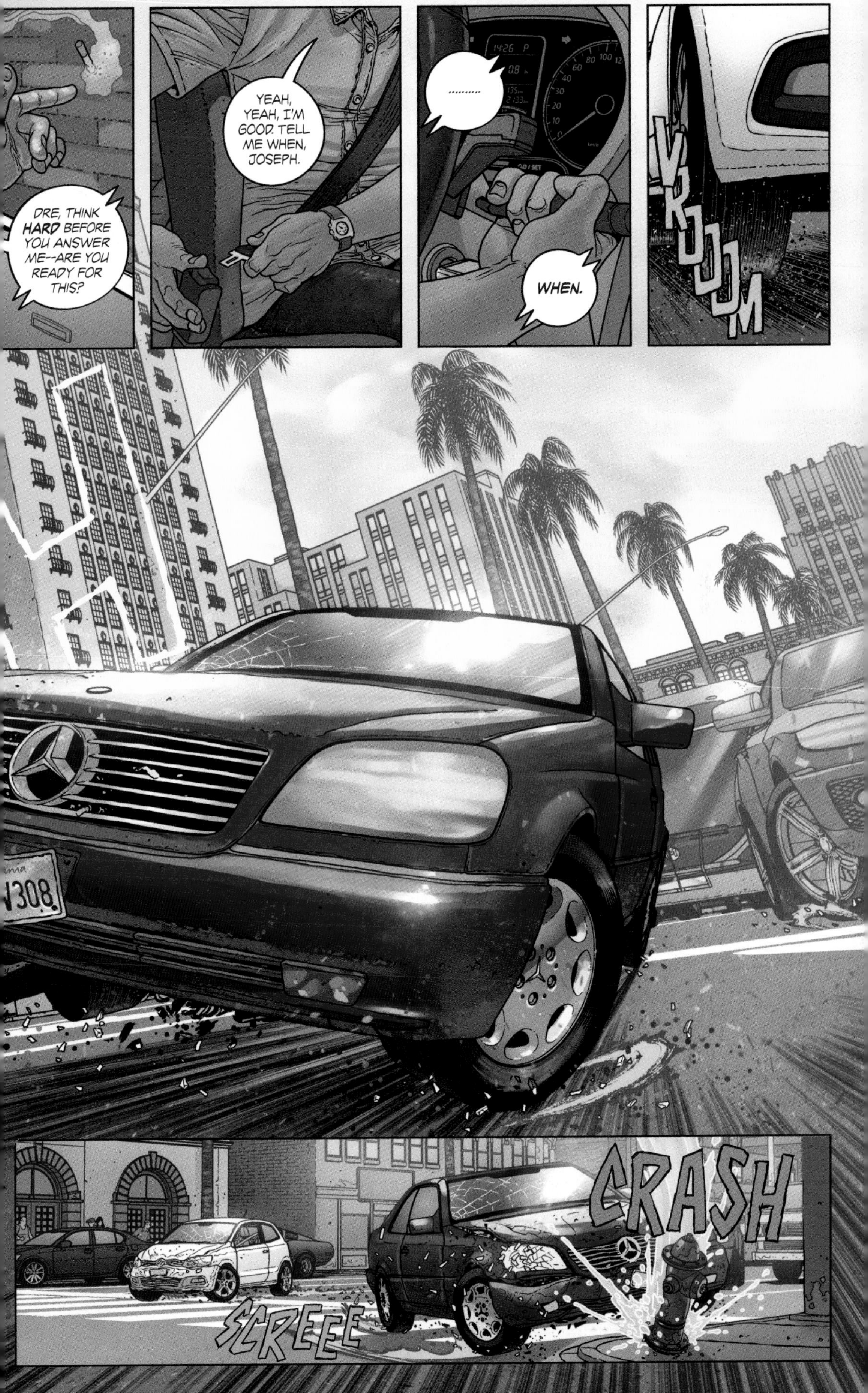
DRE, THINK HARD BEFORE YOU ANSWER ME--ARE YOU READY FOR THIS?
YEAH, YEAH, I'M GOOD. TELL ME WHEN, JOSEPH.
....
WHEN.
VROOOOM
CRASH
SCREEEE

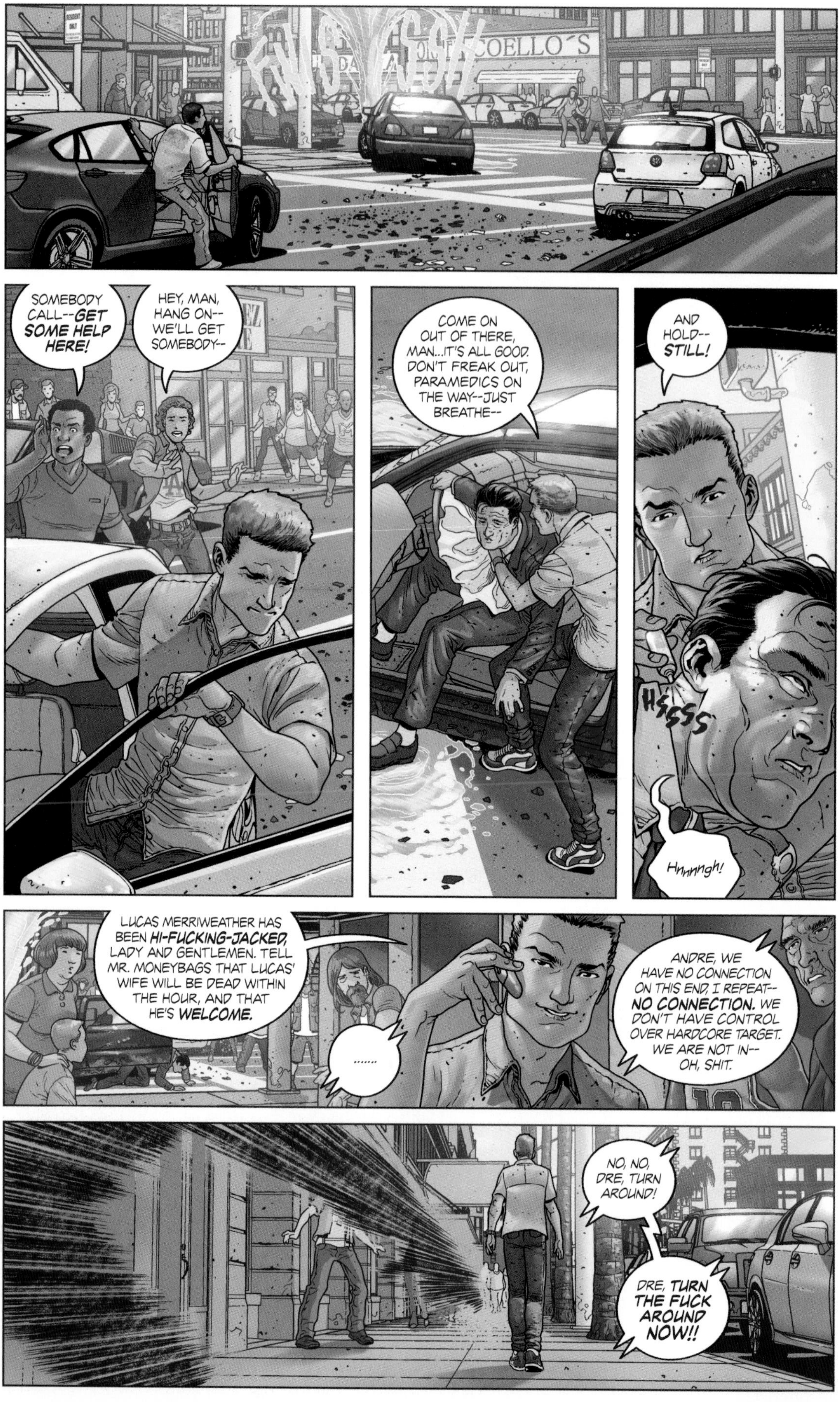
FWSSSSH
COELLO'S
SOMEBODY CALL--GET SOME HELP HERE!
HEY, MAN, HANG ON-- WE'LL GET SOMEBODY--
COME ON OUT OF THERE, MAN...IT'S ALL GOOD. DON'T FREAK OUT, PARAMEDICS ON THE WAY--JUST BREATHE--
AND HOLD-- STILL!
HSSSS
Hnnnngh!
LUCAS MERRIWEATHER HAS BEEN HI-FUCKING-JACKED, LADY AND GENTLEMEN. TELL MR. MONEYBAGS THAT LUCAS' WIFE WILL BE DEAD WITHIN THE HOUR, AND THAT HE'S WELCOME.
....
ANDRE, WE HAVE NO CONNECTION ON THIS END, I REPEAT-- NO CONNECTION. WE DON'T HAVE CONTROL OVER HARDCORE TARGET. WE ARE NOT IN-- OH, SHIT.
NO, NO, DRE, TURN AROUND!
DRE, TURN THE FUCK AROUND NOW!!

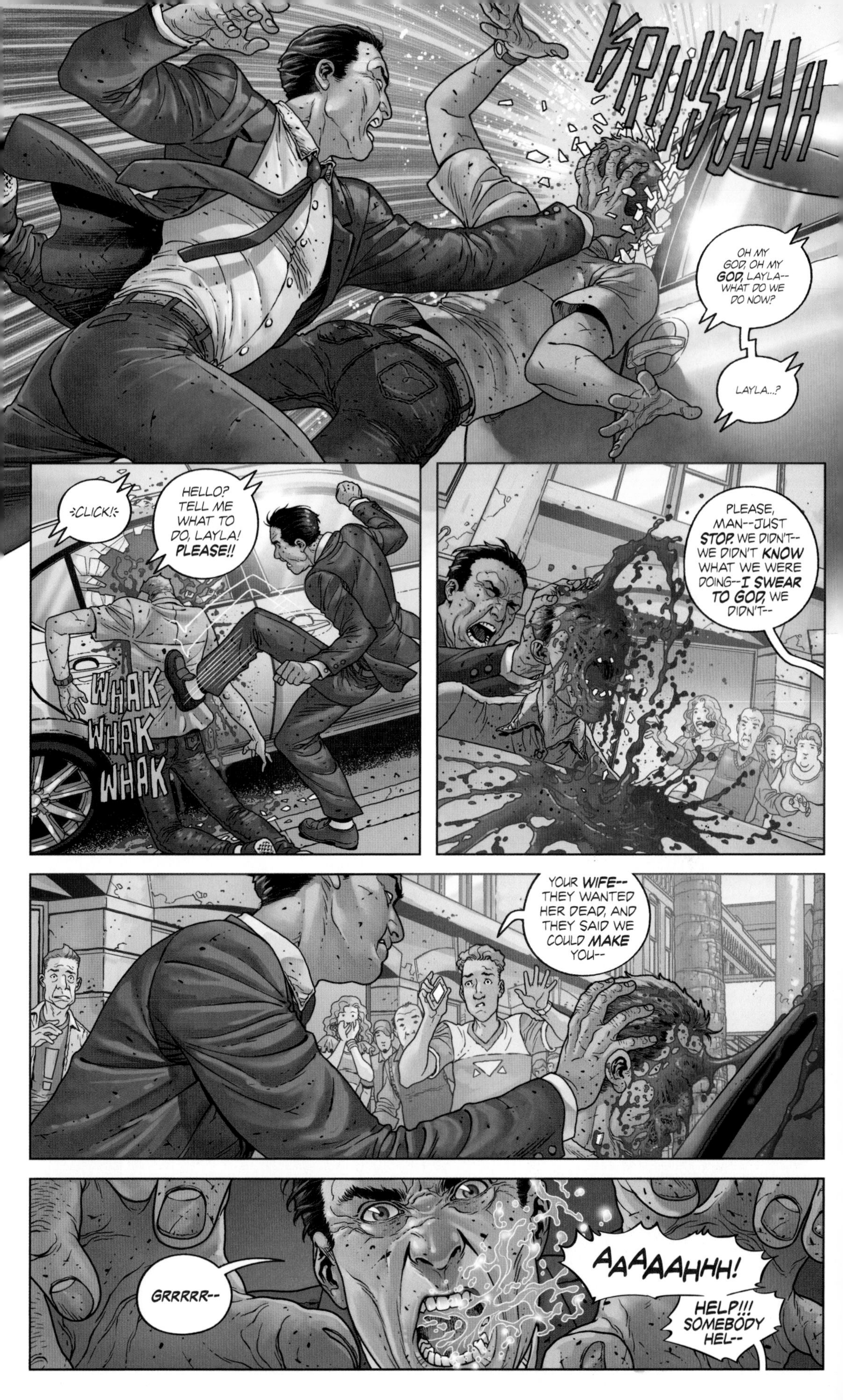
KRUSSHH
OH MY GOD, OH MY GOD, LAYLA-- WHAT DO WE DO NOW?
LAYLA...?
CLICK!
HELLO? TELL ME WHAT TO DO, LAYLA! PLEASE!!
WHAK WHAK WHAK
PLEASE, MAN--JUST STOP. WE DIDN'T-- WE DIDN'T KNOW WHAT WE WERE DOING--I SWEAR TO GOD, WE DIDN'T--
YOUR WIFE-- THEY WANTED HER DEAD, AND THEY SAID WE COULD MAKE YOU--
GRRRRR--
AAAAAHHH!
HELP!!! SOMEBODY HEL--

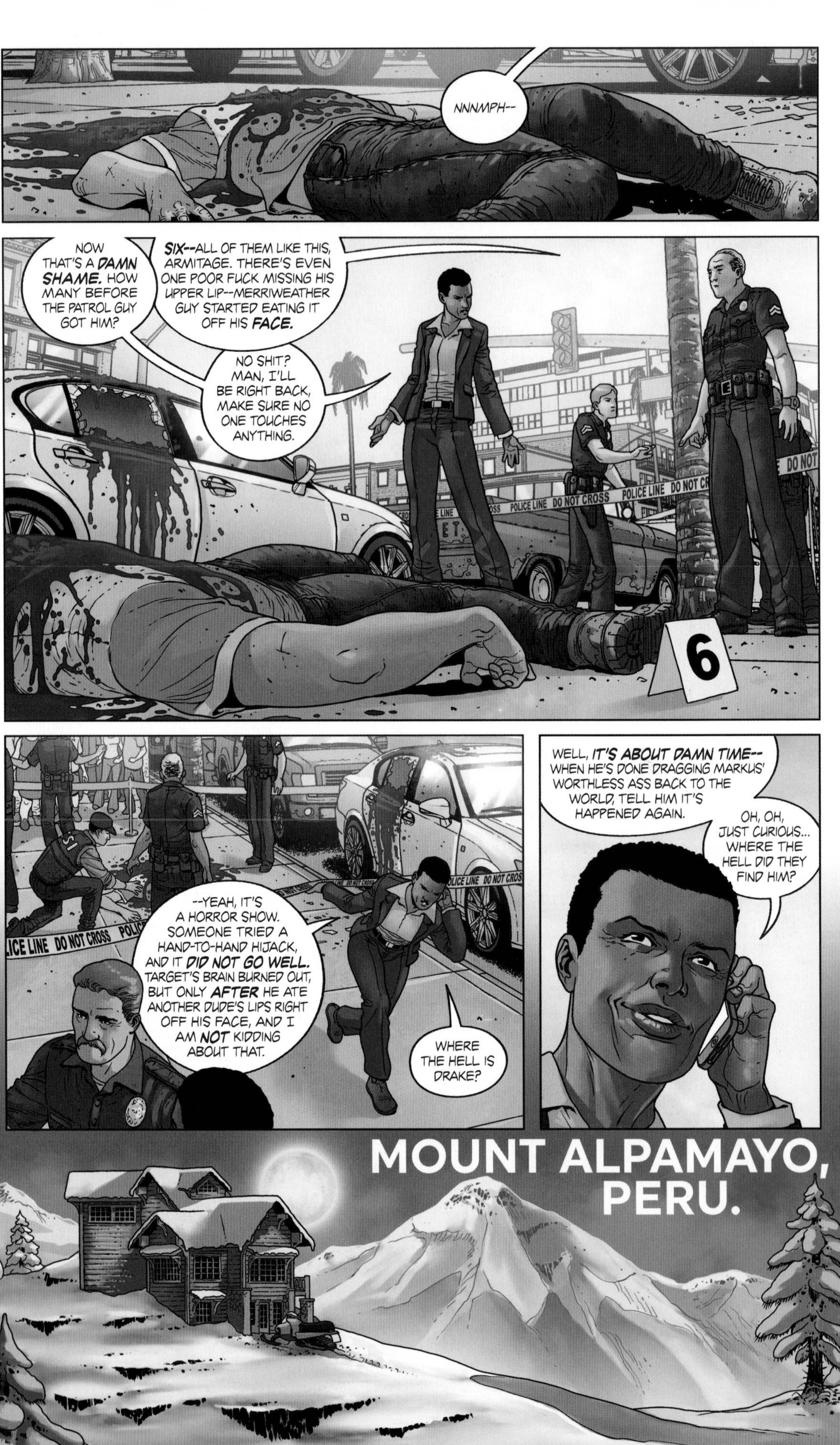
NNNMPH--
NOW THAT'S A DAMN SHAME. HOW MANY BEFORE THE PATROL GUY GOT HIM?
SIX--ALL OF THEM LIKE THIS, ARMITAGE. THERE'S EVEN ONE POOR FUCK MISSING HIS UPPER LIP--MERRIWEATHER GUY STARTED EATING IT OFF HIS FACE.
NO SHIT? MAN, I'LL BE RIGHT BACK, MAKE SURE NO ONE TOUCHES ANYTHING.
POLICE LINE DO NOT CROSS
6
--YEAH, IT'S A HORROR SHOW. SOMEONE TRIED A HAND-TO-HAND HIJACK, AND IT DID NOT GO WELL. TARGET'S BRAIN BURNED OUT, BUT ONLY AFTER HE ATE ANOTHER DUDE'S LIPS RIGHT OFF HIS FACE, AND I AM NOT KIDDING ABOUT THAT.
WHERE THE HELL IS DRAKE?
WELL, IT'S ABOUT DAMN TIME-- WHEN HE'S DONE DRAGGING MARKUS' WORTHLESS ASS BACK TO THE WORLD, TELL HIM IT'S HAPPENED AGAIN.
OH, OH, JUST CURIOUS... WHERE THE HELL DID THEY FIND HIM?
MOUNT ALPAMAYO, PERU.

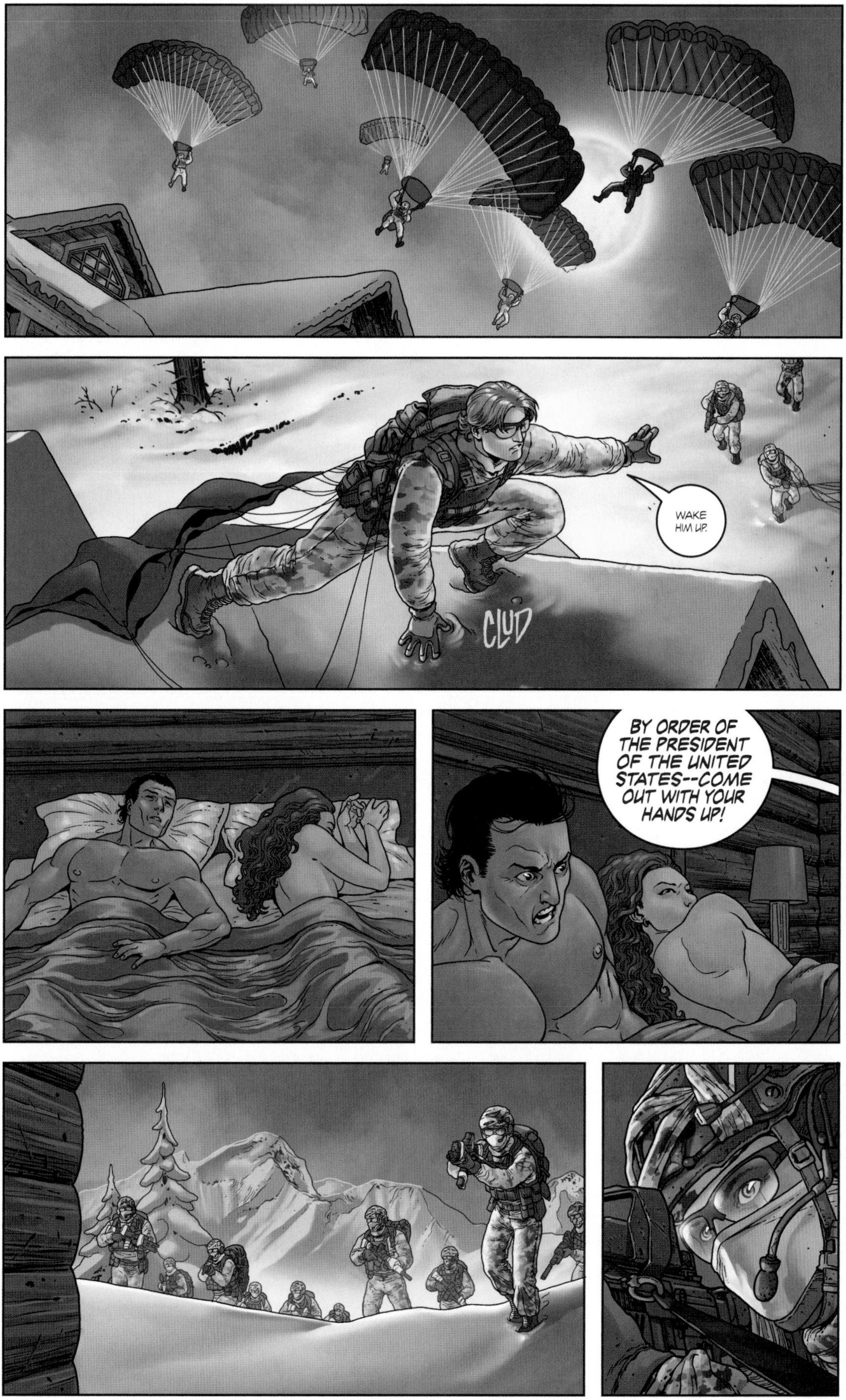
WAKE HIM UP.
CLUD
BY ORDER OF THE PRESIDENT OF THE UNITED STATES--COME OUT WITH YOUR HANDS UP!

squelch
BAM
BAM

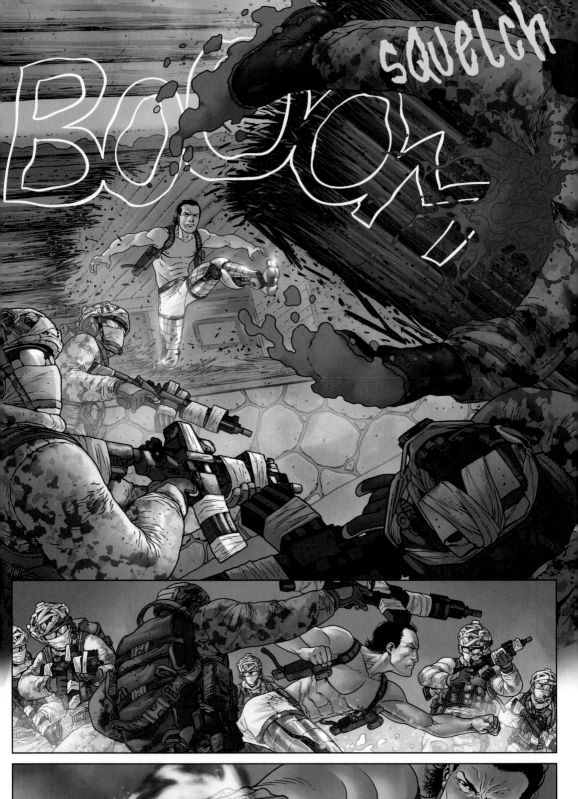

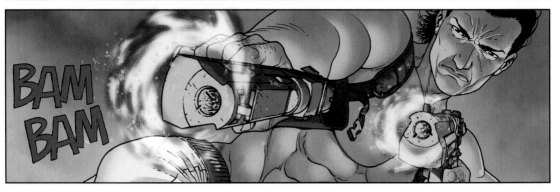

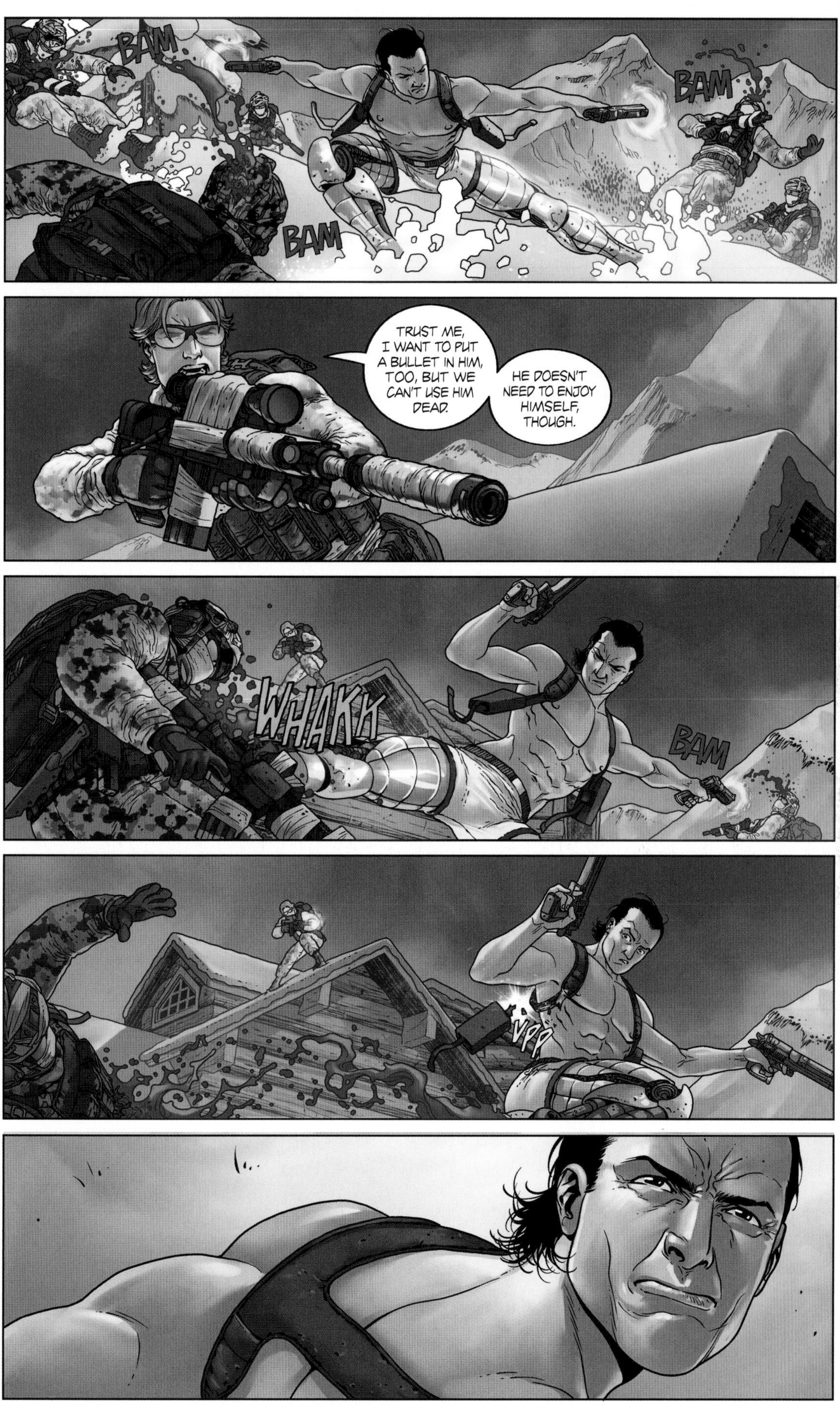
BAM
BAM
BAM
TRUST ME, I WANT TO PUT A BULLET IN HIM, TOO, BUT WE CAN'T USE HIM DEAD.
HE DOESN'T NEED TO ENJOY HIMSELF, THOUGH.
WHAKK
BAM
VPP

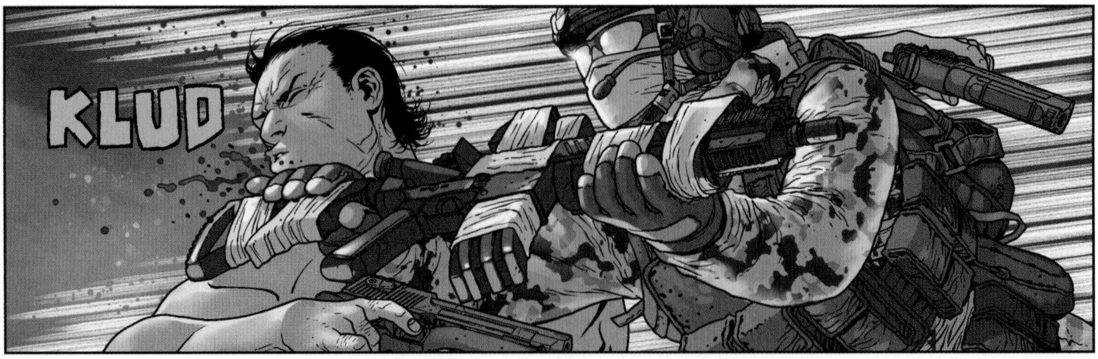
KLUD

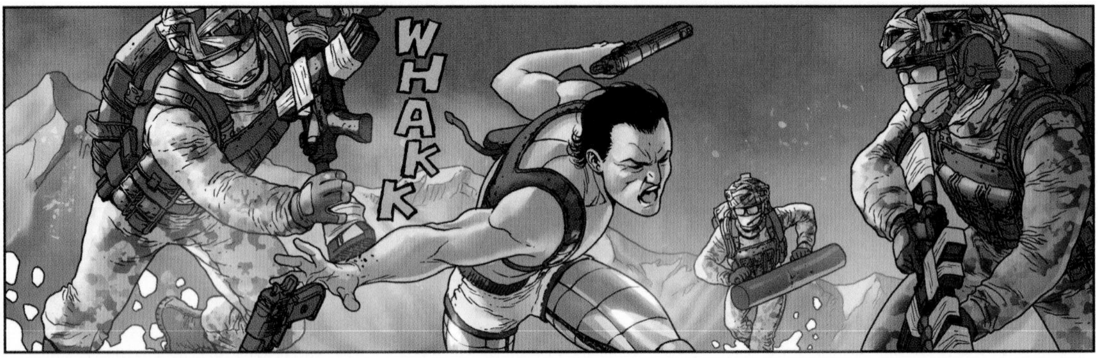
WHAKK

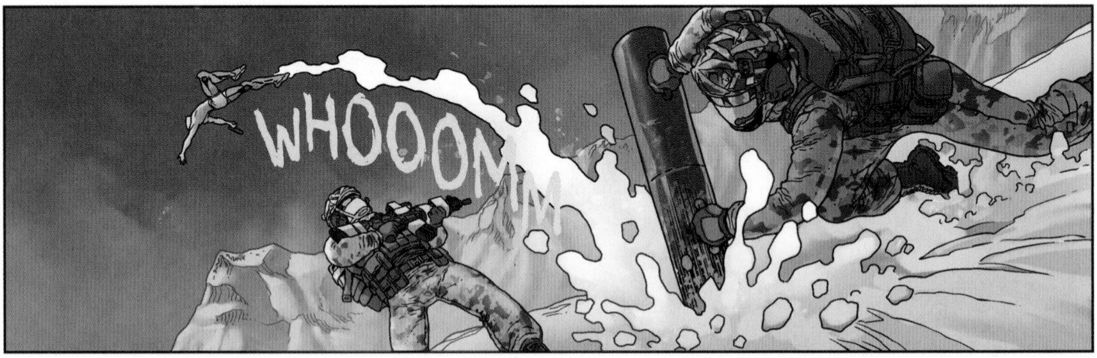
WHOOOMM

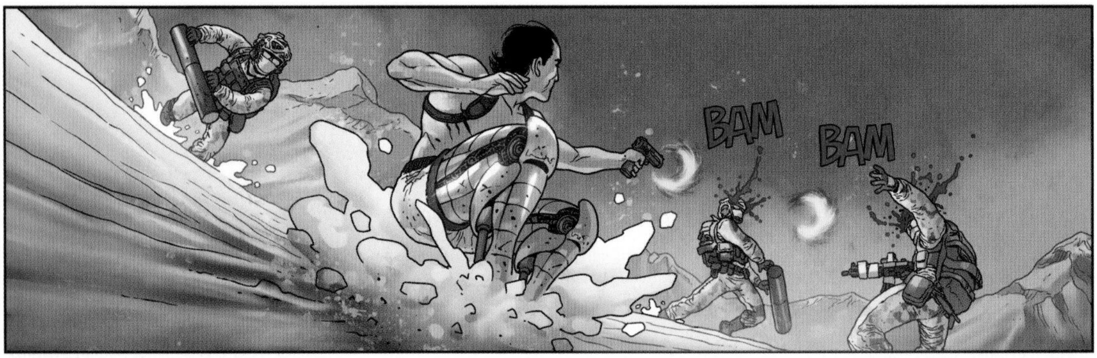
BAM
BAM

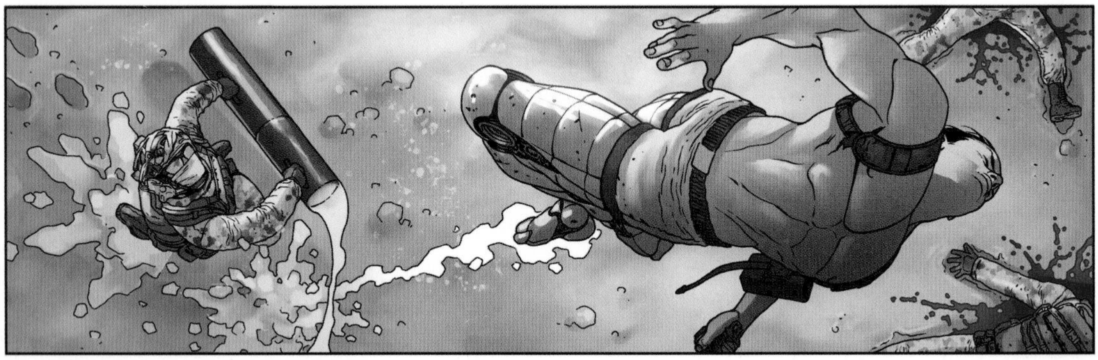

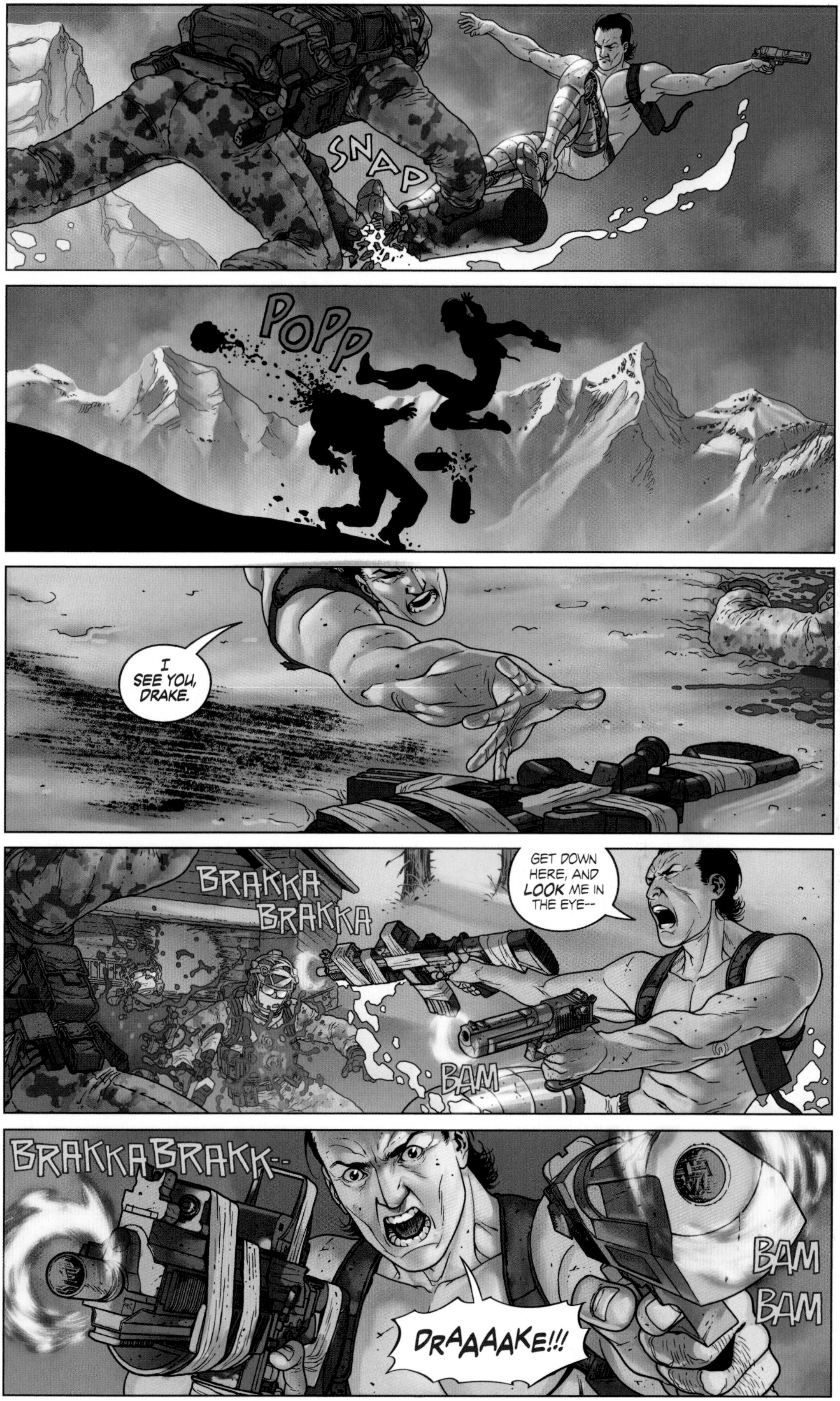
SNAP
POPP
I SEE YOU, DRAKE.
BRAKKA BRAKKA
GET DOWN HERE, AND **LOOK** ME IN THE EYE--
BAM
BRAKKA BRAKK--
BAM BAM
DRAAAAKE!!!

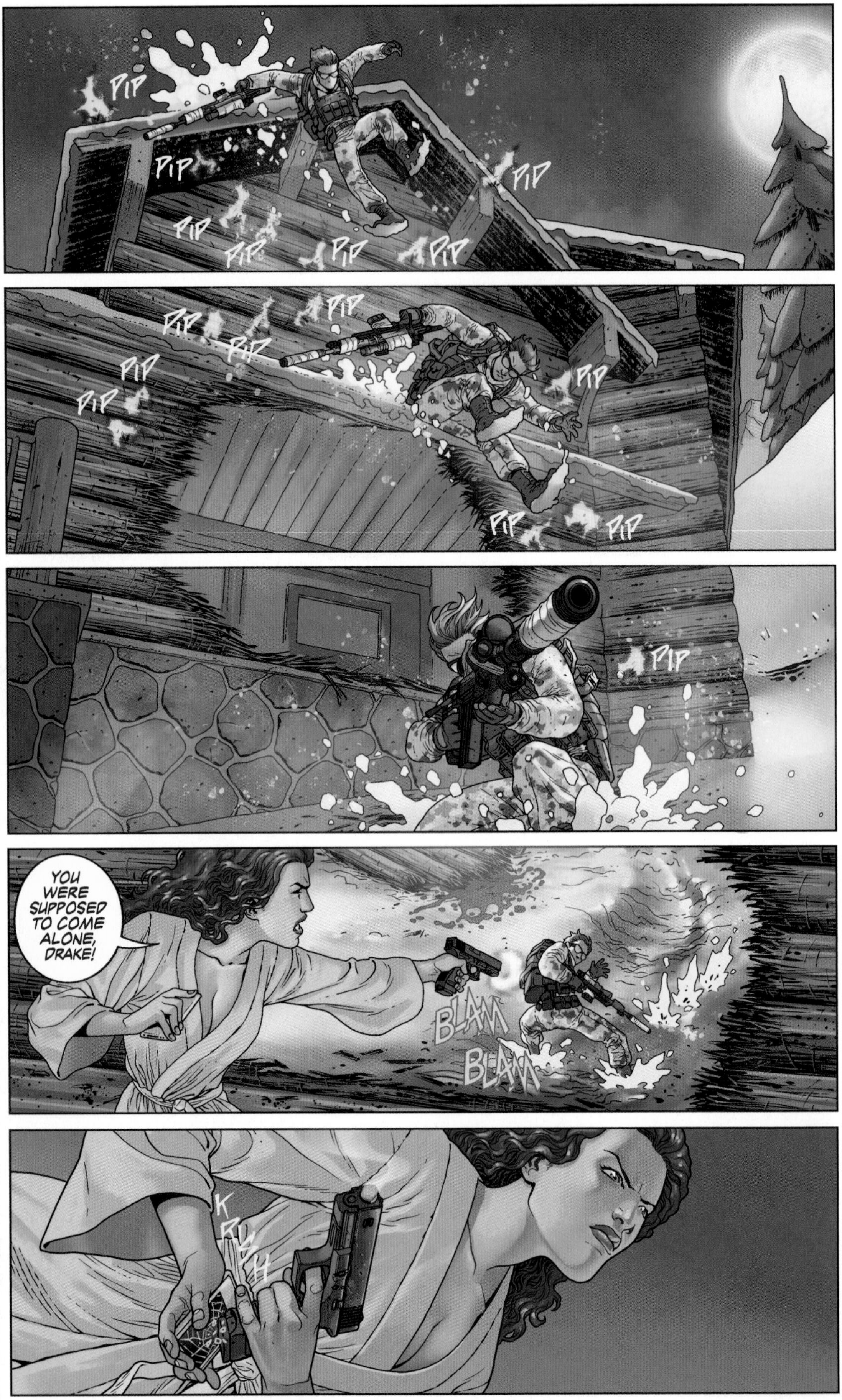
PIP
PIP
PIP
PIP
PIP
PIP
PIP
PIP
PIP
PIP
PIP
PIP
PIP
PIP
PIP
PIP
YOU WERE SUPPOSED TO COME ALONE, DRAKE!
BLAM
BLAM
KRUSH

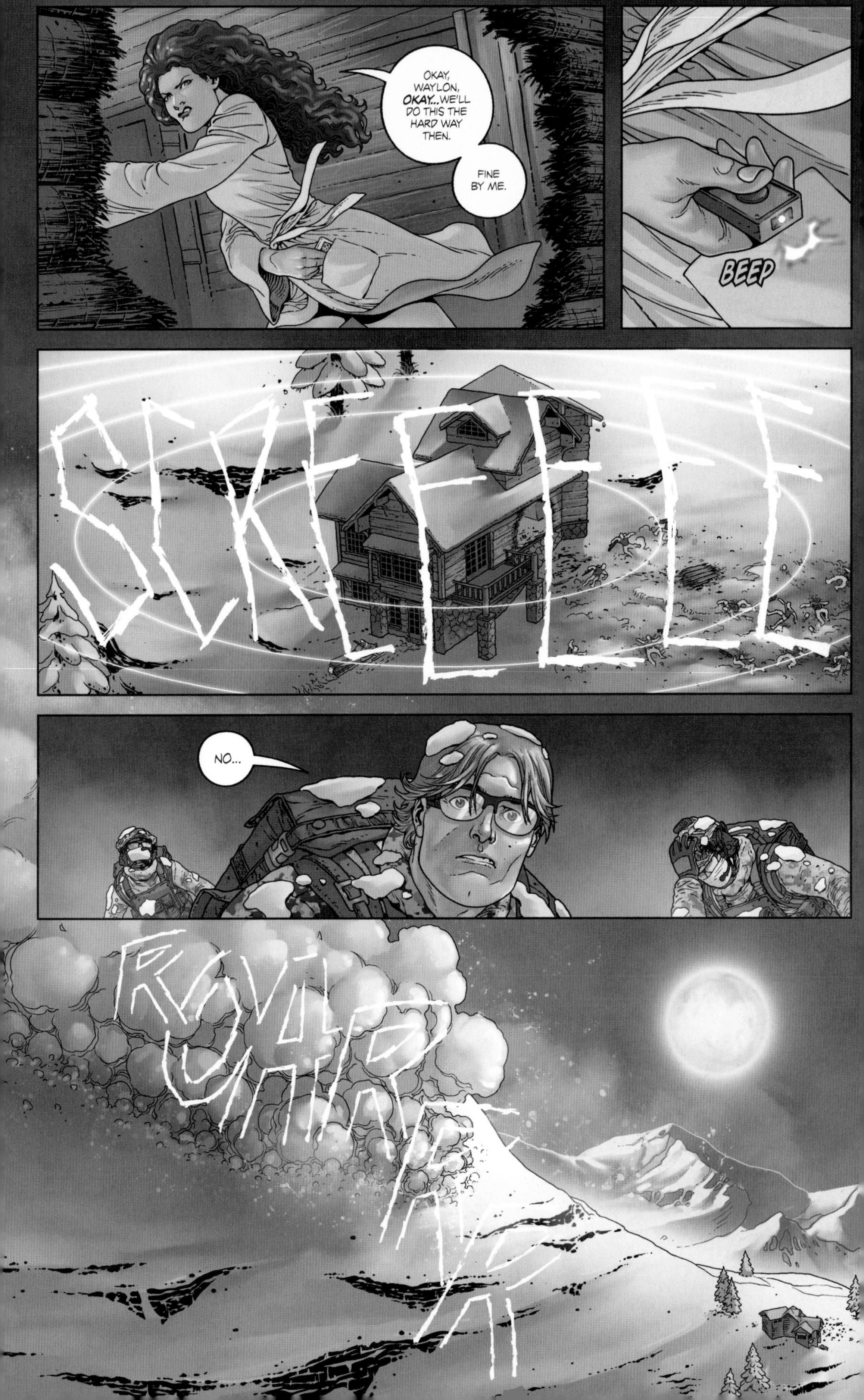

OKAY, WAYLON, **OKAY...** WE'LL DO THIS THE HARD WAY THEN.
FINE BY ME.
BEEP
NO...

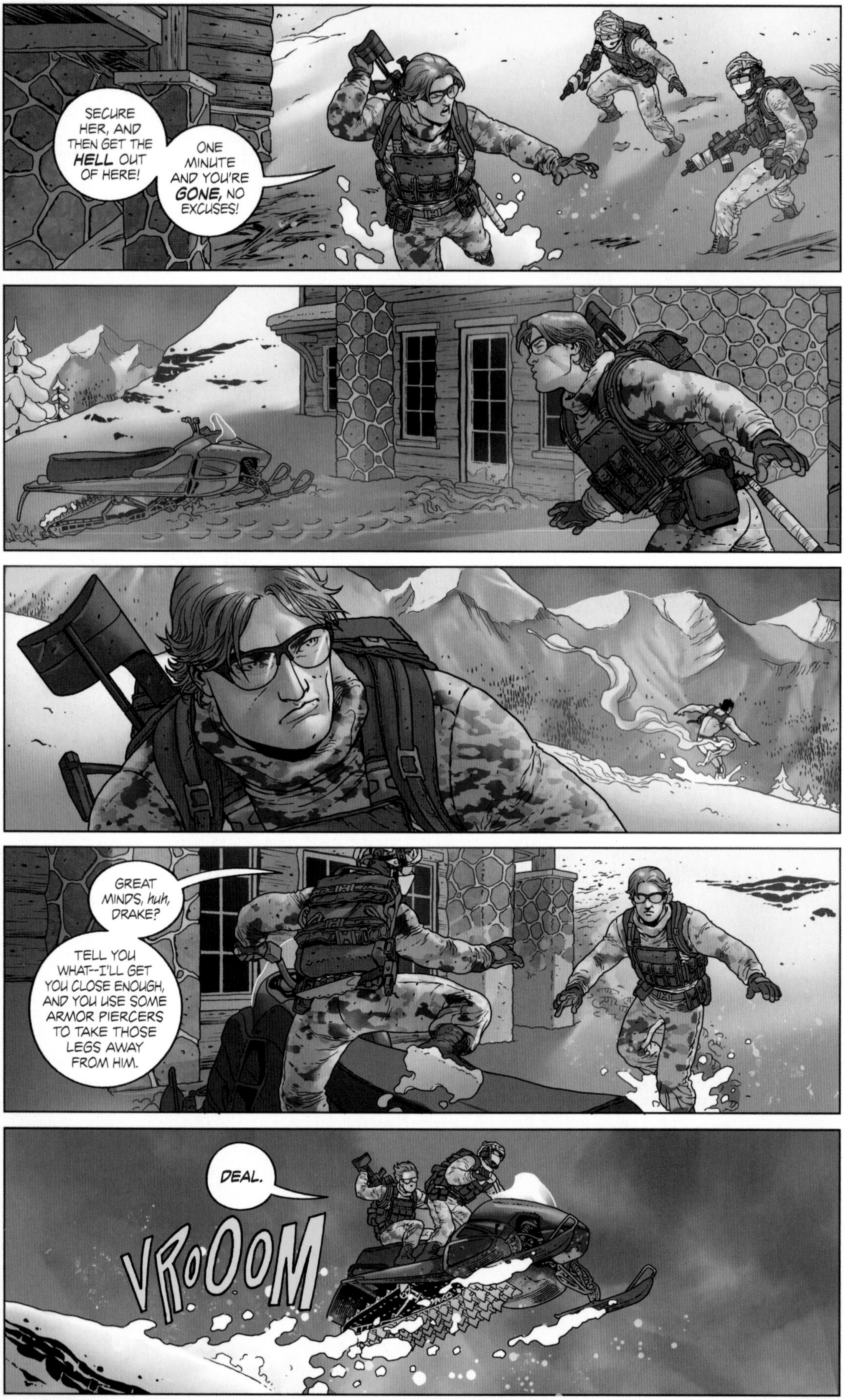

SECURE HER, AND THEN GET THE **HELL** OUT OF HERE!
ONE MINUTE AND YOU'RE **GONE,** NO EXCUSES!
GREAT MINDS, *huh,* DRAKE?
TELL YOU WHAT--I'LL GET YOU CLOSE ENOUGH, AND YOU USE SOME ARMOR PIERCERS TO TAKE THOSE LEGS AWAY FROM HIM.
DEAL.
VROOOM

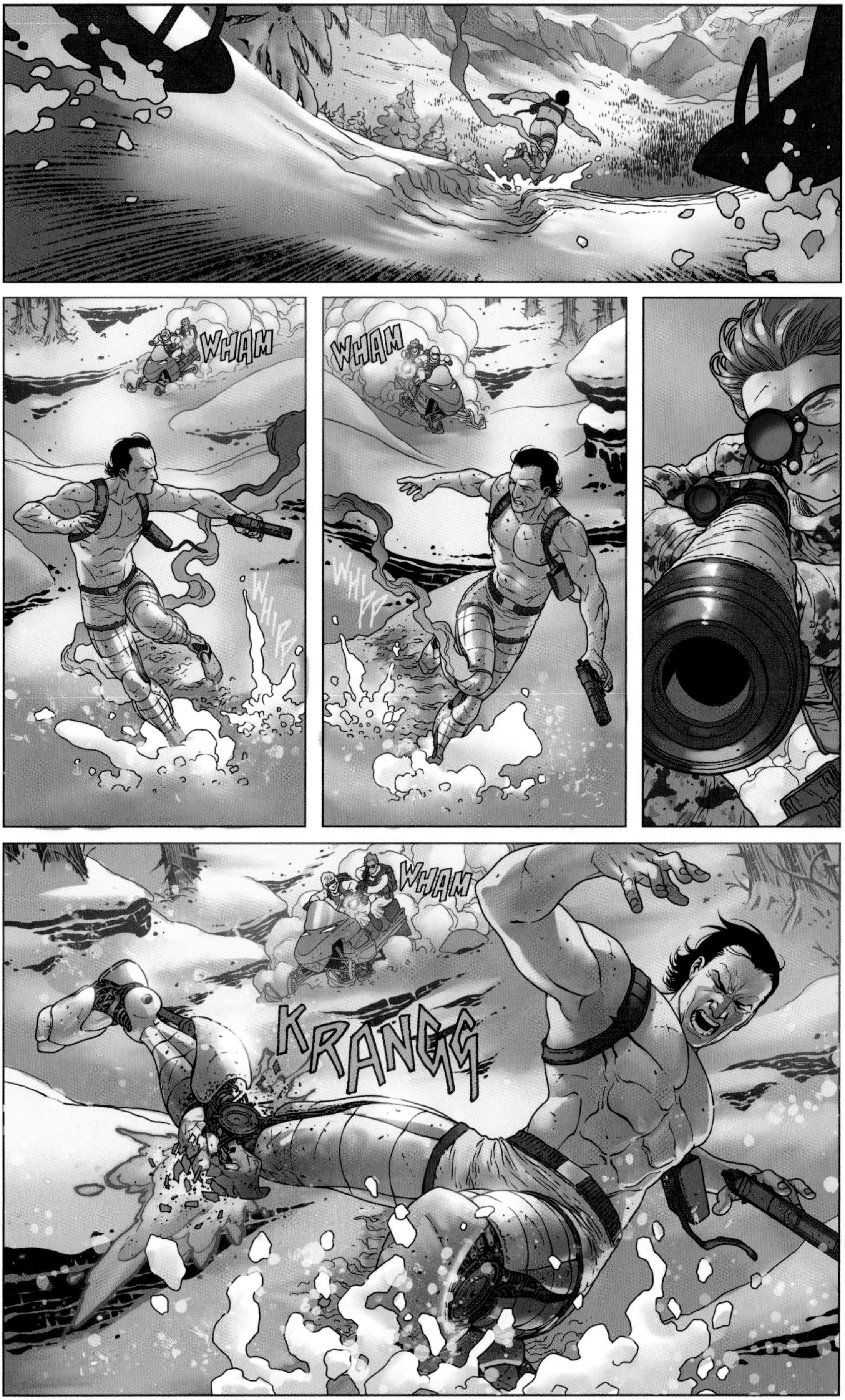
WHAM
WHIPP
WHAM
WHIPP
WHAM
KRANGG

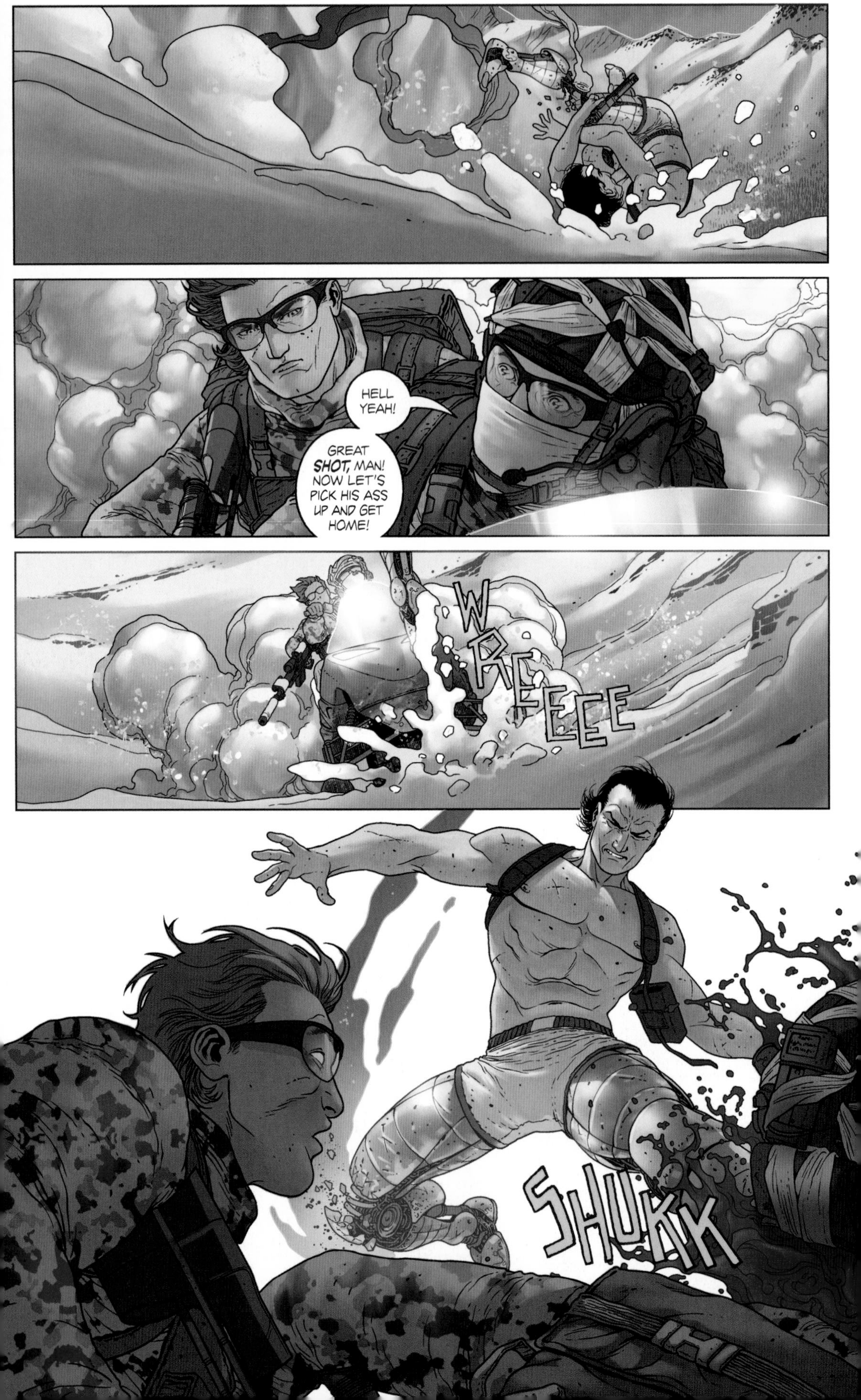
HELL YEAH!
GREAT **SHOT,** MAN! NOW LET'S PICK HIS ASS UP AND GET HOME!
WREEEEE
SHUKK

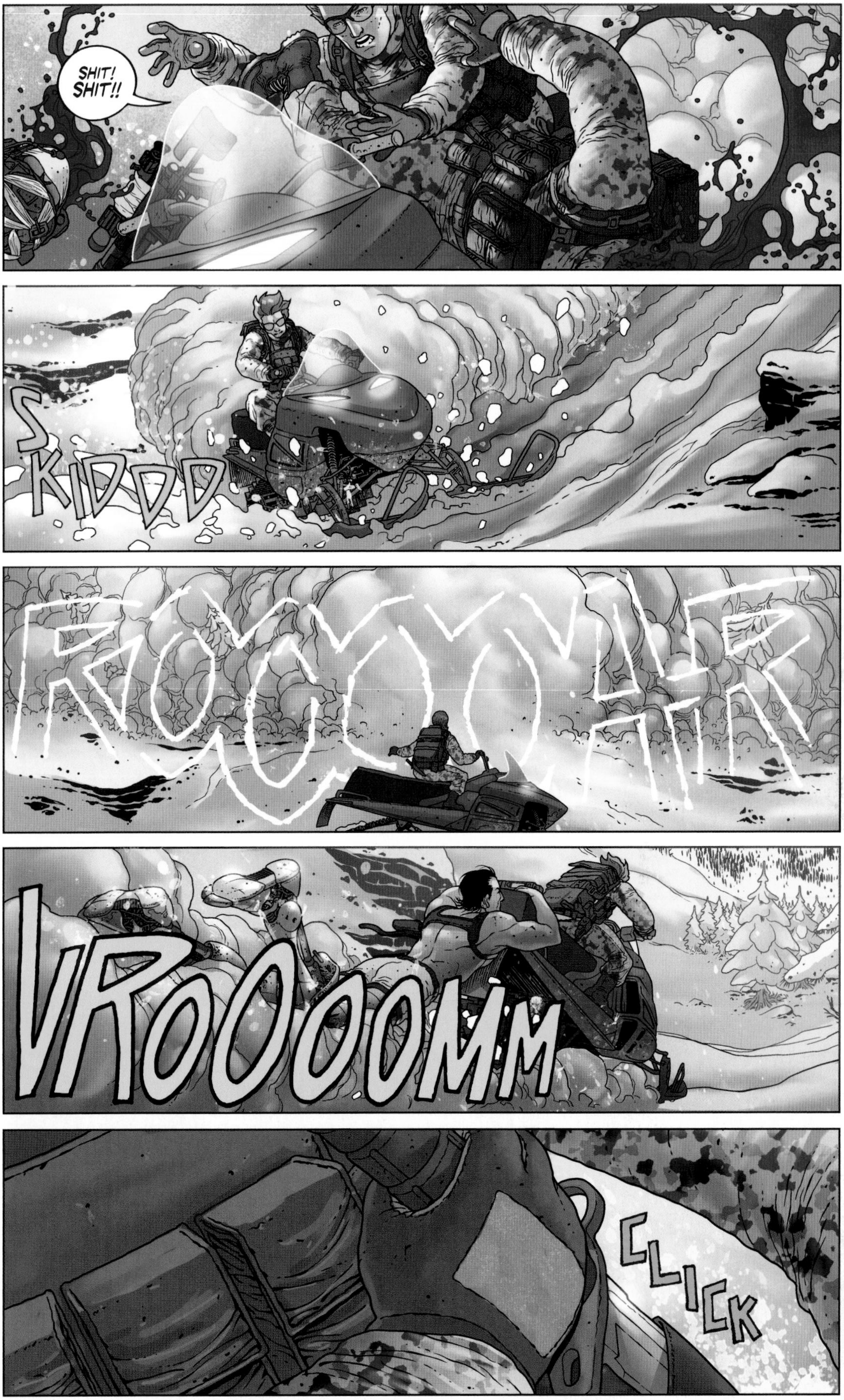
SHIT! SHIT!!
SKIDDD
ROOOOOAR
VROOOOMM
CLICK

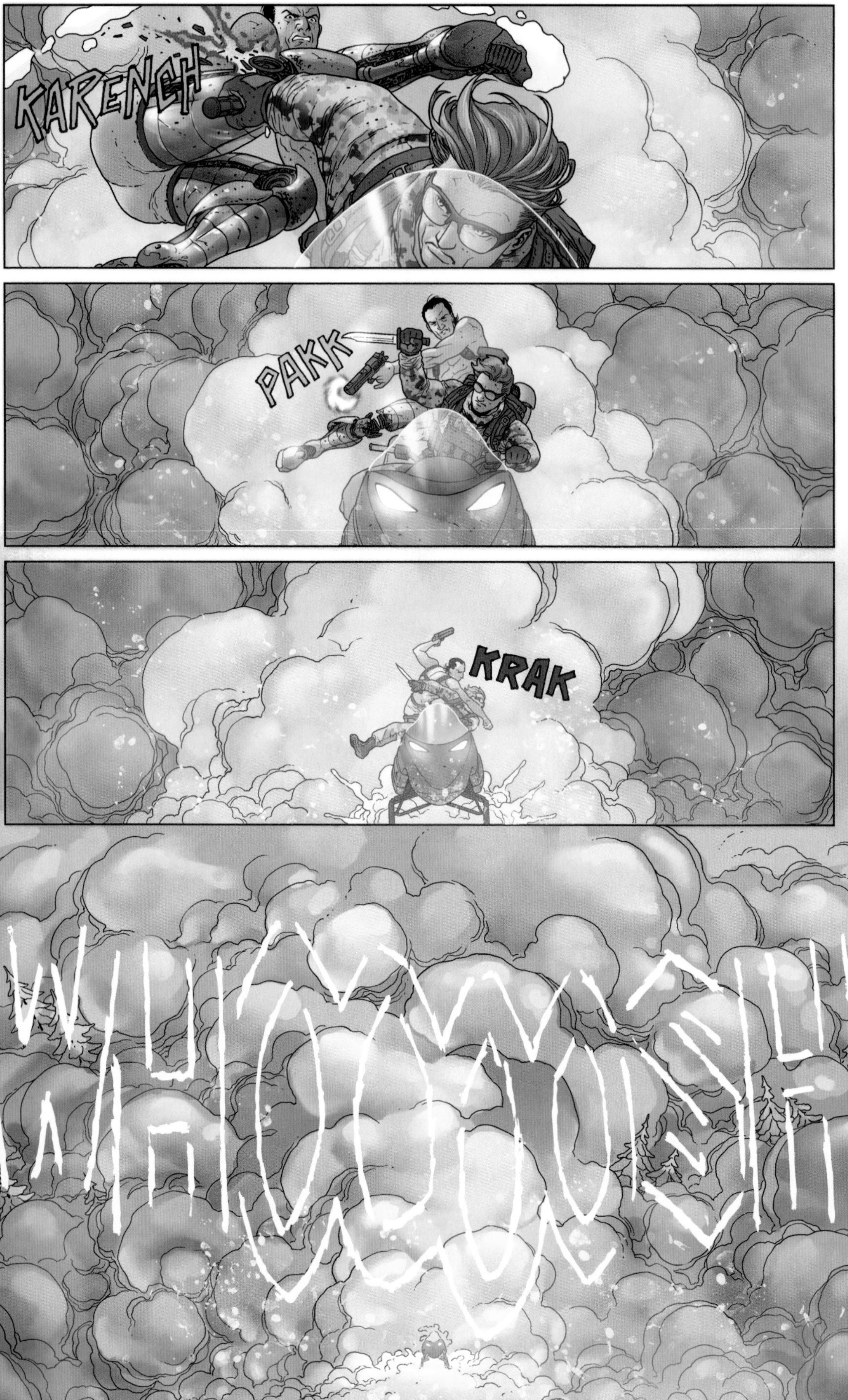
KARENCH
PAKK
KRAK
WHOOOOSH

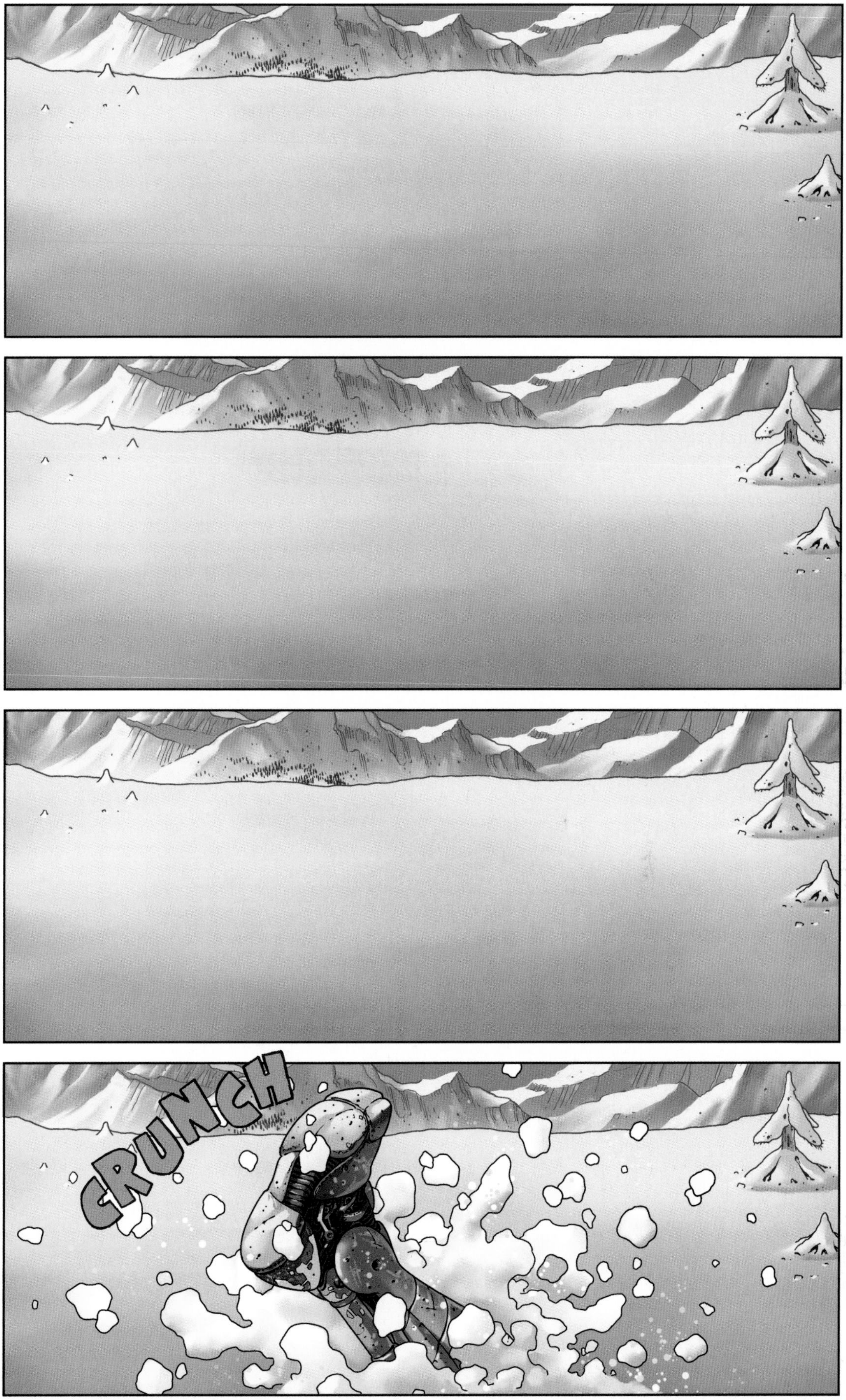
CRUNCH

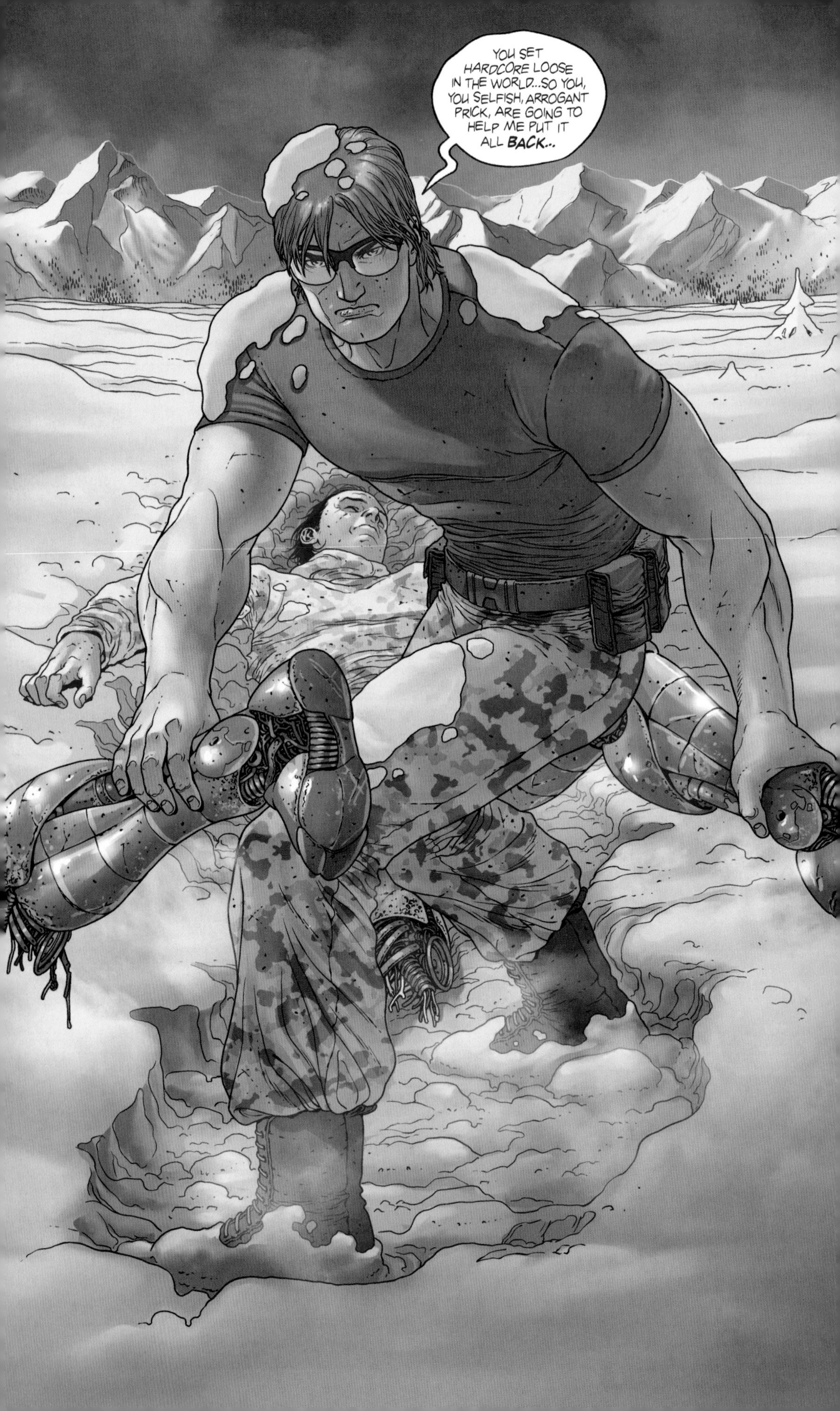
YOU SET HARDCORE LOOSE IN THE WORLD...SO YOU, YOU SELFISH, ARROGANT PRICK, ARE GOING TO HELP ME PUT IT ALL BACK...

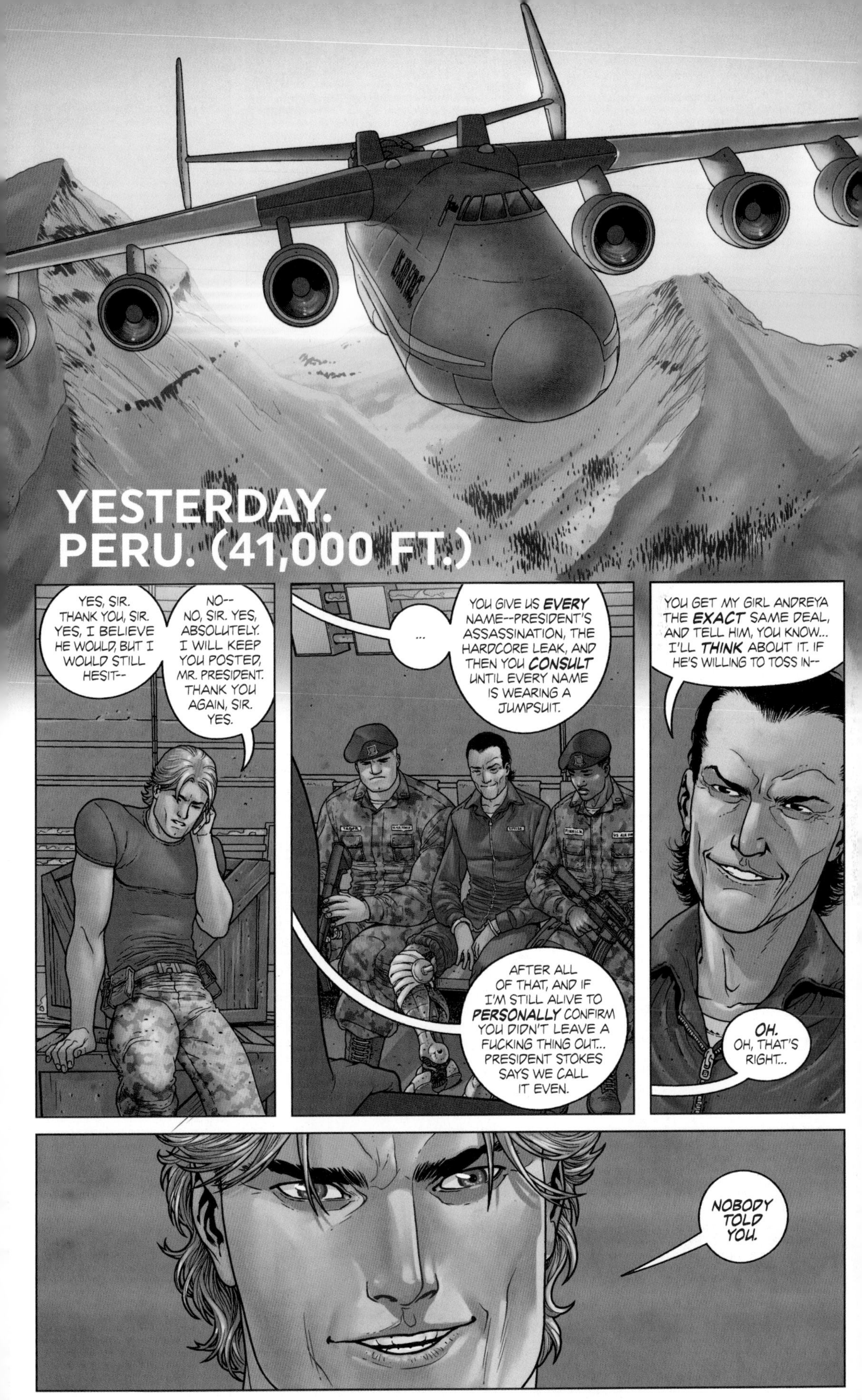
YESTERDAY.
PERU. (41,000 FT.)
YES, SIR. THANK YOU, SIR. YES, I BELIEVE HE WOULD, BUT I WOULD STILL HESIT--
NO-- NO, SIR. YES, ABSOLUTELY. I WILL KEEP YOU POSTED, MR. PRESIDENT. THANK YOU AGAIN, SIR. YES.
...
YOU GIVE US EVERY NAME--PRESIDENT'S ASSASSINATION, THE HARDCORE LEAK, AND THEN YOU CONSULT UNTIL EVERY NAME IS WEARING A JUMPSUIT.
AFTER ALL OF THAT, AND IF I'M STILL ALIVE TO PERSONALLY CONFIRM YOU DIDN'T LEAVE A FUCKING THING OUT... PRESIDENT STOKES SAYS WE CALL IT EVEN.
YOU GET MY GIRL ANDREYA THE EXACT SAME DEAL, AND TELL HIM, YOU KNOW... I'LL THINK ABOUT IT. IF HE'S WILLING TO TOSS IN--
OH. OH, THAT'S RIGHT...
NOBODY TOLD YOU.

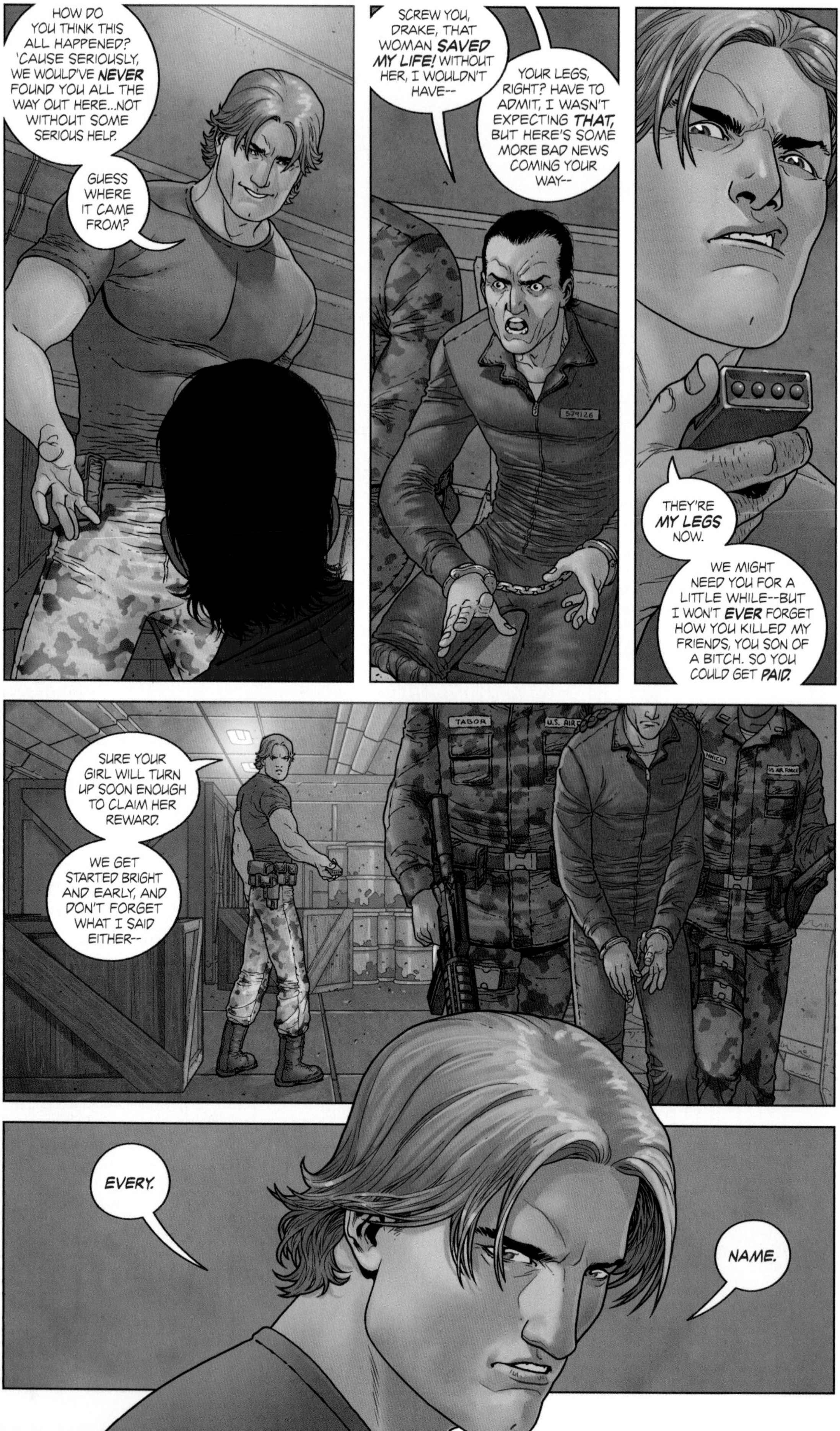
HOW DO YOU THINK THIS ALL HAPPENED? 'CAUSE SERIOUSLY, WE WOULD'VE NEVER FOUND YOU ALL THE WAY OUT HERE...NOT WITHOUT SOME SERIOUS HELP.
GUESS WHERE IT CAME FROM?
SCREW YOU, DRAKE, THAT WOMAN SAVED MY LIFE! WITHOUT HER, I WOULDN'T HAVE--
YOUR LEGS, RIGHT? HAVE TO ADMIT, I WASN'T EXPECTING THAT, BUT HERE'S SOME MORE BAD NEWS COMING YOUR WAY--
THEY'RE MY LEGS NOW.
WE MIGHT NEED YOU FOR A LITTLE WHILE--BUT I WON'T EVER FORGET HOW YOU KILLED MY FRIENDS, YOU SON OF A BITCH. SO YOU COULD GET PAID.
SURE YOUR GIRL WILL TURN UP SOON ENOUGH TO CLAIM HER REWARD.
WE GET STARTED BRIGHT AND EARLY, AND DON'T FORGET WHAT I SAID EITHER--
EVERY.
NAME.

TODAY.

SCOTTIE! SCOTT, IS MY CASE DOWN THERE!?

PASADENA, CALIFORNIA.
HOME OF JUSTIN & SCOTT HALIK.

YEAH! YOU LEFT IT IN THE NOOK!

KISS THE COOK

KKSSSS

HEY, HEY, DON'T FORGET YOUR COFFEE!

SHIT, WHAT WOULD I EVER DO?

HAVE A GOOD DAY.

DON'T FORGET YOUR DOCTOR'S APPOINTMENT!

WORLD'S GREATEST LOVER

CLICK

KISS THE COOK

YES. YES, ABSOLUTELY. THE TOXIN WILL BUILD UP IN HIS SYSTEM OVER THE NEXT SIX HOURS. NO, HE'LL HAVE *NO* IDEA.

THINK HE'S JUST COMING DOWN WITH SOMETHING.

YES, WE ARE GETTING QUITE A BIT BETTER AT THIS. LATENCY FEELS ALMOST NON-EXISTENT.

WE GET THE INTEL IN DRAKE'S HEAD, AND WE'LL TRULY BE READY FOR THE NEXT AGE.

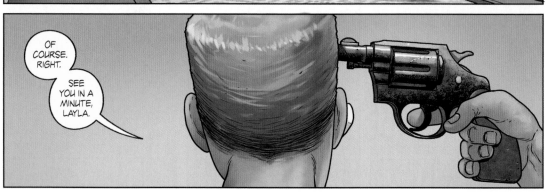

OF COURSE. RIGHT.

SEE YOU IN A MINUTE, LAYLA.

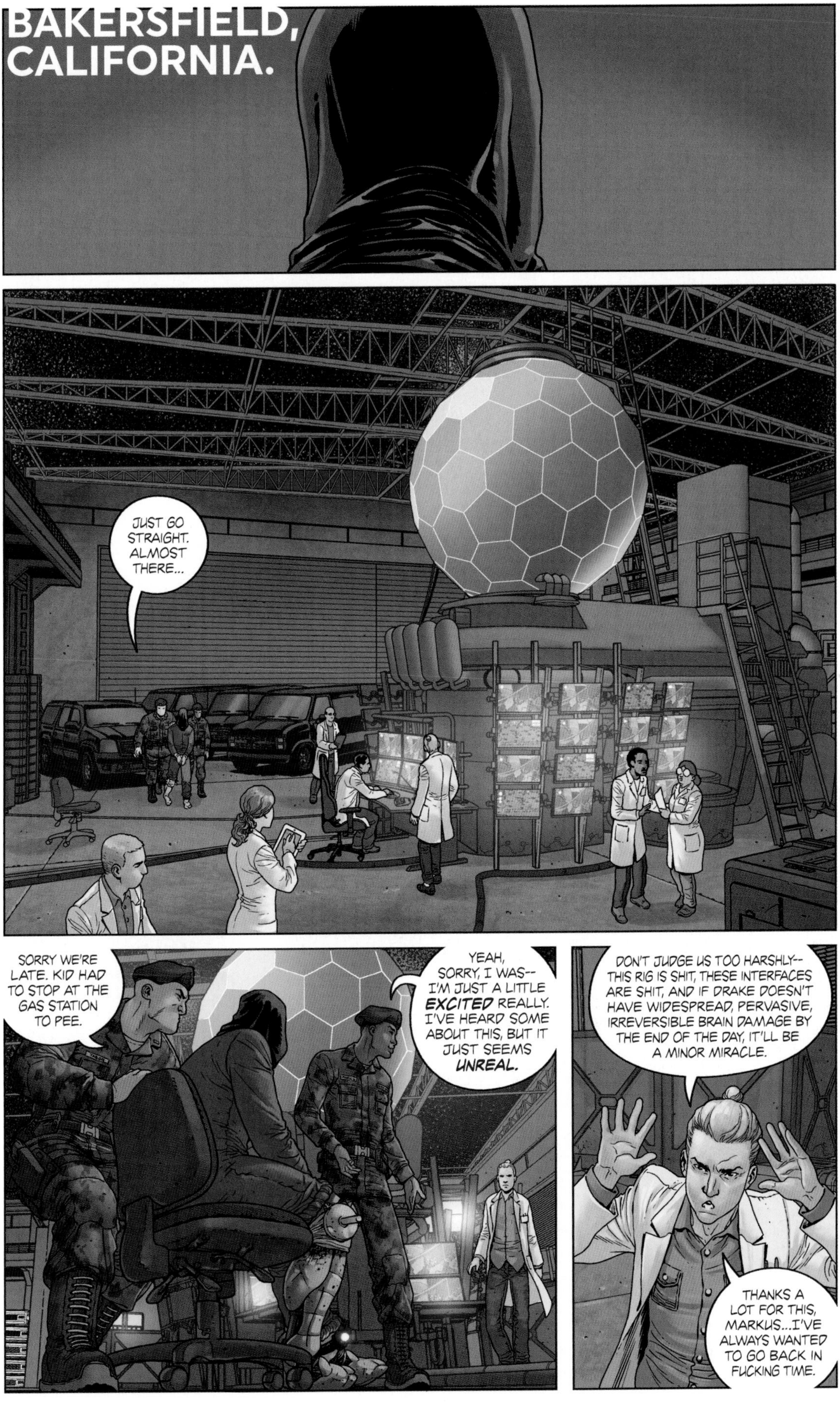

BAKERSFIELD, CALIFORNIA.
JUST GO STRAIGHT. ALMOST THERE...
SORRY WE'RE LATE. KID HAD TO STOP AT THE GAS STATION TO PEE.
YEAH, SORRY, I WAS-- I'M JUST A LITTLE EXCITED REALLY. I'VE HEARD SOME ABOUT THIS, BUT IT JUST SEEMS UNREAL.
DON'T JUDGE US TOO HARSHLY-- THIS RIG IS SHIT, THESE INTERFACES ARE SHIT, AND IF DRAKE DOESN'T HAVE WIDESPREAD, PERVASIVE, IRREVERSIBLE BRAIN DAMAGE BY THE END OF THE DAY, IT'LL BE A MINOR MIRACLE.
THANKS A LOT FOR THIS, MARKUS...I'VE ALWAYS WANTED TO GO BACK IN FUCKING TIME.

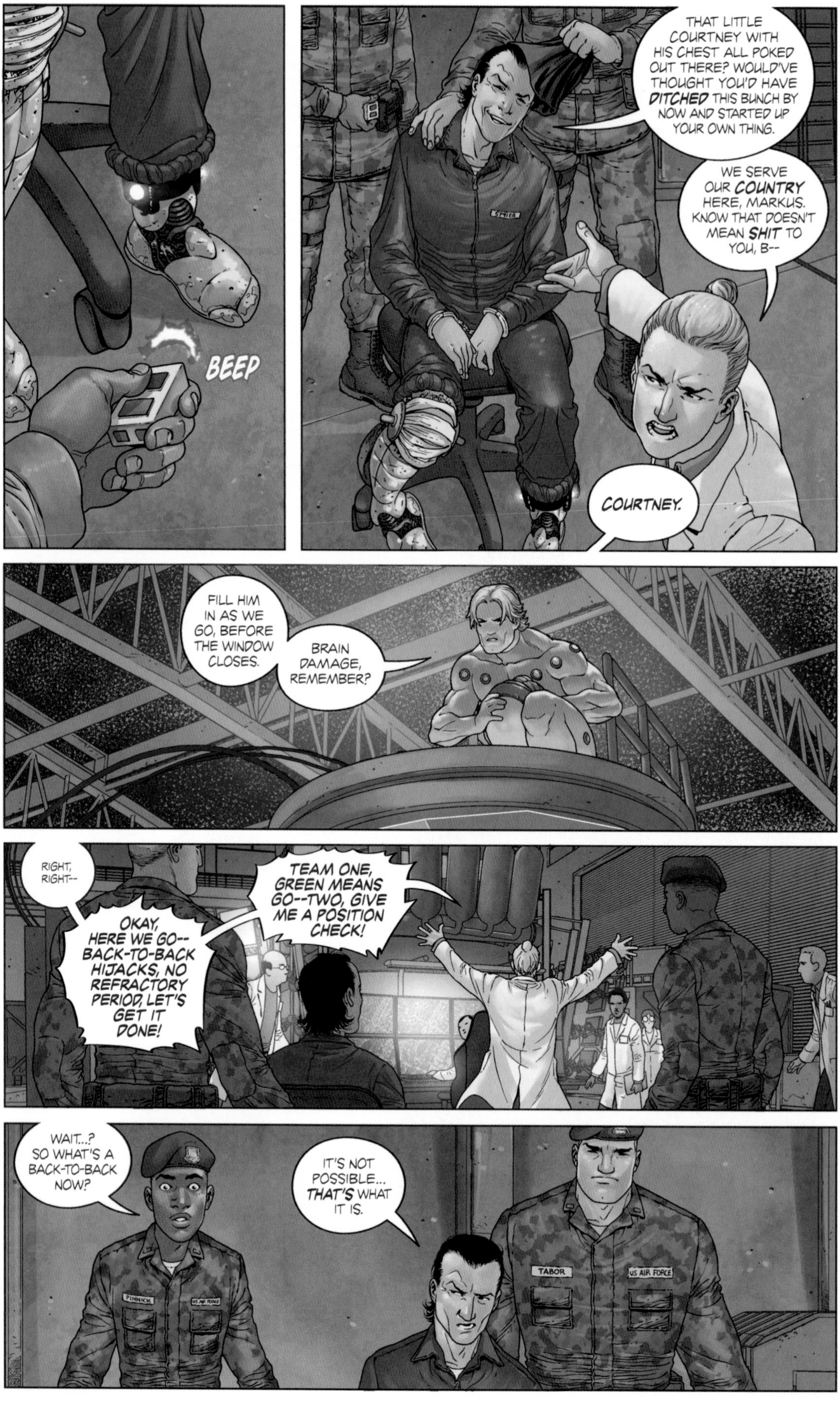
BEEP
THAT LITTLE COURTNEY WITH HIS CHEST ALL POKED OUT THERE? WOULD'VE THOUGHT YOU'D HAVE DITCHED THIS BUNCH BY NOW AND STARTED UP YOUR OWN THING.
WE SERVE OUR COUNTRY HERE, MARKUS. KNOW THAT DOESN'T MEAN SHIT TO YOU, B--
COURTNEY.
FILL HIM IN AS WE GO, BEFORE THE WINDOW CLOSES.
BRAIN DAMAGE, REMEMBER?
RIGHT, RIGHT--
OKAY, HERE WE GO--BACK-TO-BACK HIJACKS, NO REFRACTORY PERIOD, LET'S GET IT DONE!
TEAM ONE, GREEN MEANS GO--TWO, GIVE ME A POSITION CHECK!
WAIT...? SO WHAT'S A BACK-TO-BACK NOW?
IT'S NOT POSSIBLE... THAT'S WHAT IT IS.
PINNICK
US AIR FORCE
TABOR
US AIR FORCE

DRAKE'S CONTINUED EXPOSURE TO THE HARDCORE TECH HAS LEFT HIM WITH A SERIES OF CALLOUSES IN HIS NEURAL PATHWAYS, SO HIS HEAD CAN DO SHIT OTHERS CAN'T.

DRAKE, DIAGNOSTICS ARE LOOKING PRETTY CLEAN OVERALL, BUT I WANT TO KEEP THE NEURAL GUARDS UP A LITTLE HIGHER THAN NORMAL, TO MAKE THE TRANSITION A LITTLE SMOOTHER.

CLOSE EYE ON YOUR PHYSICAL RESPONSE, THOUGH-- MIGHT FEEL SOME TIME DELAY--

WHAT'S TIME DELAY MEAN?

I-I DON'T KNOW *WHAT* THE HELL THAT IS...

BUT I THOUGHT YOU USED TO WORK ON HARDCORE, AND THAT'S HOW--

THAT'S ENOUGH CHATTERING BACK THERE. NEXT PART IS IMPORTANT.

DRAKE, HOW WE DOING?

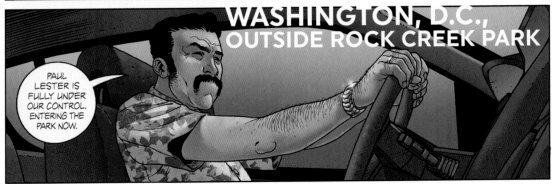

WASHINGTON, D.C., OUTSIDE ROCK CREEK PARK

PAUL LESTER IS FULLY UNDER OUR CONTROL. ENTERING THE PARK NOW.

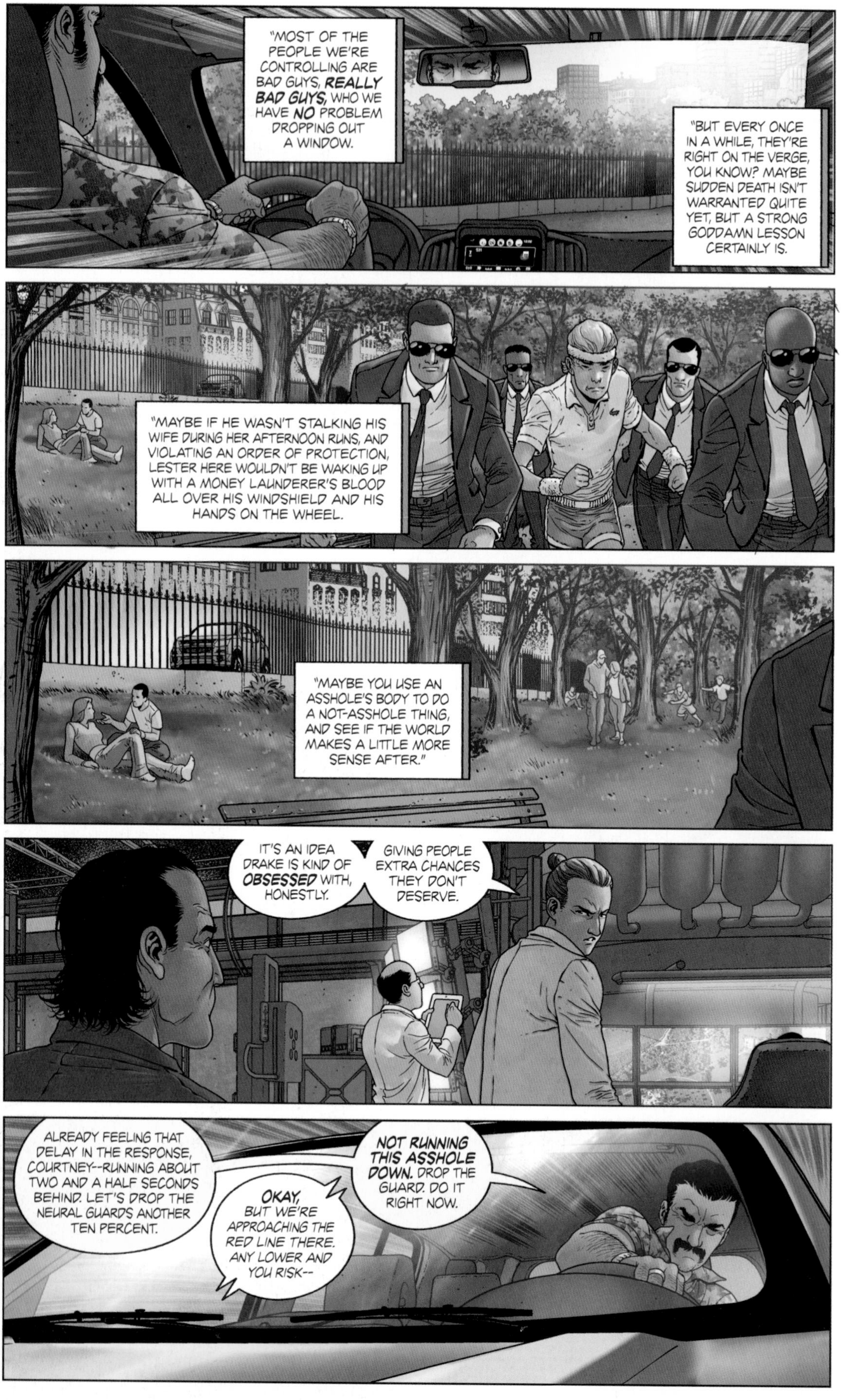
"MOST OF THE PEOPLE WE'RE CONTROLLING ARE BAD GUYS, **REALLY BAD GUYS,** WHO WE HAVE **NO** PROBLEM DROPPING OUT A WINDOW.
"BUT EVERY ONCE IN A WHILE, THEY'RE RIGHT ON THE VERGE, YOU KNOW? MAYBE SUDDEN DEATH ISN'T WARRANTED QUITE YET, BUT A STRONG GODDAMN LESSON CERTAINLY IS.
"MAYBE IF HE WASN'T STALKING HIS WIFE DURING HER AFTERNOON RUNS, AND VIOLATING AN ORDER OF PROTECTION, LESTER HERE WOULDN'T BE WAKING UP WITH A MONEY LAUNDERER'S BLOOD ALL OVER HIS WINDSHIELD AND HIS HANDS ON THE WHEEL.
"MAYBE YOU USE AN ASSHOLE'S BODY TO DO A NOT-ASSHOLE THING, AND SEE IF THE WORLD MAKES A LITTLE MORE SENSE AFTER."
IT'S AN IDEA DRAKE IS KIND OF **OBSESSED** WITH, HONESTLY.
GIVING PEOPLE EXTRA CHANCES THEY DON'T DESERVE.
ALREADY FEELING THAT DELAY IN THE RESPONSE, COURTNEY--RUNNING ABOUT TWO AND A HALF SECONDS BEHIND. LET'S DROP THE NEURAL GUARDS ANOTHER TEN PERCENT.
NOT RUNNING THIS ASSHOLE DOWN. DROP THE GUARD. DO IT RIGHT NOW.
OKAY, BUT WE'RE APPROACHING THE RED LINE THERE. ANY LOWER AND YOU RISK--

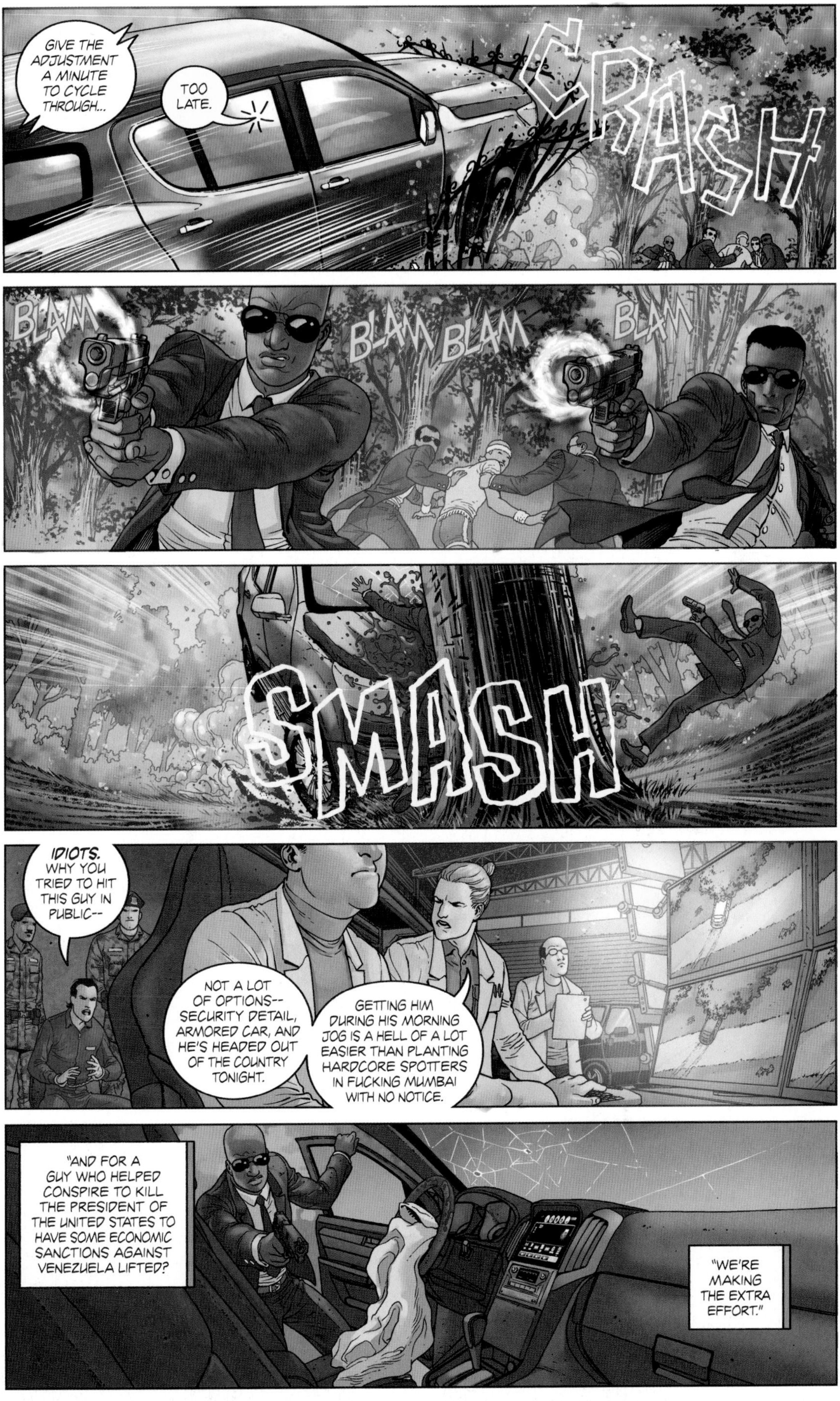

GIVE THE ADJUSTMENT A MINUTE TO CYCLE THROUGH...
TOO LATE.
CRASH
BLAM
BLAM BLAM
BLAM
SMASH
IDIOTS. WHY YOU TRIED TO HIT THIS GUY IN PUBLIC--
NOT A LOT OF OPTIONS-- SECURITY DETAIL, ARMORED CAR, AND HE'S HEADED OUT OF THE COUNTRY TONIGHT.
GETTING HIM DURING HIS MORNING JOG IS A HELL OF A LOT EASIER THAN PLANTING HARDCORE SPOTTERS IN FUCKING MUMBAI WITH NO NOTICE.
"AND FOR A GUY WHO HELPED CONSPIRE TO KILL THE PRESIDENT OF THE UNITED STATES TO HAVE SOME ECONOMIC SANCTIONS AGAINST VENEZUELA LIFTED?
"WE'RE MAKING THE EXTRA EFFORT."

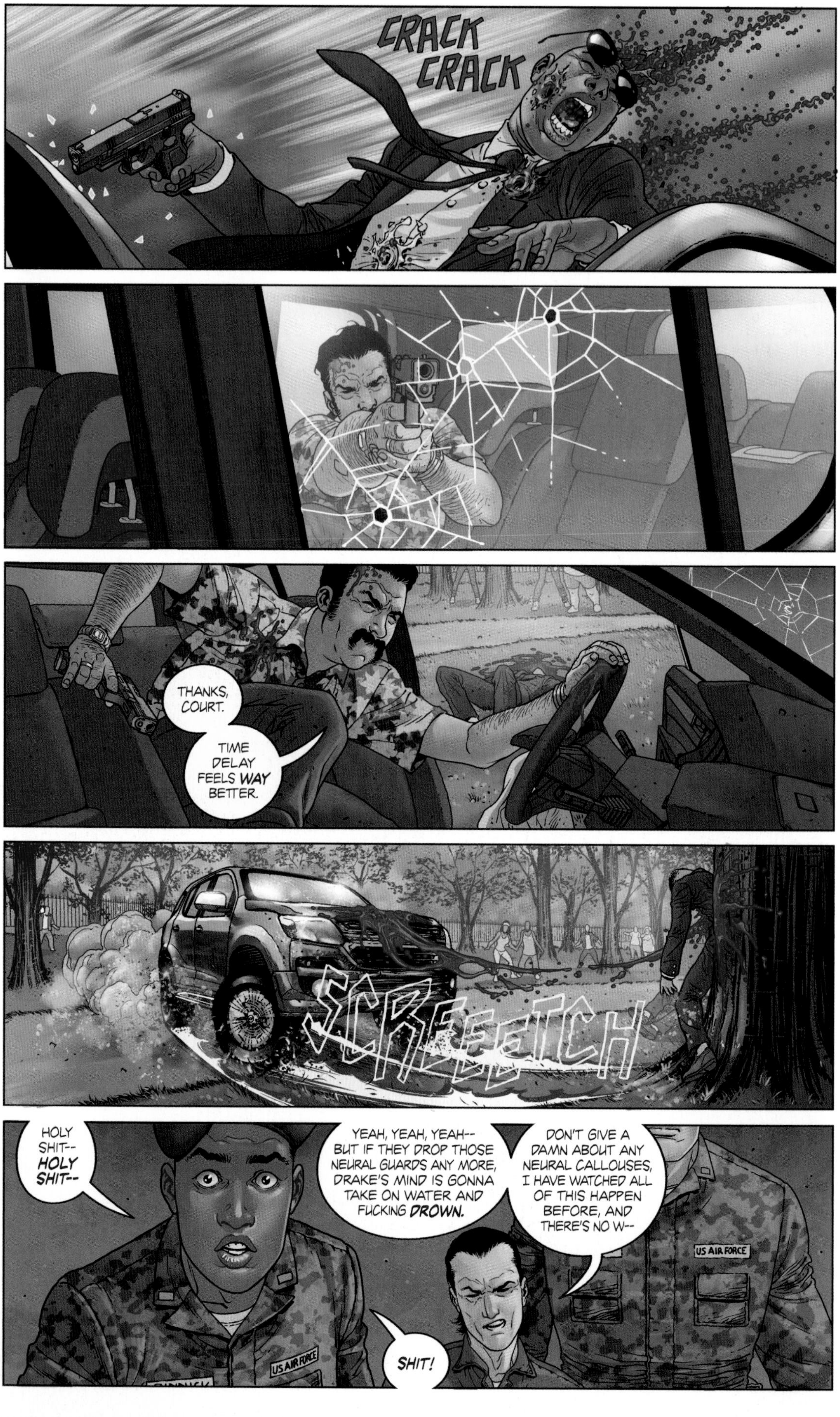

CRACK CRACK
THANKS, COURT.
TIME DELAY FEELS **WAY** BETTER.
SCREEETCH
HOLY SHIT-- ***HOLY SHIT--***
YEAH, YEAH, YEAH-- BUT IF THEY DROP THOSE NEURAL GUARDS ANY MORE, DRAKE'S MIND IS GONNA TAKE ON WATER AND FUCKING **DROWN.**
DON'T GIVE A DAMN ABOUT ANY NEURAL CALLOUSES, I HAVE WATCHED ALL OF THIS HAPPEN BEFORE, AND THERE'S NO W--
SHIT!
US AIR FORCE
US AIR FORCE

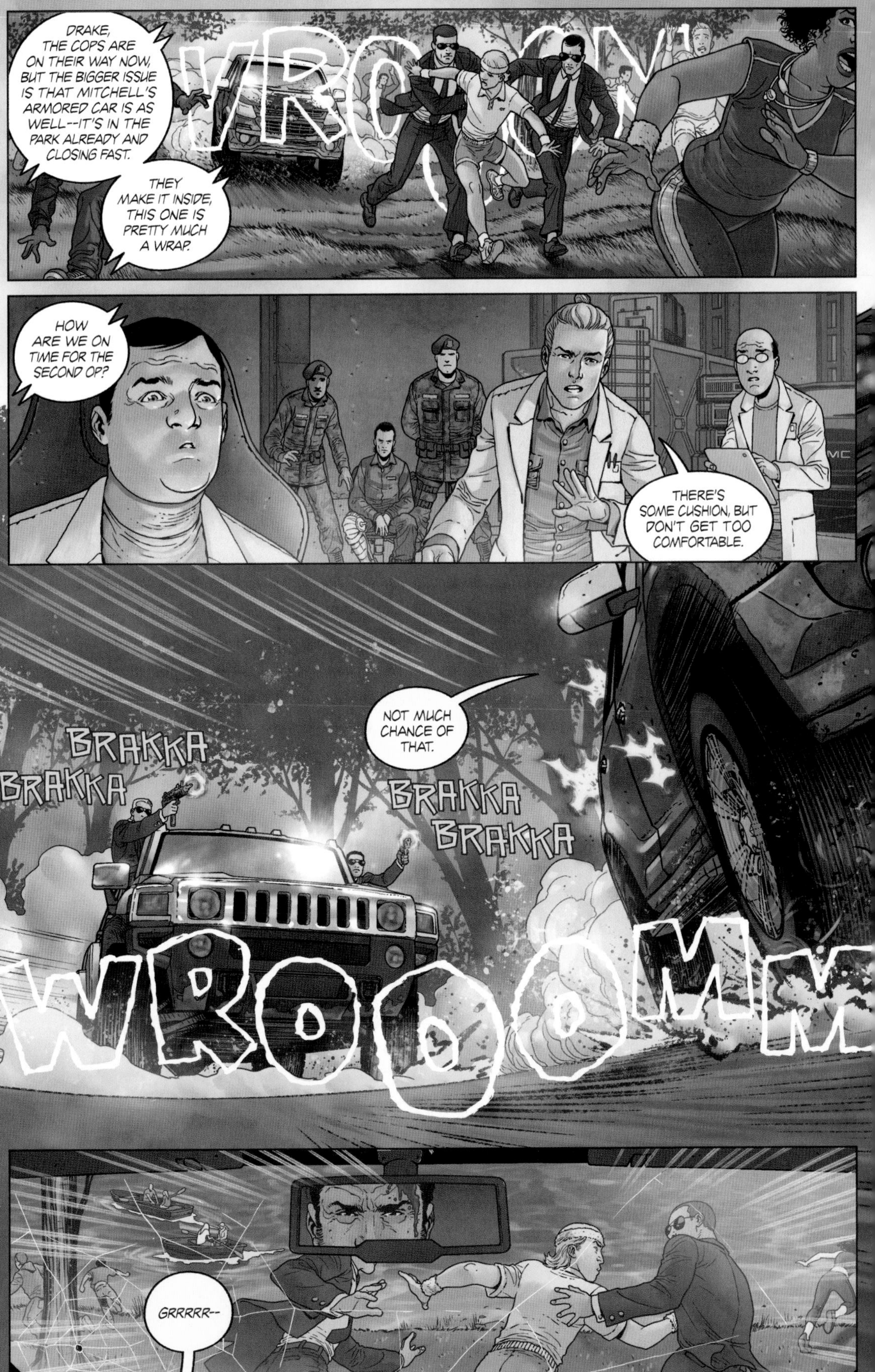
DRAKE, THE COPS ARE ON THEIR WAY NOW, BUT THE BIGGER ISSUE IS THAT MITCHELL'S ARMORED CAR IS AS WELL--IT'S IN THE PARK ALREADY AND CLOSING FAST.
THEY MAKE IT INSIDE, THIS ONE IS PRETTY MUCH A WRAP.
HOW ARE WE ON TIME FOR THE SECOND OP?
THERE'S SOME CUSHION, BUT DON'T GET TOO COMFORTABLE.
NOT MUCH CHANCE OF THAT.
BRAKKA BRAKKA
BRAKKA BRAKKA
WROOOMM
GRRRRR--

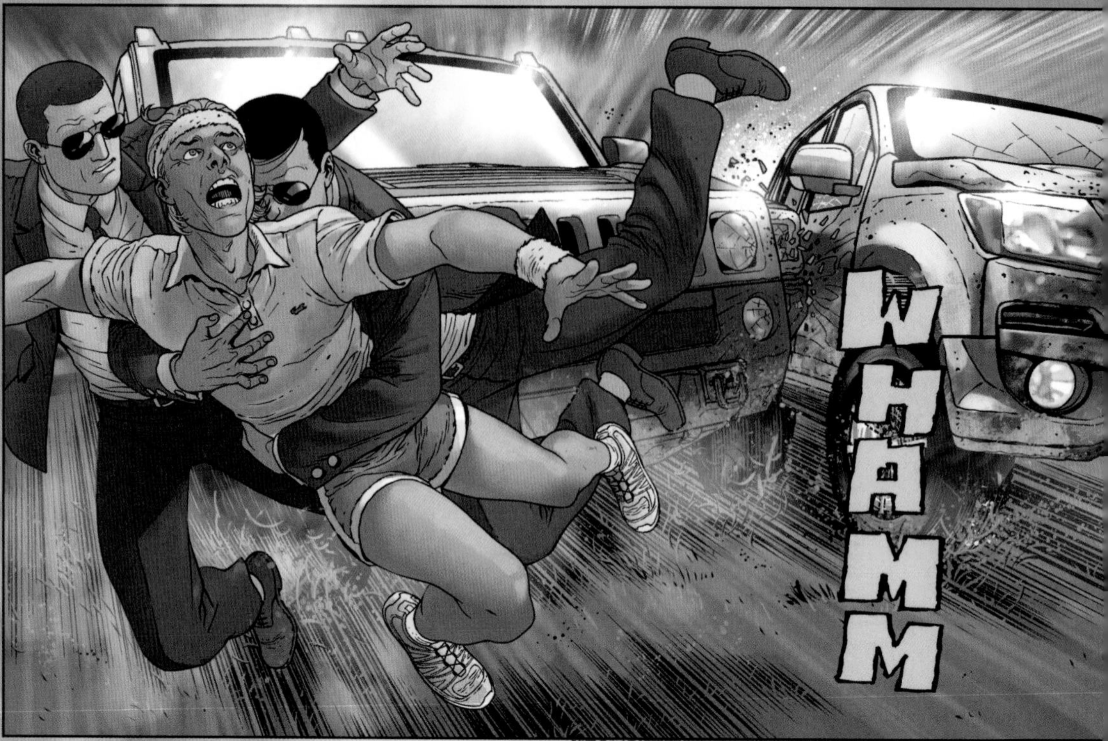
WHAMM

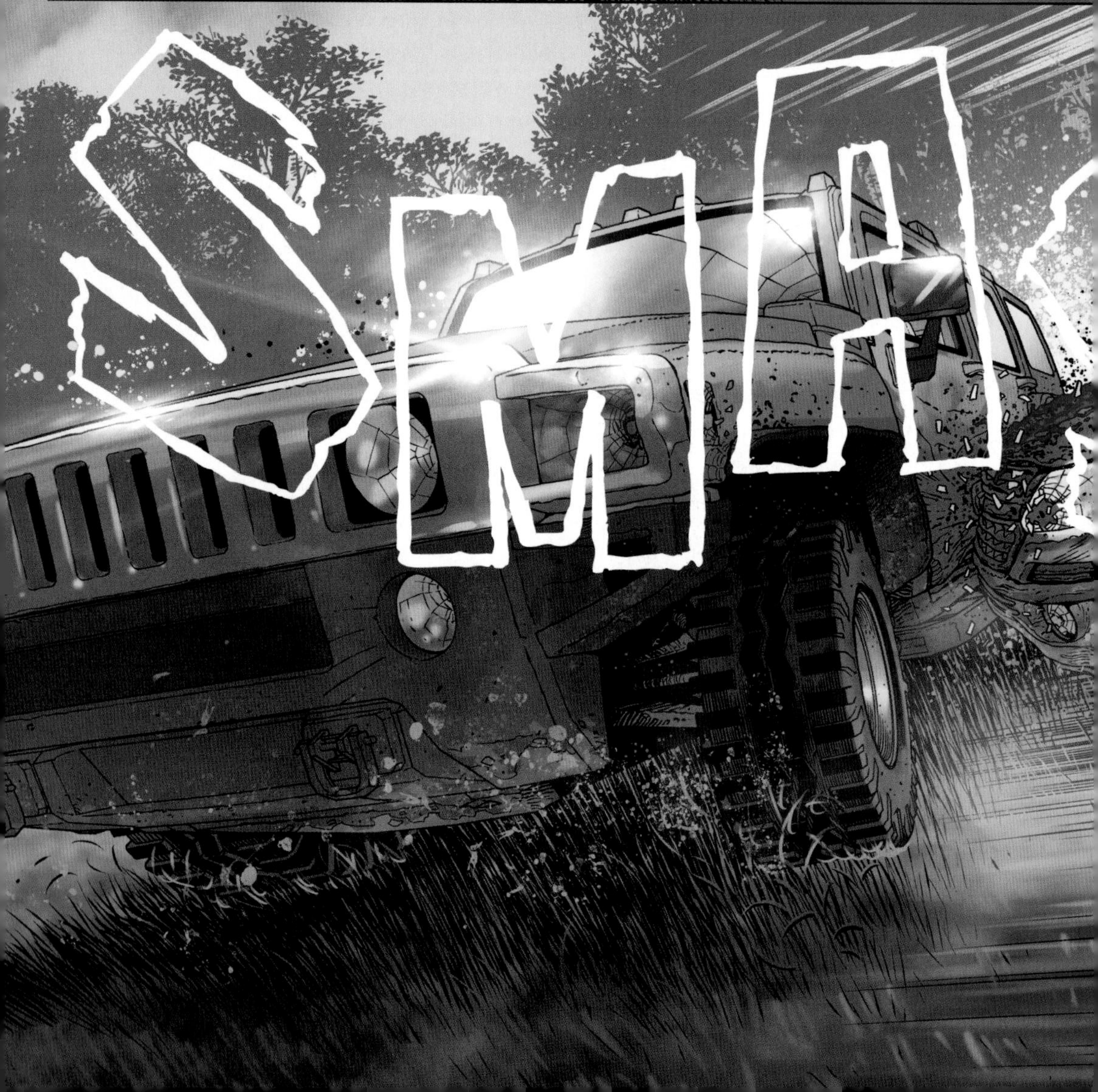
SMA

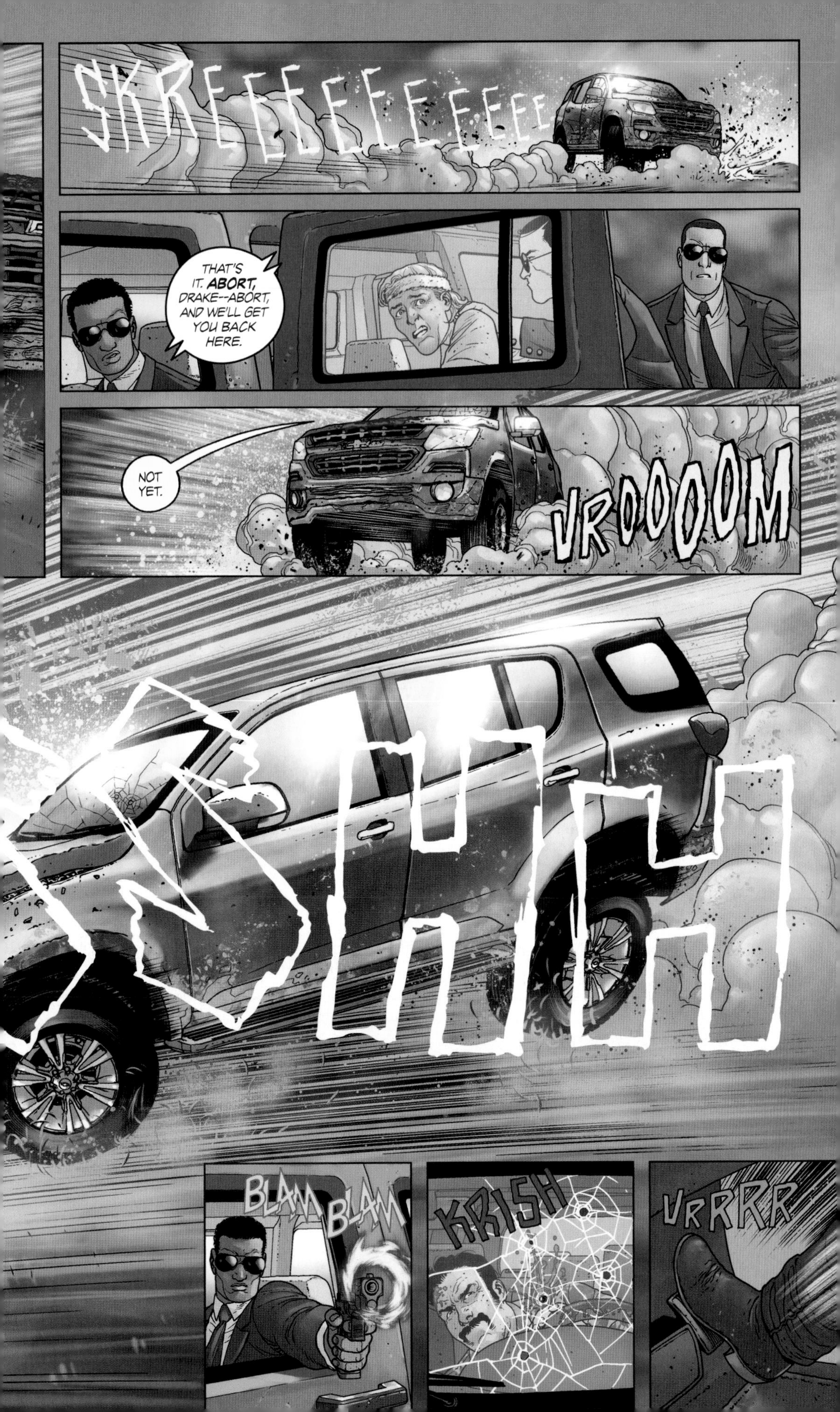
SKREEEEEEEEEEE
THAT'S IT. **ABORT,** DRAKE--ABORT, AND WE'LL GET YOU BACK HERE.
NOT YET.
VROOOOM
SMASH
BLAM BLAM
KRISH
VRRRR

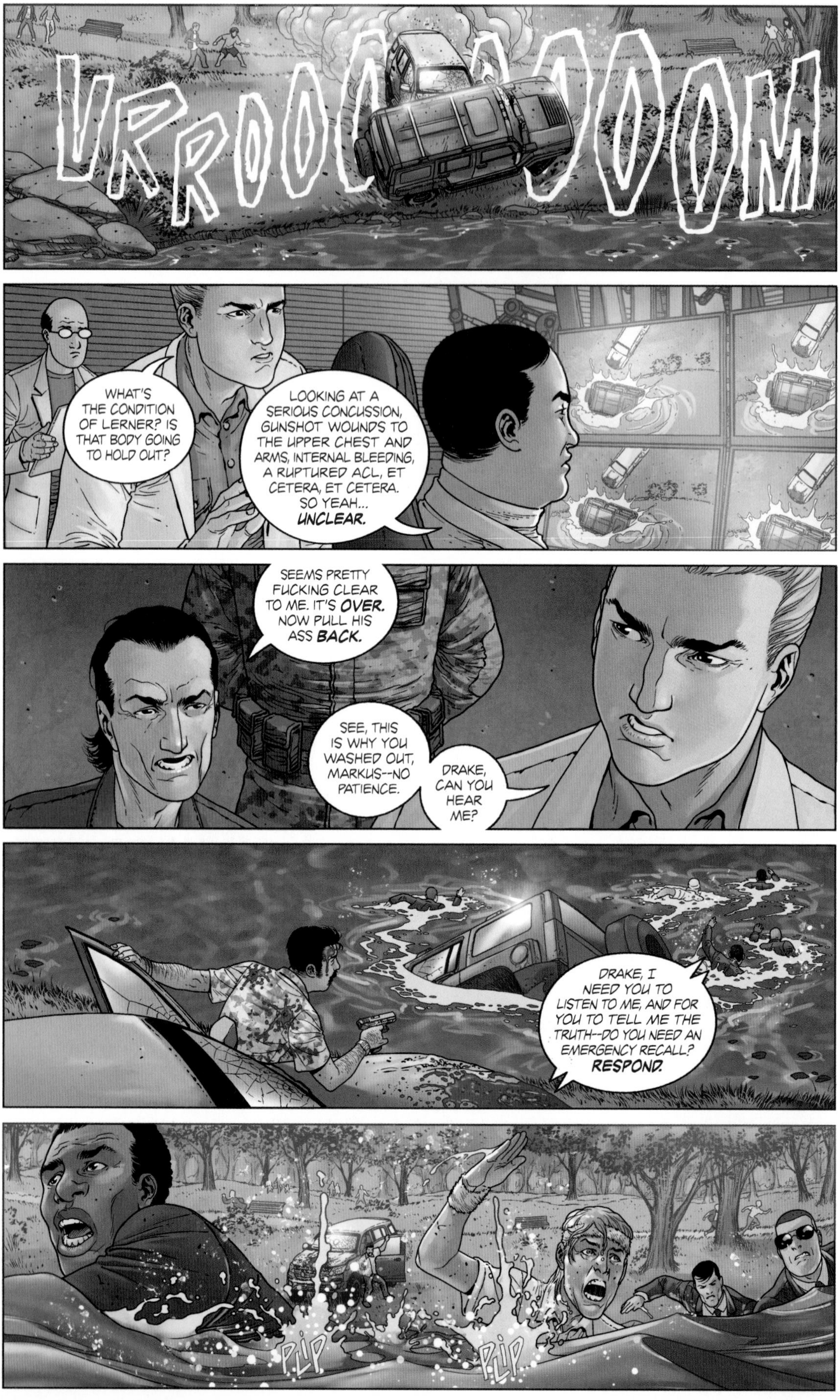
VRROOOOOOOOOM
WHAT'S THE CONDITION OF LERNER? IS THAT BODY GOING TO HOLD OUT?
LOOKING AT A SERIOUS CONCUSSION, GUNSHOT WOUNDS TO THE UPPER CHEST AND ARMS, INTERNAL BLEEDING, A RUPTURED ACL, ET CETERA, ET CETERA. SO YEAH... UNCLEAR.
SEEMS PRETTY FUCKING CLEAR TO ME. IT'S OVER. NOW PULL HIS ASS BACK.
SEE, THIS IS WHY YOU WASHED OUT, MARKUS--NO PATIENCE.
DRAKE, CAN YOU HEAR ME?
DRAKE, I NEED YOU TO LISTEN TO ME, AND FOR YOU TO TELL ME THE TRUTH--DO YOU NEED AN EMERGENCY RECALL? RESPOND.
PLIP
PLIP

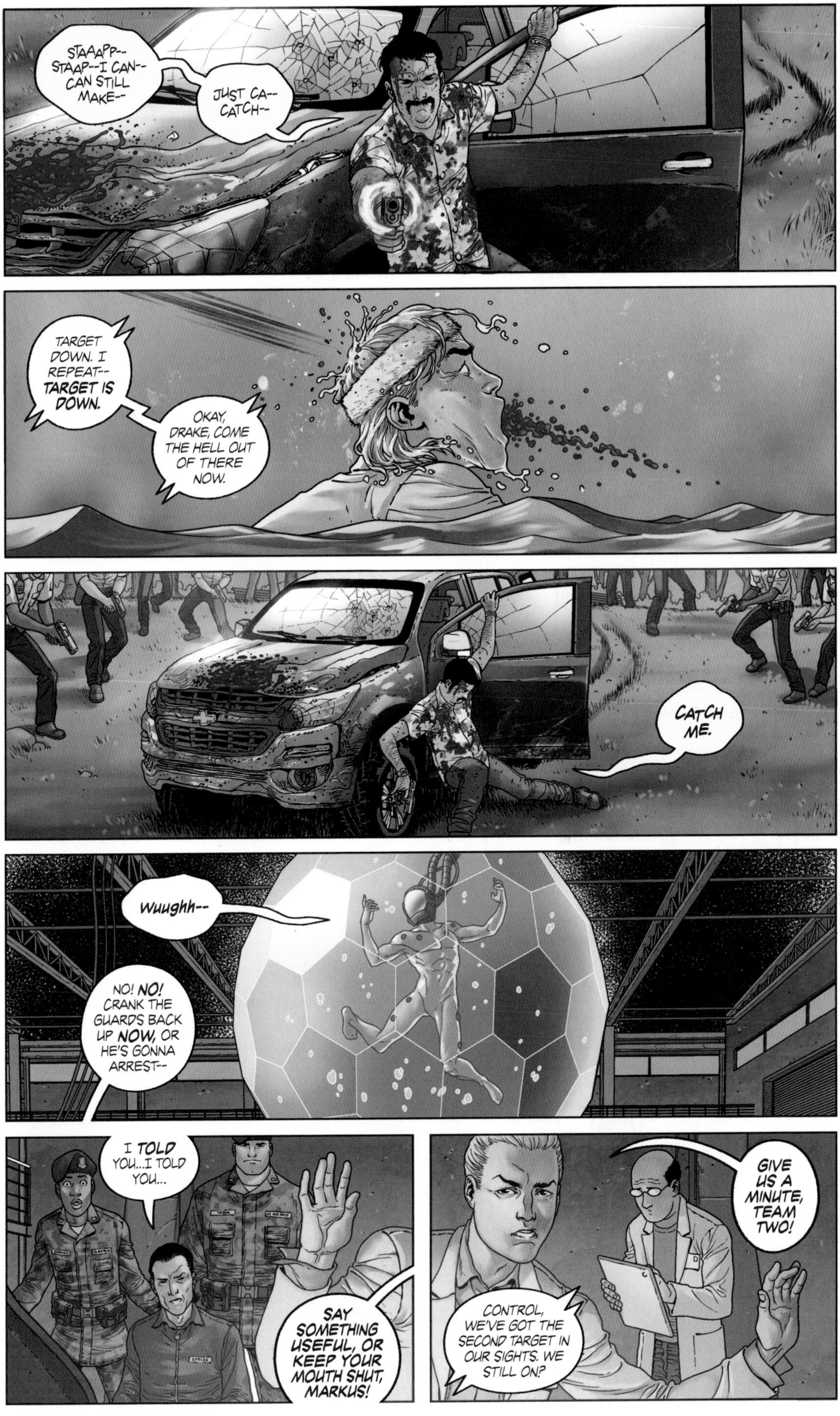
STAAAPP-- STAAP--I CAN-- CAN STILL MAKE--
JUST CA-- CATCH--
TARGET DOWN. I REPEAT-- TARGET IS DOWN.
OKAY, DRAKE, COME THE HELL OUT OF THERE NOW.
CATCH ME.
wuughh--
NO! NO! CRANK THE GUARDS BACK UP NOW, OR HE'S GONNA ARREST--
I TOLD YOU...I TOLD YOU...
SAY SOMETHING USEFUL, OR KEEP YOUR MOUTH SHUT, MARKUS!
GIVE US A MINUTE, TEAM TWO!
CONTROL, WE'VE GOT THE SECOND TARGET IN OUR SIGHTS. WE STILL ON?

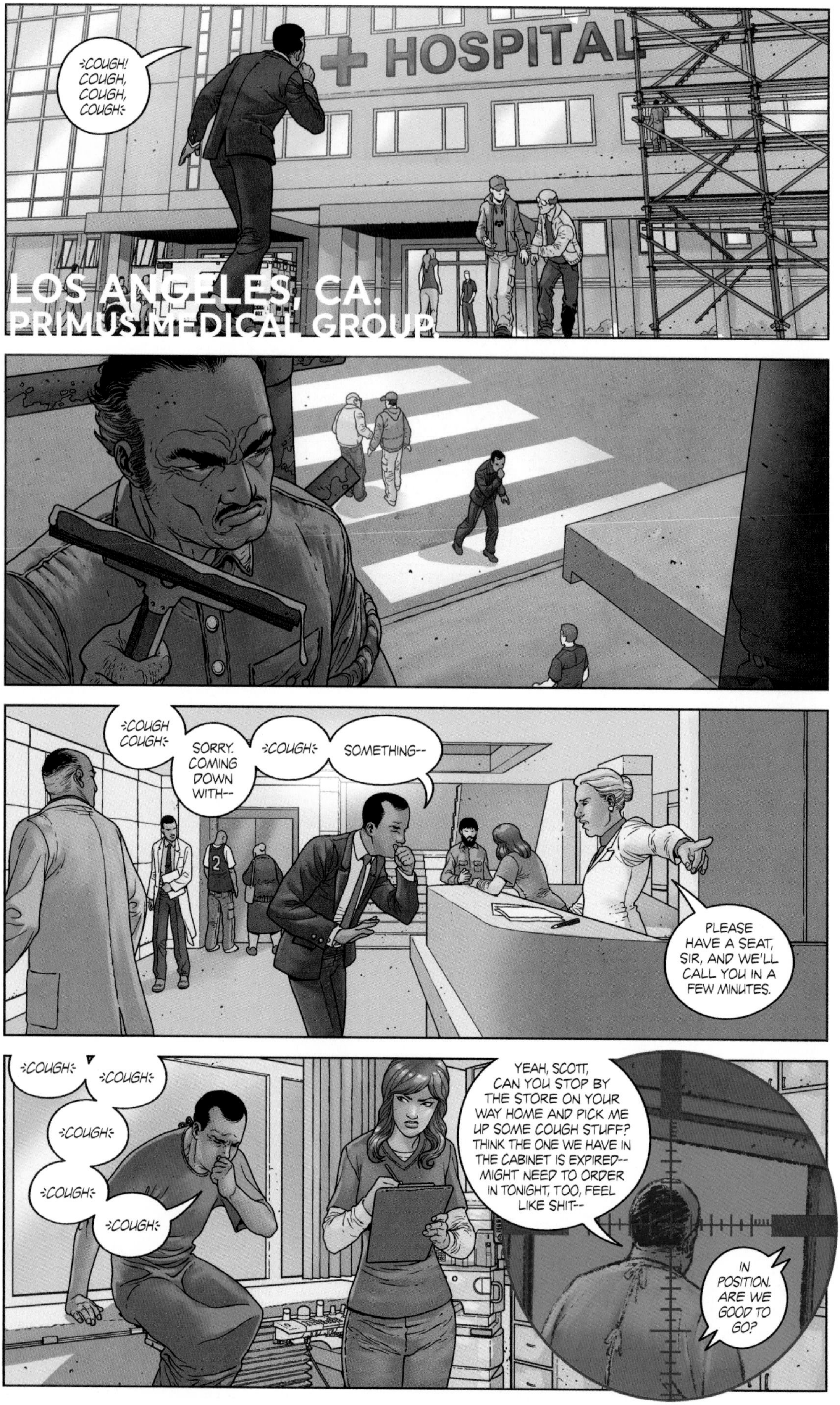

>COUGH! COUGH, COUGH, COUGH<
+ HOSPITAL
LOS ANGELES, CA.
PRIMUS MEDICAL GROUP.
>COUGH COUGH<
SORRY. COMING DOWN WITH--
>COUGH<
SOMETHING--
PLEASE HAVE A SEAT, SIR, AND WE'LL CALL YOU IN A FEW MINUTES.
>COUGH<
>COUGH<
>COUGH<
>COUGH<
>COUGH<
YEAH, SCOTT, CAN YOU STOP BY THE STORE ON YOUR WAY HOME AND PICK ME UP SOME COUGH STUFF? THINK THE ONE WE HAVE IN THE CABINET IS EXPIRED-- MIGHT NEED TO ORDER IN TONIGHT, TOO, FEEL LIKE SHIT--
IN POSITION. ARE WE GOOD TO GO?

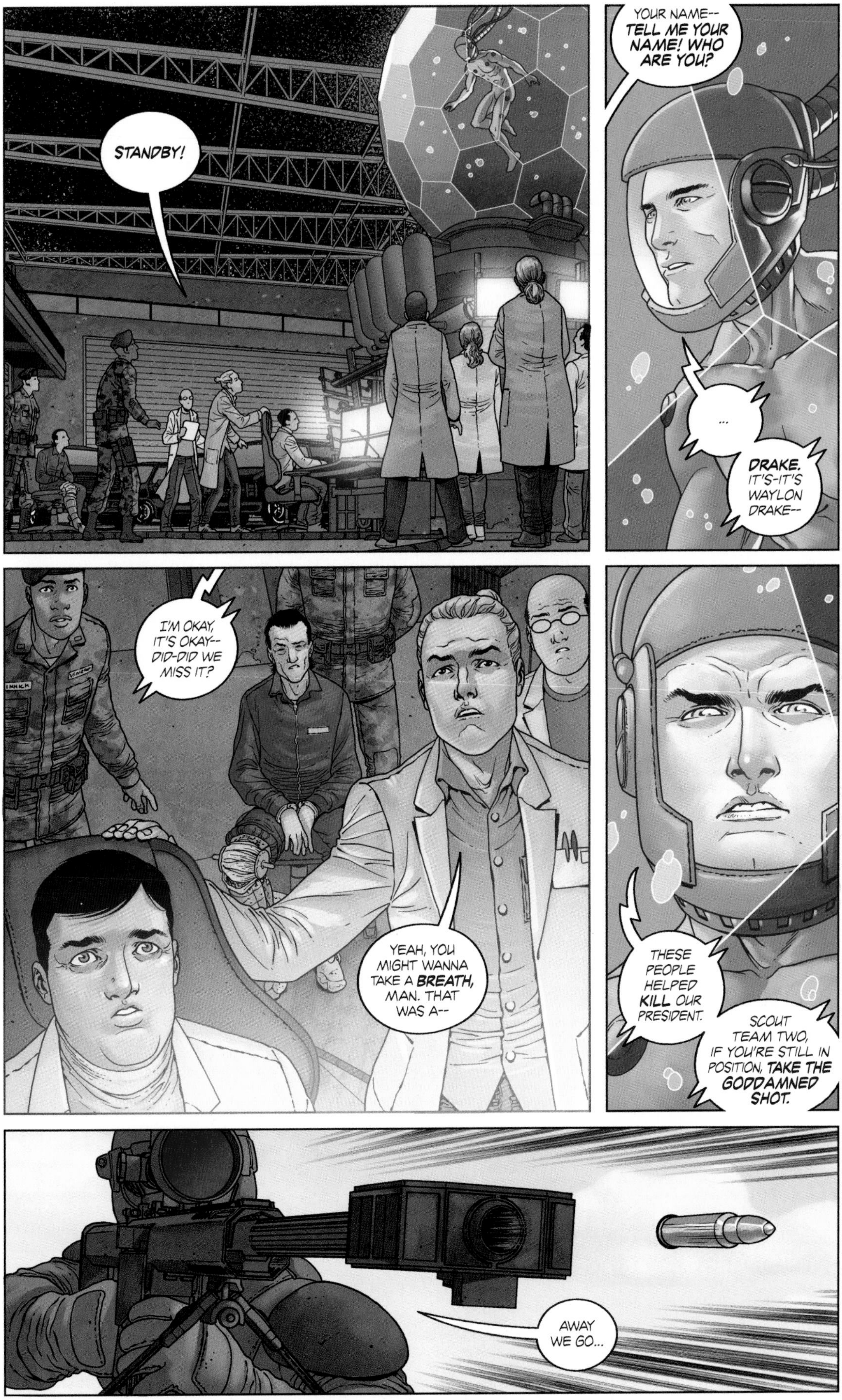
STANDBY!
YOUR NAME-- TELL ME YOUR NAME! WHO ARE YOU?
...
DRAKE. IT'S--IT'S WAYLON DRAKE--
I'M OKAY, IT'S OKAY-- DID-DID WE MISS IT?
YEAH, YOU MIGHT WANNA TAKE A BREATH, MAN. THAT WAS A--
THESE PEOPLE HELPED KILL OUR PRESIDENT.
SCOUT TEAM TWO, IF YOU'RE STILL IN POSITION, TAKE THE GODDAMNED SHOT.
AWAY WE GO...

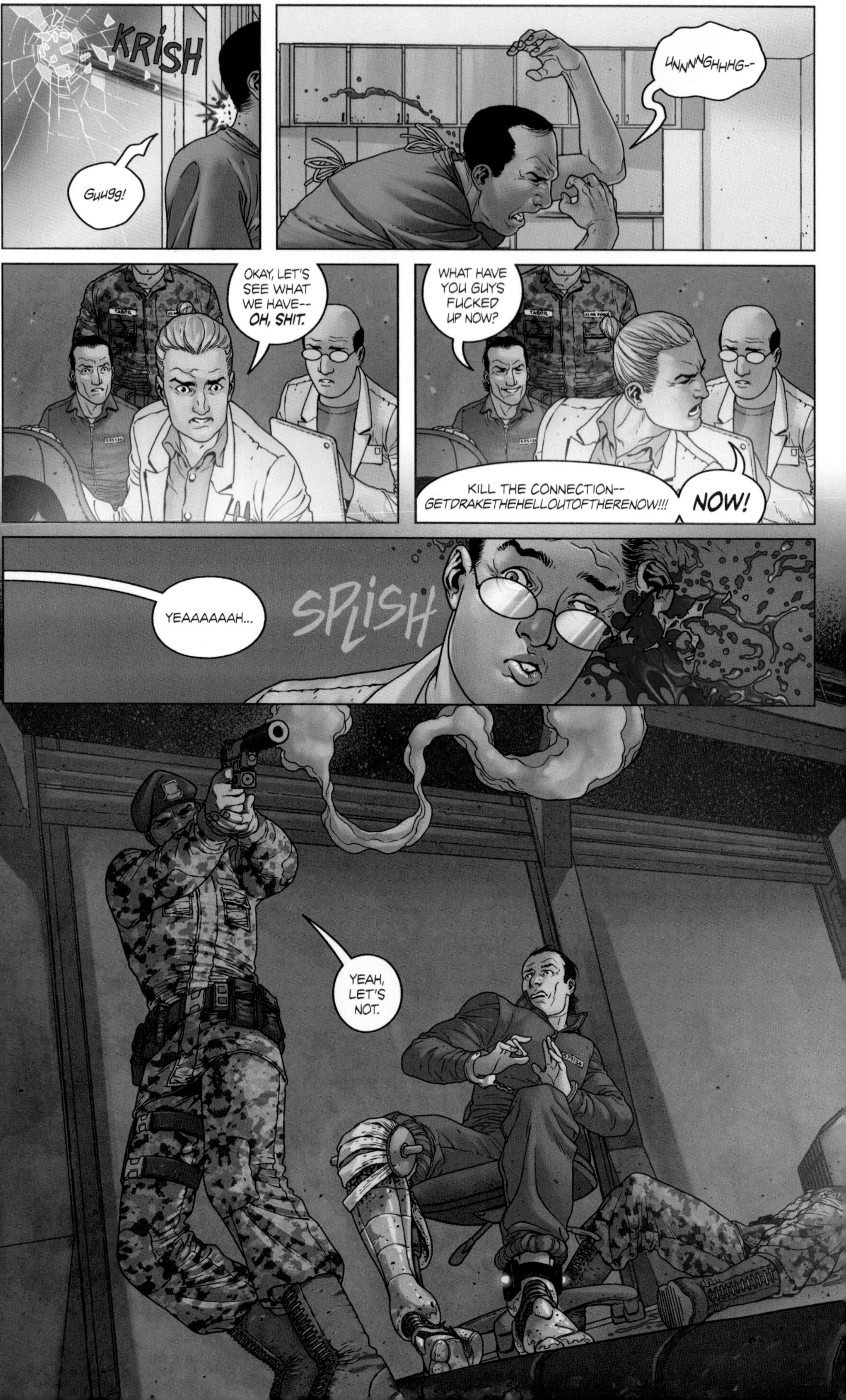
KRISH
Guugg!
UNNNNGHHHG--
OKAY, LET'S SEE WHAT WE HAVE-- OH, SHIT.
WHAT HAVE YOU GUYS FUCKED UP NOW?
KILL THE CONNECTION-- GETDRAKETHEHELLOUTOFTHERENOW!!!
NOW!
YEAAAAAAH...
SPLISH
YEAH, LET'S NOT.

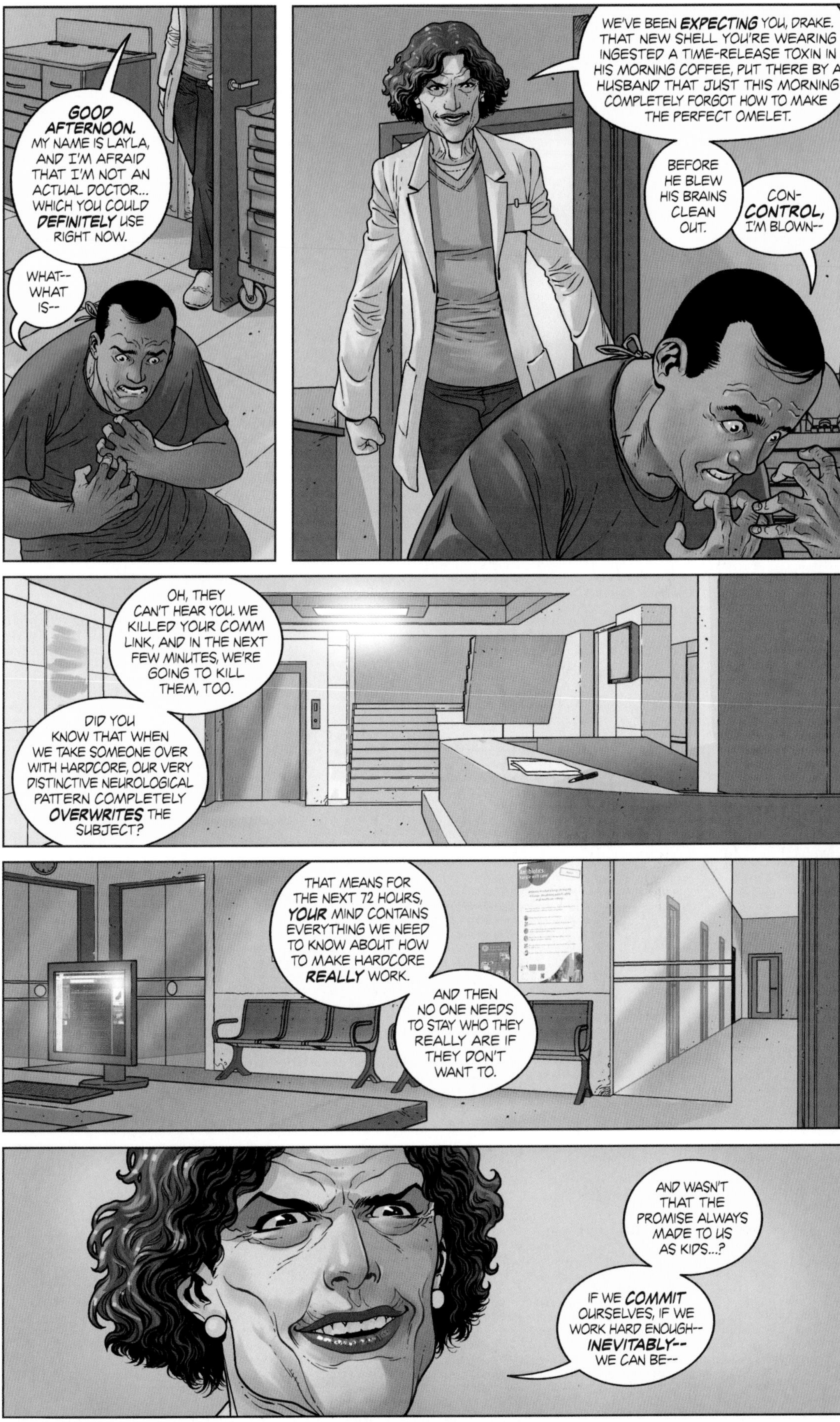
GOOD AFTERNOON. MY NAME IS LAYLA, AND I'M AFRAID THAT I'M NOT AN ACTUAL DOCTOR... WHICH YOU COULD DEFINITELY USE RIGHT NOW.
WHAT-- WHAT IS--
WE'VE BEEN EXPECTING YOU, DRAKE. THAT NEW SHELL YOU'RE WEARING INGESTED A TIME-RELEASE TOXIN IN HIS MORNING COFFEE, PUT THERE BY A HUSBAND THAT JUST THIS MORNING COMPLETELY FORGOT HOW TO MAKE THE PERFECT OMELET.
BEFORE HE BLEW HIS BRAINS CLEAN OUT.
CON-CONTROL, I'M BLOWN--
OH, THEY CAN'T HEAR YOU. WE KILLED YOUR COMM LINK, AND IN THE NEXT FEW MINUTES, WE'RE GOING TO KILL THEM, TOO.
DID YOU KNOW THAT WHEN WE TAKE SOMEONE OVER WITH HARDCORE, OUR VERY DISTINCTIVE NEUROLOGICAL PATTERN COMPLETELY OVERWRITES THE SUBJECT?
THAT MEANS FOR THE NEXT 72 HOURS, YOUR MIND CONTAINS EVERYTHING WE NEED TO KNOW ABOUT HOW TO MAKE HARDCORE REALLY WORK.
AND THEN NO ONE NEEDS TO STAY WHO THEY REALLY ARE IF THEY DON'T WANT TO.
AND WASN'T THAT THE PROMISE ALWAYS MADE TO US AS KIDS...?
IF WE COMMIT OURSELVES, IF WE WORK HARD ENOUGH-- INEVITABLY-- WE CAN BE--

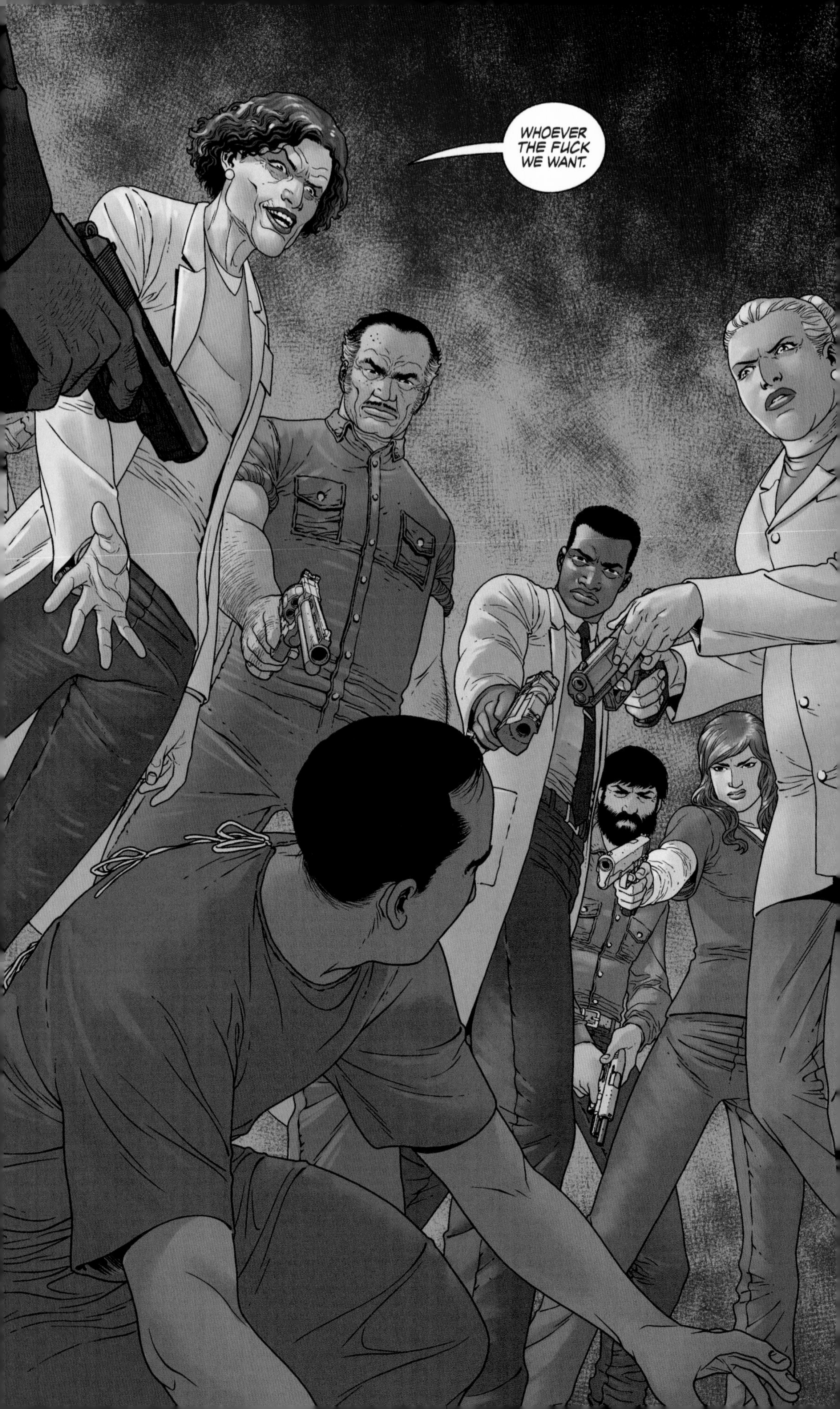
WHOEVER THE FUCK WE WANT.

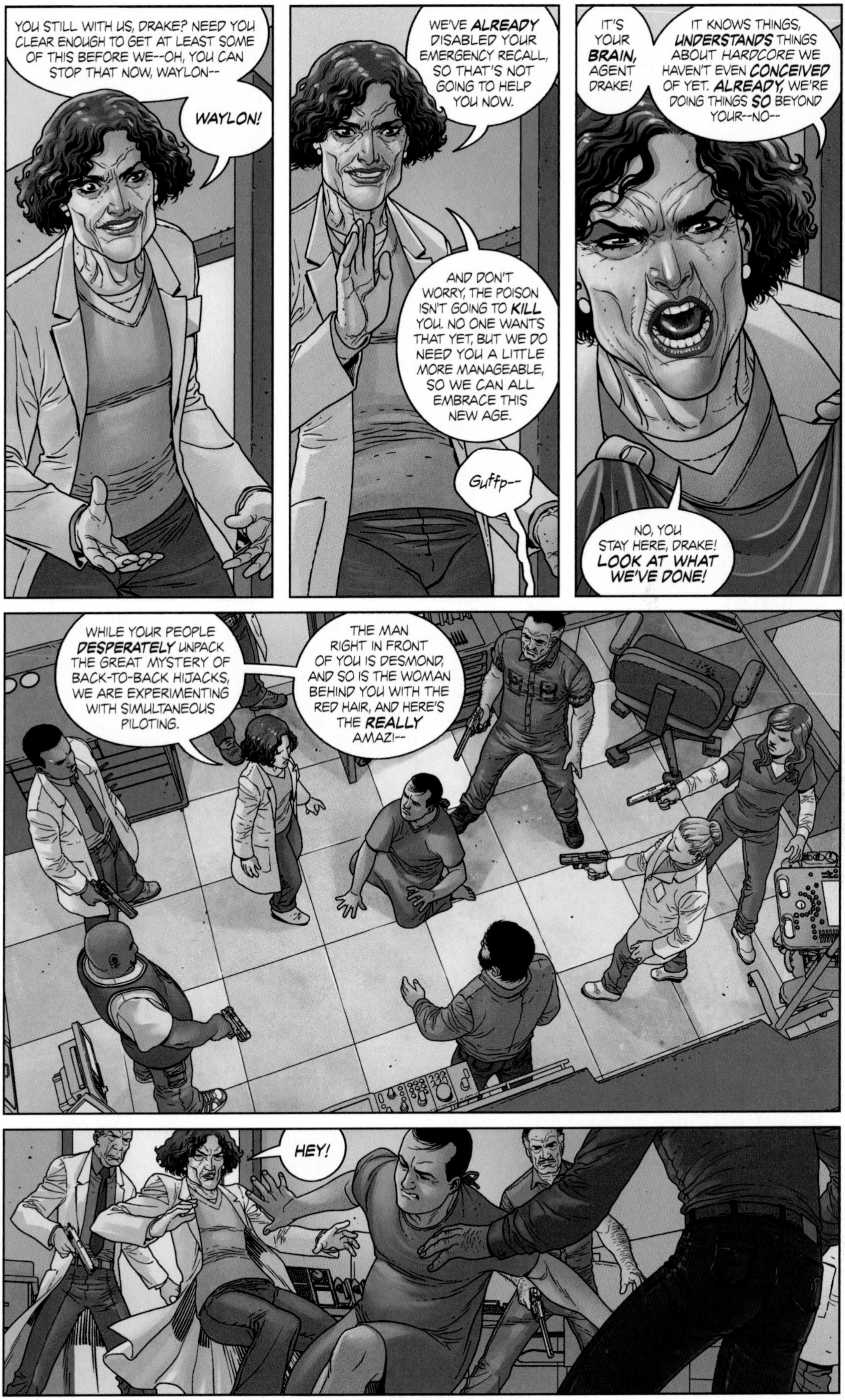
YOU STILL WITH US, DRAKE? NEED YOU CLEAR ENOUGH TO GET AT LEAST SOME OF THIS BEFORE WE--OH, YOU CAN STOP THAT NOW, WAYLON--
WAYLON!
WE'VE ALREADY DISABLED YOUR EMERGENCY RECALL, SO THAT'S NOT GOING TO HELP YOU NOW.
AND DON'T WORRY, THE POISON ISN'T GOING TO KILL YOU. NO ONE WANTS THAT YET, BUT WE DO NEED YOU A LITTLE MORE MANAGEABLE, SO WE CAN ALL EMBRACE THIS NEW AGE.
Guffp--
IT'S YOUR BRAIN, AGENT DRAKE!
IT KNOWS THINGS, UNDERSTANDS THINGS ABOUT HARDCORE WE HAVEN'T EVEN CONCEIVED OF YET. ALREADY, WE'RE DOING THINGS SO BEYOND YOUR--NO--
NO, YOU STAY HERE, DRAKE! LOOK AT WHAT WE'VE DONE!
WHILE YOUR PEOPLE DESPERATELY UNPACK THE GREAT MYSTERY OF BACK-TO-BACK HIJACKS, WE ARE EXPERIMENTING WITH SIMULTANEOUS PILOTING.
THE MAN RIGHT IN FRONT OF YOU IS DESMOND, AND SO IS THE WOMAN BEHIND YOU WITH THE RED HAIR, AND HERE'S THE REALLY AMAZI--
HEY!

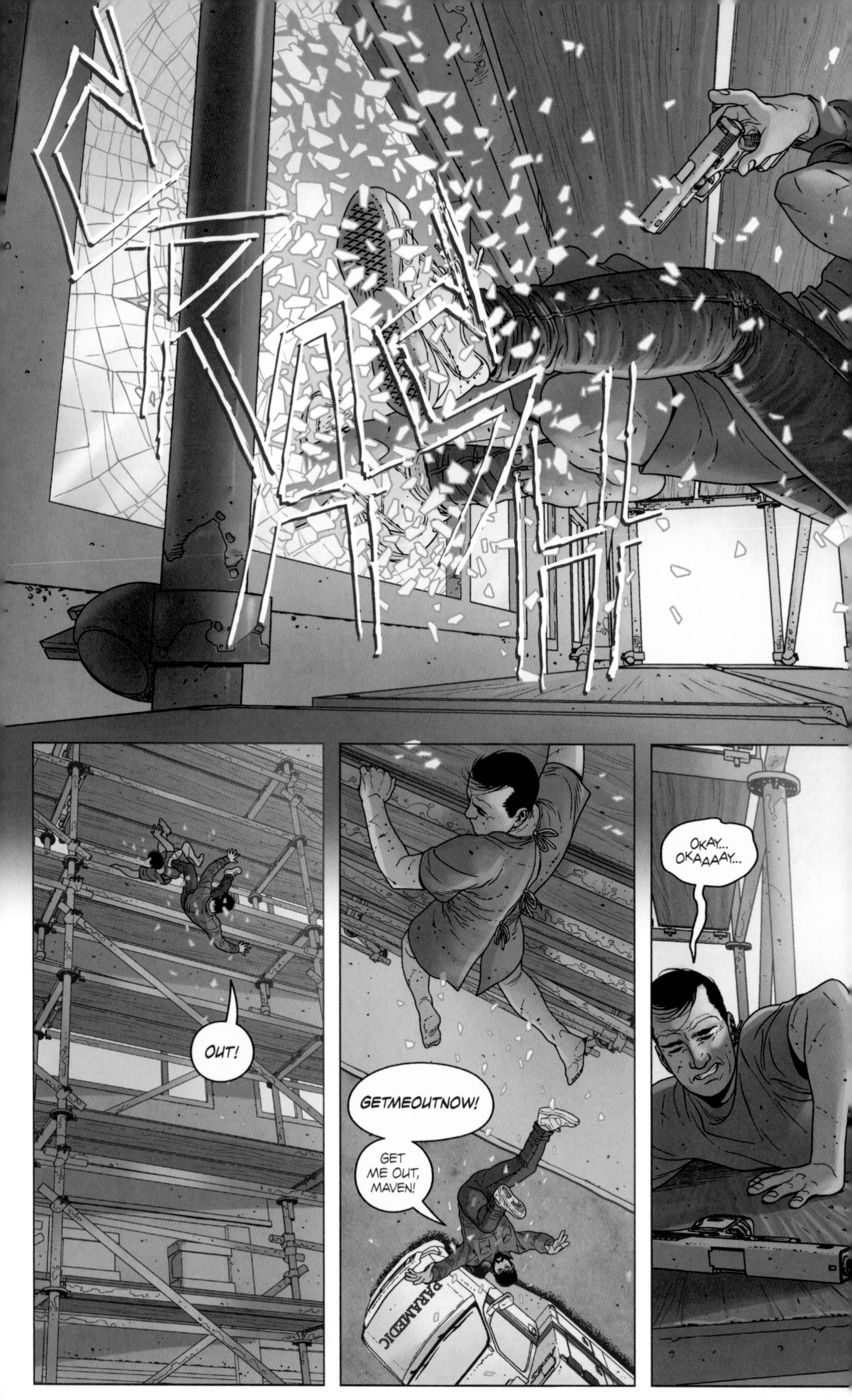
CRASSHH
OUT!
GETMEOUTNOW!
GET ME OUT, MAVEN!
PARAMEDIC
OKAY... OKAAAAY...

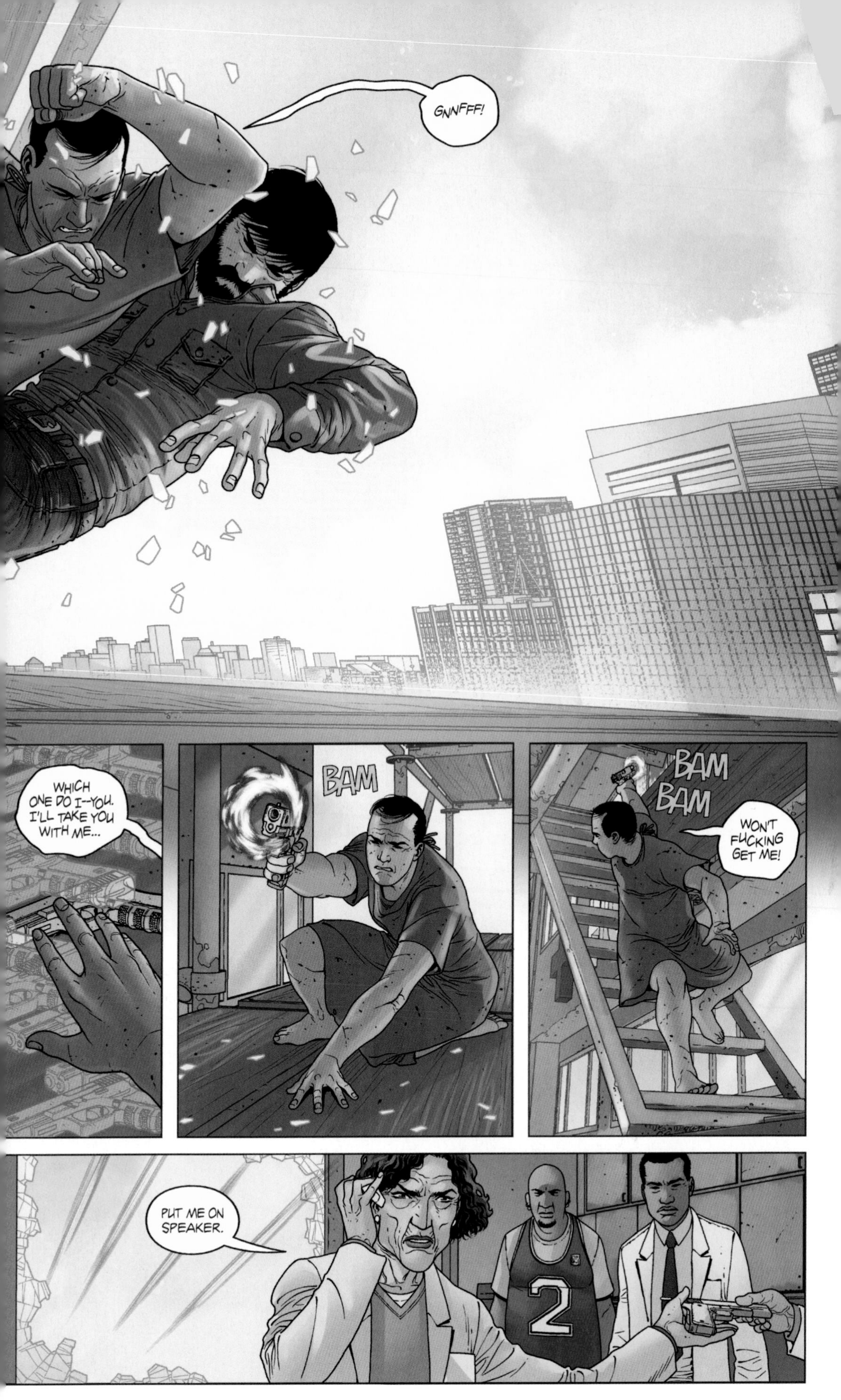
GNNFFF!
WHICH ONE DO I--YOU. I'LL TAKE YOU WITH ME...
BAM
BAM BAM
WON'T FUCKING GET ME!
PUT ME ON SPEAKER.

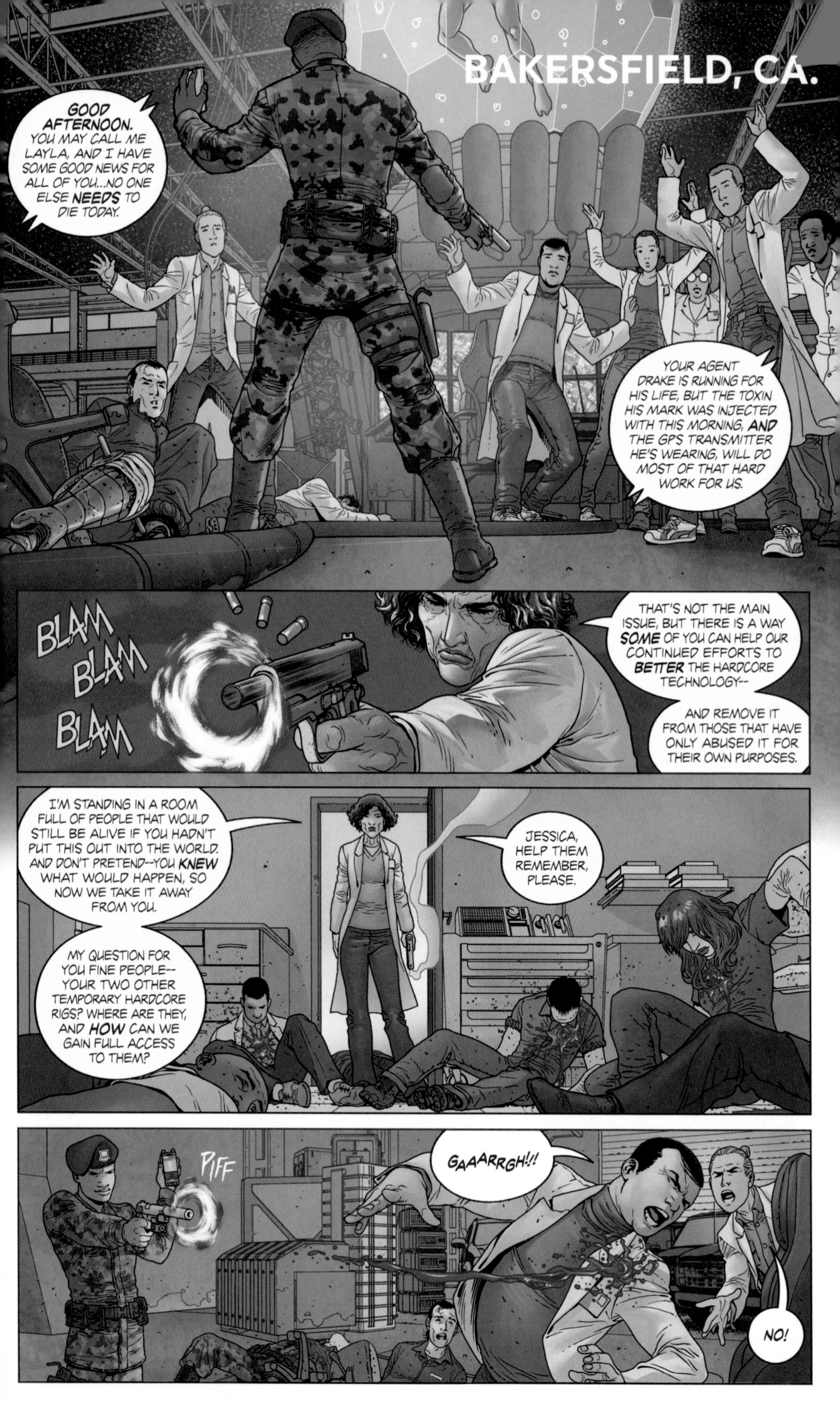
BAKERSFIELD, CA.
GOOD AFTERNOON. YOU MAY CALL ME LAYLA, AND I HAVE SOME GOOD NEWS FOR ALL OF YOU...NO ONE ELSE NEEDS TO DIE TODAY.
YOUR AGENT DRAKE IS RUNNING FOR HIS LIFE, BUT THE TOXIN HIS MARK WAS INJECTED WITH THIS MORNING, AND THE GPS TRANSMITTER HE'S WEARING, WILL DO MOST OF THAT HARD WORK FOR US.
BLAM BLAM BLAM
THAT'S NOT THE MAIN ISSUE, BUT THERE IS A WAY SOME OF YOU CAN HELP OUR CONTINUED EFFORTS TO BETTER THE HARDCORE TECHNOLOGY--
AND REMOVE IT FROM THOSE THAT HAVE ONLY ABUSED IT FOR THEIR OWN PURPOSES.
I'M STANDING IN A ROOM FULL OF PEOPLE THAT WOULD STILL BE ALIVE IF YOU HADN'T PUT THIS OUT INTO THE WORLD. AND DON'T PRETEND--YOU KNEW WHAT WOULD HAPPEN, SO NOW WE TAKE IT AWAY FROM YOU.
MY QUESTION FOR YOU FINE PEOPLE--YOUR TWO OTHER TEMPORARY HARDCORE RIGS? WHERE ARE THEY, AND HOW CAN WE GAIN FULL ACCESS TO THEM?
JESSICA, HELP THEM REMEMBER, PLEASE.
PIFF
GAAARRGH!!!
NO!

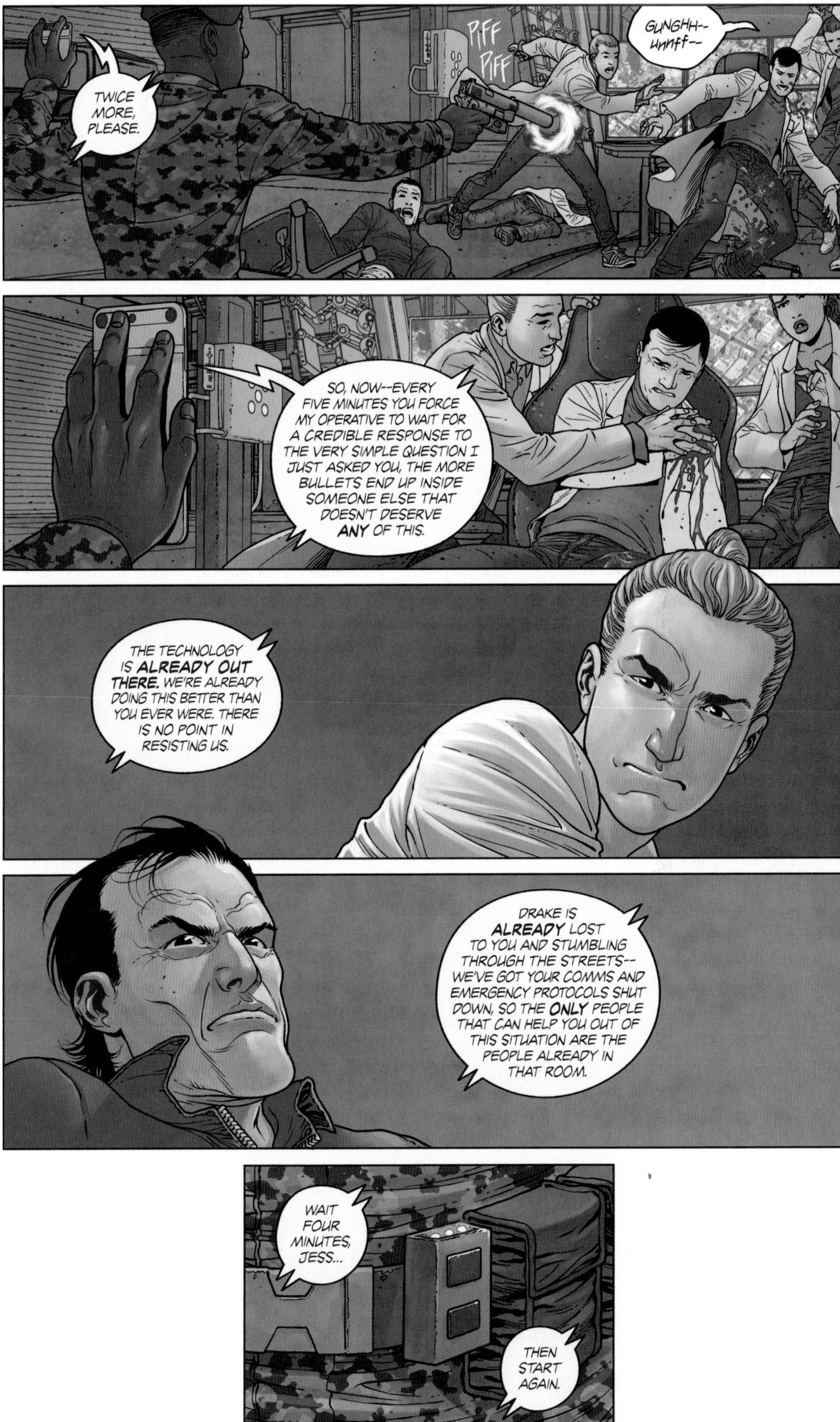
TWICE MORE, PLEASE.
PIFF PIFF
GUNGHH-- unnff--
SO, NOW--EVERY FIVE MINUTES YOU FORCE MY OPERATIVE TO WAIT FOR A CREDIBLE RESPONSE TO THE VERY SIMPLE QUESTION I JUST ASKED YOU, THE MORE BULLETS END UP INSIDE SOMEONE ELSE THAT DOESN'T DESERVE **ANY** OF THIS.
THE TECHNOLOGY IS **ALREADY OUT THERE.** WE'RE ALREADY DOING THIS BETTER THAN YOU EVER WERE. THERE IS NO POINT IN RESISTING US.
DRAKE IS **ALREADY** LOST TO YOU AND STUMBLING THROUGH THE STREETS-- WE'VE GOT YOUR COMMS AND EMERGENCY PROTOCOLS SHUT DOWN, SO THE **ONLY** PEOPLE THAT CAN HELP YOU OUT OF THIS SITUATION ARE THE PEOPLE ALREADY IN THAT ROOM.
WAIT FOUR MINUTES, JESS...
THEN START AGAIN.

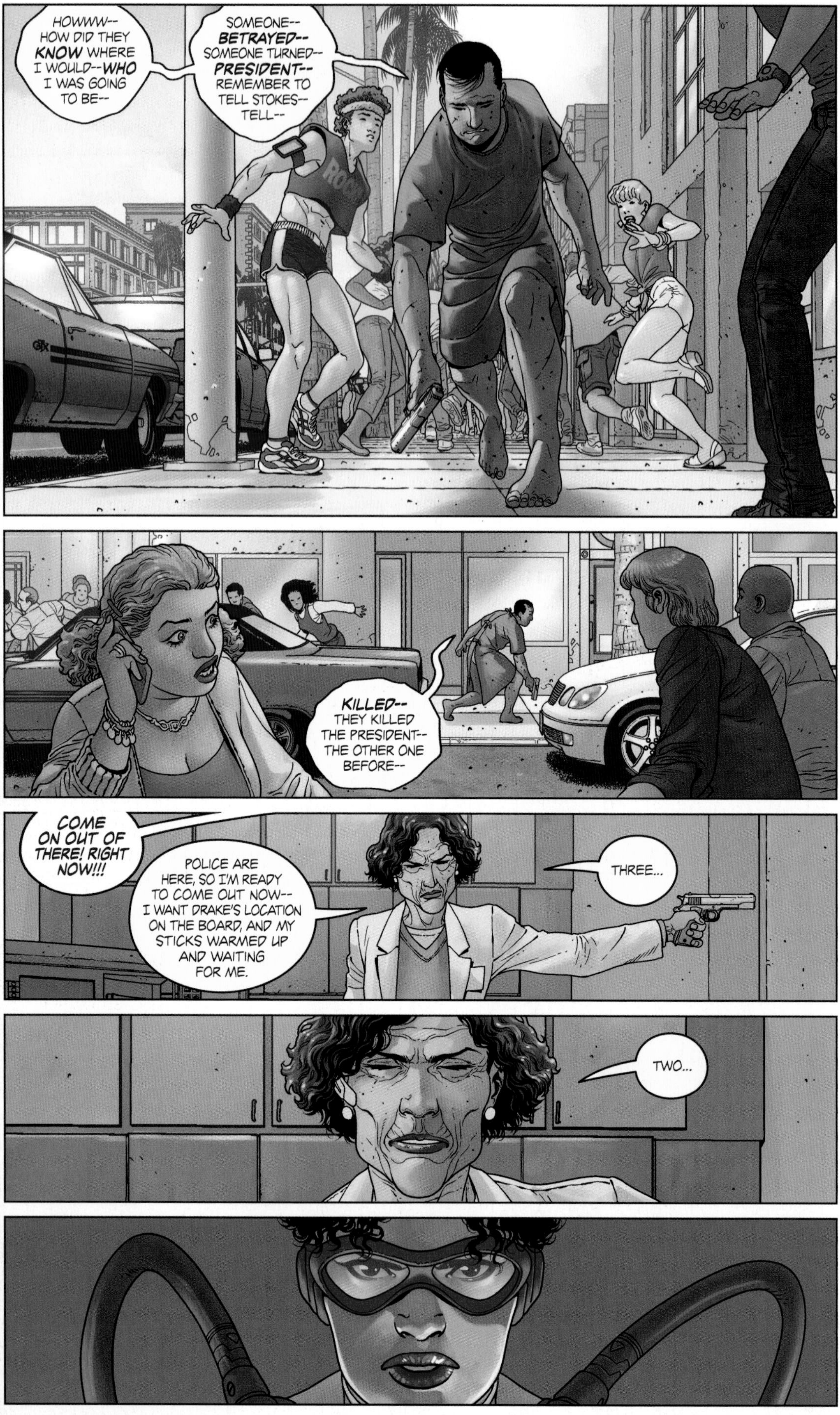
HOWWW-- HOW DID THEY KNOW WHERE I WOULD--WHO I WAS GOING TO BE--
SOMEONE-- BETRAYED-- SOMEONE TURNED-- PRESIDENT-- REMEMBER TO TELL STOKES-- TELL--
KILLED-- THEY KILLED THE PRESIDENT-- THE OTHER ONE BEFORE--
COME ON OUT OF THERE! RIGHT NOW!!!
POLICE ARE HERE, SO I'M READY TO COME OUT NOW-- I WANT DRAKE'S LOCATION ON THE BOARD, AND MY STICKS WARMED UP AND WAITING FOR ME.
THREE...
TWO...

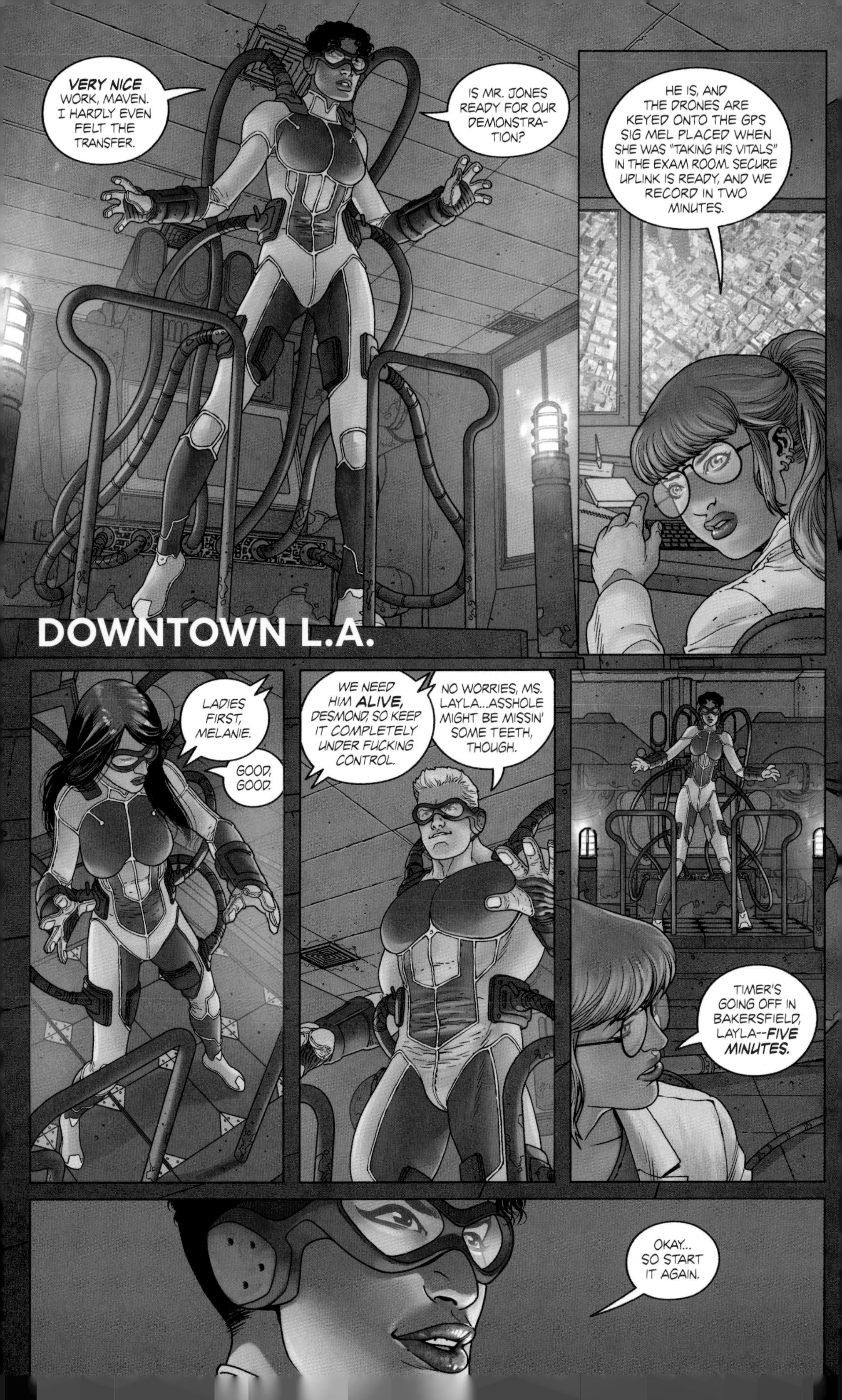
VERY NICE WORK, MAVEN. I HARDLY EVEN FELT THE TRANSFER.
IS MR. JONES READY FOR OUR DEMONSTRATION?
HE IS, AND THE DRONES ARE KEYED ONTO THE GPS SIG MEL PLACED WHEN SHE WAS "TAKING HIS VITALS" IN THE EXAM ROOM. SECURE UPLINK IS READY, AND WE RECORD IN TWO MINUTES.
DOWNTOWN L.A.
LADIES FIRST, MELANIE.
GOOD, GOOD.
WE NEED HIM ALIVE, DESMOND, SO KEEP IT COMPLETELY UNDER FUCKING CONTROL.
NO WORRIES, MS. LAYLA...ASSHOLE MIGHT BE MISSIN' SOME TEETH, THOUGH.
TIMER'S GOING OFF IN BAKERSFIELD, LAYLA--FIVE MINUTES.
OKAY... SO START IT AGAIN.

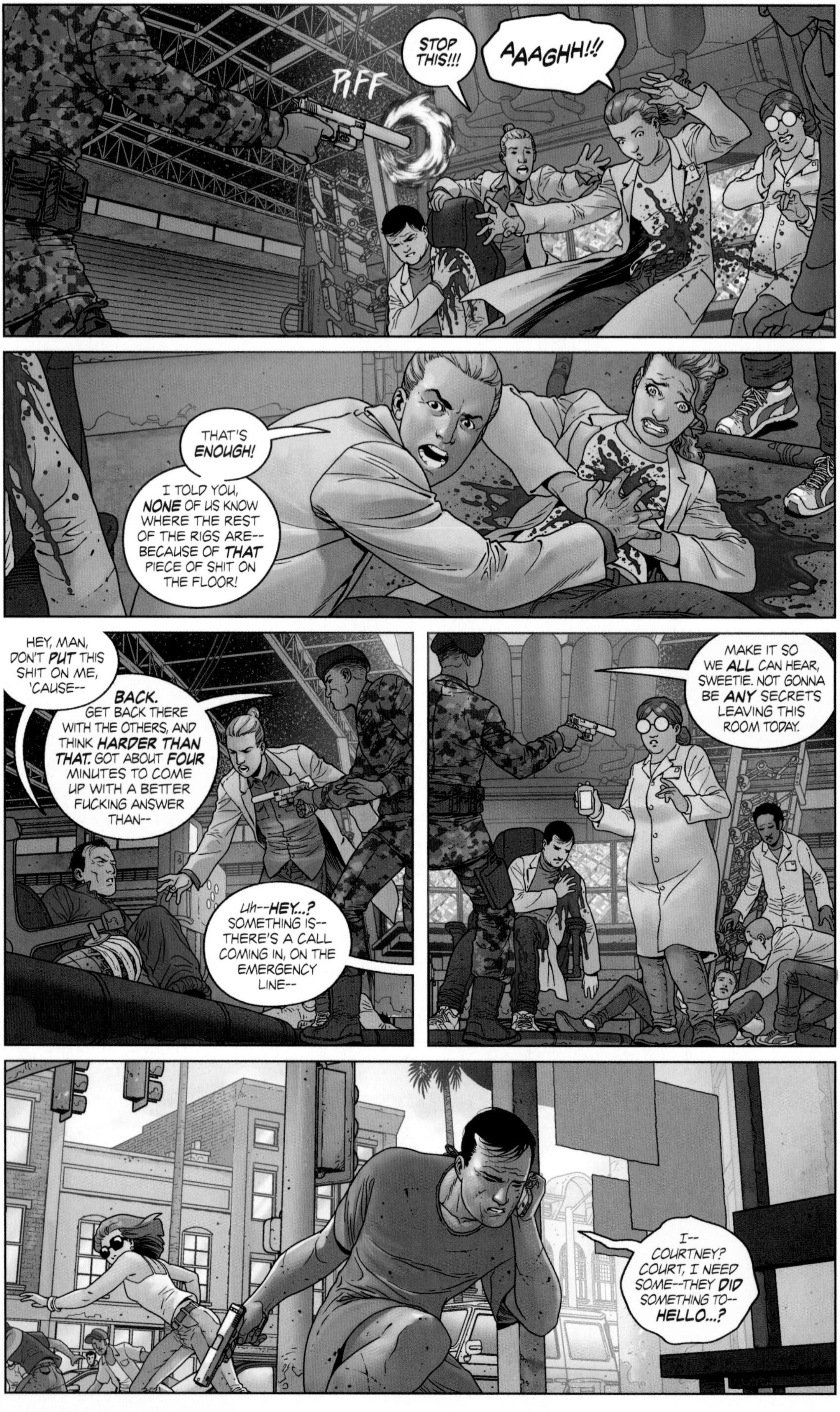
PIFF
STOP THIS!!!
AAAGHH!!!
THAT'S ENOUGH!
I TOLD YOU, NONE OF US KNOW WHERE THE REST OF THE RIGS ARE-- BECAUSE OF THAT PIECE OF SHIT ON THE FLOOR!
HEY, MAN, DON'T PUT THIS SHIT ON ME, 'CAUSE--
BACK. GET BACK THERE WITH THE OTHERS, AND THINK HARDER THAN THAT. GOT ABOUT FOUR MINUTES TO COME UP WITH A BETTER FUCKING ANSWER THAN--
UH--HEY...? SOMETHING IS-- THERE'S A CALL COMING IN, ON THE EMERGENCY LINE--
MAKE IT SO WE ALL CAN HEAR, SWEETIE. NOT GONNA BE ANY SECRETS LEAVING THIS ROOM TODAY.
I-- COURTNEY? COURT, I NEED SOME--THEY DID SOMETHING TO-- HELLO...?

COURTNEY!
THEY'RE SENDING IN THE FUCKING BIRDS, MAN!
GET OUT! GET OUT OF HERE!!!
BAM BAM
"MR. JONES, HARDCORE ALLOWS US TO TARGET, INFECT, AND THEN CONTROL ANYONE WE WANT, AND THE CREATORS OF THIS GROUNDBREAKING TECHNOLOGY HAVE ONLY SCRATCHED THE VERY SURFACE OF ITS POTENTIAL APPLICATION AND DEPLOYMENT.
"IT'S ALL PROTOCOLS AND GUIDE MANUALS AND SAFETY CHECKS WITH THESE PEOPLE, BUT OUR APPROACH IS MORE...ASPIRATIONAL.
"NONE OF US ARE SAFE. HAVEN'T BEEN FOR A LONG TIME, BUT THIS ONLY REINFORCES THE FACT, AND IN THE WAKE OF THAT REVELATION THERE'S ONLY ONE MOVE LEFT--TO ENRICH OURSELVES FOR HOWEVER MUCH TIME WE ALL HAVE LEFT.
AHH!
"WE'VE GONE TO SOME LENGTHS TO ARRANGE THIS DEMONSTRATION, AND WE'RE HOPING THAT IF YOU LIKE WHAT YOU SEE HERE TODAY--
THIS IS MELANIE, BACK IN PLAY. PURSUING TARGET.

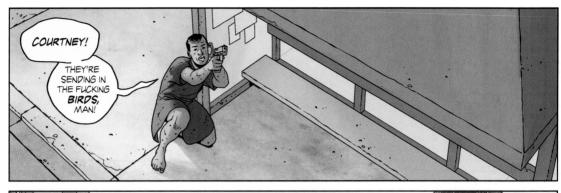

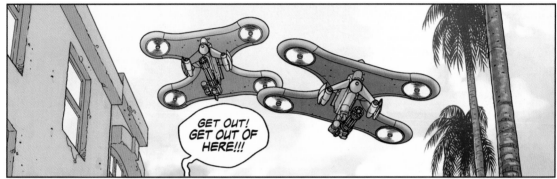

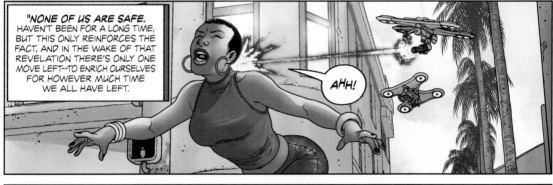

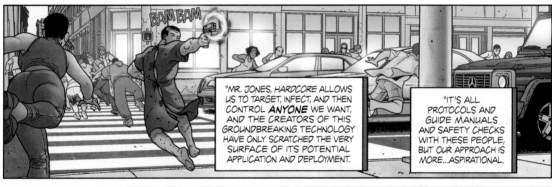

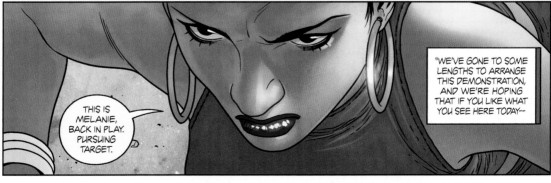

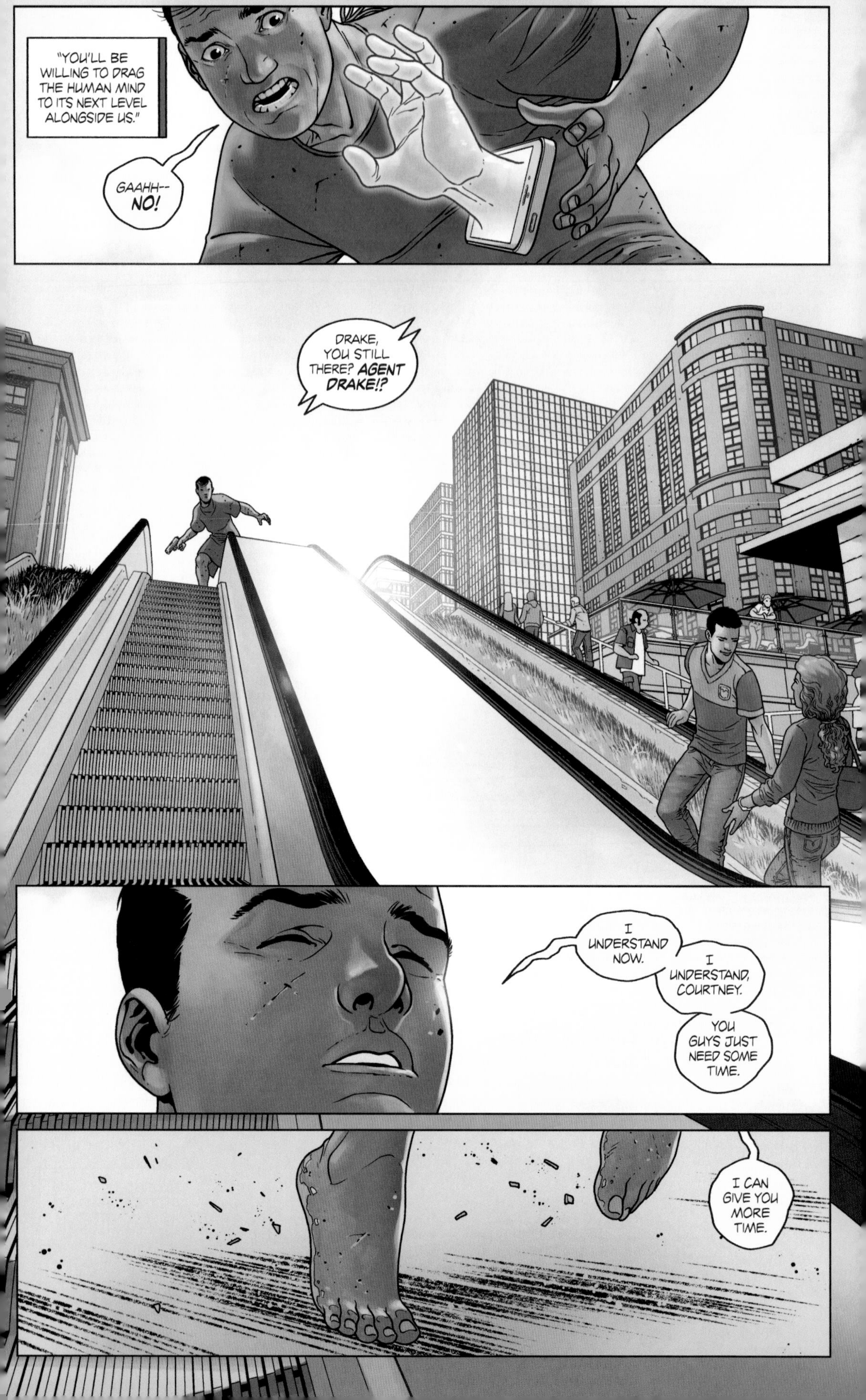
"YOU'LL BE WILLING TO DRAG THE HUMAN MIND TO ITS NEXT LEVEL ALONGSIDE US."
GAAHH-- NO!
DRAKE, YOU STILL THERE? AGENT DRAKE!?
I UNDERSTAND NOW.
I UNDERSTAND, COURTNEY.
YOU GUYS JUST NEED SOME TIME.
I CAN GIVE YOU MORE TIME.

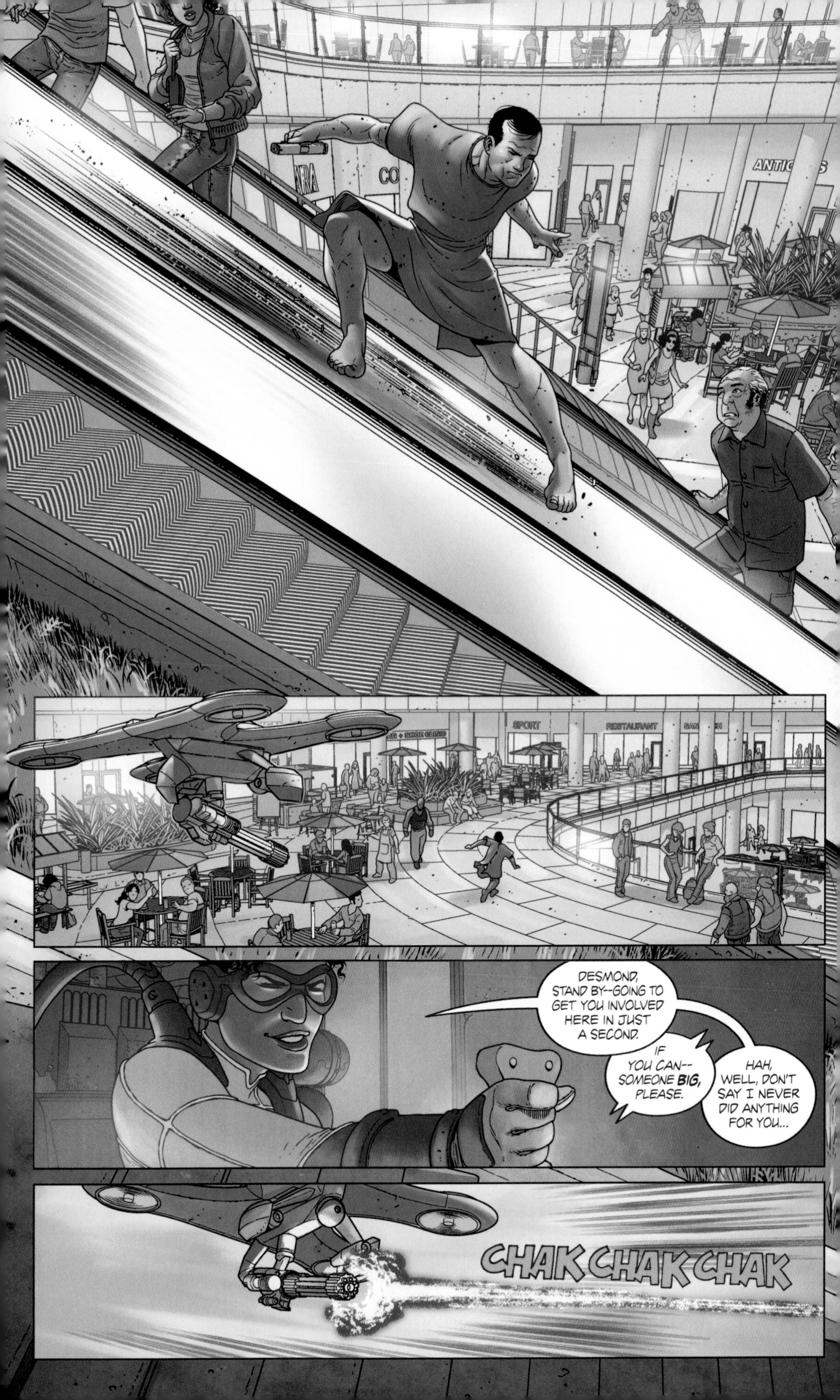
SPORT
RESTAURANT
DESMOND, STAND BY--GOING TO GET YOU INVOLVED HERE IN JUST A SECOND.
IF YOU CAN-- SOMEONE BIG, PLEASE.
HAH, WELL, DON'T SAY I NEVER DID ANYTHING FOR YOU...
CHAK CHAK CHAK

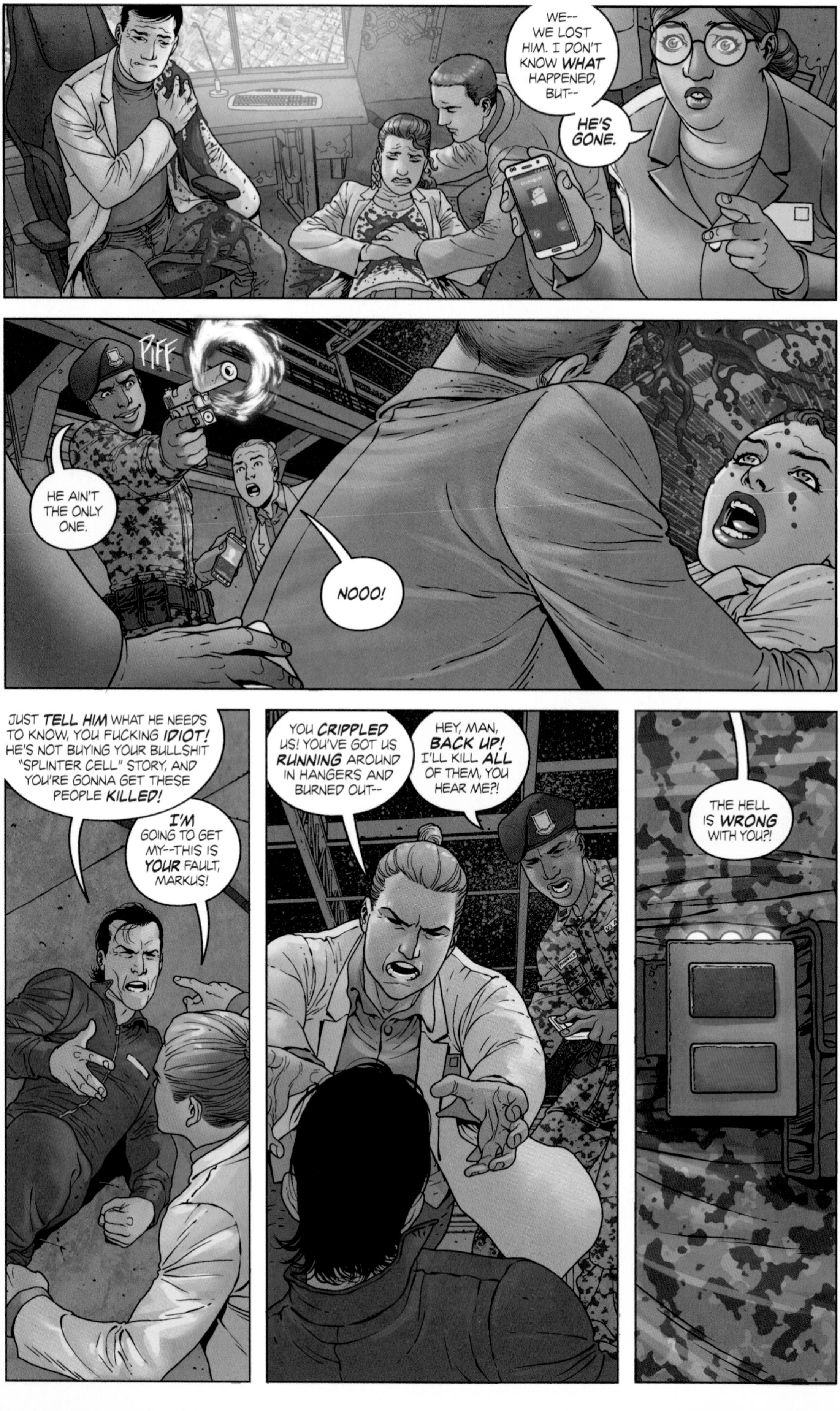
WE-- WE LOST HIM. I DON'T KNOW WHAT HAPPENED, BUT--
HE'S GONE.
PIFF
HE AIN'T THE ONLY ONE.
NOOO!
JUST TELL HIM WHAT HE NEEDS TO KNOW, YOU FUCKING IDIOT! HE'S NOT BUYING YOUR BULLSHIT "SPLINTER CELL" STORY, AND YOU'RE GONNA GET THESE PEOPLE KILLED!
I'M GOING TO GET MY--THIS IS YOUR FAULT, MARKUS!
YOU CRIPPLED US! YOU'VE GOT US RUNNING AROUND IN HANGERS AND BURNED OUT--
HEY, MAN, BACK UP! I'LL KILL ALL OF THEM, YOU HEAR ME?!
THE HELL IS WRONG WITH YOU?!

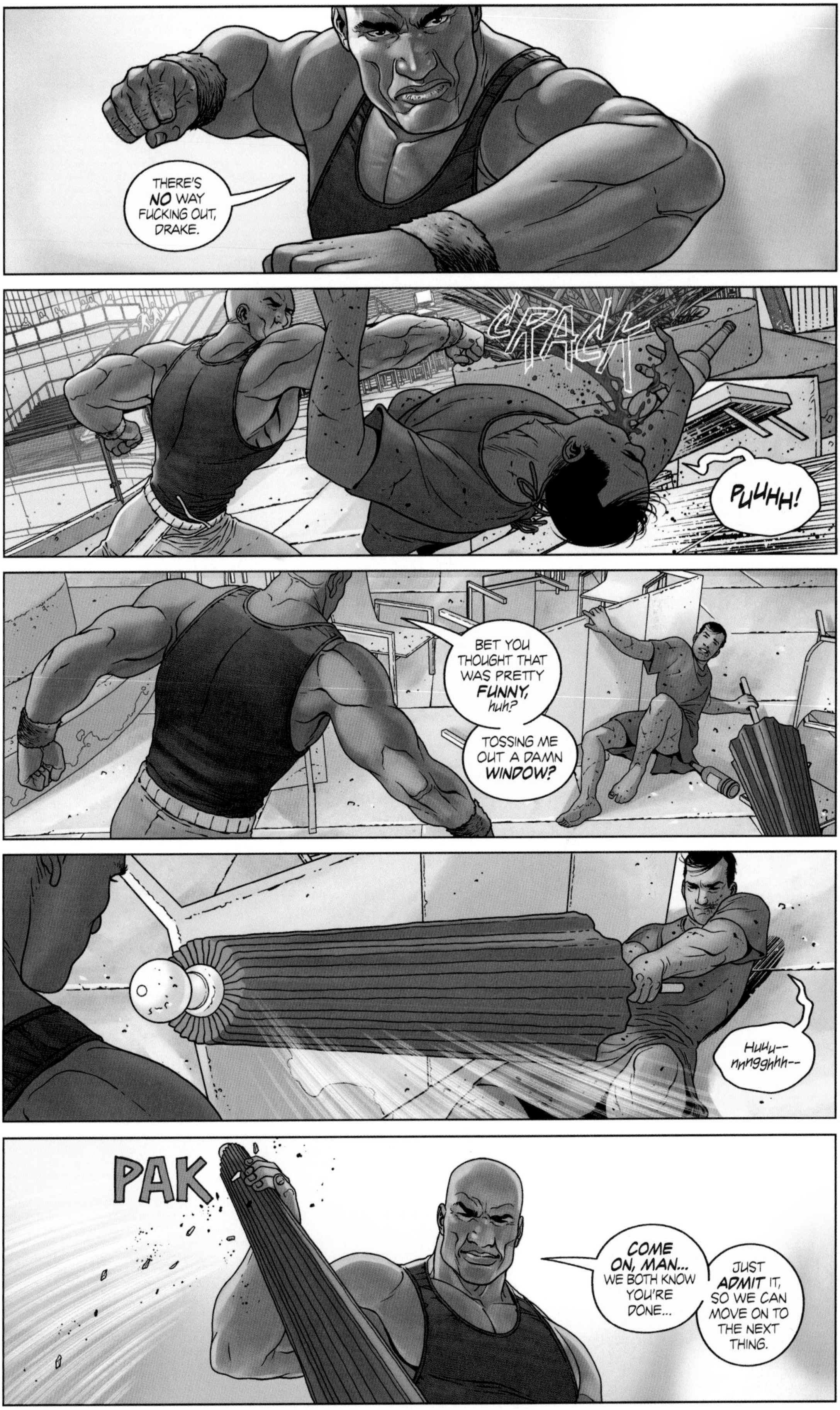
THERE'S NO WAY FUCKING OUT, DRAKE.
CRACK
PUUHH!
BET YOU THOUGHT THAT WAS PRETTY FUNNY, huh?
TOSSING ME OUT A DAMN WINDOW?
Huuu-- nnngghhh--
PAK
COME ON, MAN... WE BOTH KNOW YOU'RE DONE...
JUST ADMIT IT, SO WE CAN MOVE ON TO THE NEXT THING.

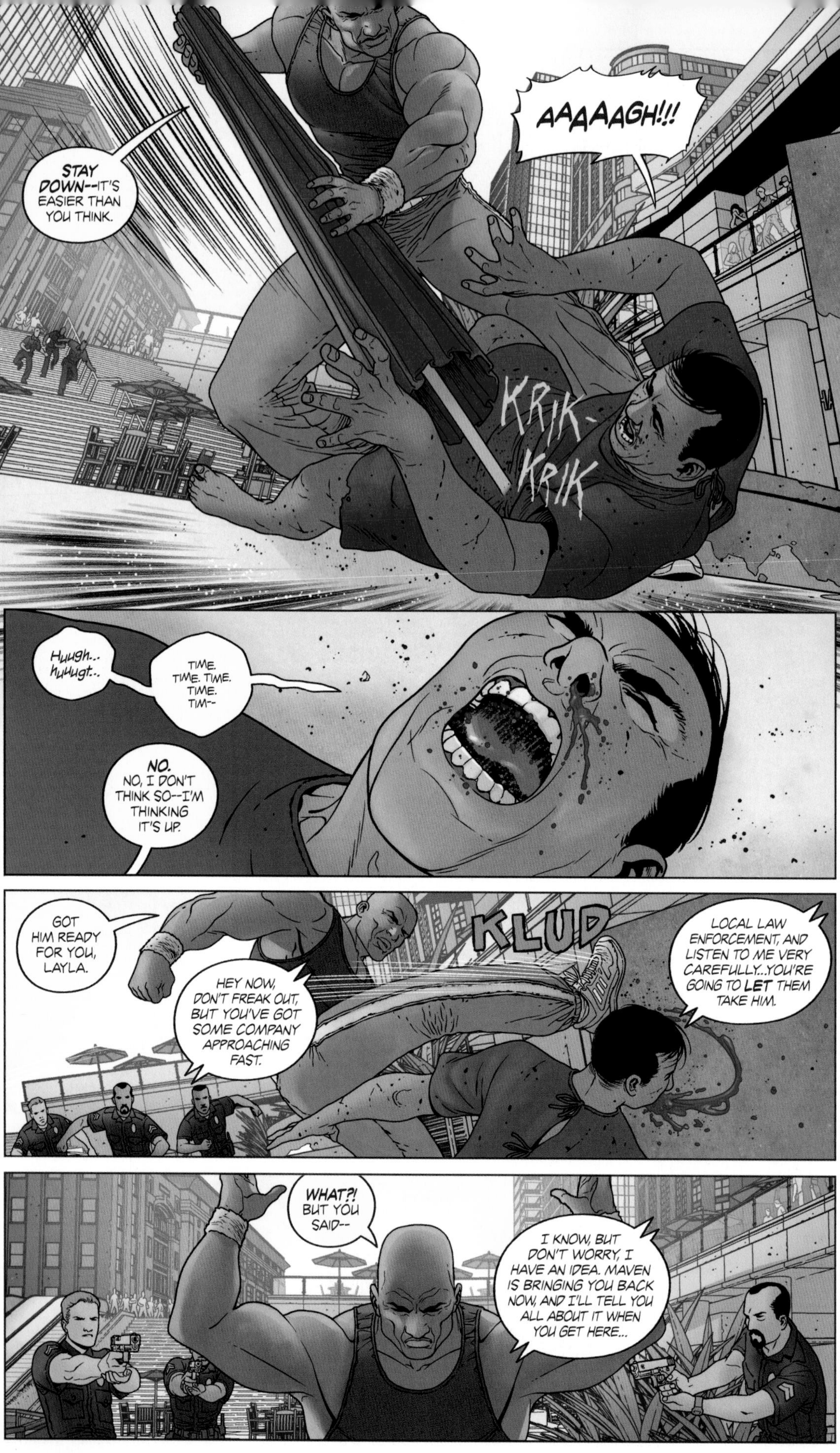
STAY DOWN--IT'S EASIER THAN YOU THINK.
AAAAAGH!!!
KRIK-KRIK
Huugh... huuugt...
TIME. TIME. TIME. TIME. TIM--
NO. NO, I DON'T THINK SO--I'M THINKING IT'S UP.
GOT HIM READY FOR YOU, LAYLA.
KLUD
HEY NOW, DON'T FREAK OUT, BUT YOU'VE GOT SOME COMPANY APPROACHING FAST.
LOCAL LAW ENFORCEMENT, AND LISTEN TO ME VERY CAREFULLY...YOU'RE GOING TO LET THEM TAKE HIM.
WHAT?! BUT YOU SAID--
I KNOW, BUT DON'T WORRY, I HAVE AN IDEA. MAVEN IS BRINGING YOU BACK NOW, AND I'LL TELL YOU ALL ABOUT IT WHEN YOU GET HERE...

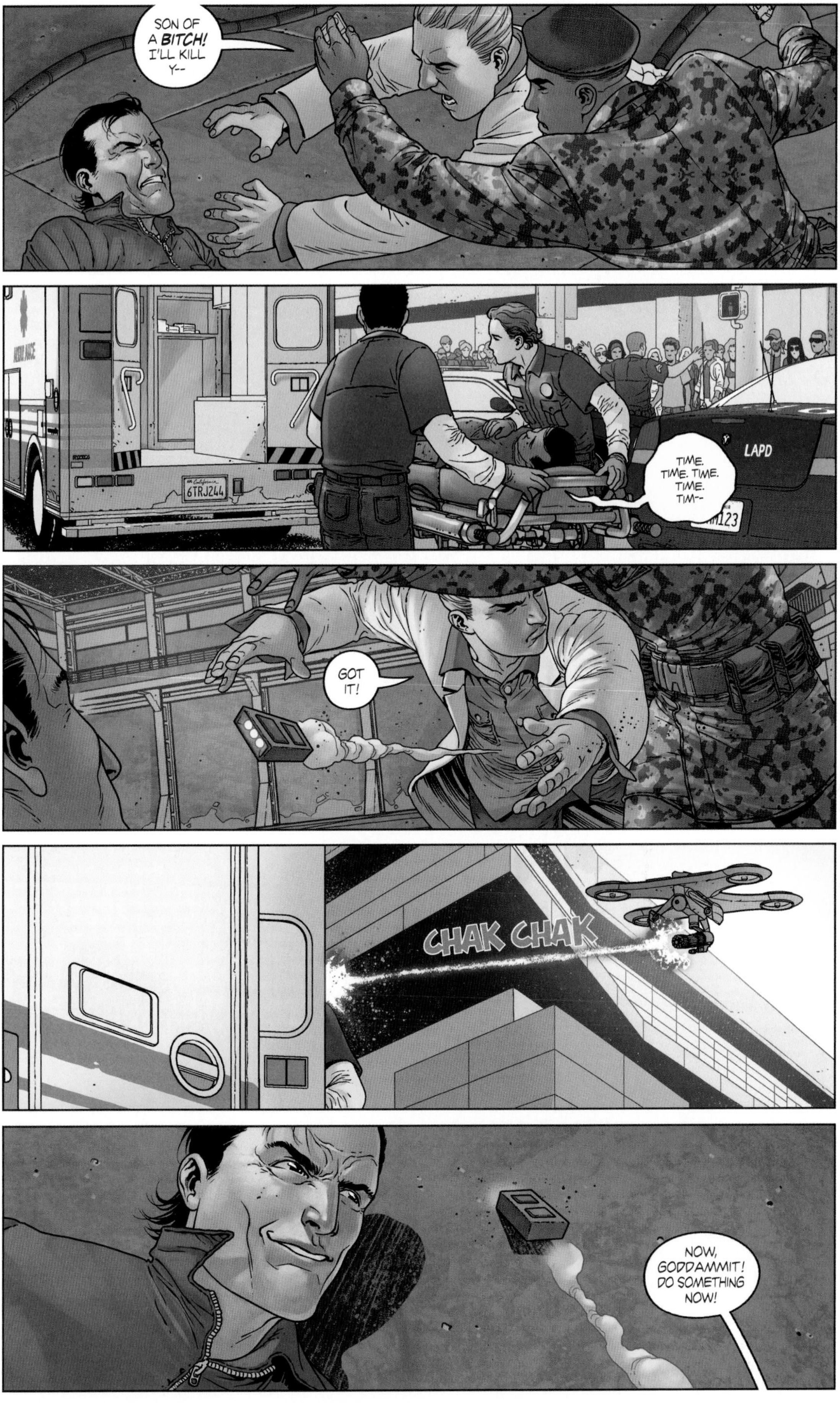
SON OF A BITCH! I'LL KILL Y--
TIME. TIME. TIME. TIME. TIM--
LAPD
6TRJ244
GOT IT!
CHAK CHAK
NOW, GODDAMMIT! DO SOMETHING NOW!

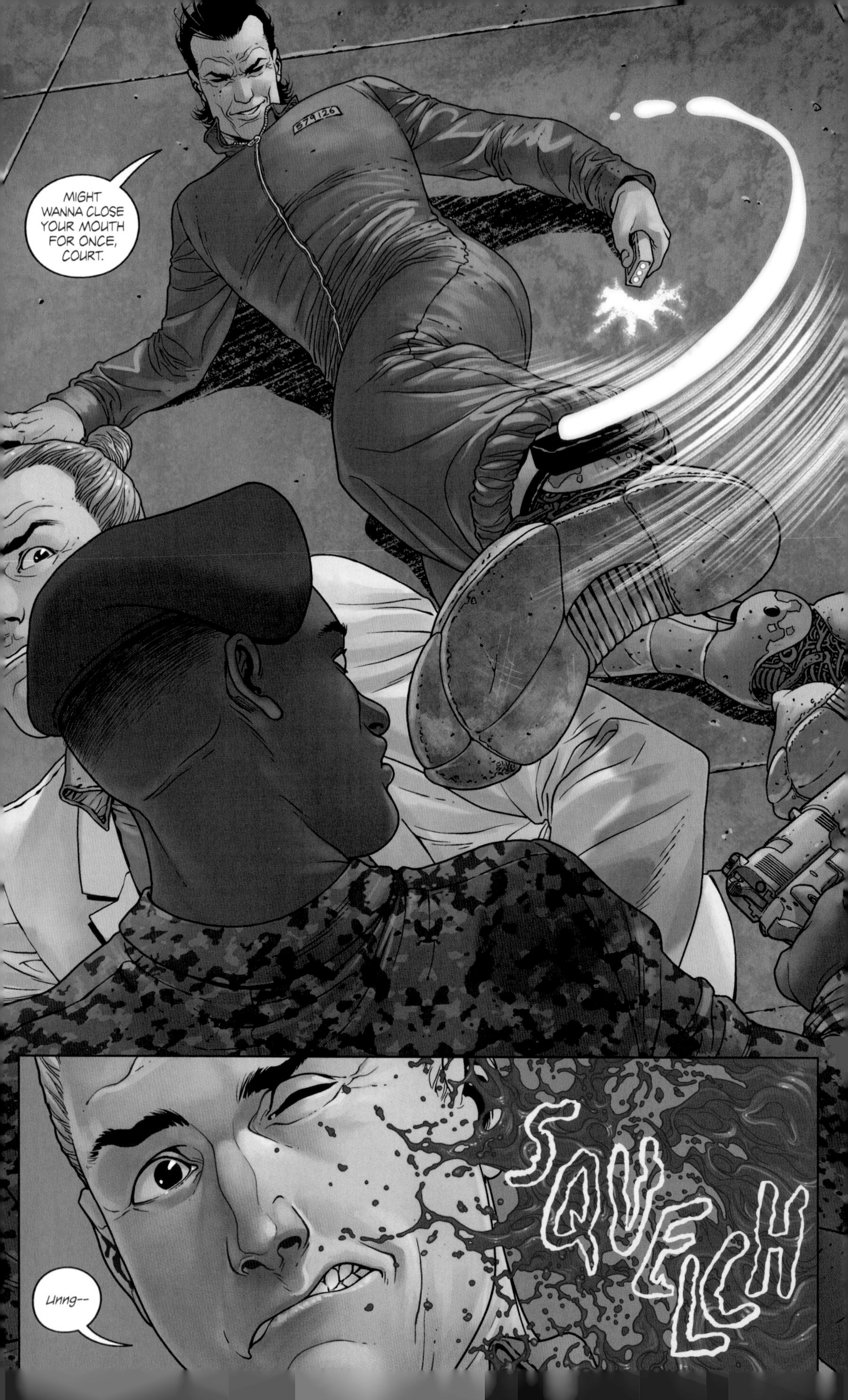
MIGHT WANNA CLOSE YOUR MOUTH FOR ONCE, COURT.
SQUELCH
Unng--

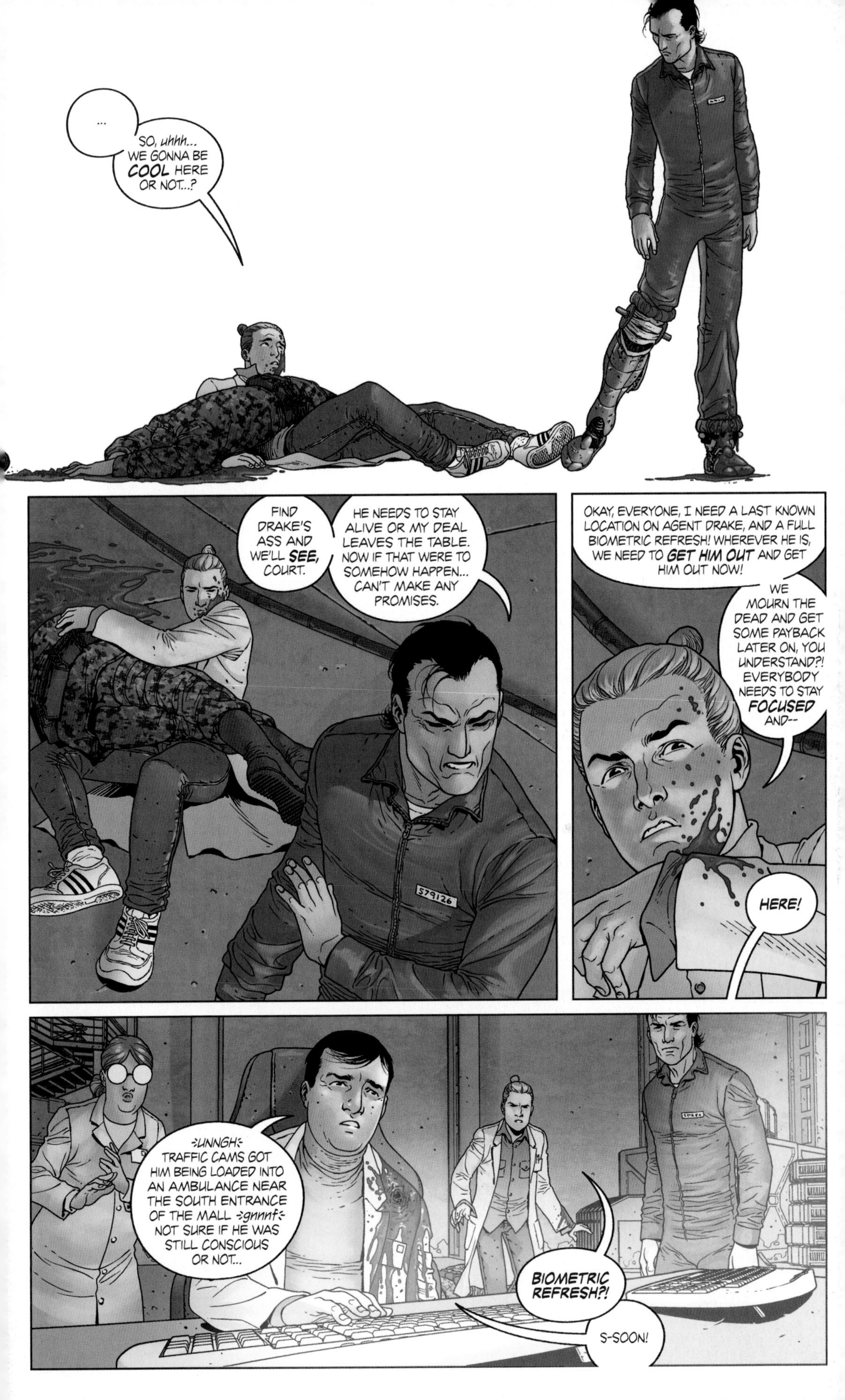

...
SO, uhhh... WE GONNA BE COOL HERE OR NOT...?
FIND DRAKE'S ASS AND WE'LL SEE, COURT.
HE NEEDS TO STAY ALIVE OR MY DEAL LEAVES THE TABLE. NOW IF THAT WERE TO SOMEHOW HAPPEN... CAN'T MAKE ANY PROMISES.
579126
OKAY, EVERYONE, I NEED A LAST KNOWN LOCATION ON AGENT DRAKE, AND A FULL BIOMETRIC REFRESH! WHEREVER HE IS, WE NEED TO GET HIM OUT AND GET HIM OUT NOW!
WE MOURN THE DEAD AND GET SOME PAYBACK LATER ON, YOU UNDERSTAND?! EVERYBODY NEEDS TO STAY FOCUSED AND--
HERE!
UNNGH TRAFFIC CAMS GOT HIM BEING LOADED INTO AN AMBULANCE NEAR THE SOUTH ENTRANCE OF THE MALL gnnnf NOT SURE IF HE WAS STILL CONSCIOUS OR NOT...
BIOMETRIC REFRESH?!
S-SOON!

"GOOD, NOW *FIND THAT DAMN AMBULANCE!*"

HANG ON! HANG ON, WE'RE ALMOST THERE!

HNNNNGGG--

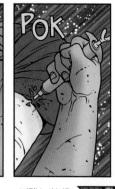

POK

POK

POK

POK

POK

WE'LL HAVE TO PUNCH HIM TO RE-ESTABLISH FULL NEURAL CONNECTION.

ONLY WAY. GO.

AAAAAAA!!!

"EMERGENCY RECALL... *NOW.*"

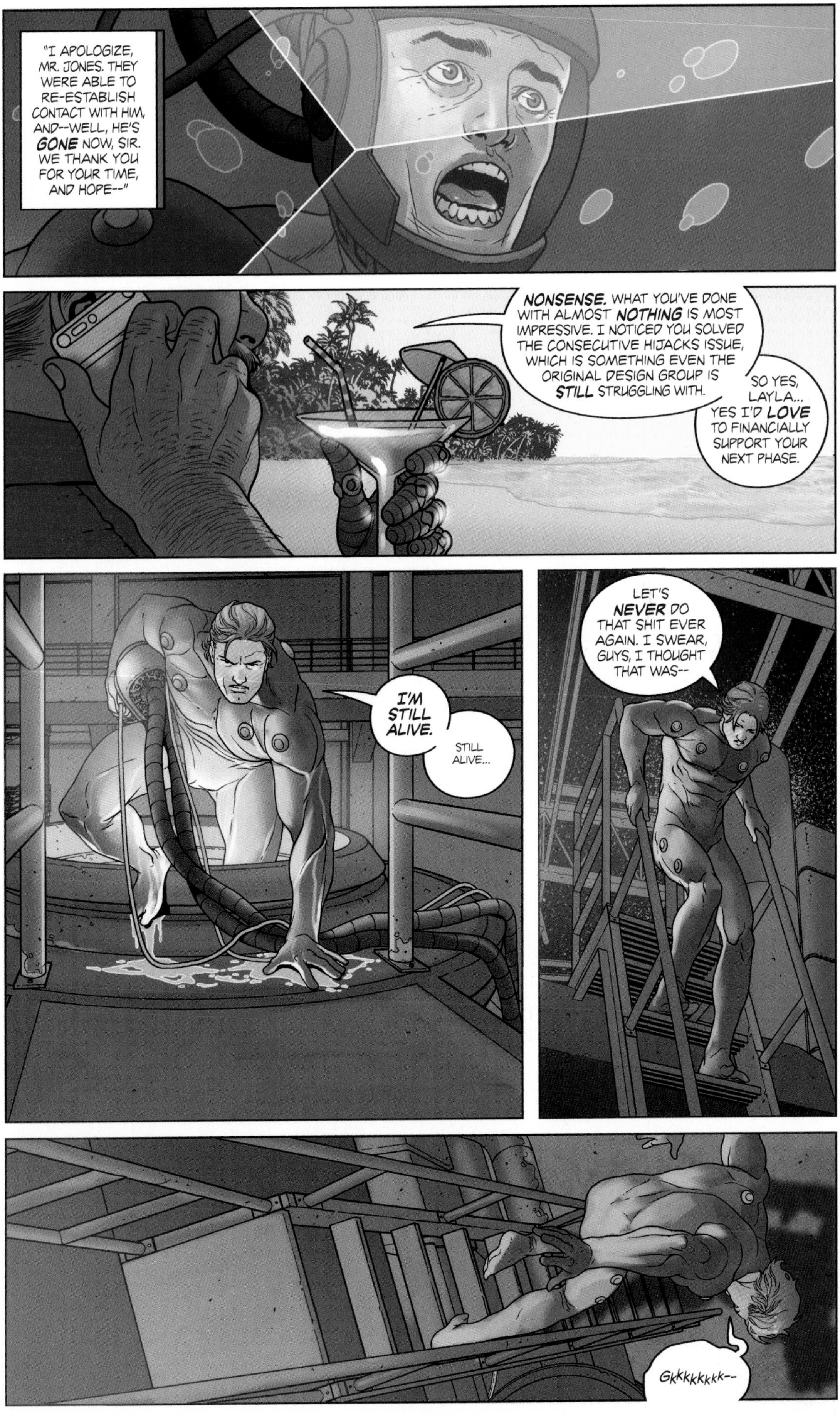
"I APOLOGIZE, MR. JONES. THEY WERE ABLE TO RE-ESTABLISH CONTACT WITH HIM, AND--WELL, HE'S GONE NOW, SIR. WE THANK YOU FOR YOUR TIME, AND HOPE--"
NONSENSE. WHAT YOU'VE DONE WITH ALMOST NOTHING IS MOST IMPRESSIVE. I NOTICED YOU SOLVED THE CONSECUTIVE HIJACKS ISSUE, WHICH IS SOMETHING EVEN THE ORIGINAL DESIGN GROUP IS STILL STRUGGLING WITH.
SO YES, LAYLA... YES I'D LOVE TO FINANCIALLY SUPPORT YOUR NEXT PHASE.
I'M STILL ALIVE.
STILL ALIVE...
LET'S NEVER DO THAT SHIT EVER AGAIN. I SWEAR, GUYS, I THOUGHT THAT WAS--
Gkkkkkkkk--

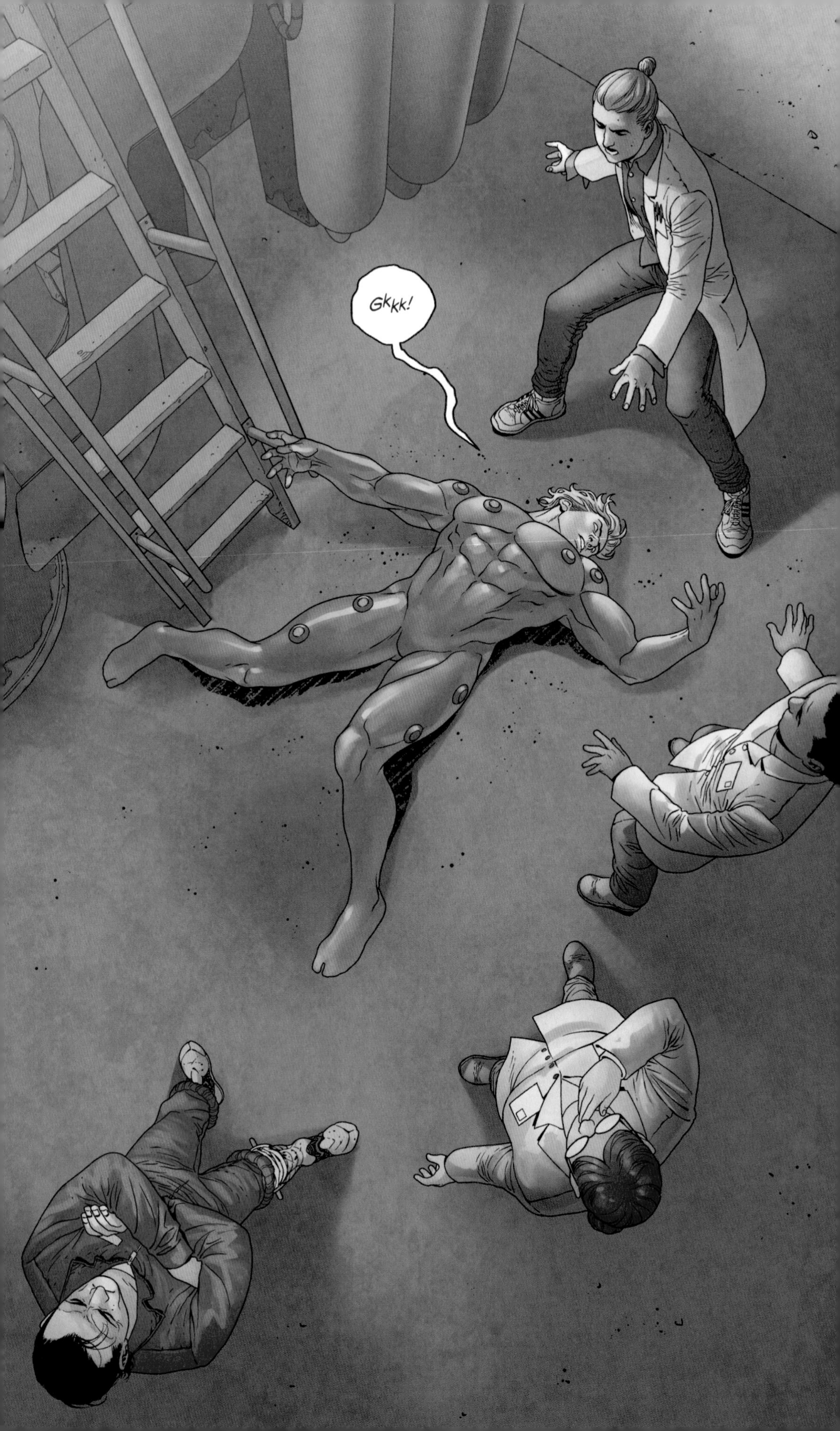
GKKK!

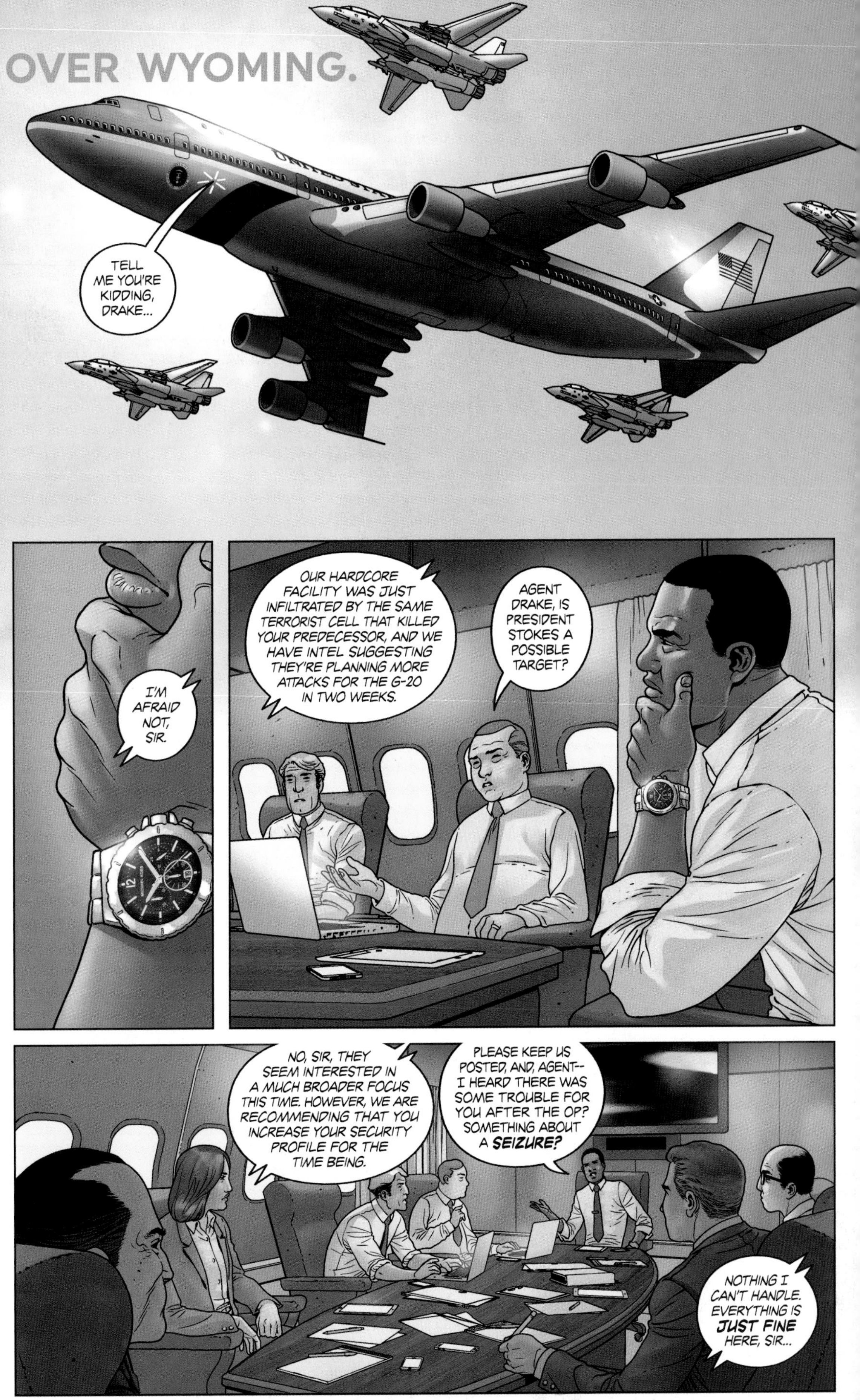
OVER WYOMING.
TELL ME YOU'RE KIDDING, DRAKE...
I'M AFRAID NOT, SIR.
OUR HARDCORE FACILITY WAS JUST INFILTRATED BY THE SAME TERRORIST CELL THAT KILLED YOUR PREDECESSOR, AND WE HAVE INTEL SUGGESTING THEY'RE PLANNING MORE ATTACKS FOR THE G-20 IN TWO WEEKS.
AGENT DRAKE, IS PRESIDENT STOKES A POSSIBLE TARGET?
NO, SIR, THEY SEEM INTERESTED IN A MUCH BROADER FOCUS THIS TIME. HOWEVER, WE ARE RECOMMENDING THAT YOU INCREASE YOUR SECURITY PROFILE FOR THE TIME BEING.
PLEASE KEEP US POSTED, AND, AGENT-- I HEARD THERE WAS SOME TROUBLE FOR YOU AFTER THE OP? SOMETHING ABOUT A **SEIZURE?**
NOTHING I CAN'T HANDLE. EVERYTHING IS **JUST FINE** HERE, SIR...

THANK YOU, MR. PRESIDENT.

WE WILL. THANK YOU, SIR. *CLIK*

OKAY, WE'RE CLEAR... GO ON, DR. SAUNDERS.

NO FURTHER CONTACT WITH HARDCORE TECH FOR AT MINIMUM SIX MONTHS, WHICH SHOULD GIVE THE NEUROLOGICAL SCARRING A CHANCE TO HEAL ON ITS OWN, OR...WE'LL BE FORCED TO PURSUE MUCH MORE AGGRESSIVE MEASURES.

WHEN WE CATCH ALL OF THE PEOPLE INVOLVED IN THE ASSASSINATION OF OUR PRESIDENT, THEN YEAH, I'LL MAYBE DO THAT... BUT NOT A SECOND BEFORE.

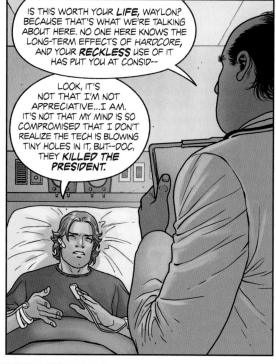

IS THIS WORTH YOUR LIFE, WAYLON? BECAUSE THAT'S WHAT WE'RE TALKING ABOUT HERE. NO ONE HERE KNOWS THE LONG-TERM EFFECTS OF HARDCORE, AND YOUR RECKLESS USE OF IT HAS PUT YOU AT CONSID--

LOOK, IT'S NOT THAT I'M NOT APPRECIATIVE...I AM. IT'S NOT THAT MY MIND IS SO COMPROMISED THAT I DON'T REALIZE THE TECH IS BLOWING TINY HOLES IN IT, BUT--DOC, THEY KILLED THE PRESIDENT.

MAYBE YOU CAN LET THAT GO, BUT WHATEVER IT COSTS--ALL OF THEM GET FOUND, AND DEALT WITH.

COURTNEY, YEAH, CAN YOU HEAR ME? DOC SAYS I'M GOOD TO GO. WE'VE GOT TWO WHOLE WEEKS BEFORE THE G-20, SO LET'S USE 'EM RIGHT.

TWO WEEKS LATER. BEFORE.

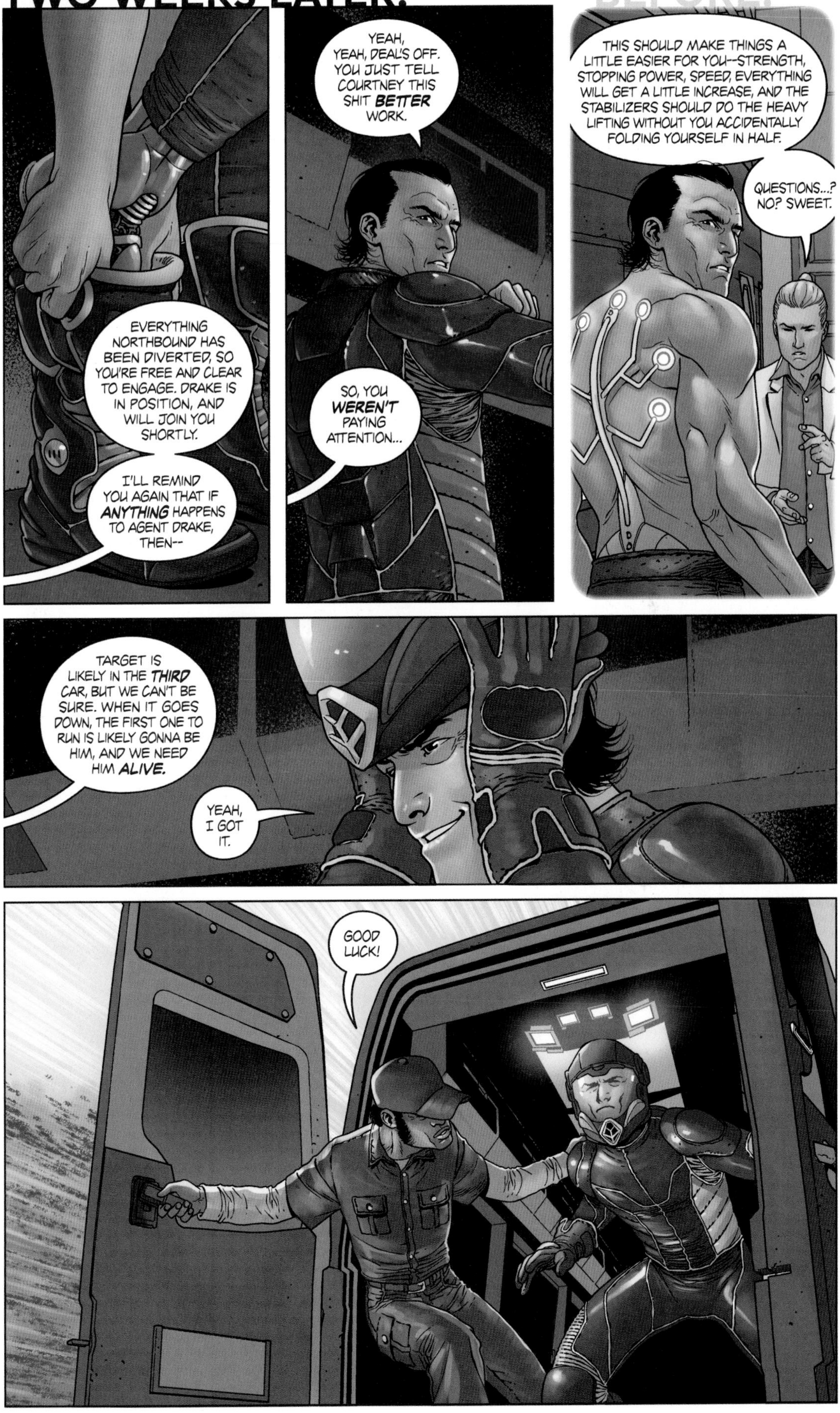

EVERYTHING NORTHBOUND HAS BEEN DIVERTED, SO YOU'RE FREE AND CLEAR TO ENGAGE. DRAKE IS IN POSITION, AND WILL JOIN YOU SHORTLY.
I'LL REMIND YOU AGAIN THAT IF ANYTHING HAPPENS TO AGENT DRAKE, THEN--
YEAH, YEAH, DEAL'S OFF. YOU JUST TELL COURTNEY THIS SHIT BETTER WORK.
SO, YOU WEREN'T PAYING ATTENTION...
THIS SHOULD MAKE THINGS A LITTLE EASIER FOR YOU--STRENGTH, STOPPING POWER, SPEED, EVERYTHING WILL GET A LITTLE INCREASE, AND THE STABILIZERS SHOULD DO THE HEAVY LIFTING WITHOUT YOU ACCIDENTALLY FOLDING YOURSELF IN HALF.
QUESTIONS...? NO? SWEET.
TARGET IS LIKELY IN THE THIRD CAR, BUT WE CAN'T BE SURE. WHEN IT GOES DOWN, THE FIRST ONE TO RUN IS LIKELY GONNA BE HIM, AND WE NEED HIM ALIVE.
YEAH, I GOT IT.
GOOD LUCK!

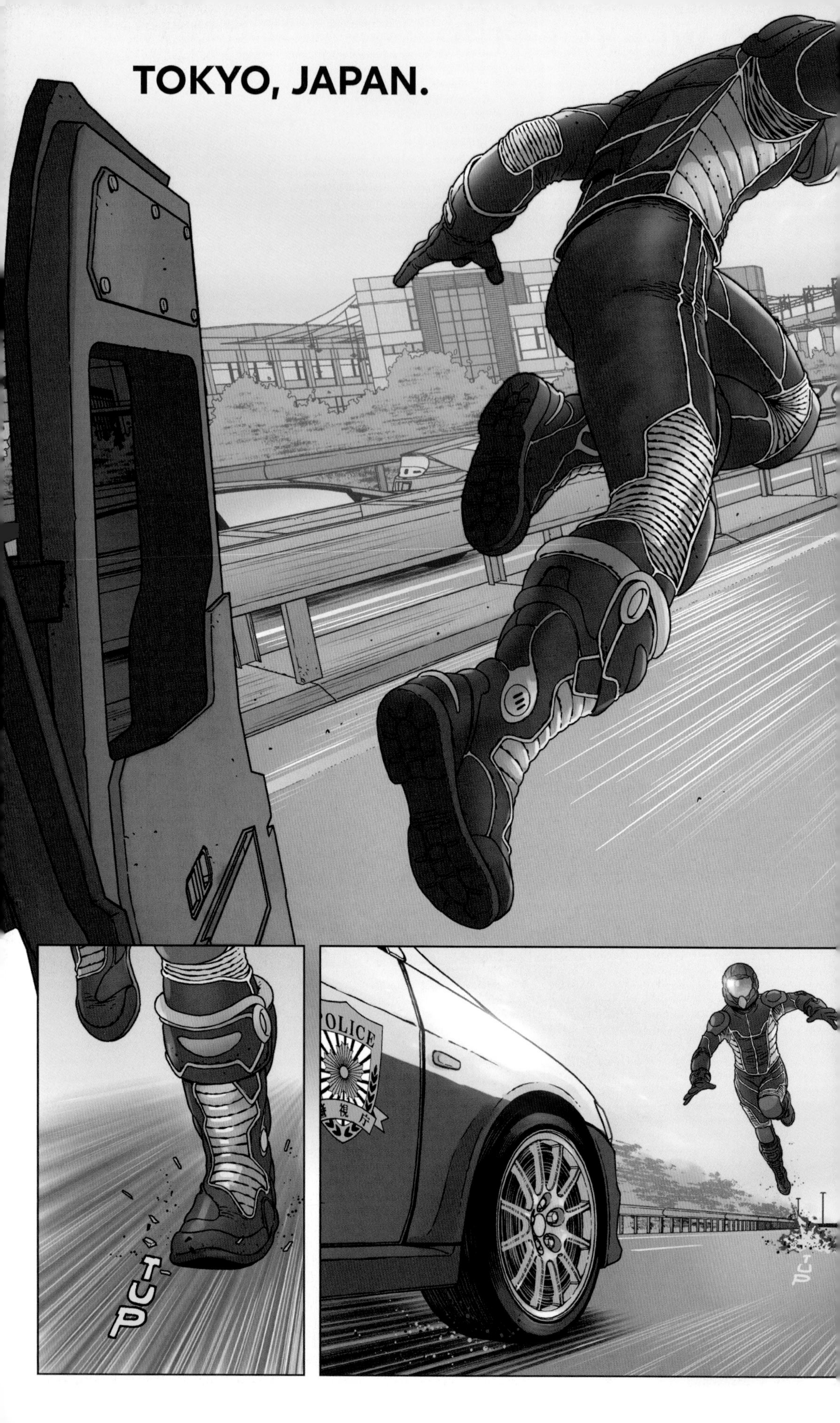
TOKYO, JAPAN.
TUP
POLICE
警視庁
TUP

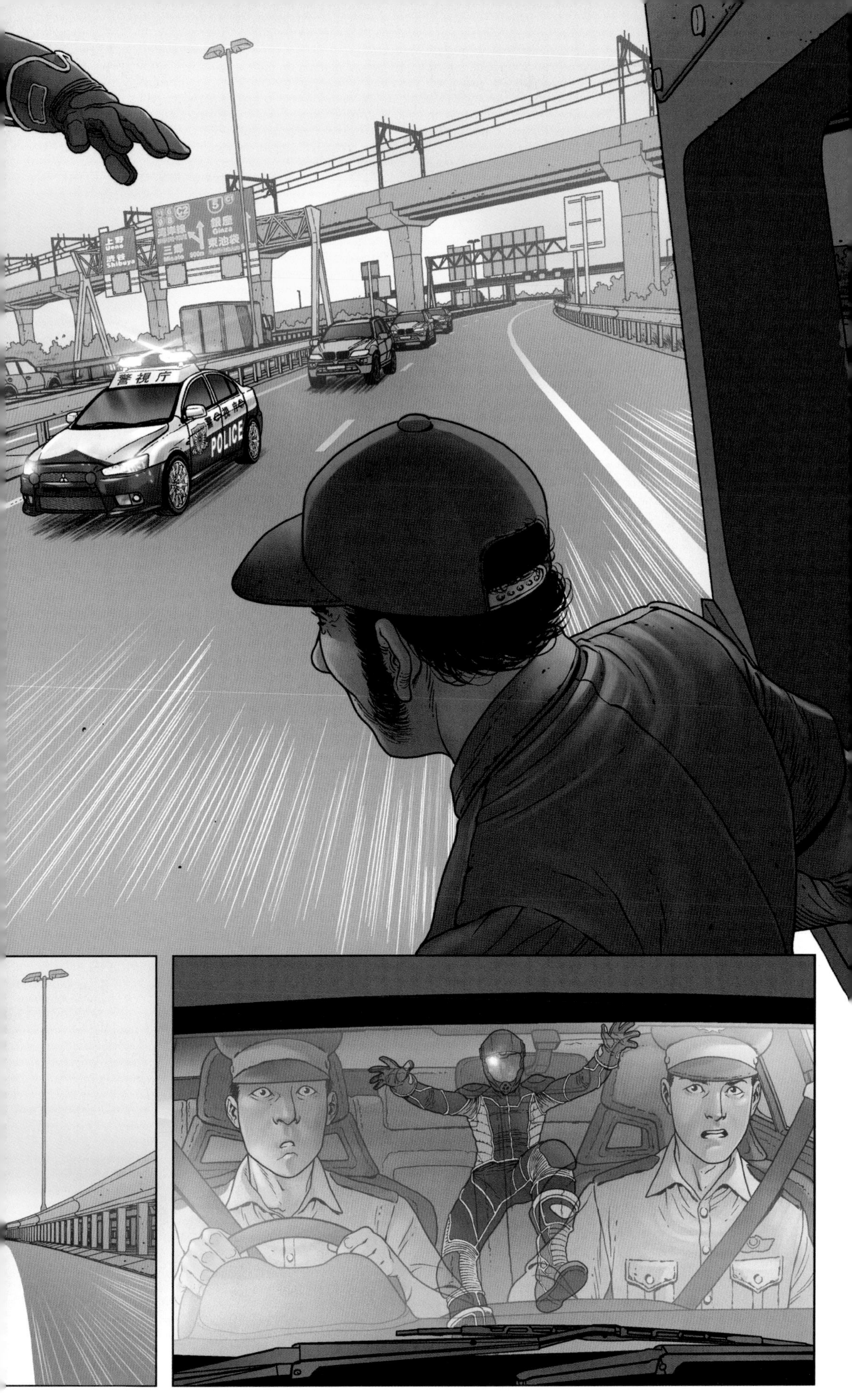

上野
Ueno
Shibuya
C2
5
銀座
東池袋
警視庁
POLICE

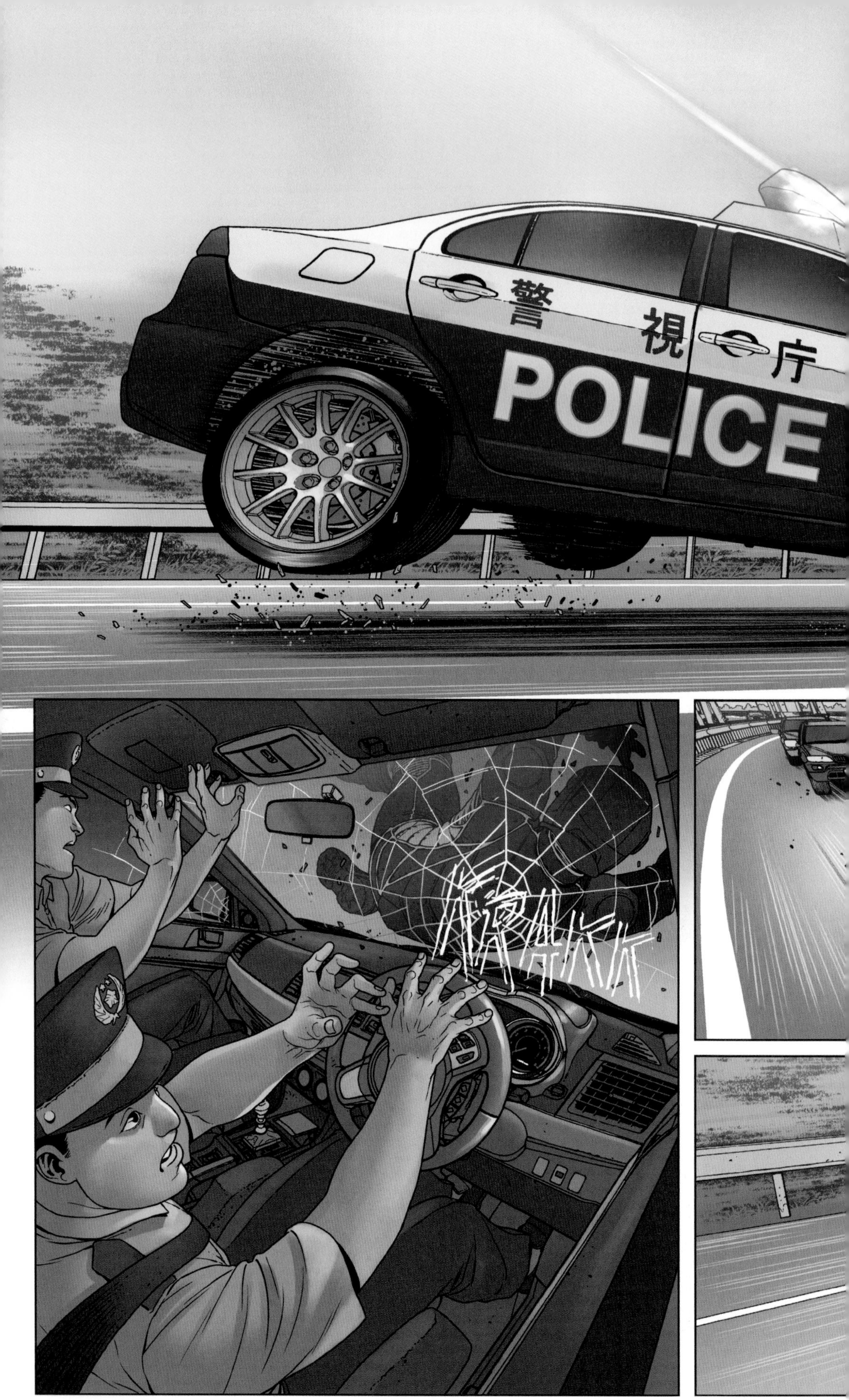
警視庁
POLICE

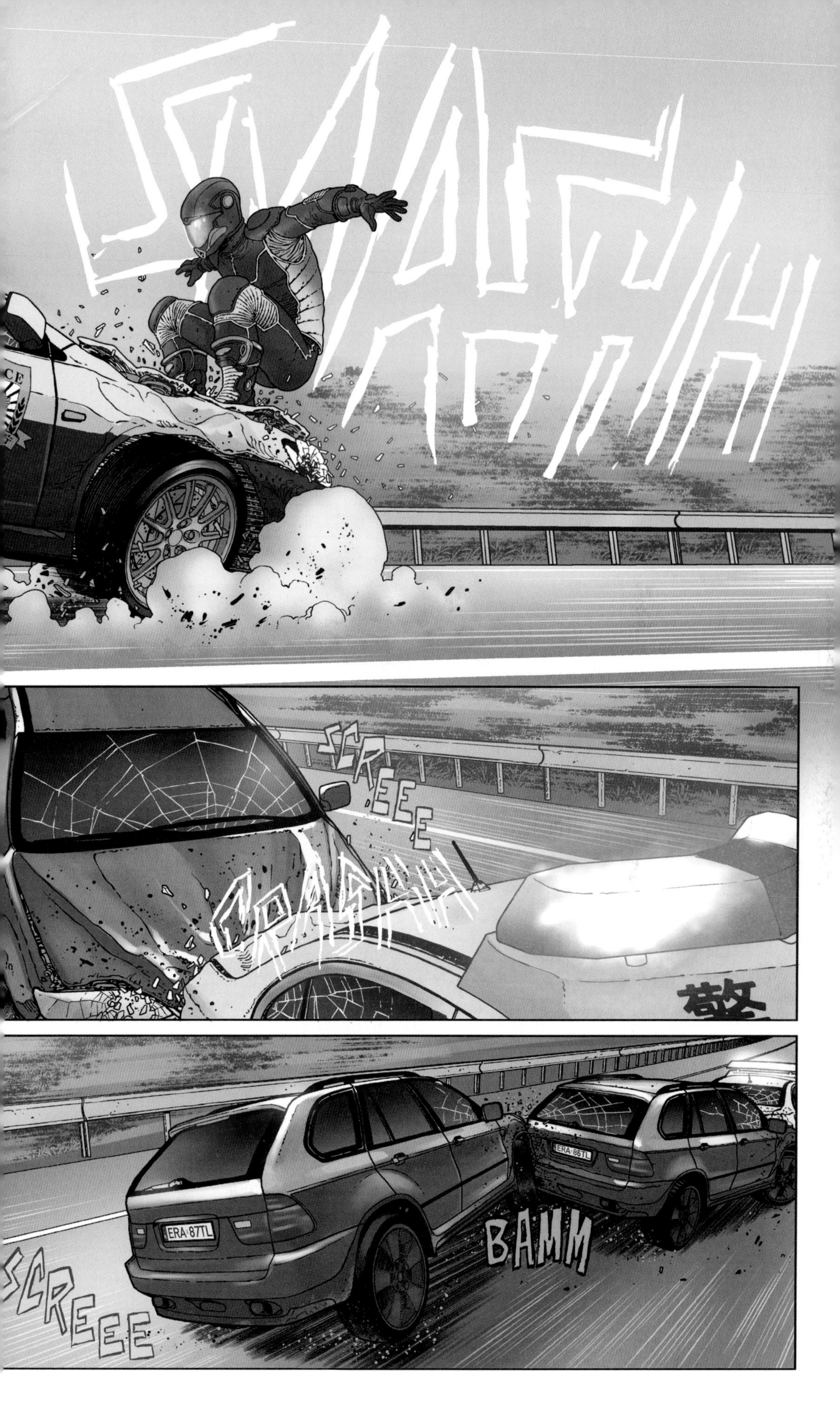
SCREEE
CRASHH
警
ERA 87TL
ERA 86TL
BAMM
SCREEE

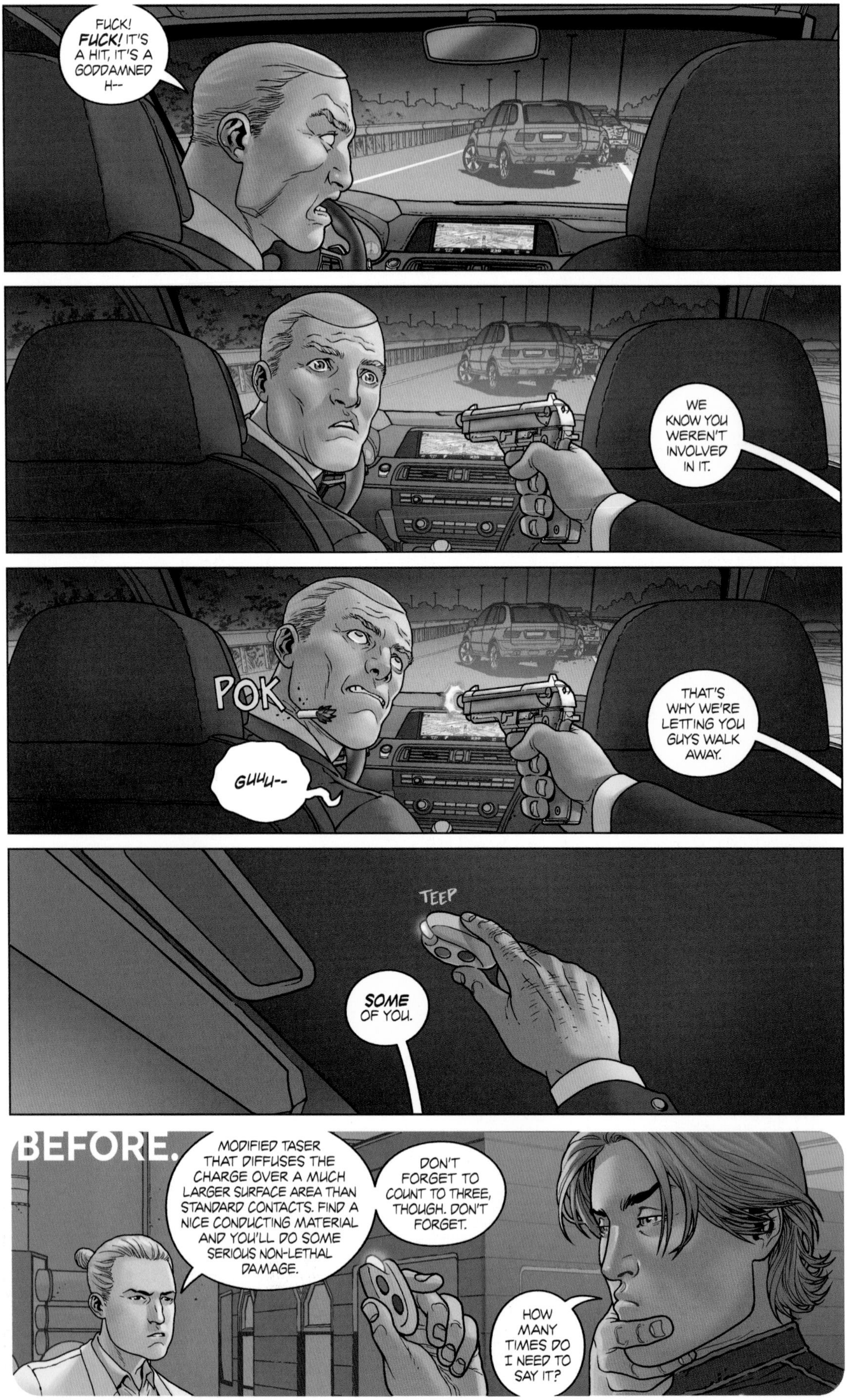
FUCK! FUCK! IT'S A HIT, IT'S A GODDAMNED H--
WE KNOW YOU WEREN'T INVOLVED IN IT.
POK
THAT'S WHY WE'RE LETTING YOU GUYS WALK AWAY.
GUUU--
TEEP
SOME OF YOU.
BEFORE.
MODIFIED TASER THAT DIFFUSES THE CHARGE OVER A MUCH LARGER SURFACE AREA THAN STANDARD CONTACTS. FIND A NICE CONDUCTING MATERIAL AND YOU'LL DO SOME SERIOUS NON-LETHAL DAMAGE.
DON'T FORGET TO COUNT TO THREE, THOUGH. DON'T FORGET.
HOW MANY TIMES DO I NEED TO SAY IT?

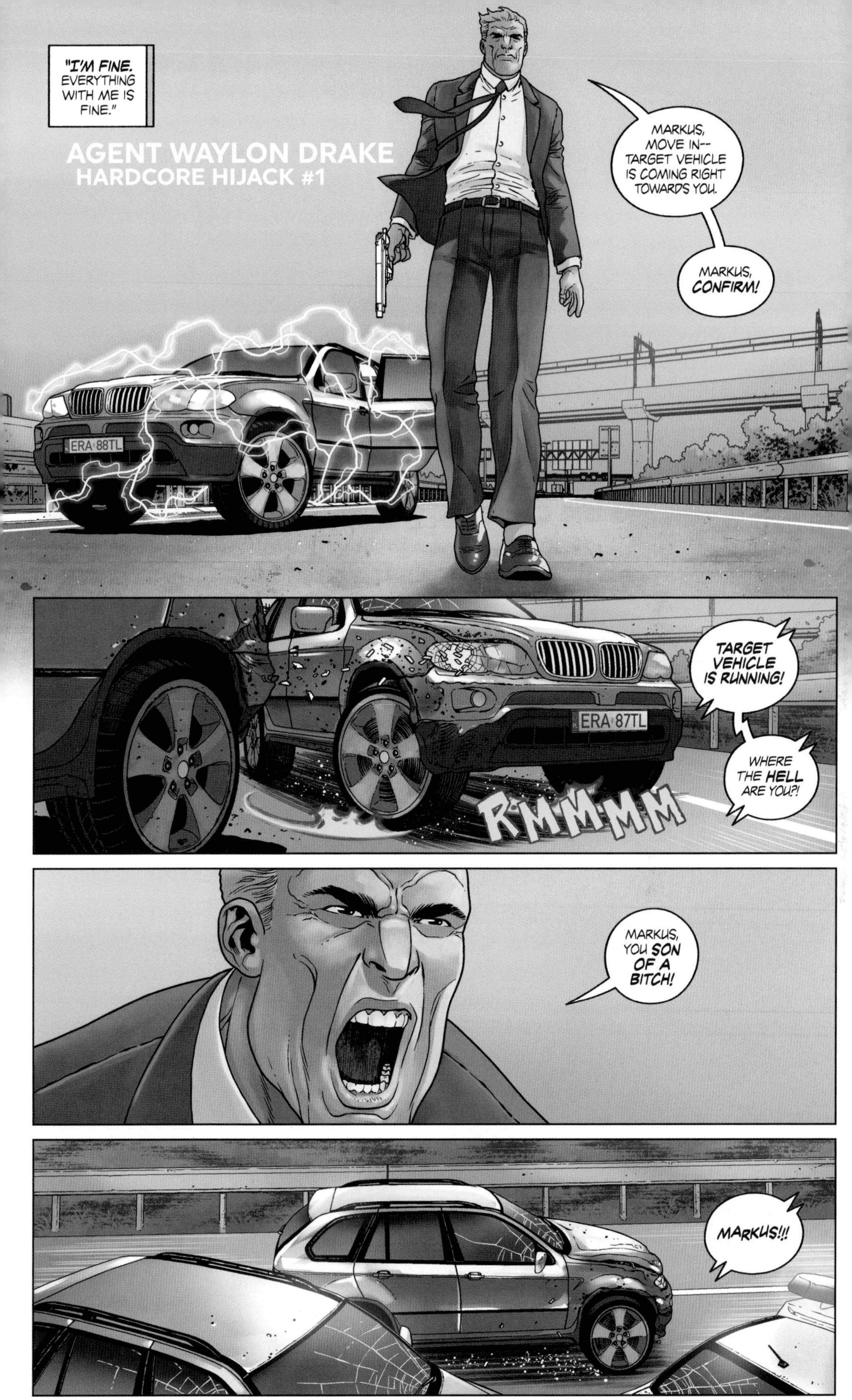
"I'M FINE. EVERYTHING WITH ME IS FINE."
AGENT WAYLON DRAKE
HARDCORE HIJACK #1
MARKUS, MOVE IN-- TARGET VEHICLE IS COMING RIGHT TOWARDS YOU.
MARKUS, CONFIRM!
ERA 88TL
ERA 87TL
TARGET VEHICLE IS RUNNING!
WHERE THE HELL ARE YOU?!
RMMMMM
MARKUS, YOU SON OF A BITCH!
MARKUS!!!

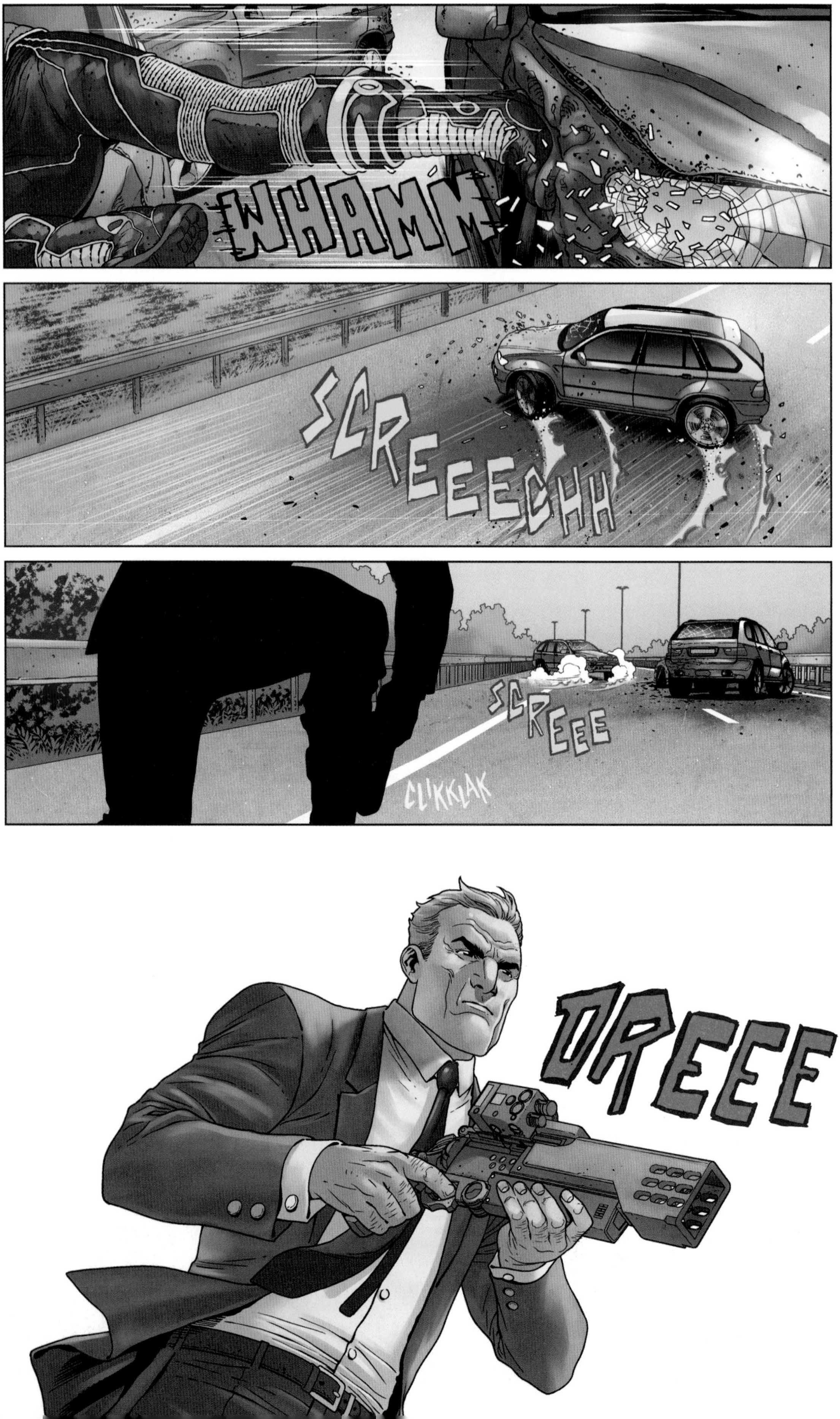
WHAMM
SCREEECHH
SCREEE
CLIKKLAK
DREEE

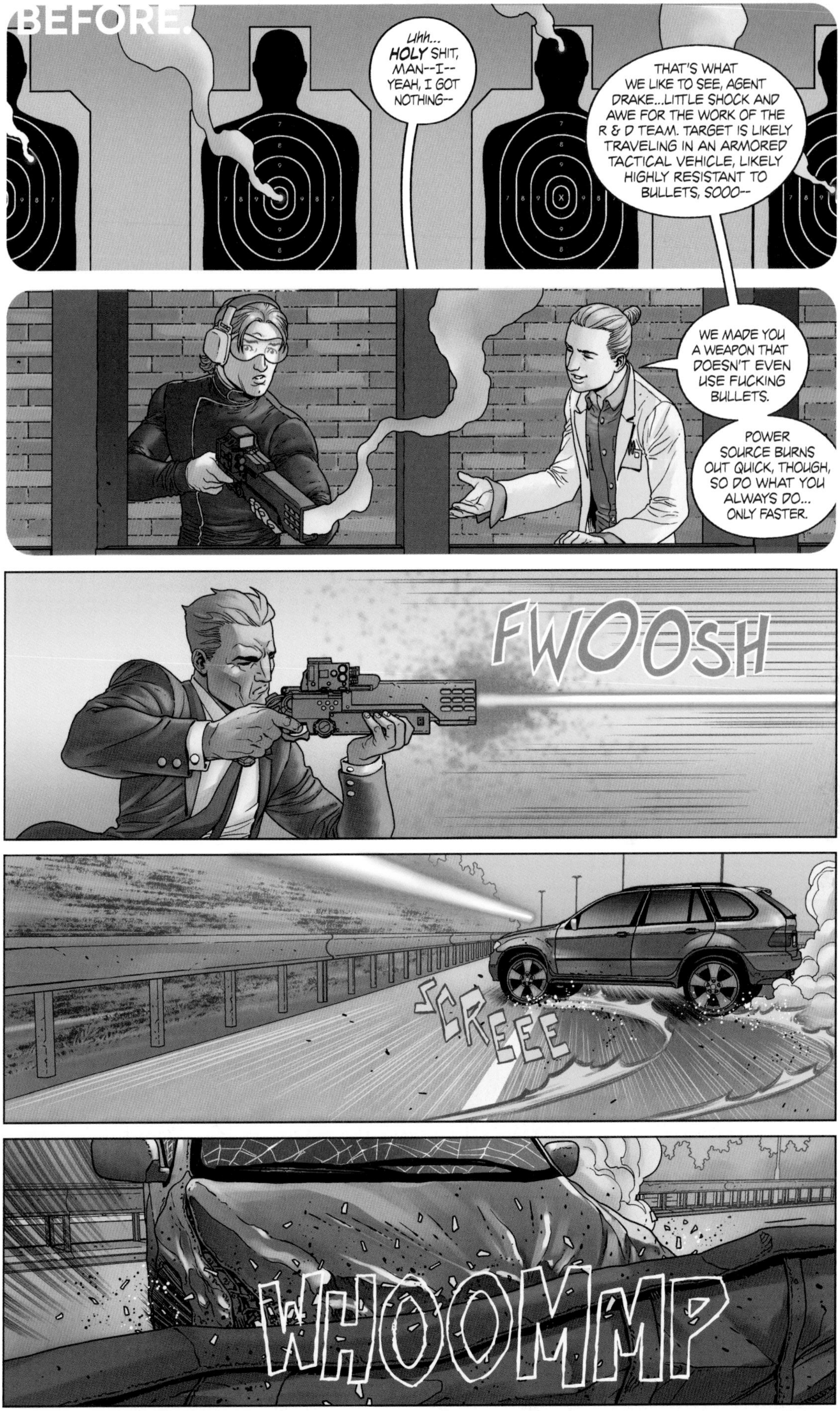
BEFORE.
UHH... HOLY SHIT, MAN--I-- YEAH, I GOT NOTHING--
THAT'S WHAT WE LIKE TO SEE, AGENT DRAKE...LITTLE SHOCK AND AWE FOR THE WORK OF THE R & D TEAM. TARGET IS LIKELY TRAVELING IN AN ARMORED TACTICAL VEHICLE, LIKELY HIGHLY RESISTANT TO BULLETS, SOOO--
WE MADE YOU A WEAPON THAT DOESN'T EVEN USE FUCKING BULLETS.
POWER SOURCE BURNS OUT QUICK, THOUGH, SO DO WHAT YOU ALWAYS DO... ONLY FASTER.
FWOOSH
SCREEEE
WHOOMMP

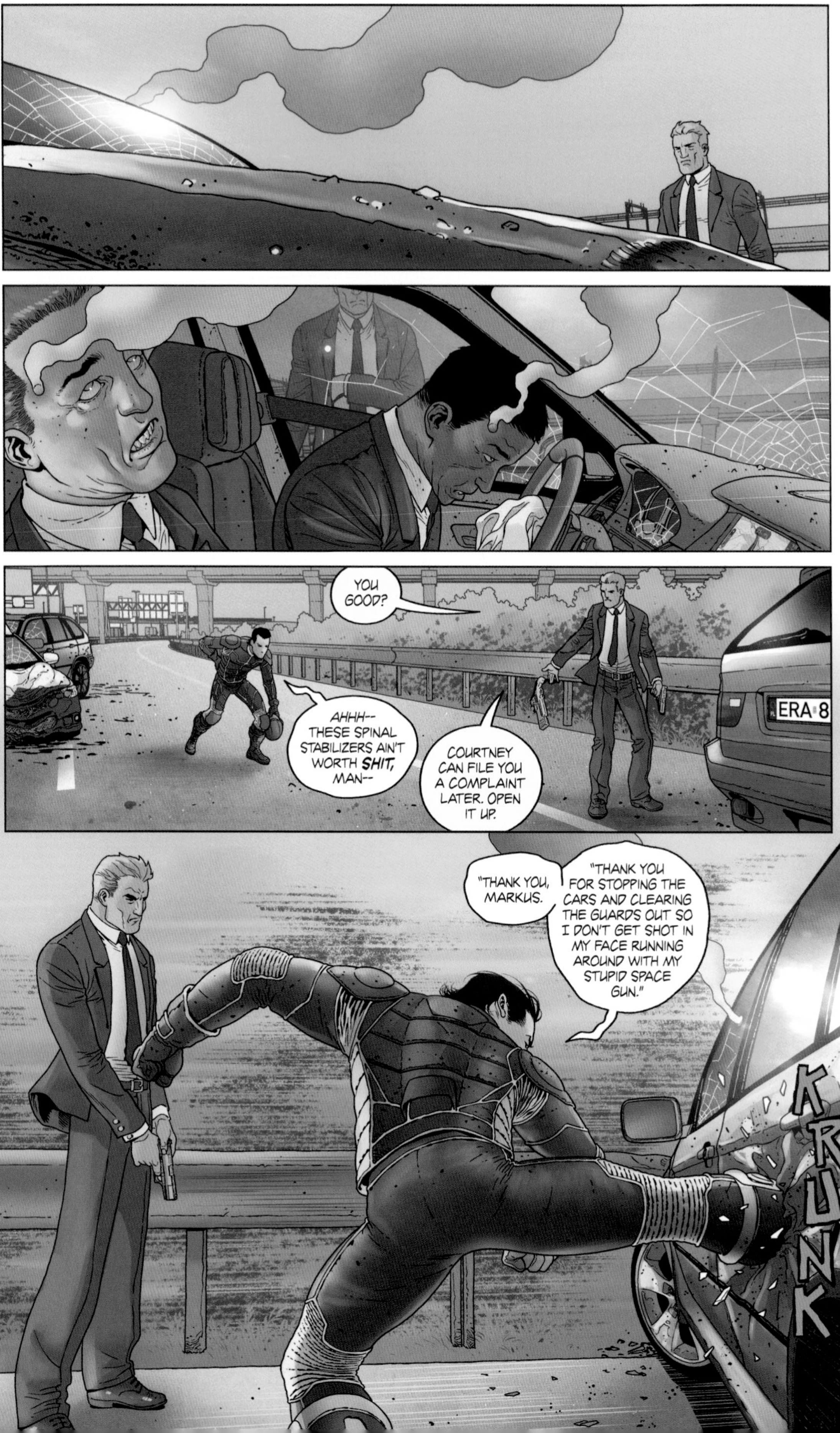
YOU GOOD?
AHHH-- THESE SPINAL STABILIZERS AIN'T WORTH **SHIT,** MAN--
COURTNEY CAN FILE YOU A COMPLAINT LATER. OPEN IT UP.
ERA 8
"THANK YOU, MARKUS.
"THANK YOU FOR STOPPING THE CARS AND CLEARING THE GUARDS OUT SO I DON'T GET SHOT IN MY FACE RUNNING AROUND WITH MY STUPID SPACE GUN."
KRUNK

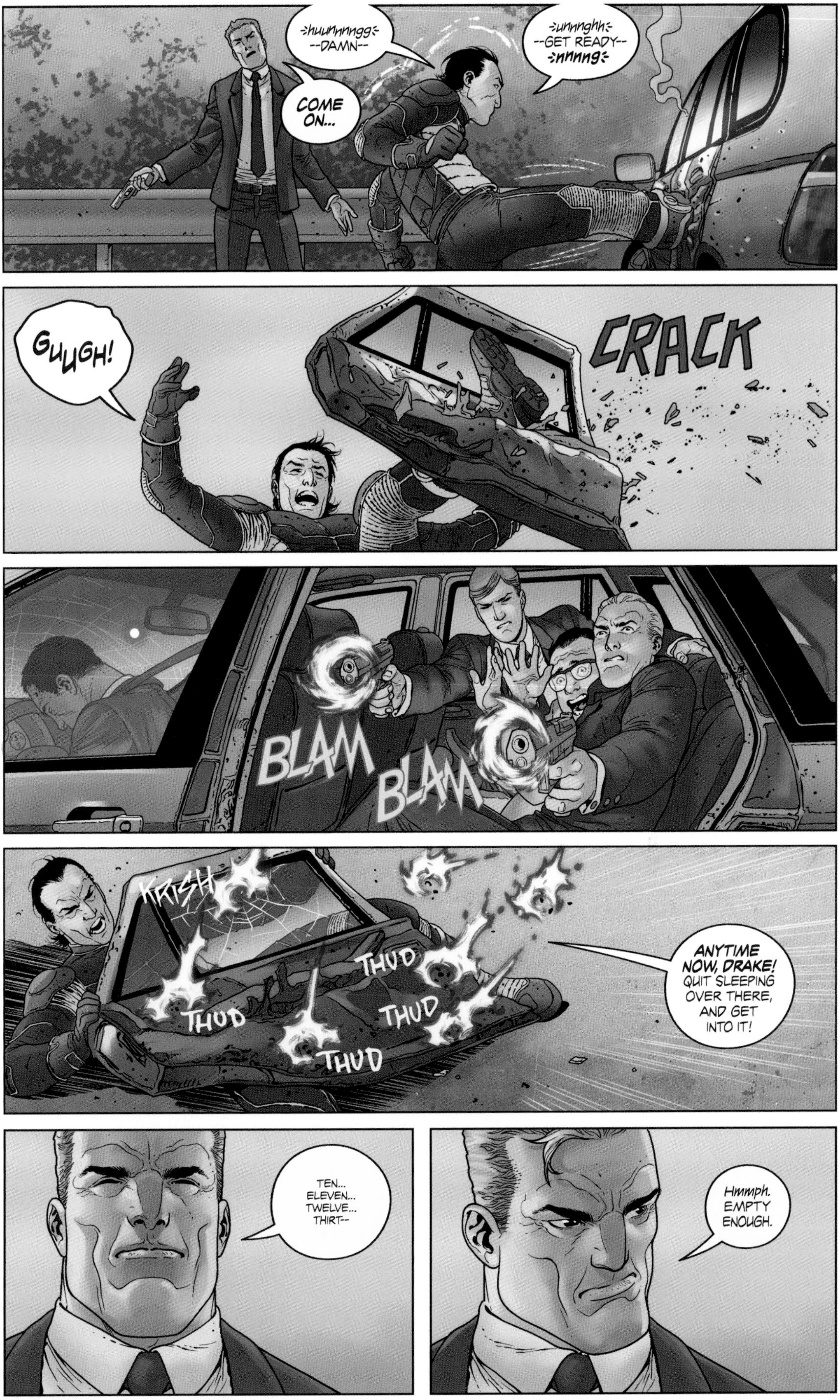

-huuunnnngg- --DAMN--
COME ON...
-unnnghh- --GET READY-- -nnnng-
GUUGH!
CRACK
BLAM
BLAM
KRISH
THUD
THUD
THUD
THUD
ANYTIME NOW, DRAKE! QUIT SLEEPING OVER THERE, AND GET INTO IT!
TEN... ELEVEN... TWELVE... THIRT--
Hmmph. EMPTY ENOUGH.

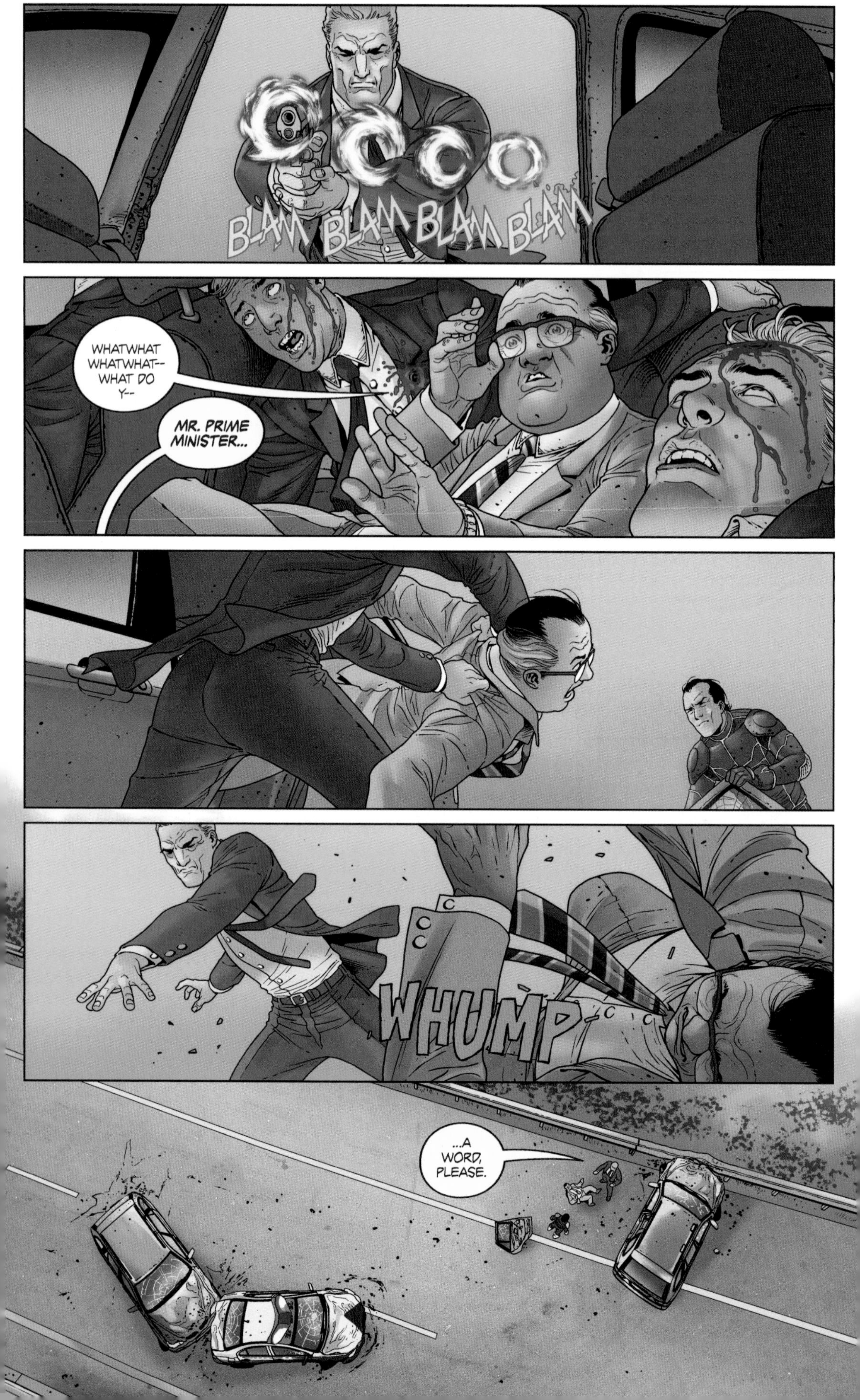
BLAM BLAM BLAM BLAM
WHATWHAT WHATWHAT-- WHAT DO Y--
MR. PRIME MINISTER...
WHUMP
...A WORD, PLEASE.

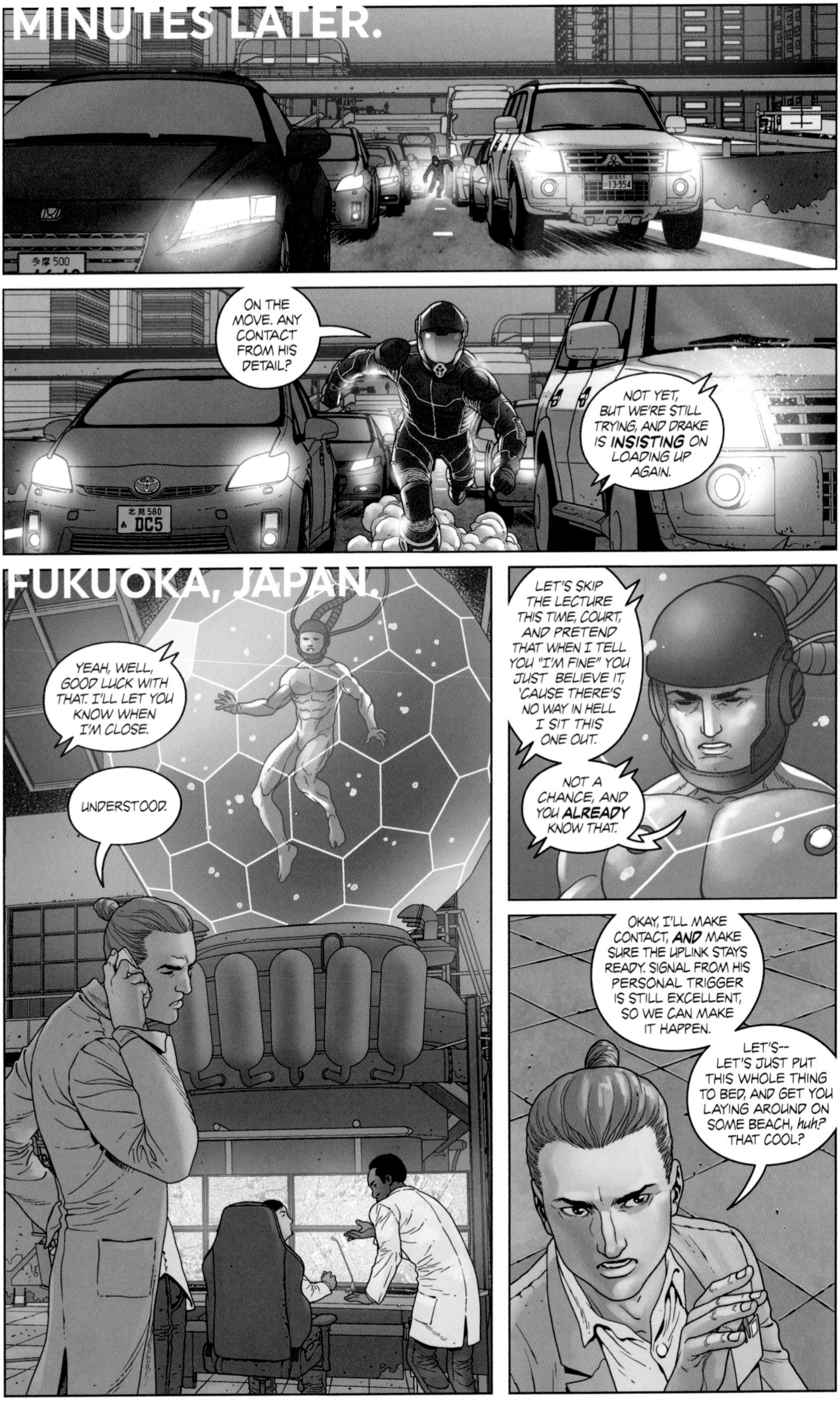
MINUTES LATER.
ON THE MOVE. ANY CONTACT FROM HIS DETAIL?
NOT YET, BUT WE'RE STILL TRYING, AND DRAKE IS **INSISTING** ON LOADING UP AGAIN.
FUKUOKA, JAPAN.
YEAH, WELL, GOOD LUCK WITH THAT. I'LL LET YOU KNOW WHEN I'M CLOSE.
UNDERSTOOD.
LET'S SKIP THE LECTURE THIS TIME, COURT, AND PRETEND THAT WHEN I TELL YOU "I'M FINE" YOU JUST BELIEVE IT, 'CAUSE THERE'S NO WAY IN HELL I SIT THIS ONE OUT.
NOT A CHANCE, AND YOU **ALREADY** KNOW THAT.
OKAY, I'LL MAKE CONTACT, **AND** MAKE SURE THE UPLINK STAYS READY. SIGNAL FROM HIS PERSONAL TRIGGER IS STILL EXCELLENT, SO WE CAN MAKE IT HAPPEN.
LET'S-- LET'S JUST PUT THIS WHOLE THING TO BED, AND GET YOU LAYING AROUND ON SOME BEACH, *huh?* THAT COOL?

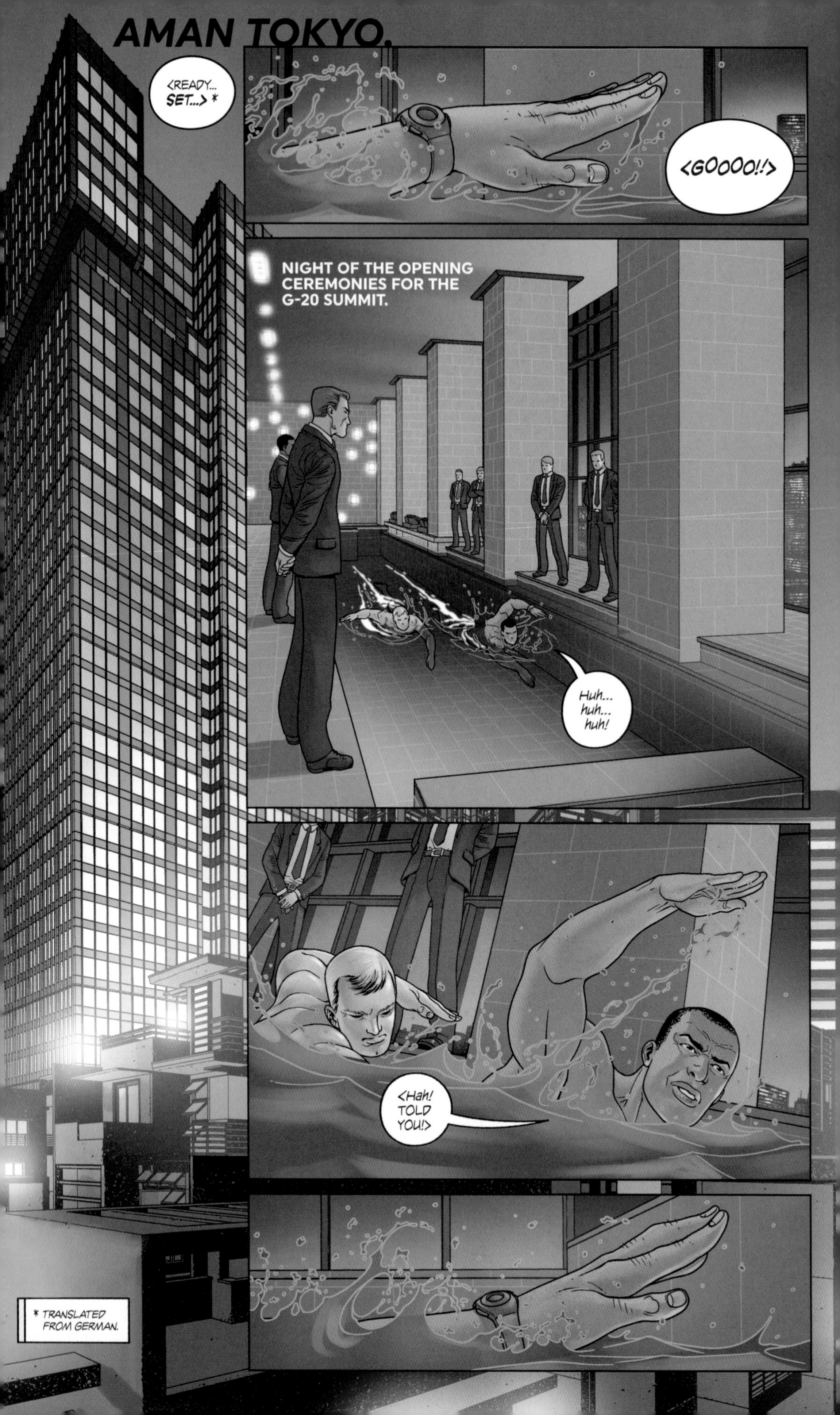
AMAN TOKYO.
<READY... SET...> *
<GOOOO!!>
NIGHT OF THE OPENING CEREMONIES FOR THE G-20 SUMMIT.
Huh... huh... huh!
<Hah! TOLD YOU!>
* TRANSLATED FROM GERMAN.

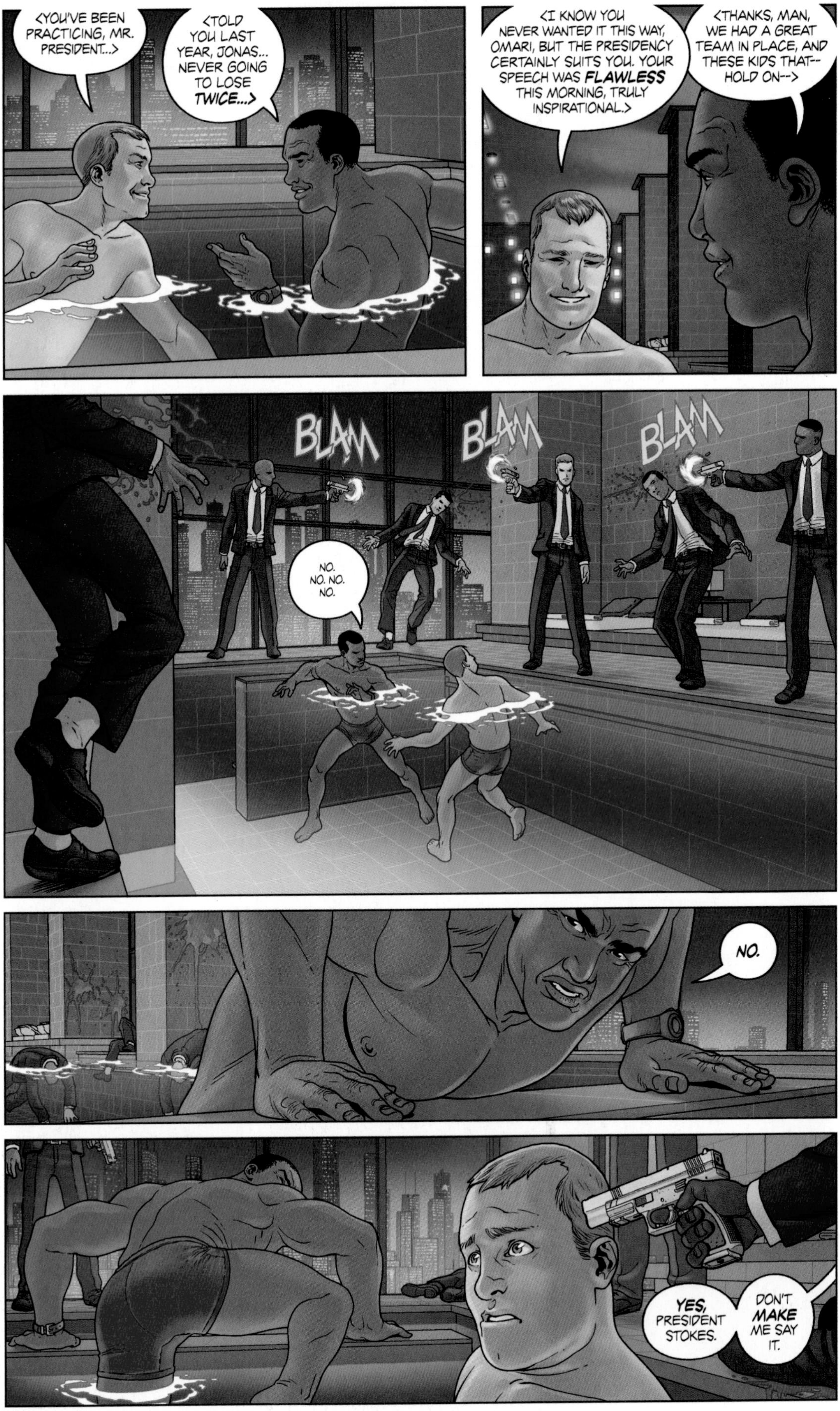
<YOU'VE BEEN PRACTICING, MR. PRESIDENT...>
<TOLD YOU LAST YEAR, JONAS... NEVER GOING TO LOSE TWICE...>
<I KNOW YOU NEVER WANTED IT THIS WAY, OMARI, BUT THE PRESIDENCY CERTAINLY SUITS YOU. YOUR SPEECH WAS FLAWLESS THIS MORNING, TRULY INSPIRATIONAL.>
<THANKS, MAN, WE HAD A GREAT TEAM IN PLACE, AND THESE KIDS THAT-- HOLD ON-->
BLAM
BLAM
BLAM
NO. NO. NO. NO.
NO.
YES, PRESIDENT STOKES.
DON'T MAKE ME SAY IT.

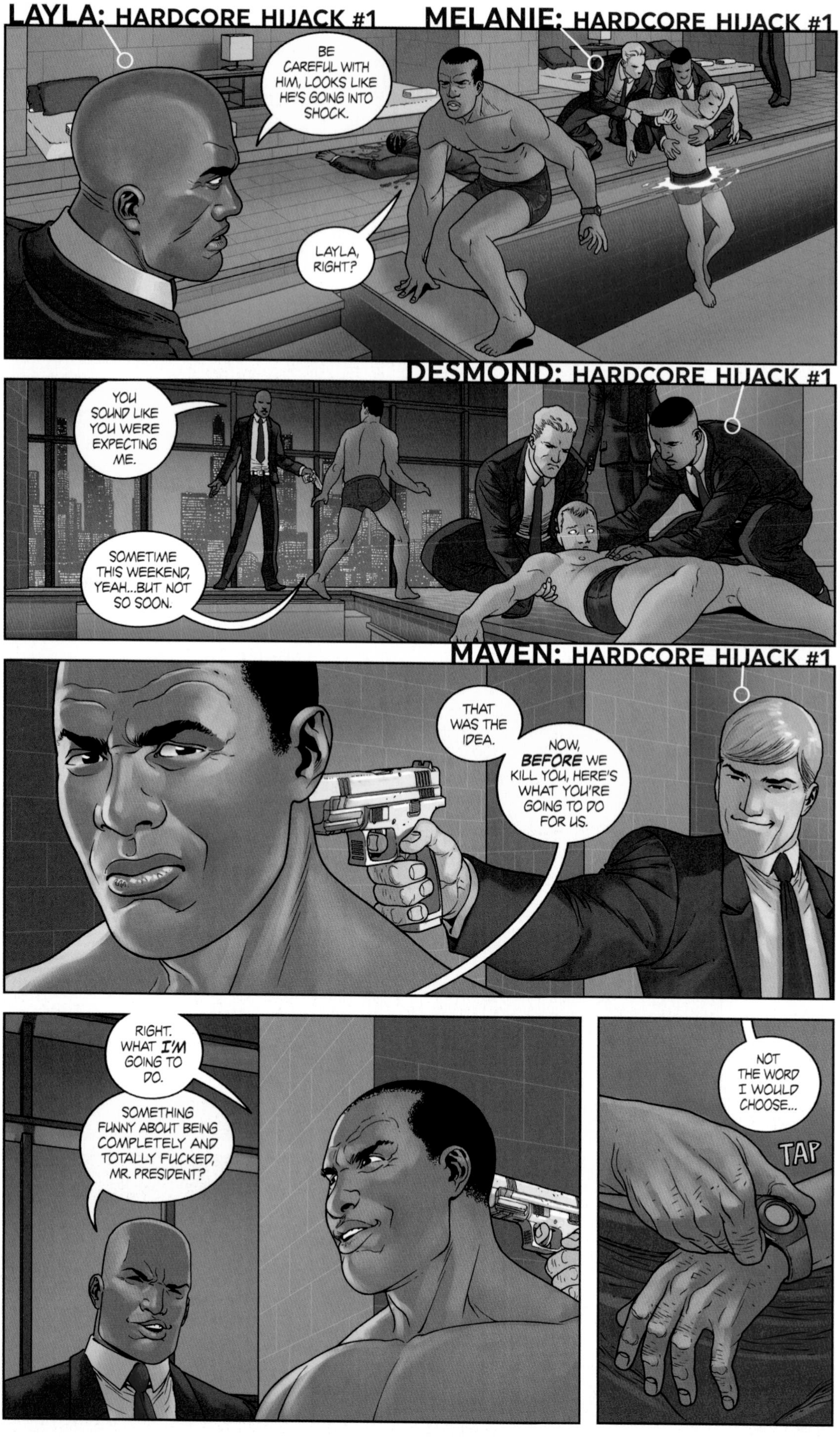
LAYLA: HARDCORE HIJACK #1
MELANIE: HARDCORE HIJACK #1
BE CAREFUL WITH HIM, LOOKS LIKE HE'S GOING INTO SHOCK.
LAYLA, RIGHT?
DESMOND: HARDCORE HIJACK #1
YOU SOUND LIKE YOU WERE EXPECTING ME.
SOMETIME THIS WEEKEND, YEAH...BUT NOT SO SOON.
MAVEN: HARDCORE HIJACK #1
THAT WAS THE IDEA.
NOW, BEFORE WE KILL YOU, HERE'S WHAT YOU'RE GOING TO DO FOR US.
RIGHT. WHAT I'M GOING TO DO.
SOMETHING FUNNY ABOUT BEING COMPLETELY AND TOTALLY FUCKED, MR. PRESIDENT?
NOT THE WORD I WOULD CHOOSE...
TAP

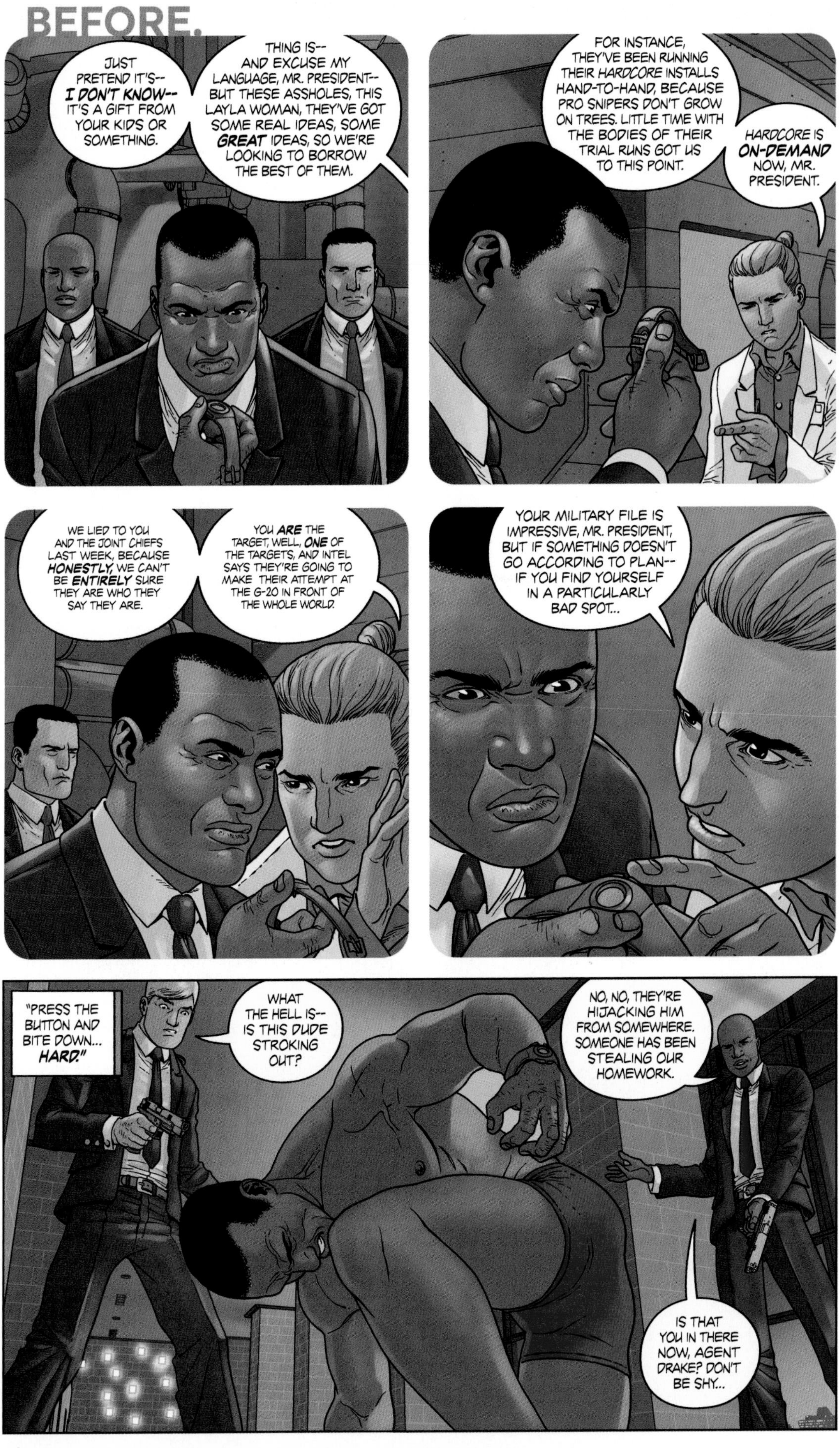
BEFORE.
JUST PRETEND IT'S-- I DON'T KNOW-- IT'S A GIFT FROM YOUR KIDS OR SOMETHING.
THING IS-- AND EXCUSE MY LANGUAGE, MR. PRESIDENT-- BUT THESE ASSHOLES, THIS LAYLA WOMAN, THEY'VE GOT SOME REAL IDEAS, SOME GREAT IDEAS, SO WE'RE LOOKING TO BORROW THE BEST OF THEM.
FOR INSTANCE, THEY'VE BEEN RUNNING THEIR HARDCORE INSTALLS HAND-TO-HAND, BECAUSE PRO SNIPERS DON'T GROW ON TREES. LITTLE TIME WITH THE BODIES OF THEIR TRIAL RUNS GOT US TO THIS POINT.
HARDCORE IS ON-DEMAND NOW, MR. PRESIDENT.
WE LIED TO YOU AND THE JOINT CHIEFS LAST WEEK, BECAUSE HONESTLY, WE CAN'T BE ENTIRELY SURE THEY ARE WHO THEY SAY THEY ARE.
YOU ARE THE TARGET, WELL, ONE OF THE TARGETS, AND INTEL SAYS THEY'RE GOING TO MAKE THEIR ATTEMPT AT THE G-20 IN FRONT OF THE WHOLE WORLD.
YOUR MILITARY FILE IS IMPRESSIVE, MR. PRESIDENT, BUT IF SOMETHING DOESN'T GO ACCORDING TO PLAN-- IF YOU FIND YOURSELF IN A PARTICULARLY BAD SPOT...
"PRESS THE BUTTON AND BITE DOWN... HARD."
WHAT THE HELL IS-- IS THIS DUDE STROKING OUT?
NO, NO, THEY'RE HIJACKING HIM FROM SOMEWHERE. SOMEONE HAS BEEN STEALING OUR HOMEWORK.
IS THAT YOU IN THERE NOW, AGENT DRAKE? DON'T BE SHY...

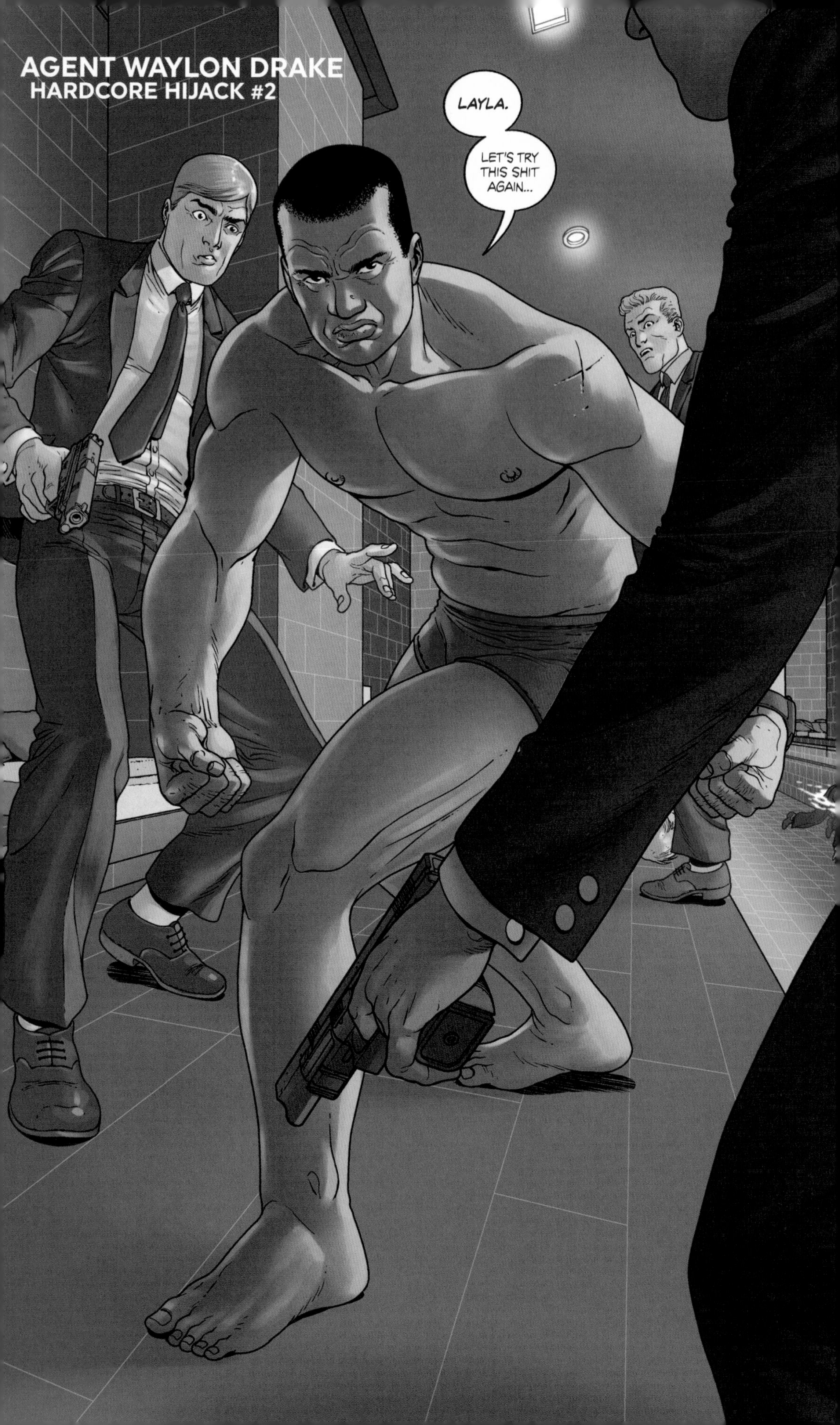
AGENT WAYLON DRAKE
HARDCORE HIJACK #2
LAYLA.
LET'S TRY THIS SHIT AGAIN...

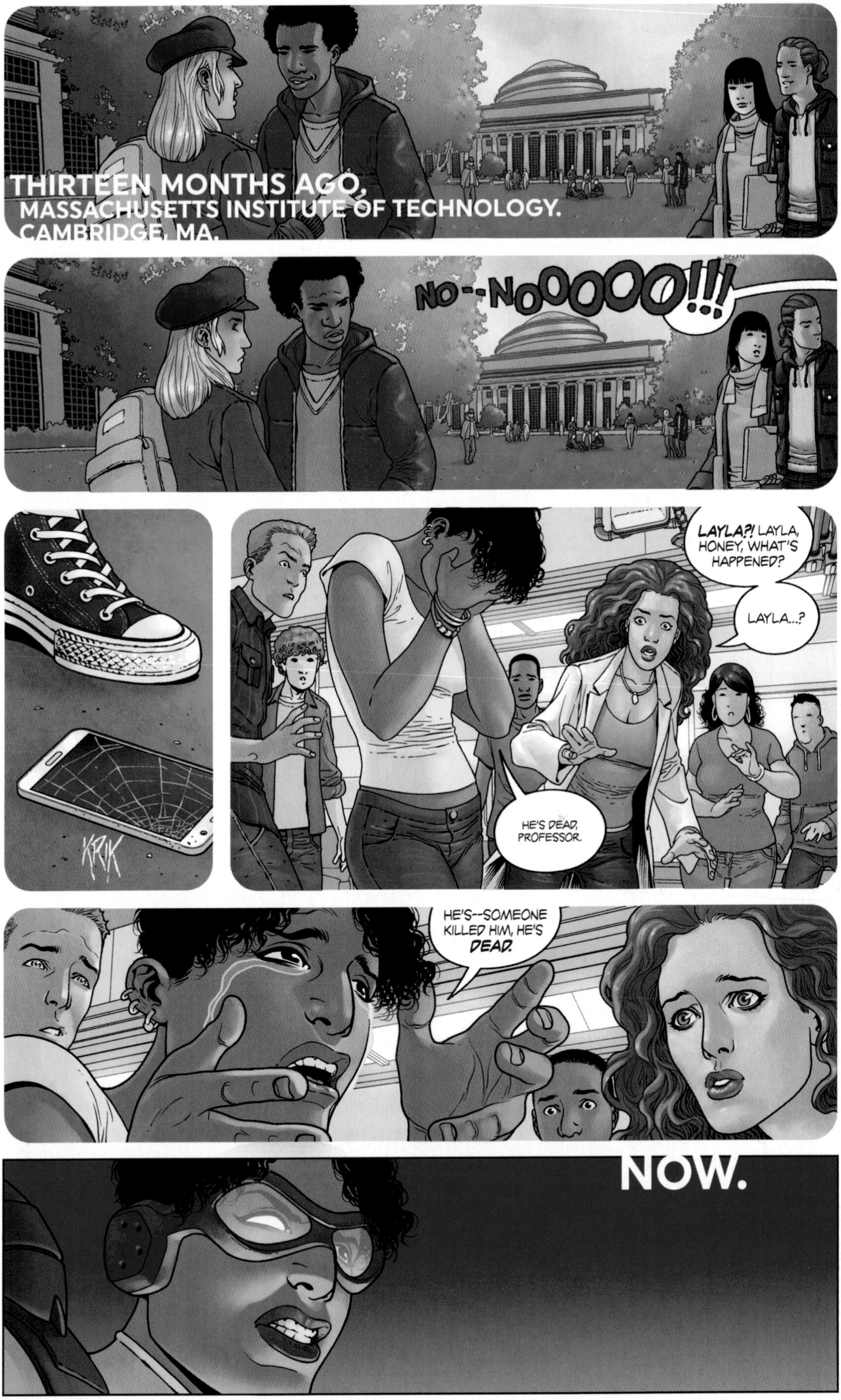
THIRTEEN MONTHS AGO.
MASSACHUSETTS INSTITUTE OF TECHNOLOGY.
CAMBRIDGE, MA.
NO--NOOOOO!!!
KRIK
LAYLA?! LAYLA, HONEY, WHAT'S HAPPENED?
LAYLA...?
HE'S DEAD, PROFESSOR.
HE'S--SOMEONE KILLED HIM, HE'S DEAD.
NOW.

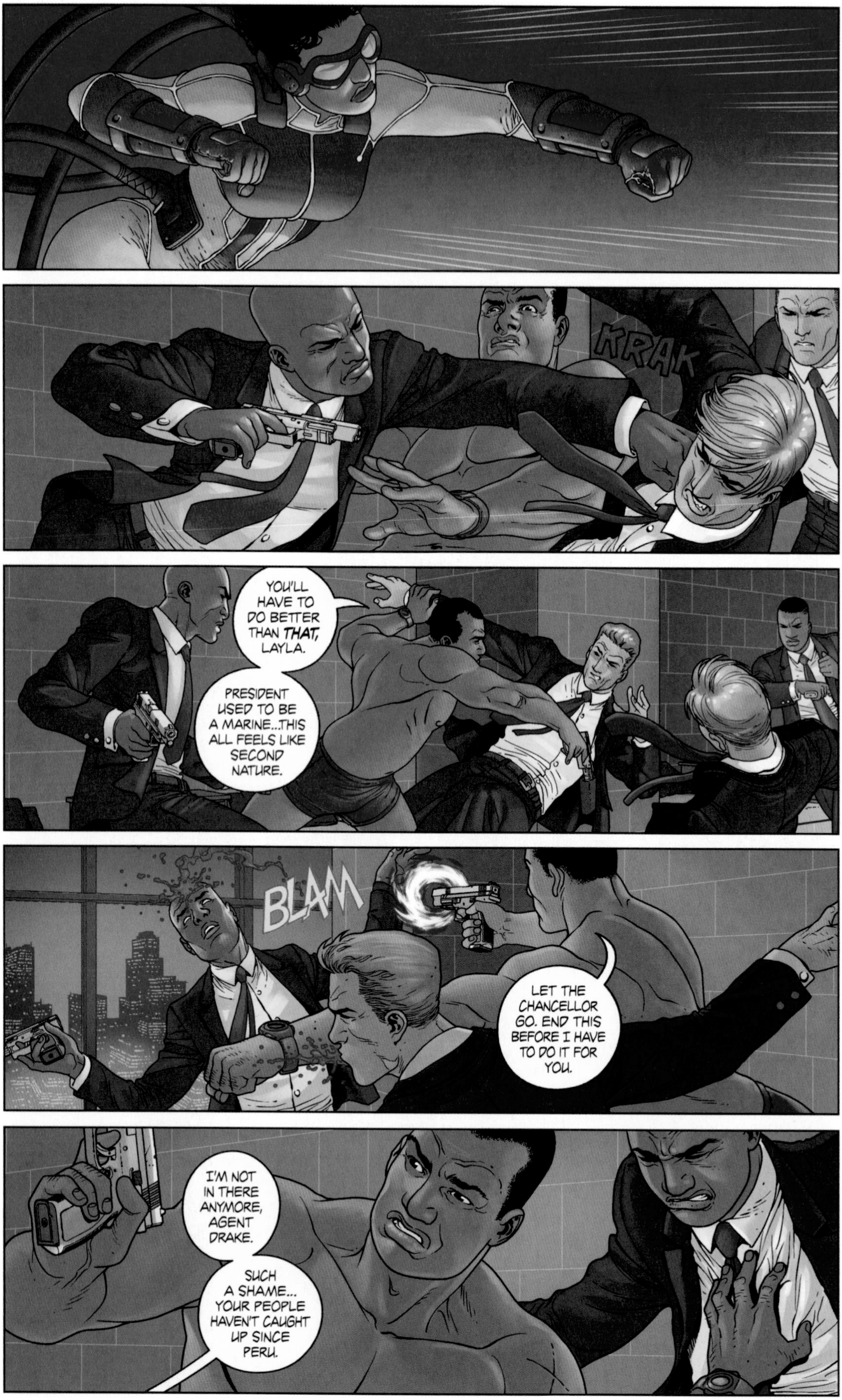
KRAK
YOU'LL HAVE TO DO BETTER THAN *THAT,* LAYLA.
PRESIDENT USED TO BE A MARINE...THIS ALL FEELS LIKE SECOND NATURE.
BLAM
LET THE CHANCELLOR GO. END THIS BEFORE I HAVE TO DO IT FOR YOU.
I'M NOT IN THERE ANYMORE, AGENT DRAKE.
SUCH A SHAME... YOUR PEOPLE HAVEN'T CAUGHT UP SINCE PERU.

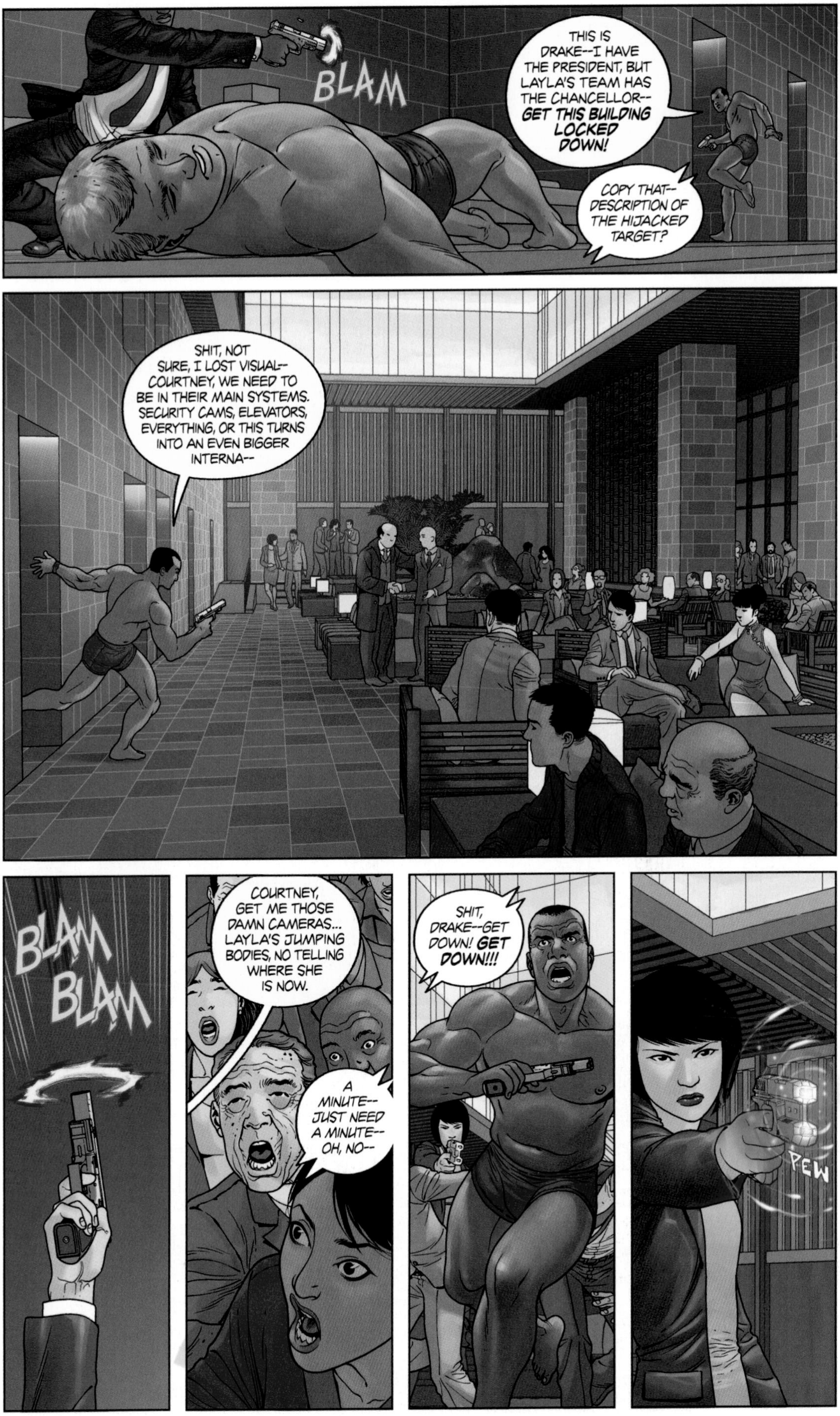
BLAM
THIS IS DRAKE--I HAVE THE PRESIDENT, BUT LAYLA'S TEAM HAS THE CHANCELLOR-- GET THIS BUILDING LOCKED DOWN!
COPY THAT-- DESCRIPTION OF THE HIJACKED TARGET?
SHIT, NOT SURE, I LOST VISUAL-- COURTNEY, WE NEED TO BE IN THEIR MAIN SYSTEMS. SECURITY CAMS, ELEVATORS, EVERYTHING, OR THIS TURNS INTO AN EVEN BIGGER INTERNA--
BLAM BLAM
COURTNEY, GET ME THOSE DAMN CAMERAS... LAYLA'S JUMPING BODIES, NO TELLING WHERE SHE IS NOW.
A MINUTE-- JUST NEED A MINUTE-- OH, NO--
SHIT, DRAKE--GET DOWN! GET DOWN!!!
PEW

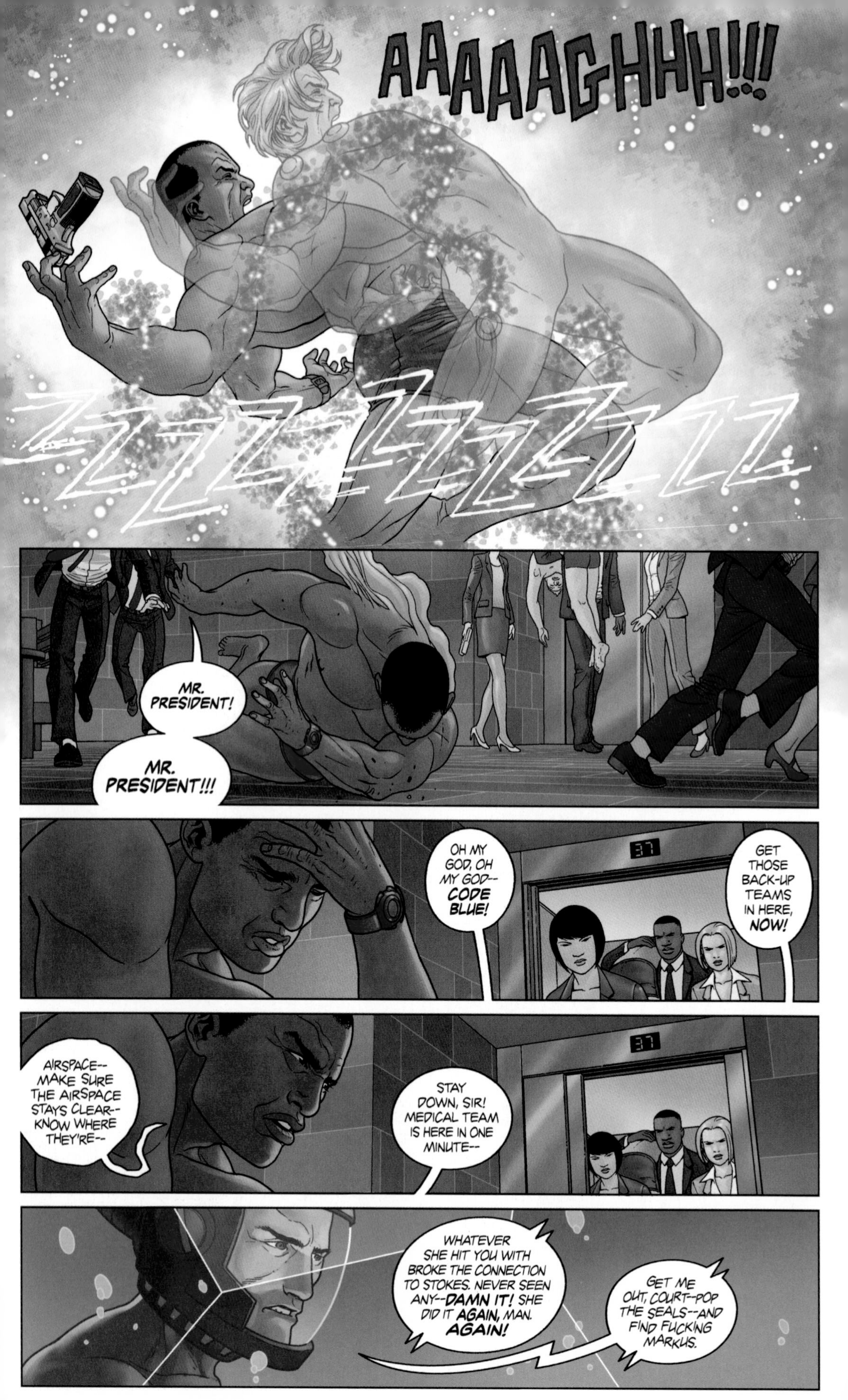
AAAAAAGHHH!!!
ZZZZZZZZZZZZZ
MR. PRESIDENT!
MR. PRESIDENT!!!
OH MY GOD, OH MY GOD-- CODE BLUE!
GET THOSE BACK-UP TEAMS IN HERE, NOW!
AIRSPACE-- MAKE SURE THE AIRSPACE STAYS CLEAR-- KNOW WHERE THEY'RE--
STAY DOWN, SIR! MEDICAL TEAM IS HERE IN ONE MINUTE--
WHATEVER SHE HIT YOU WITH BROKE THE CONNECTION TO STOKES. NEVER SEEN ANY--DAMN IT! SHE DID IT AGAIN, MAN. AGAIN!
GET ME OUT, COURT--POP THE SEALS--AND FIND FUCKING MARKUS.

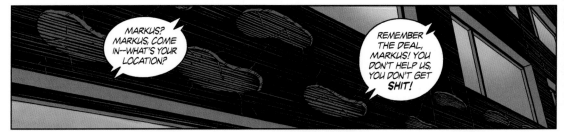

MARKUS? MARKUS, COME IN--WHAT'S YOUR LOCATION?

REMEMBER THE DEAL, MARKUS! YOU DON'T HELP US, YOU DON'T GET *SHIT!*

MR. PRESIDENT, MR. PRESIDENT, WE **NEED** TO GET YOU A--

NO.

NO, NOT YET.

CAMPBELL, I NEED YOUR FIREARM AND YOUR CELL.

JADEN, O'KEEFE-- ELEVATORS.

THIS IS THE PRESIDENT. IS AGENT DRAKE STILL FUNCTIONAL?

THANK HIM FOR THAT LITTLE ASSIST, AND TELL HIM TO GET UPSTAIRS. **NOW.**

HOTEL SUB-BASEMENT.
CLOSED FOR REMODELING.

YES, SIR, MR. PRESIDENT. WE'LL BREAK IT ALL DOWN AND GET ALL TECH SECURED ASAP.

NONE OF THEM GO FREE, YOU UNDERSTAND? I EXPECT TO SEE HIM **AND** MARKUS UP THERE HELPING ME SAVE THE CHANCELLOR, AND PUTTING A BOW ON THIS WHOLE THING.

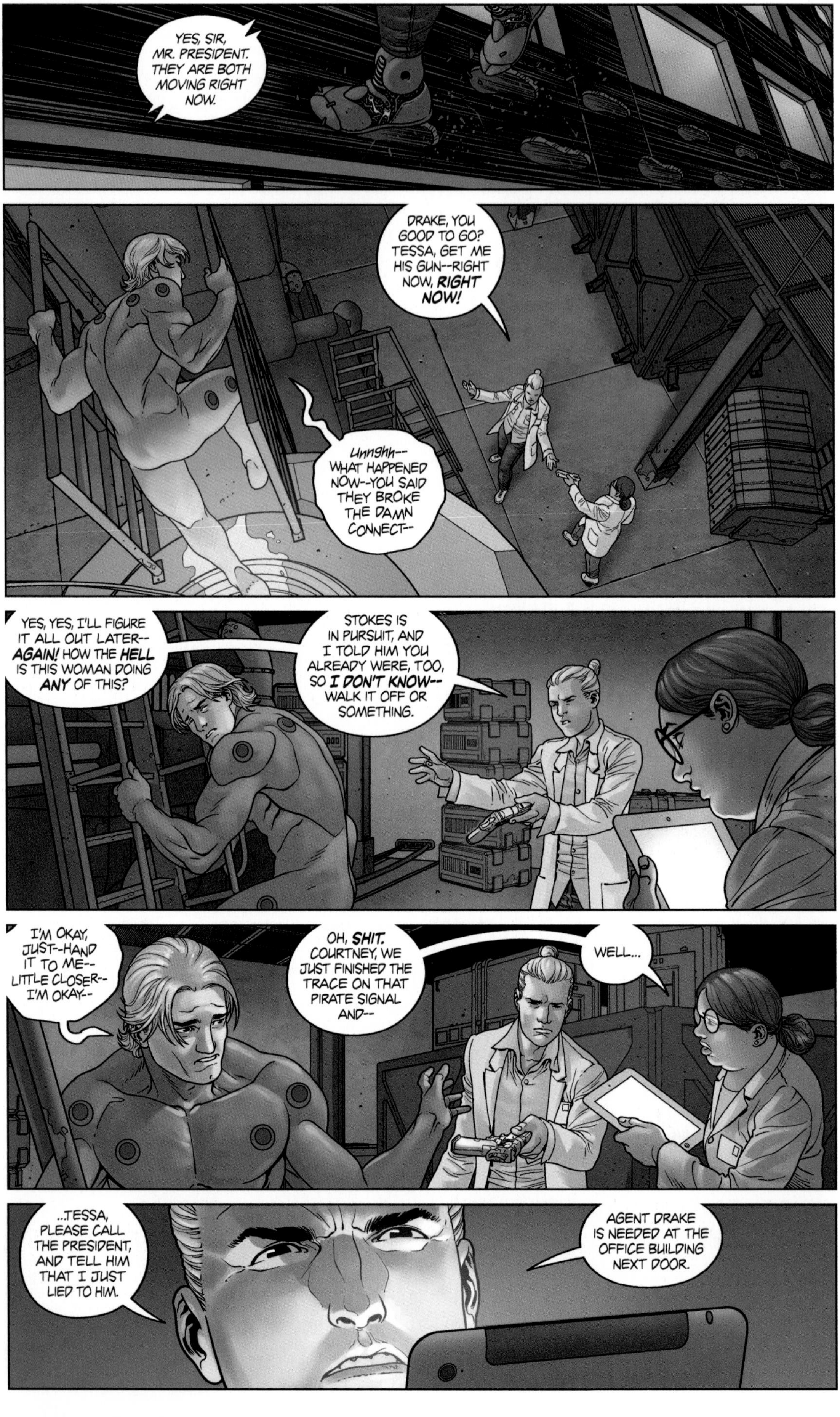
YES, SIR, MR. PRESIDENT. THEY ARE BOTH MOVING RIGHT NOW.
DRAKE, YOU GOOD TO GO? TESSA, GET ME HIS GUN--RIGHT NOW, RIGHT NOW!
Unnghh-- WHAT HAPPENED NOW--YOU SAID THEY BROKE THE DAMN CONNECT--
YES, YES, I'LL FIGURE IT ALL OUT LATER-- AGAIN! HOW THE HELL IS THIS WOMAN DOING ANY OF THIS?
STOKES IS IN PURSUIT, AND I TOLD HIM YOU ALREADY WERE, TOO, SO I DON'T KNOW-- WALK IT OFF OR SOMETHING.
I'M OKAY, JUST--HAND IT TO ME-- LITTLE CLOSER-- I'M OKAY--
OH, SHIT. COURTNEY, WE JUST FINISHED THE TRACE ON THAT PIRATE SIGNAL AND--
WELL...
...TESSA, PLEASE CALL THE PRESIDENT, AND TELL HIM THAT I JUST LIED TO HIM.
AGENT DRAKE IS NEEDED AT THE OFFICE BUILDING NEXT DOOR.

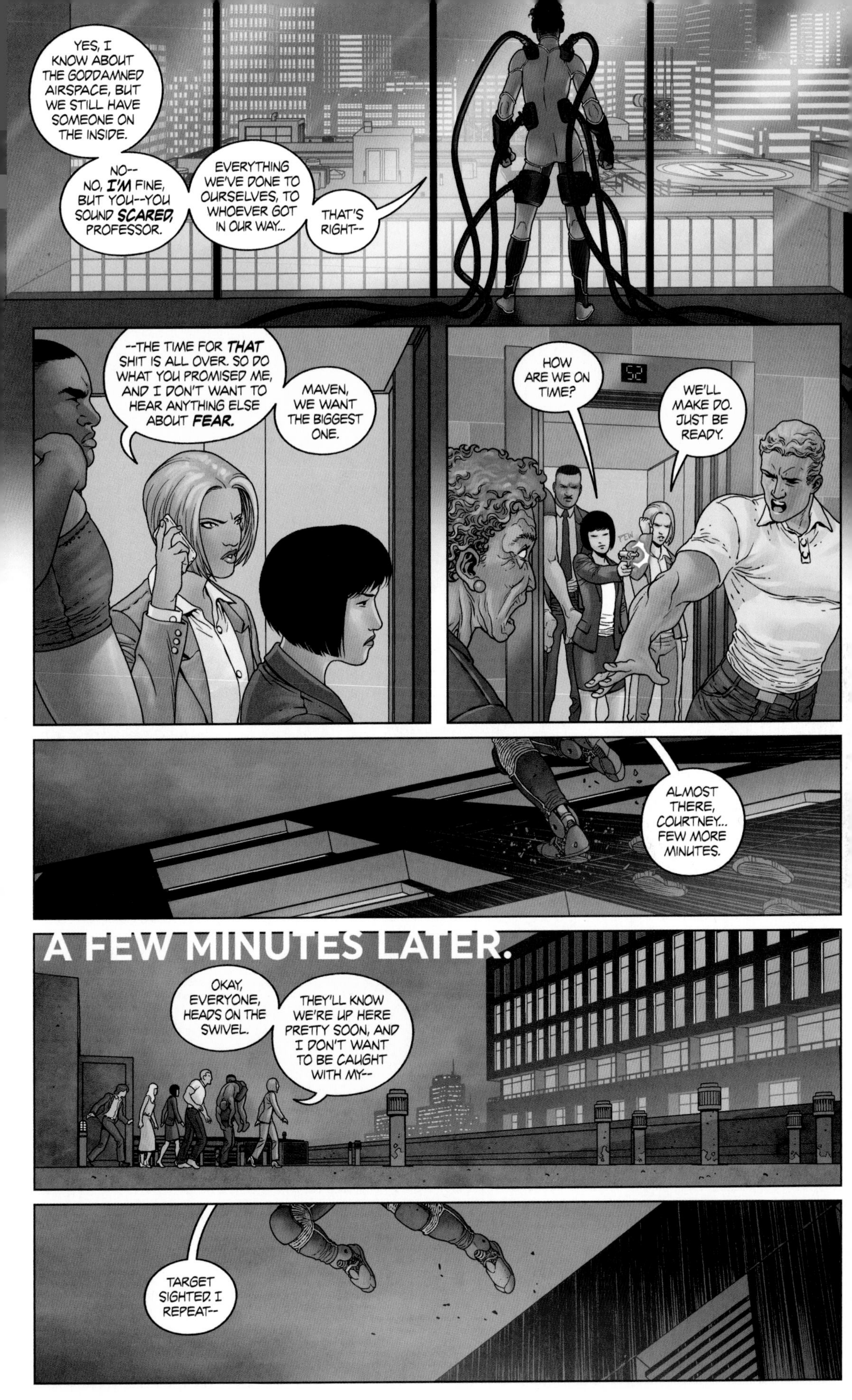
YES, I KNOW ABOUT THE GODDAMNED AIRSPACE, BUT WE STILL HAVE SOMEONE ON THE INSIDE.
NO-- NO, I'M FINE, BUT YOU--YOU SOUND SCARED, PROFESSOR.
EVERYTHING WE'VE DONE TO OURSELVES, TO WHOEVER GOT IN OUR WAY...
THAT'S RIGHT--
--THE TIME FOR THAT SHIT IS ALL OVER. SO DO WHAT YOU PROMISED ME, AND I DON'T WANT TO HEAR ANYTHING ELSE ABOUT FEAR.
MAVEN, WE WANT THE BIGGEST ONE.
52
HOW ARE WE ON TIME?
WE'LL MAKE DO. JUST BE READY.
PEW
ALMOST THERE, COURTNEY... FEW MORE MINUTES.
A FEW MINUTES LATER.
OKAY, EVERYONE, HEADS ON THE SWIVEL.
THEY'LL KNOW WE'RE UP HERE PRETTY SOON, AND I DON'T WANT TO BE CAUGHT WITH MY--
TARGET SIGHTED. I REPEAT--

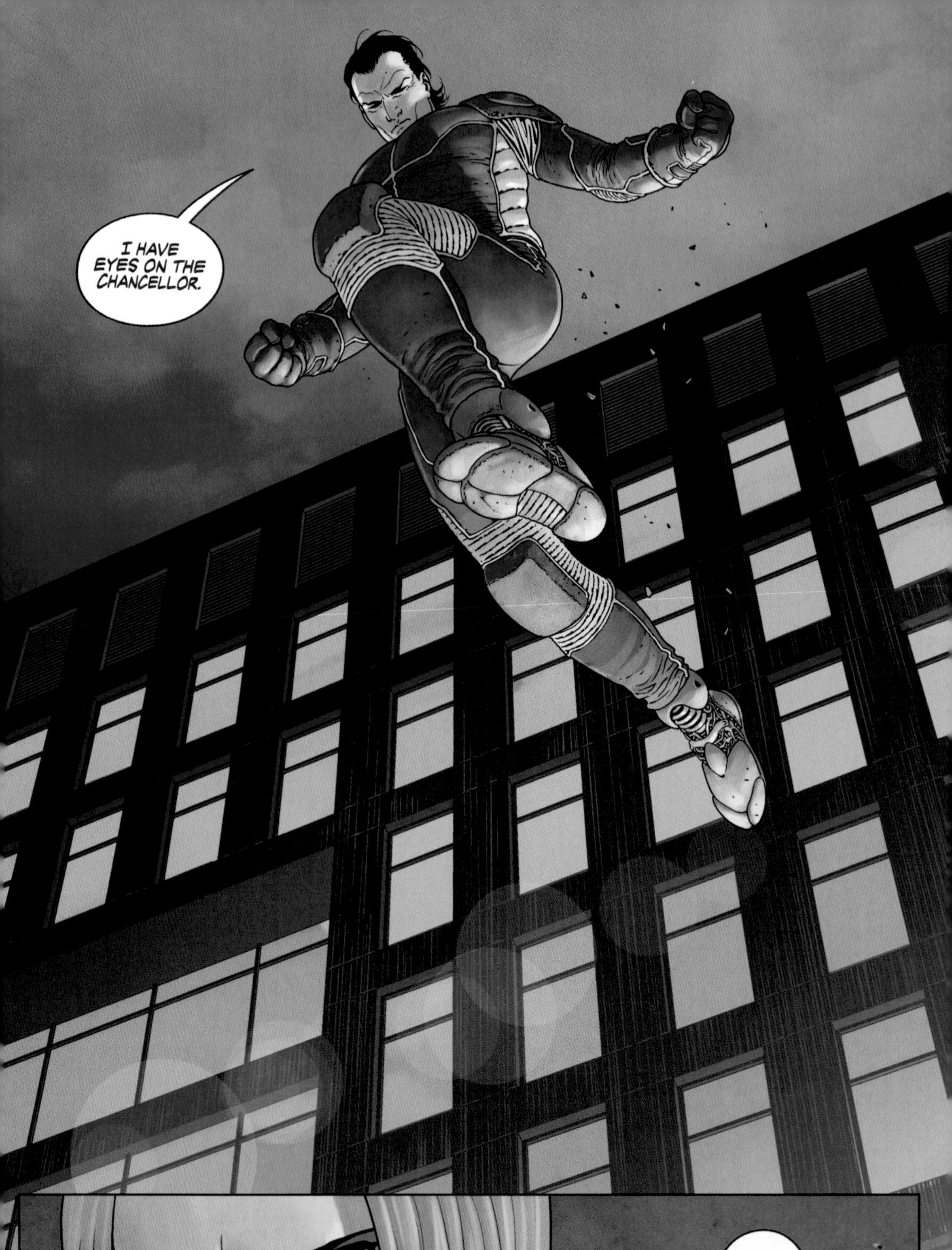
I HAVE EYES ON THE CHANCELLOR.
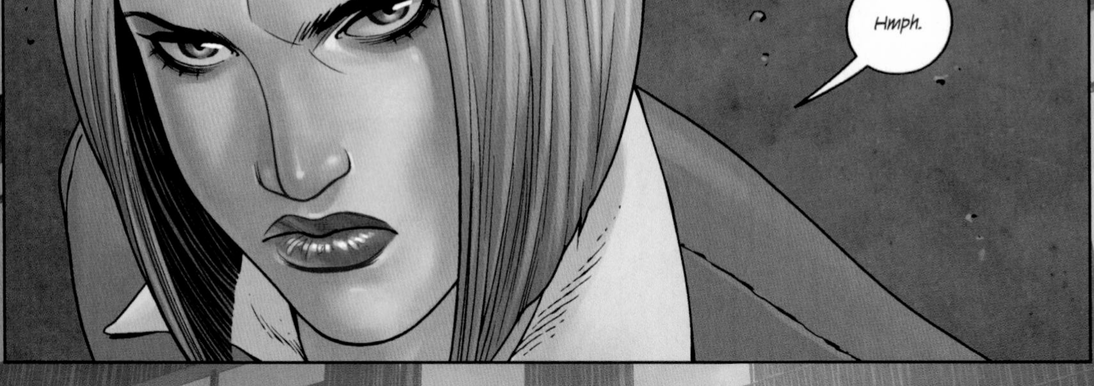
Hmph.

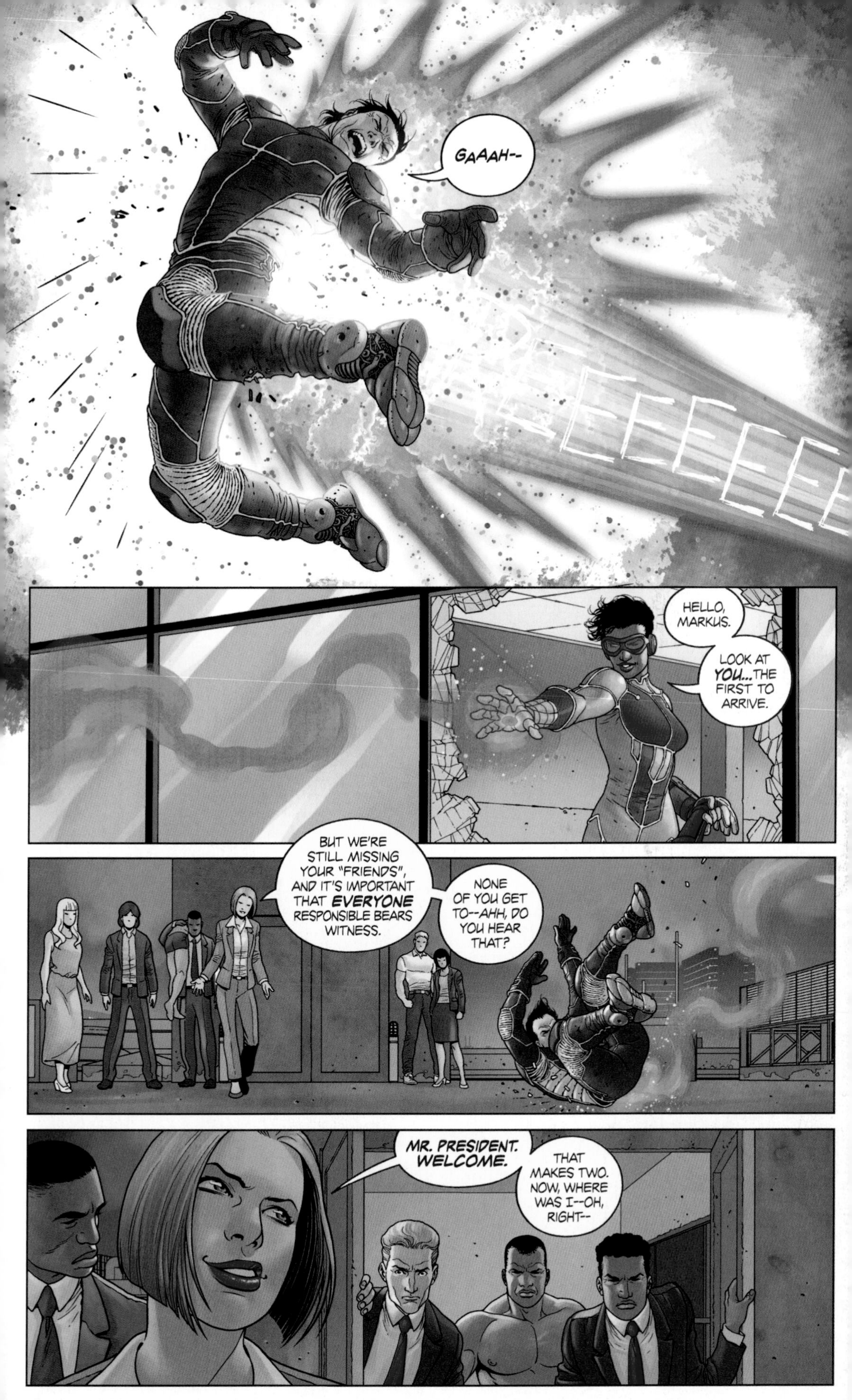
GAAAH--
HELLO, MARKUS.
LOOK AT YOU...THE FIRST TO ARRIVE.
BUT WE'RE STILL MISSING YOUR "FRIENDS", AND IT'S IMPORTANT THAT EVERYONE RESPONSIBLE BEARS WITNESS.
NONE OF YOU GET TO--AHH, DO YOU HEAR THAT?
MR. PRESIDENT. WELCOME.
THAT MAKES TWO. NOW, WHERE WAS I--OH, RIGHT--

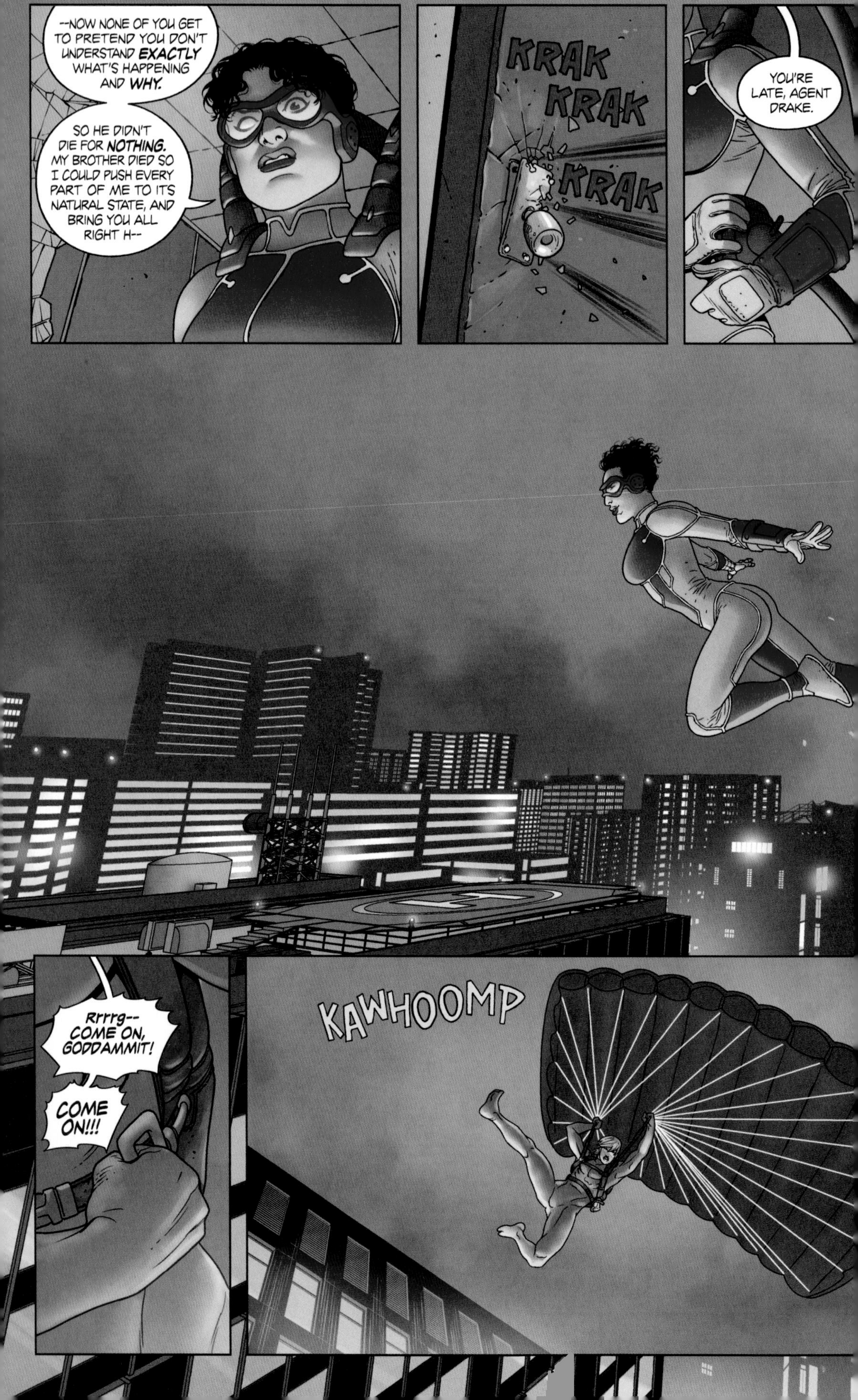
--NOW NONE OF YOU GET TO PRETEND YOU DON'T UNDERSTAND **EXACTLY** WHAT'S HAPPENING AND **WHY.**
SO HE DIDN'T DIE FOR **NOTHING.** MY BROTHER DIED SO I COULD PUSH EVERY PART OF ME TO ITS NATURAL STATE, AND BRING YOU ALL RIGHT H--
KRAK
KRAK
KRAK
YOU'RE LATE, AGENT DRAKE.
Rrrrg-- COME ON, GODDAMMIT!
COME ON!!!
KAWHOOMP

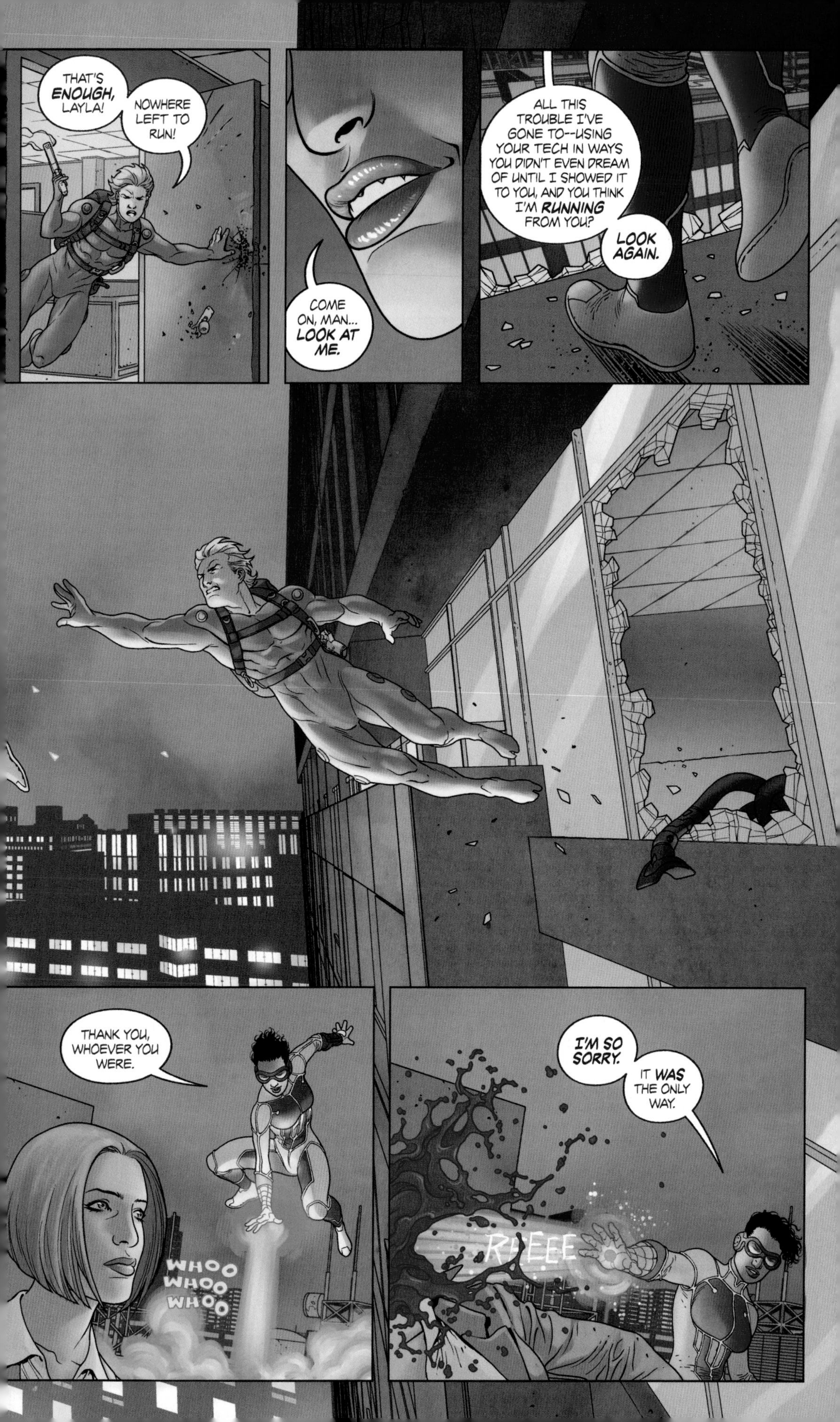
THAT'S ENOUGH, LAYLA!
NOWHERE LEFT TO RUN!
COME ON, MAN... LOOK AT ME.
ALL THIS TROUBLE I'VE GONE TO--USING YOUR TECH IN WAYS YOU DIDN'T EVEN DREAM OF UNTIL I SHOWED IT TO YOU, AND YOU THINK I'M RUNNING FROM YOU?
LOOK AGAIN.
THANK YOU, WHOEVER YOU WERE.
WHOO WHOO WHOO
I'M SO SORRY.
IT WAS THE ONLY WAY.
RIEEEE

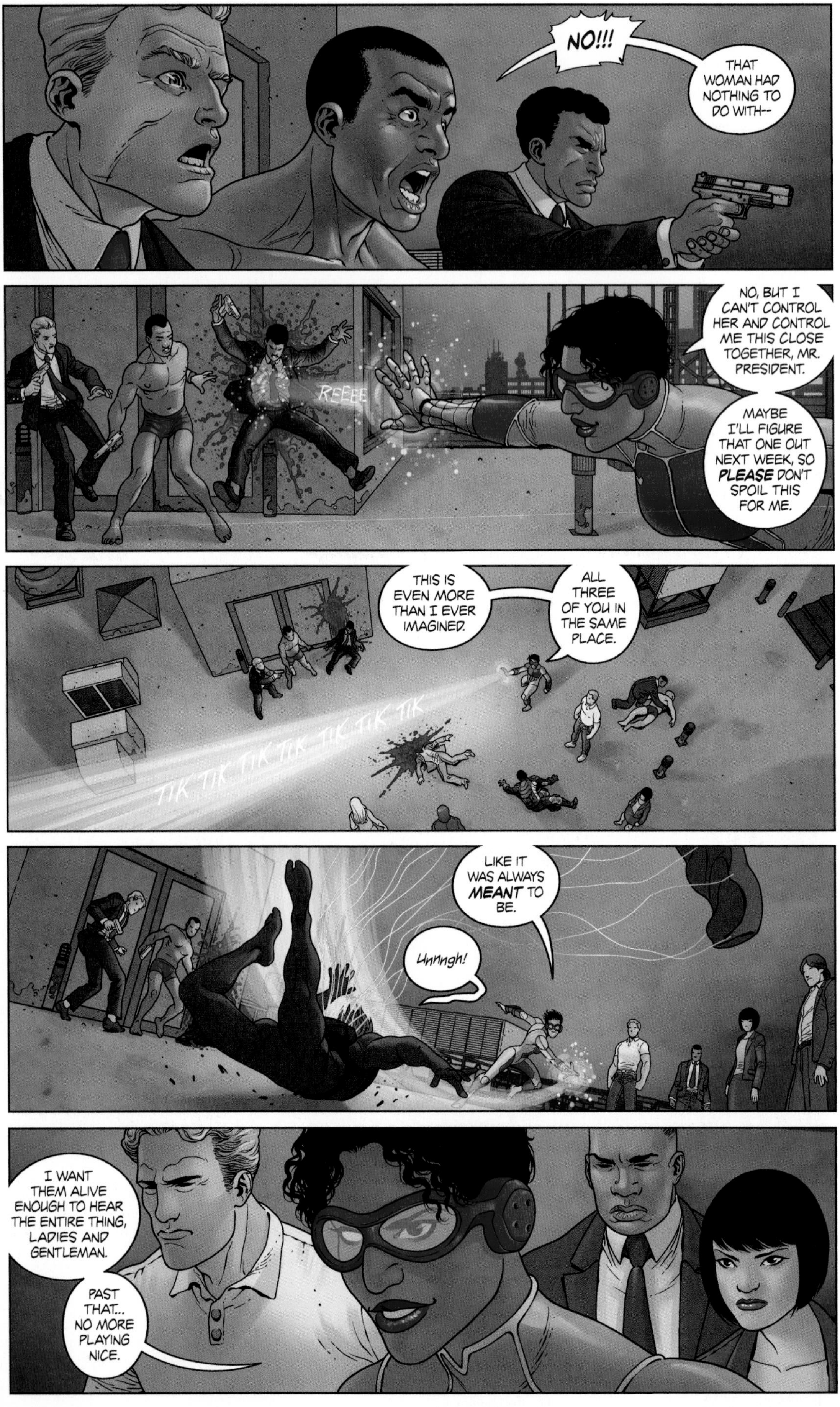
NO!!!
THAT WOMAN HAD NOTHING TO DO WITH--
NO, BUT I CAN'T CONTROL HER AND CONTROL ME THIS CLOSE TOGETHER, MR. PRESIDENT.
MAYBE I'LL FIGURE THAT ONE OUT NEXT WEEK, SO **PLEASE** DON'T SPOIL THIS FOR ME.
REEEE
THIS IS EVEN MORE THAN I EVER IMAGINED.
ALL THREE OF YOU IN THE SAME PLACE.
TIK TIK TIK TIK TIK TIK TIK TIK
LIKE IT WAS ALWAYS **MEANT** TO BE.
Unnngh!
I WANT THEM ALIVE ENOUGH TO HEAR THE ENTIRE THING, LADIES AND GENTLEMAN.
PAST THAT... NO MORE PLAYING NICE.

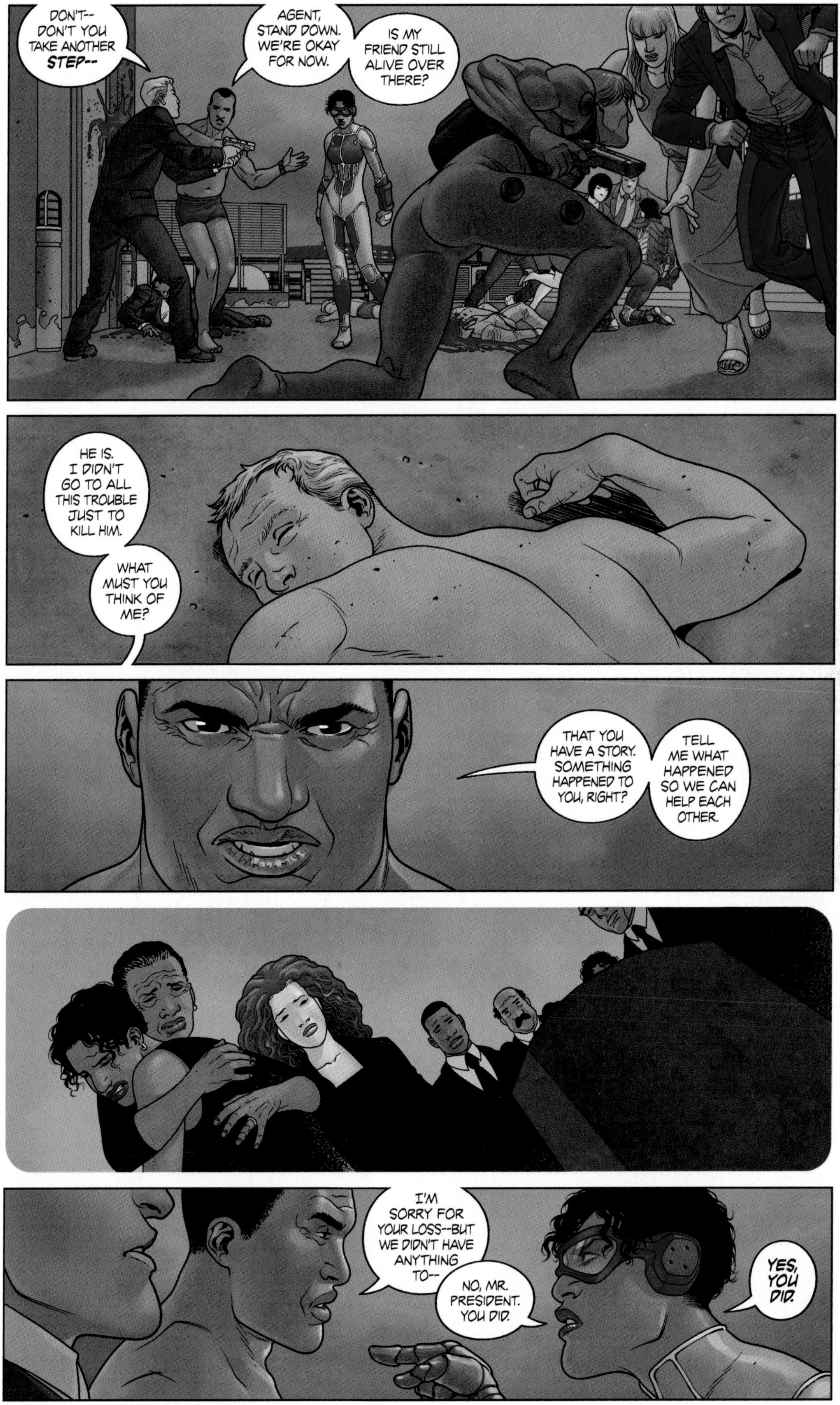
DON'T--
DON'T YOU
TAKE ANOTHER
STEP--
AGENT,
STAND DOWN.
WE'RE OKAY
FOR NOW.
IS MY
FRIEND STILL
ALIVE OVER
THERE?
HE IS.
I DIDN'T
GO TO ALL
THIS TROUBLE
JUST TO
KILL HIM.
WHAT
MUST YOU
THINK OF
ME?
THAT YOU
HAVE A STORY.
SOMETHING
HAPPENED TO
YOU, RIGHT?
TELL
ME WHAT
HAPPENED
SO WE CAN
HELP EACH
OTHER.
I'M
SORRY FOR
YOUR LOSS--BUT
WE DIDN'T HAVE
ANYTHING
TO--
NO, MR.
PRESIDENT.
YOU DID.
YES,
YOU
DID.

MARKUS HELPED CREATE IT.

DRAKE, TOO, AND WORSE THAN THAT...HE *WIELDS* IT.

"FOR THE GREATER GOOD."

BUT *YOU*, FORMER SENATOR STOKES...*YOU* ENSURED WHAT HARDCORE WOULD COME TO BE.

THE DECIDING VOTE, IF I REMEMBER CORRECTLY.

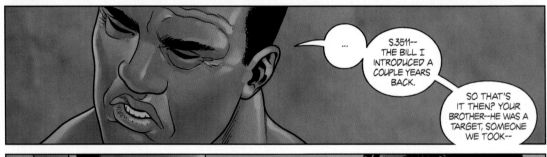

...

S.3511-- THE BILL I INTRODUCED A COUPLE YEARS BACK.

SO THAT'S IT THEN? YOUR BROTHER--HE WAS A TARGET, SOMEONE WE TOOK--

NO! *NO!* YOU DON'T GET TO DO THAT, I DON'T CARE *WHO* YOU ARE!

HE WAS AN *ACCIDENT!* MARKUS, DRAKE, *YOU*--YOU *KILLED* HIM WHILE YOU WERE OUT *KILLING* SOMEONE ELSE!!!

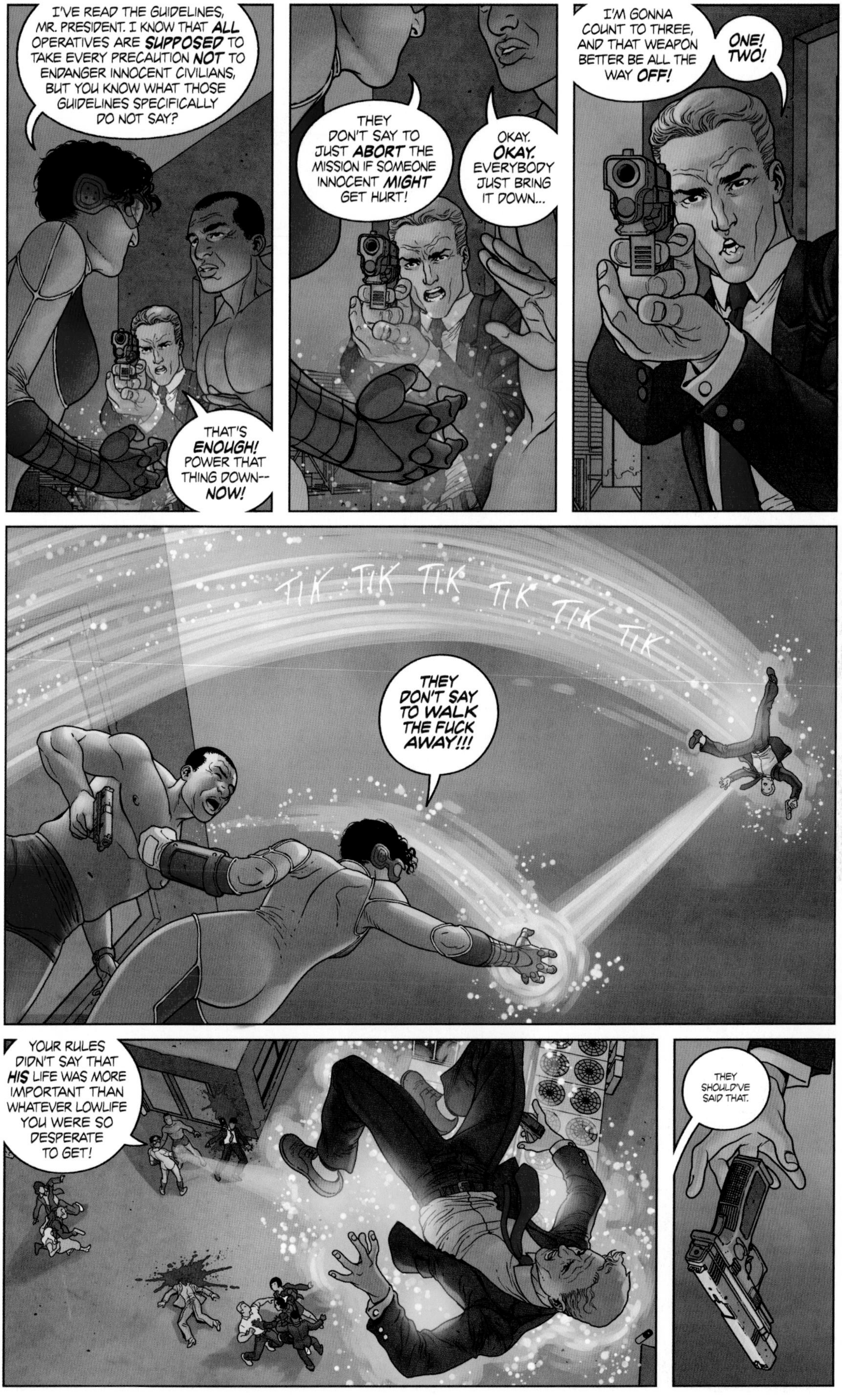
I'VE READ THE GUIDELINES, MR. PRESIDENT. I KNOW THAT ALL OPERATIVES ARE SUPPOSED TO TAKE EVERY PRECAUTION NOT TO ENDANGER INNOCENT CIVILIANS, BUT YOU KNOW WHAT THOSE GUIDELINES SPECIFICALLY DO NOT SAY?
THAT'S ENOUGH! POWER THAT THING DOWN-- NOW!
THEY DON'T SAY TO JUST ABORT THE MISSION IF SOMEONE INNOCENT MIGHT GET HURT!
OKAY. OKAY. EVERYBODY JUST BRING IT DOWN...
I'M GONNA COUNT TO THREE, AND THAT WEAPON BETTER BE ALL THE WAY OFF!
ONE! TWO!
TIK TIK TIK TIK TIK TIK
THEY DON'T SAY TO WALK THE FUCK AWAY!!!
YOUR RULES DIDN'T SAY THAT HIS LIFE WAS MORE IMPORTANT THAN WHATEVER LOWLIFE YOU WERE SO DESPERATE TO GET!
THEY SHOULD'VE SAID THAT.

MARKUS, *DON'T!*

THE PEOPLE THEY'RE CONTROLLING ARE INNOCENT!

WE CAN STILL *SAVE* THEM, MARKUS!

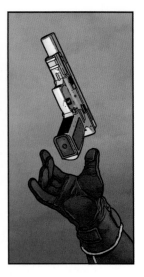

WE ARE *SUPPOSED* TO *SAVE* THEM, YOU BAS--

BLAM
BLAM

AM BLAM

NO.

DO YOU SEE NOW, MR. PRESIDENT?

Unnff!

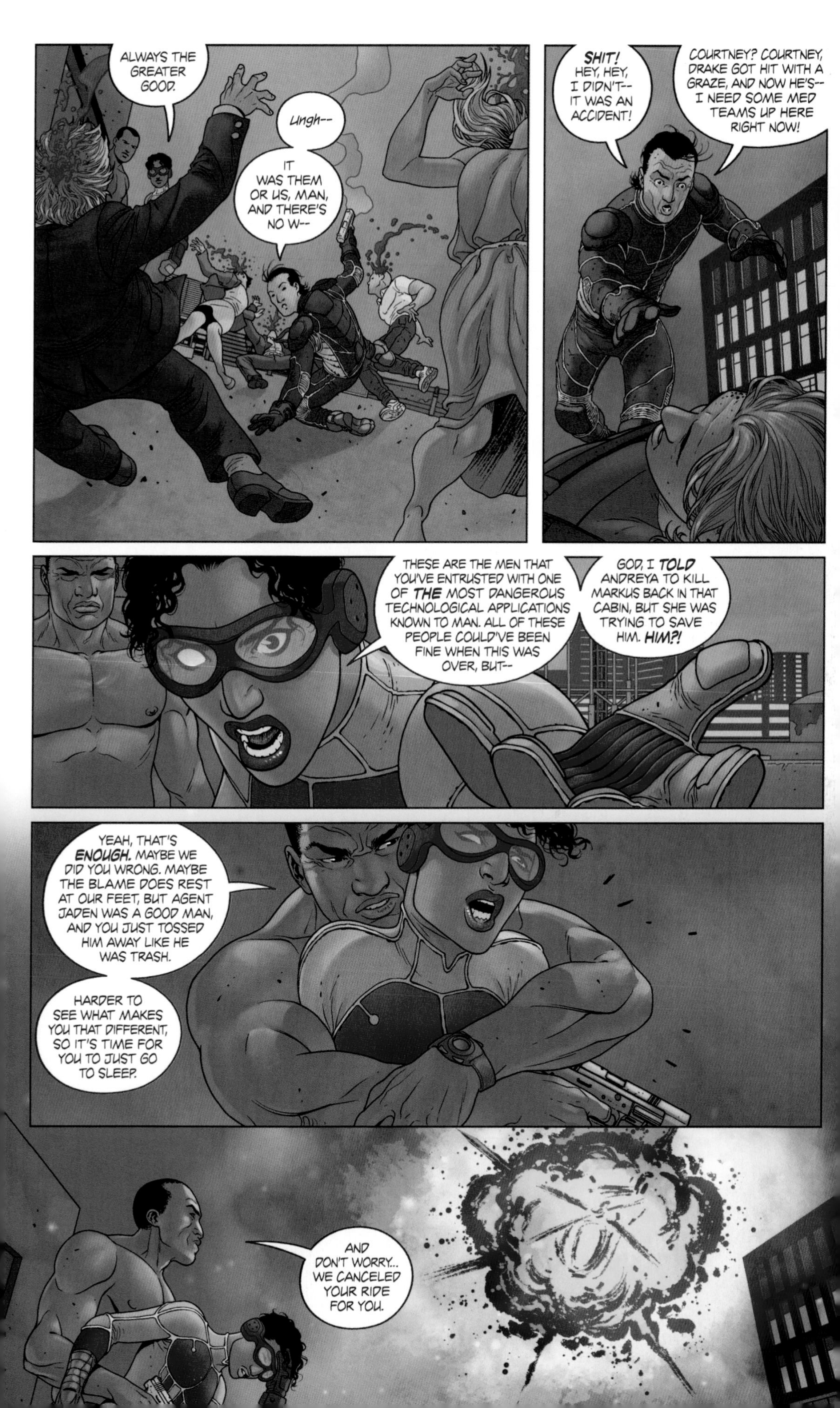
ALWAYS THE GREATER GOOD.
Ungh--
IT WAS THEM OR US, MAN, AND THERE'S NO W--
SHIT! HEY, HEY, I DIDN'T-- IT WAS AN ACCIDENT!
COURTNEY? COURTNEY, DRAKE GOT HIT WITH A GRAZE, AND NOW HE'S-- I NEED SOME MED TEAMS UP HERE RIGHT NOW!
THESE ARE THE MEN THAT YOU'VE ENTRUSTED WITH ONE OF THE MOST DANGEROUS TECHNOLOGICAL APPLICATIONS KNOWN TO MAN. ALL OF THESE PEOPLE COULD'VE BEEN FINE WHEN THIS WAS OVER, BUT--
GOD, I TOLD ANDREYA TO KILL MARKUS BACK IN THAT CABIN, BUT SHE WAS TRYING TO SAVE HIM. HIM?!
YEAH, THAT'S ENOUGH. MAYBE WE DID YOU WRONG. MAYBE THE BLAME DOES REST AT OUR FEET, BUT AGENT JADEN WAS A GOOD MAN, AND YOU JUST TOSSED HIM AWAY LIKE HE WAS TRASH.
HARDER TO SEE WHAT MAKES YOU THAT DIFFERENT, SO IT'S TIME FOR YOU TO JUST GO TO SLEEP.
AND DON'T WORRY... WE CANCELED YOUR RIDE FOR YOU.

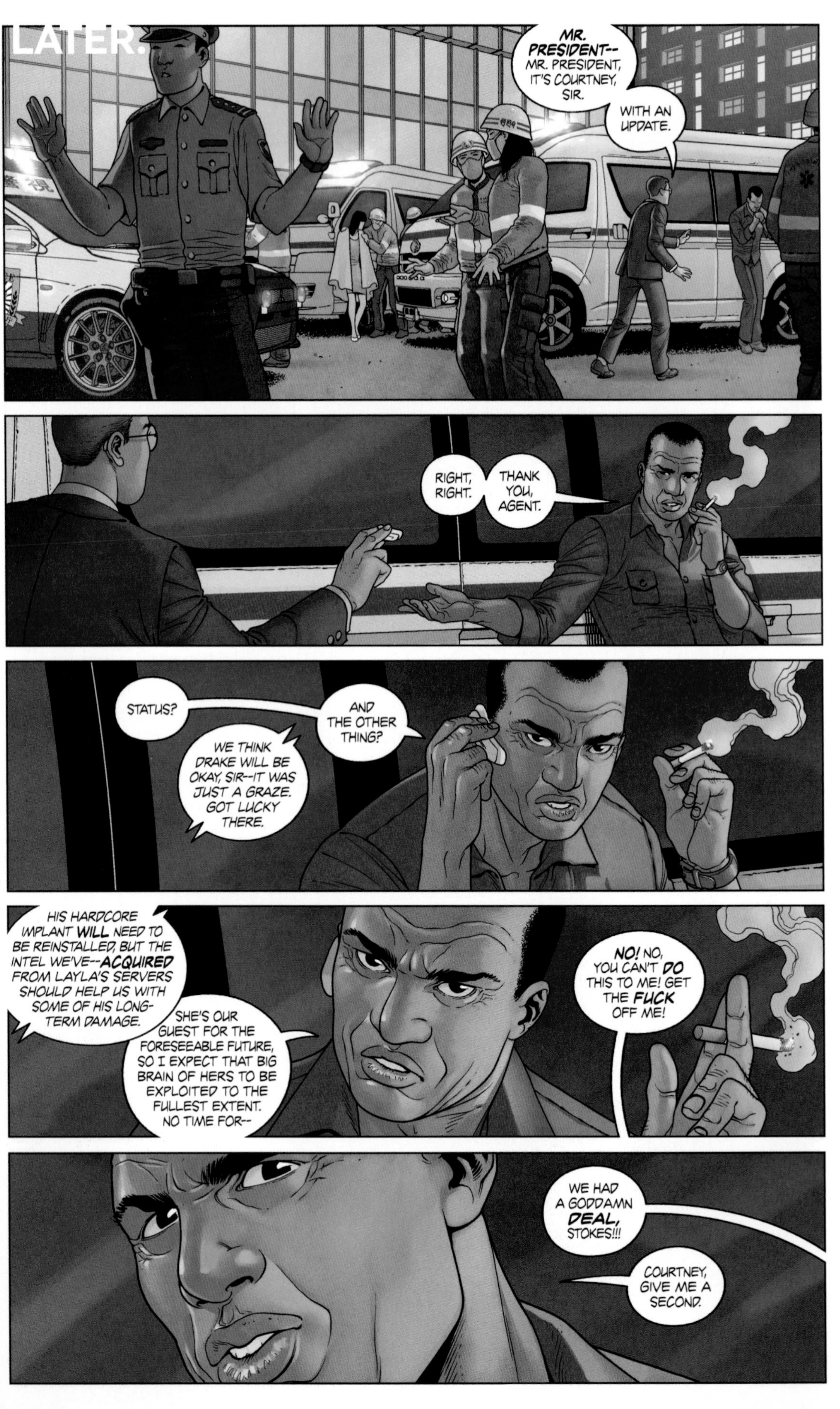

LATER.
MR. PRESIDENT-- MR. PRESIDENT, IT'S COURTNEY, SIR.
WITH AN UPDATE.
RIGHT, RIGHT.
THANK YOU, AGENT.
STATUS?
WE THINK DRAKE WILL BE OKAY, SIR--IT WAS JUST A GRAZE. GOT LUCKY THERE.
AND THE OTHER THING?
HIS HARDCORE IMPLANT WILL NEED TO BE REINSTALLED, BUT THE INTEL WE'VE--ACQUIRED FROM LAYLA'S SERVERS SHOULD HELP US WITH SOME OF HIS LONG-TERM DAMAGE.
SHE'S OUR GUEST FOR THE FORESEEABLE FUTURE, SO I EXPECT THAT BIG BRAIN OF HERS TO BE EXPLOITED TO THE FULLEST EXTENT. NO TIME FOR--
NO! NO, YOU CAN'T DO THIS TO ME! GET THE FUCK OFF ME!
WE HAD A GODDAMN DEAL, STOKES!!!
COURTNEY, GIVE ME A SECOND.

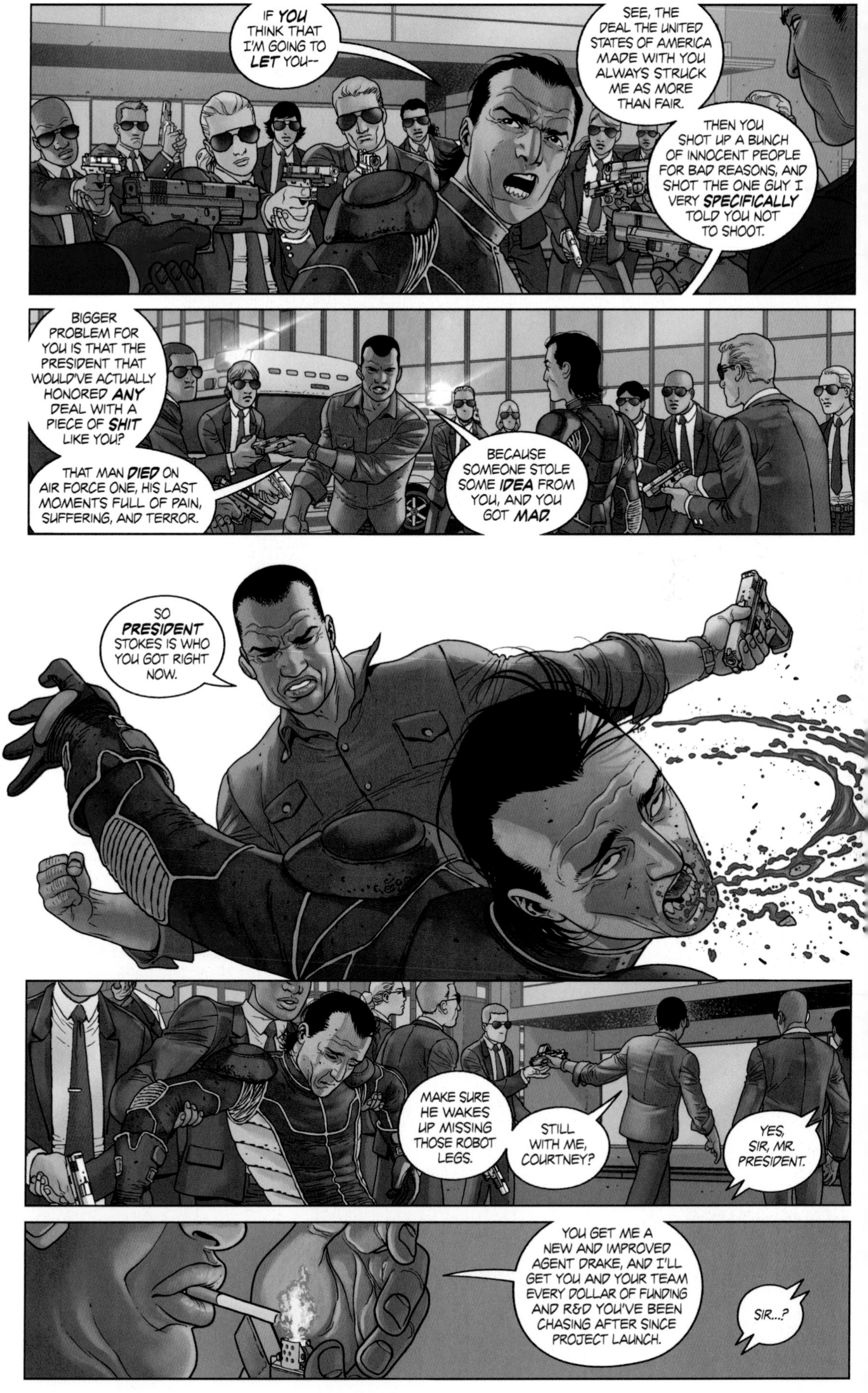
IF YOU THINK THAT I'M GOING TO LET YOU--
SEE, THE DEAL THE UNITED STATES OF AMERICA MADE WITH YOU ALWAYS STRUCK ME AS MORE THAN FAIR.
THEN YOU SHOT UP A BUNCH OF INNOCENT PEOPLE FOR BAD REASONS, AND SHOT THE ONE GUY I VERY SPECIFICALLY TOLD YOU NOT TO SHOOT.
BIGGER PROBLEM FOR YOU IS THAT THE PRESIDENT THAT WOULD'VE ACTUALLY HONORED ANY DEAL WITH A PIECE OF SHIT LIKE YOU?
THAT MAN DIED ON AIR FORCE ONE, HIS LAST MOMENTS FULL OF PAIN, SUFFERING, AND TERROR.
BECAUSE SOMEONE STOLE SOME IDEA FROM YOU, AND YOU GOT MAD.
SO PRESIDENT STOKES IS WHO YOU GOT RIGHT NOW.
MAKE SURE HE WAKES UP MISSING THOSE ROBOT LEGS.
STILL WITH ME, COURTNEY?
YES, SIR, MR. PRESIDENT.
YOU GET ME A NEW AND IMPROVED AGENT DRAKE, AND I'LL GET YOU AND YOUR TEAM EVERY DOLLAR OF FUNDING AND R&D YOU'VE BEEN CHASING AFTER SINCE PROJECT LAUNCH.
SIR...?

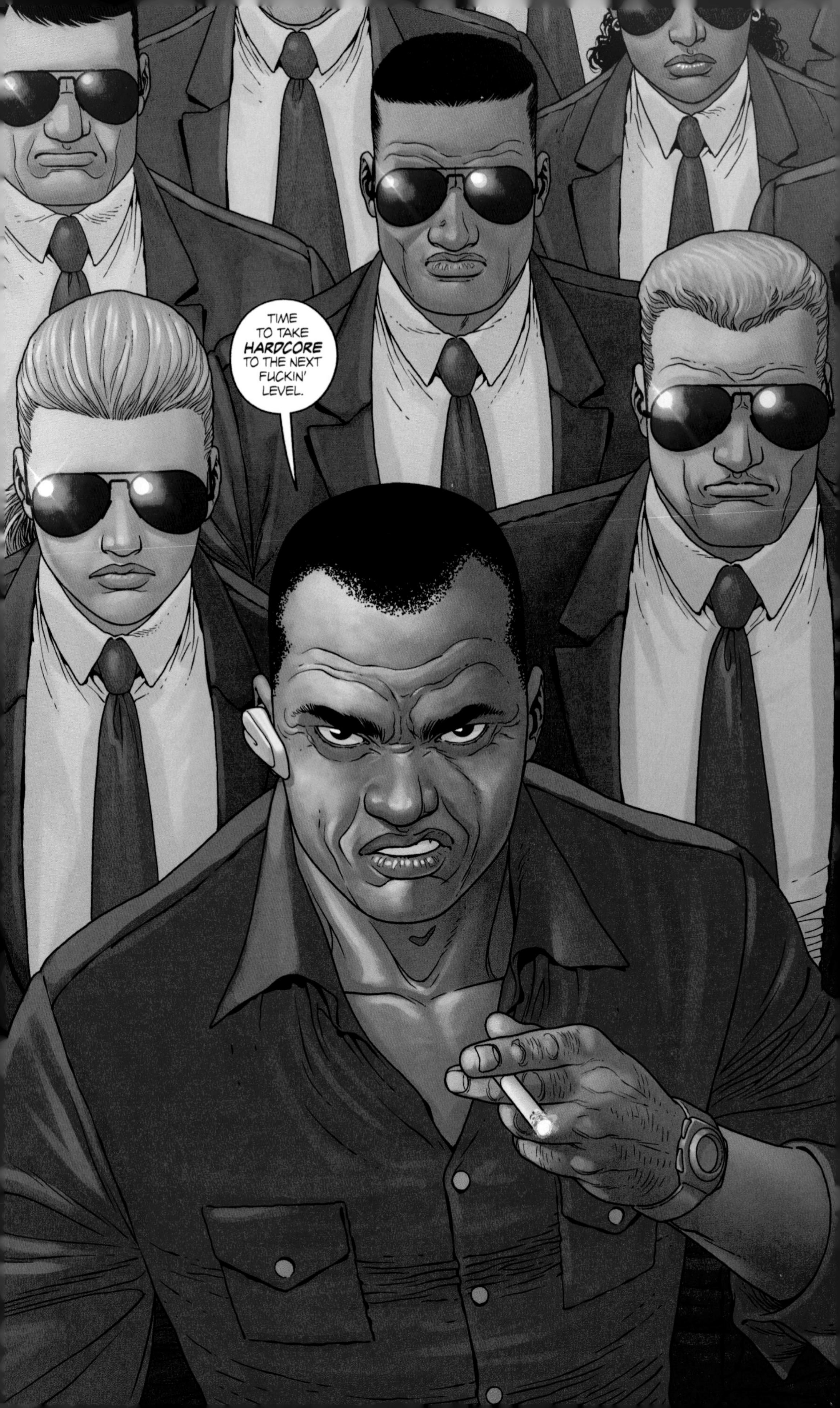
TIME TO TAKE **HARDCORE** TO THE NEXT FUCKIN' LEVEL.

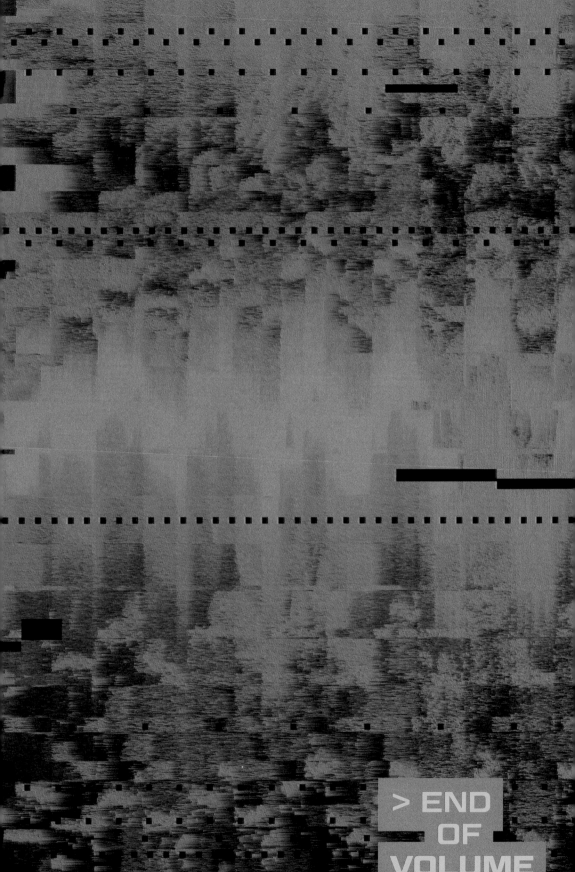

> END
> OF
> VOLUME
> TWO

COVERS BY NIC KLEIN

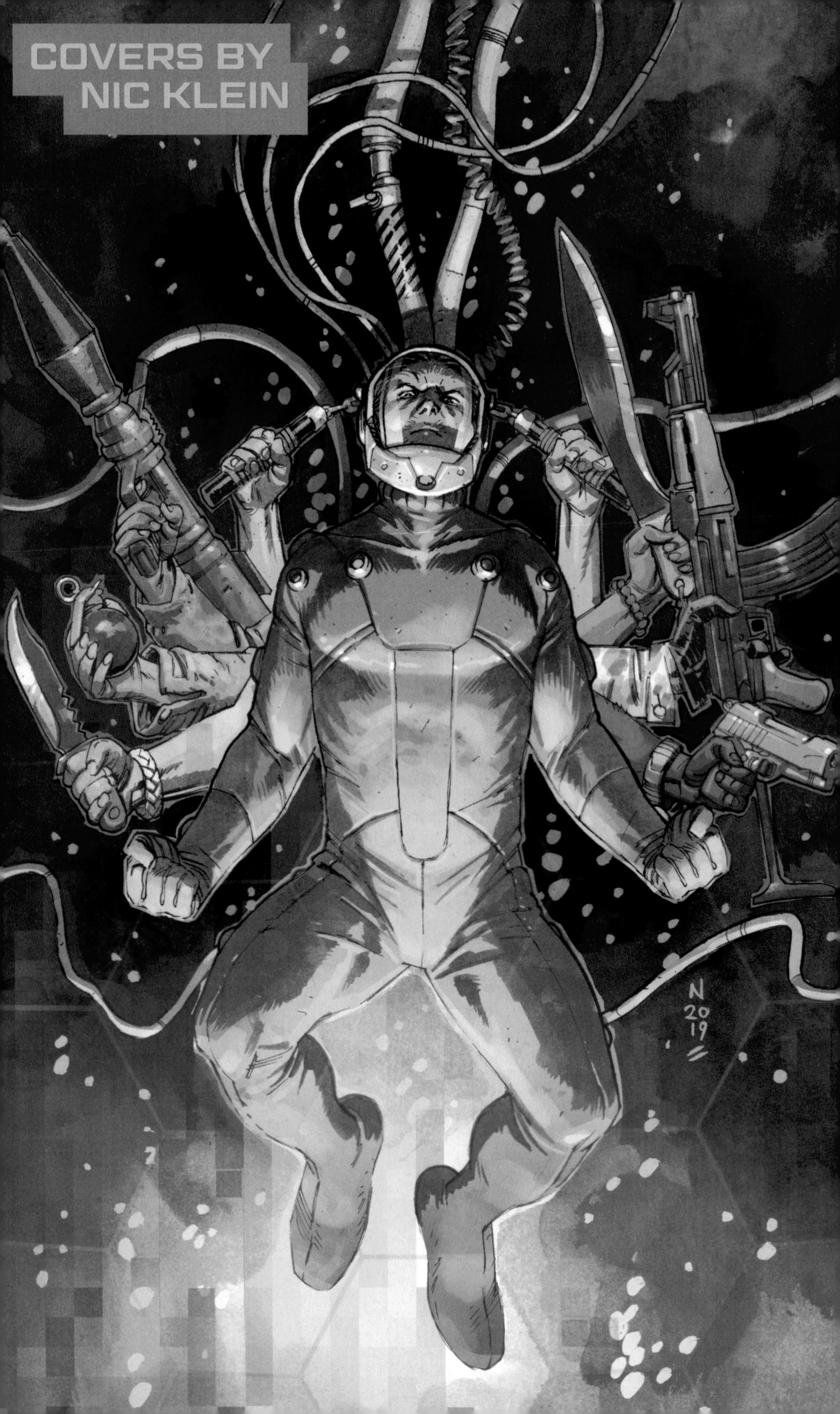
N 20 19

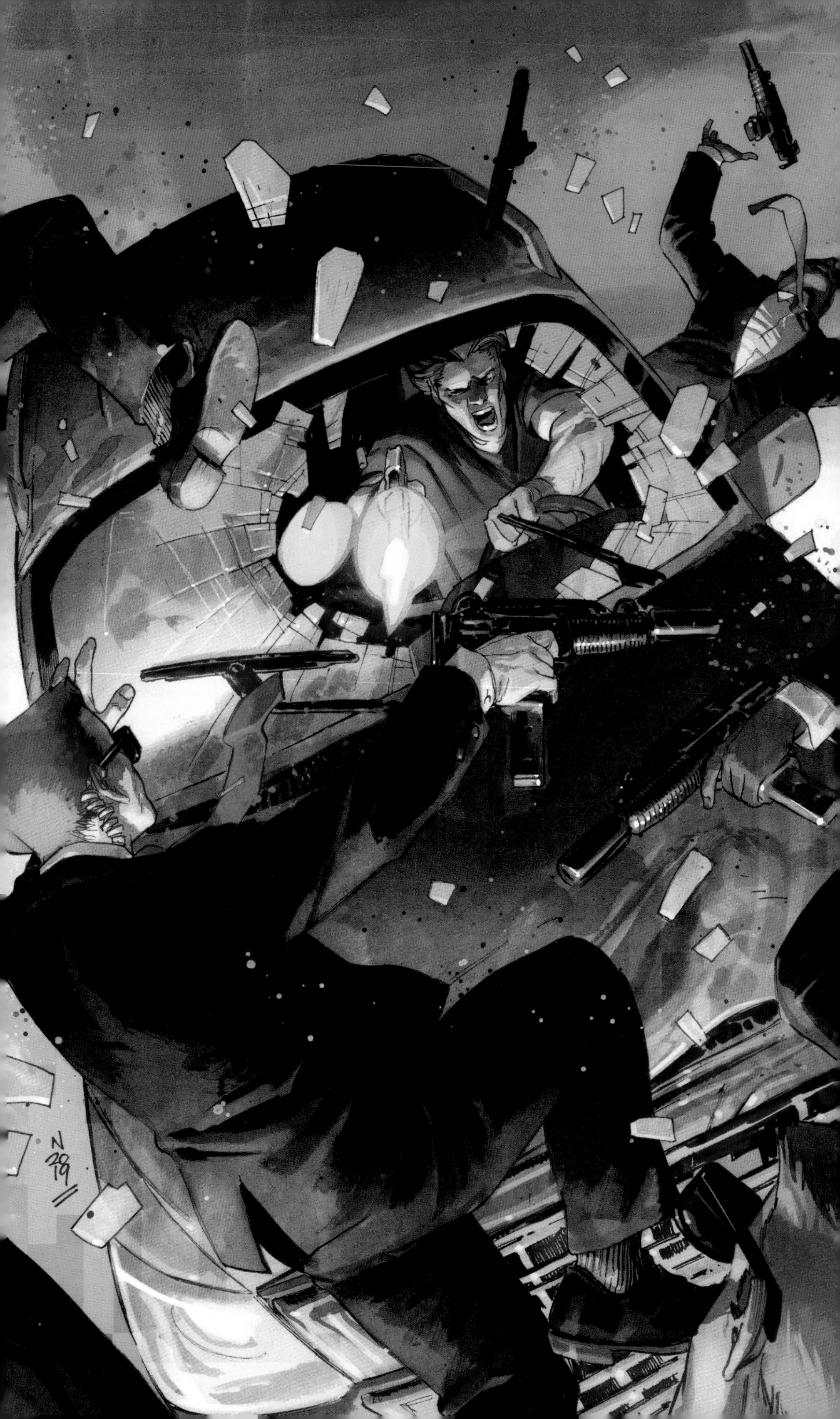

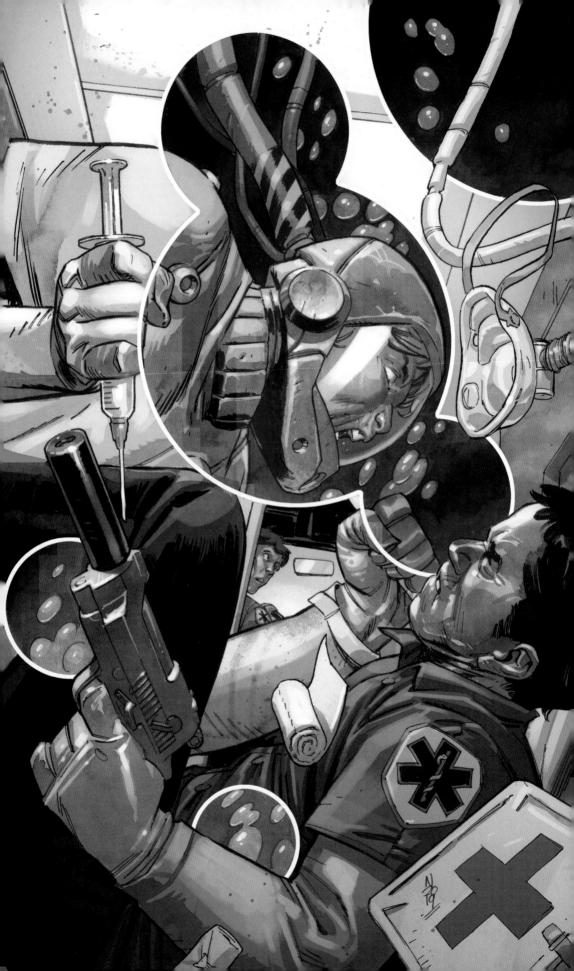

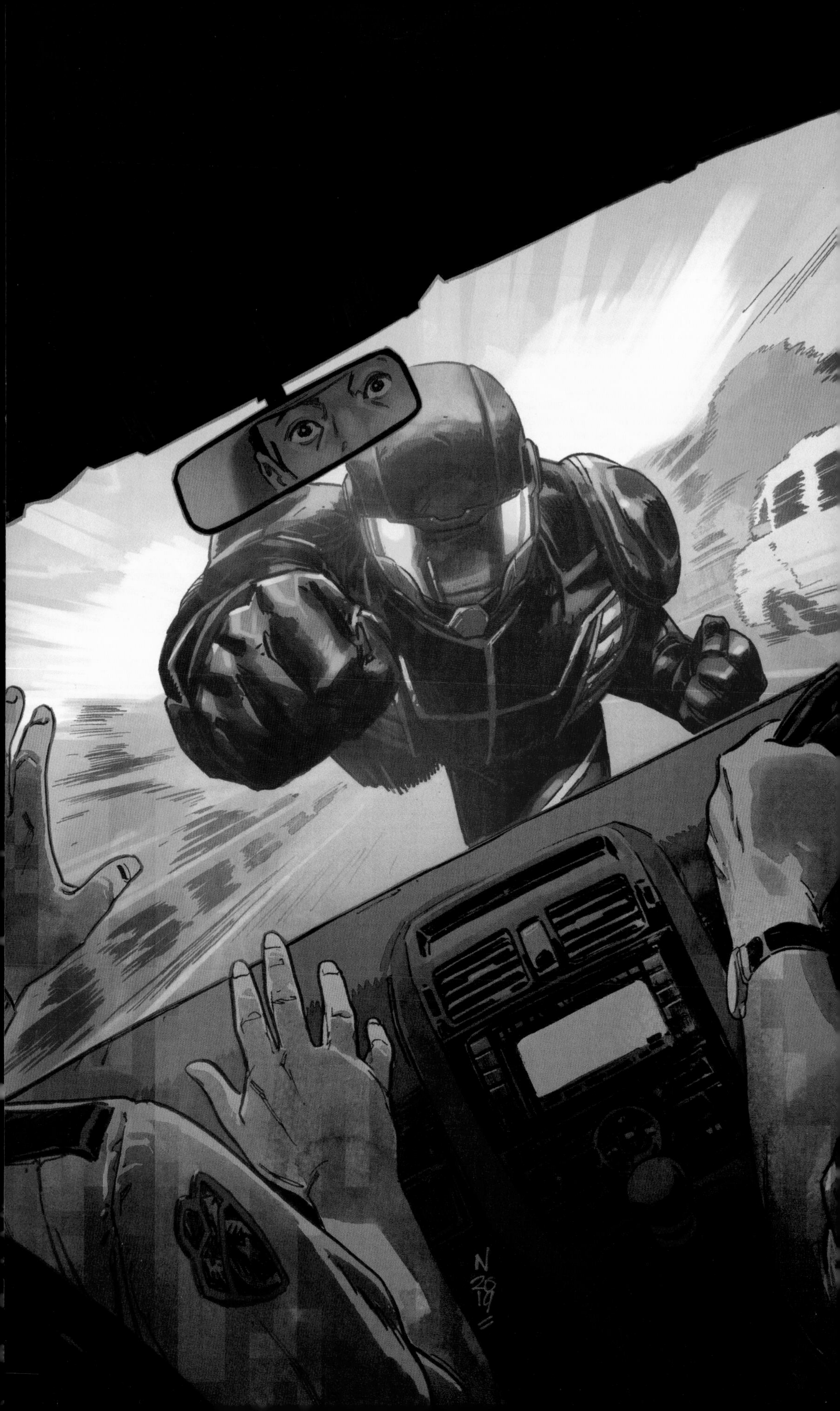

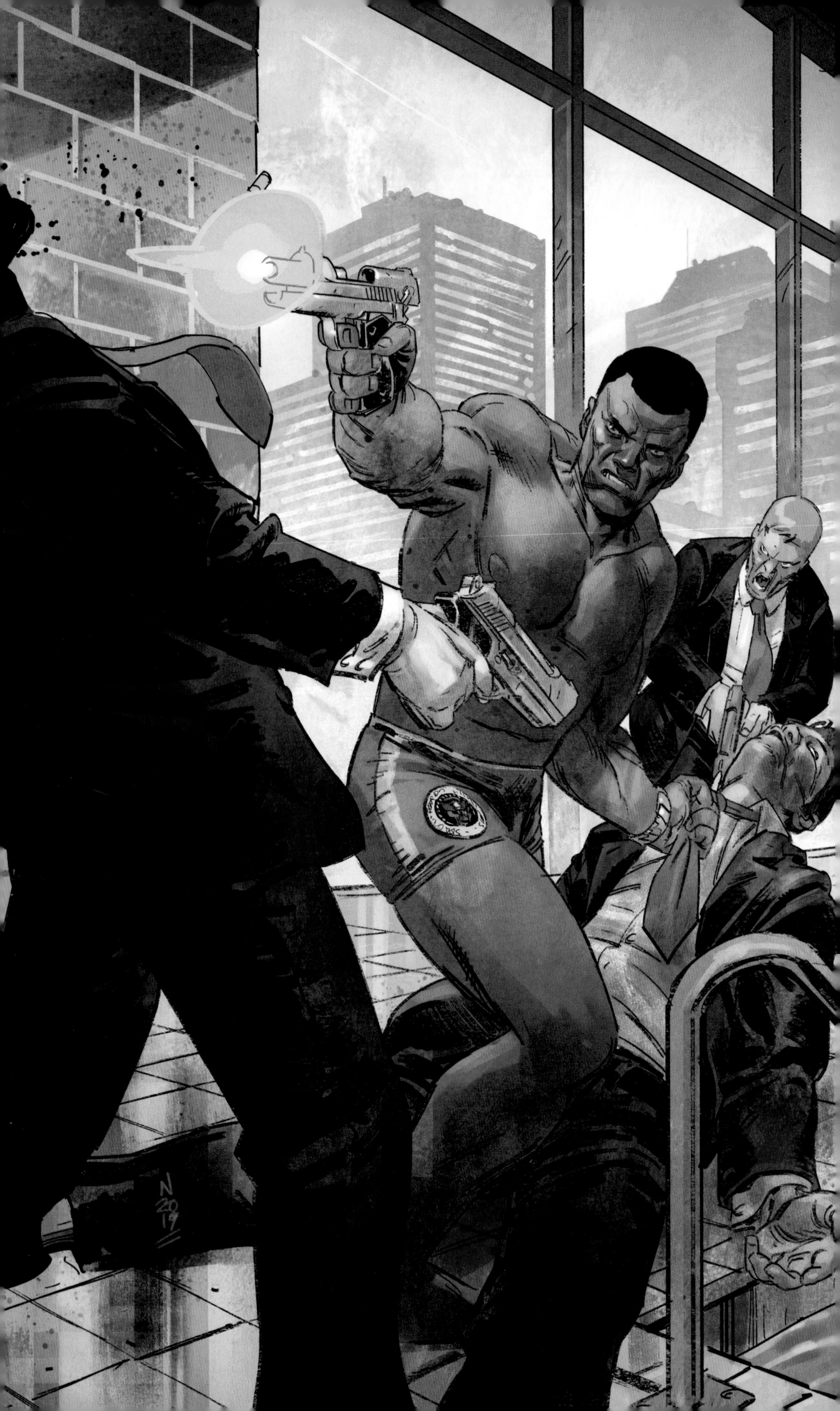

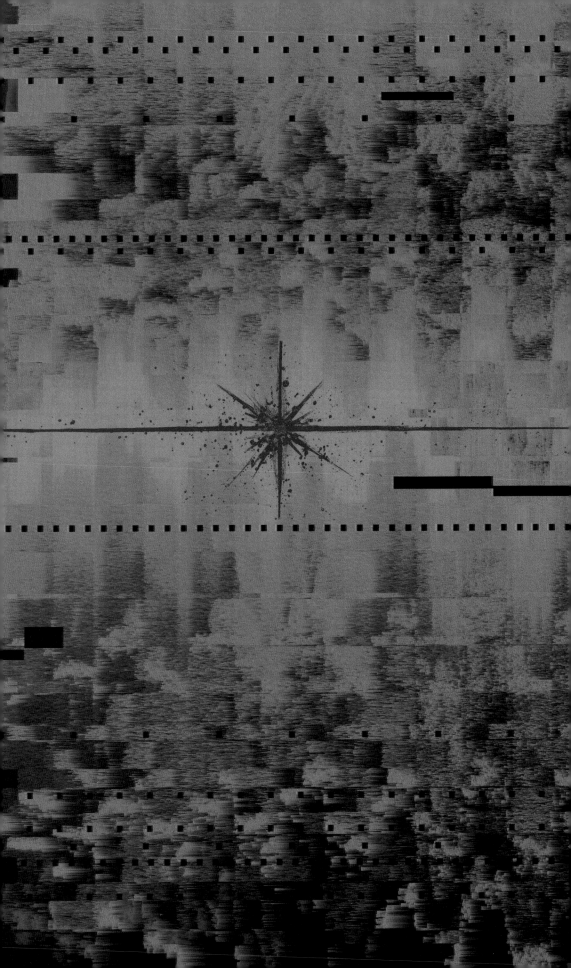

For more tales from ROBERT KIRKMAN and SKYBOUND

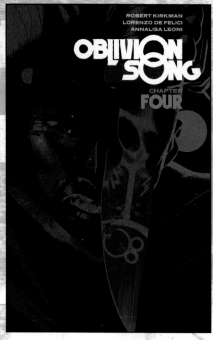

ROBERT KIRKMAN
LORENZO DE FELICI
ANNALISA LEONI

OBLIVION SONG
CHAPTER FOUR

OUTER DARKNESS
JOHN LAYMAN
AFU CHAN

VOLUME 2
CASTROPHANY OF HATE

CHAPTER ONE
ISBN: 978-1-5343-0642-4
$9.99

CHAPTER THREE
ISBN: 978-1-5343-1326-2
$16.99

VOL. 1: EACH OTHER'S THROATS
ISBN: 978-1-5343-1210-4
$16.99

VOL. 2: CASTROPHANY OF HATE
ISBN: 978-1-5343-1370-5
$16.99

CHAPTER TWO
ISBN: 978-1-5343-1057-5
$16.99

CHAPTER FOUR
ISBN: 978-1-5343-1517-4
$16.99

VOL. 1: HOMECOMING
ISBN: 978-1-63215-231-2
$9.99

VOL. 2: CALL TO ADVENTURE
ISBN: 978-1-63215-446-0
$12.99

VOL. 3: ALLIES AND ENEMIES
ISBN: 978-1-63215-683-9
$12.99

VOL. 4: FAMILY HISTORY
ISBN: 978-1-63215-871-0
$12.99

VOL. 5: BELLY OF THE BEAST
ISBN: 978-1-5343-0218-1
$12.99

VOL. 6: FATHERHOOD
ISBN: 978-1-53430-498-7
$14.99

VOL. 7: BLOOD BROTHERS
ISBN: 978-1-5343-1053-7
$14.99

VOL. 8: LIVE BY THE SWORD
ISBN: 978-1-5343-1368-2
$14.99

VOL. 1: KILL THE PAST
ISBN: 978-1-5343-1362-0
$16.99

VOL. 1: A DARKNESS SURROUNDS HIM
ISBN: 978-1-63215-053-0
$9.99

VOL. 2: A VAST AND UNENDING RUIN
ISBN: 978-1-63215-448-4
$14.99

VOL. 3: THIS LITTLE LIGHT
ISBN: 978-1-63215-693-8
$14.99

VOL. 4: UNDER DEVIL'S WING
ISBN: 978-1-5343-0050-7
$14.99

VOL. 5: THE NEW PATH
ISBN: 978-1-5343-0249-5
$16.99

VOL. 6: INVASION
ISBN: 978-1-5343-0751-3
$16.99

VOL. 7: THE DARKNESS GROWS
ISBN: 978-1-5343-1239-5
$16.99

VOL. 1: DEEP IN THE HEART
ISBN: 978-1-5343-0331-7
$16.99

VOL. 2: THE EYES UPON YOU
ISBN: 978-1-5343-0665-3
$16.99

VOL. 3: LONGHORNS
ISBN: 978-1-5343-1050-6
$16.99

VOL. 4: LONE STAR
ISBN: 978-1-5343-1367-5
$16.99